Escaping Our Reality

Escaping Our Reality

BOOK ONE

HALCIE DAWN

Published by Halcie Dawn
Edited by Elaine York/Allusion Publishing
www.allusionpublishing.com
Cover Design by Stacey Blake/Champagne Book Design, www.champagnebookdesign.com
Formatting by Elaine York/Allusion Publishing
www.allusionpublishing.com

For Kuntry, Boo, Dandy, and Big Deddy
Love isn't a big enough word.

For Granny
You left. But I know where to find you.
"Scratch my back and make me laugh…"

Escaping Our Reality is Book One in *The Reality Duet*.
This is not a standalone novel and
should immediately be followed by...

Finding Our Reality: The Reality Duet Book Two

Trust me... You'll see why.

Chapter 1

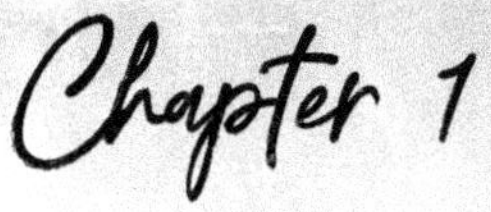

Ella

I really don't like what I hear.

Sometimes you just don't care to hear the words that come from someone's mouth. You want to pluck those words from the sky and stuff them back where they belong. Deep, deep down into the vacuum of the black abyss.

When I was little, I could cover my ears when I didn't like what someone was telling me. I don't really think that's feasible—feasible, sure, but not necessarily mature—at seventeen.

"So, unfortunately, there's really nothing further we can do until we get some new leads. New tips."

I blankly stare at Detective Marcum as he looks between me, my mom, and my dad as I try to absorb every syllable of what he's attempting to tell me, doing his best to use politically correct and placating language in front of my parents.

So, that's it? No more looking for my sister? Nothing?

Caroline Olive Hill no longer exists?

I guess I should stop thinking in *questions* and start thinking in *statements*. Statement: Bogus tips and false leads stop coming in, and Carrie is gone. Done. Finished. Pushed to the back burner by the general public who have grown weary of seeing her face splattered all over the evening news.

My eyes burn and my throat constricts as I swallow and try to contain my unshed sobs. Marcum, with his kind eyes and graying temples, shifts to gently cover my trembling hand with his own. His movement stops suddenly when my mother's shrill howl fragments the peaceful calm of the sheriff's department family room. Marcum clears his throat and passes her a box of tissues. I immediately stiffen my spine and roll my shoulders, having a visceral reaction to her hollow antics. She can't be serious with this Oscar-worthy performance, can she?

I glance in her direction, watching as her body shudders. Dad massages her back in large, exaggerated strokes. She fans her face, exclaiming loudly, "Oh, my heart. My heart is torn in two. I just can't take it anymore!"

Oh, please. Dramatic much?

She shakes her tissue in the air like a pompom and dabs the sides of her eyes—her very dry eyes, very non-bloodshot eyes. You think she'd learn by now how to make herself cry. I'm sure there's a YouTube on that very thing. I mean, someone needs to tell her that sobs without tears just look ridiculous.

Marcum tosses me a knowing look.

"Robert, this has been so hard on me. It's devastating. Truly devastating. I just don't think I can stay in this town right now, knowing that no one's looking for my baby."

Mom can play the most spectacular sympathy card with the very best of them. She's a true Vegas card shark when it comes to that. And Dad feeds on her every word and whim, like a mangy mutt eating shit from the trash can. He doesn't care where it's from, as long as the results are the same.

"Darling, I completely understand. Susan, let me take you away for a bit. I'll have Addison rearrange my surgical calendar, and we can leave for the Bahamas by lunch tomorrow."

Mom tosses him a flippant look of disgust. "Ugh, not the Bahamas again."

"Bermuda?"

She grins and nods. Thankfully she didn't have to worry about any tears going into her mouth as she smiles like the Cheshire cat at his change of venue.

"It's decided," he says, asserting a fully professional tone. "Detective Marcum, I'm taking my wife on a much-deserved and needed holiday. I have our monthly news conference scheduled for two weeks from tomorrow. I suggest that the department does all it can between now and then to find some new leads on our daughter's case. I'd hate for our local sheriff's department to be cast in such a negative light on the national platform. I'm sure you understand what I'm trying to say."

Marcum just sits there dumbfounded. He's used to their dramatics, but even this episode was a bit much.

My parents make their exit from the room, briefly pausing in the doorway when they realize they're forgetting one small, little thing—me, their other daughter.

"Ella," Dad beckons me like a master calling his pet.

I politely smile. "I'll be home soon. Remember, we drove separately."

He nods curtly, and I'm left drowning in the residue of my mother's $400 perfume. It takes only a few moments for the gravity of the situation to settle over me like a dense, heavy fog, and tears spring to my eyes. I cover my face with my hands and cry. Marcum quickly assumes the role of surrogate father, gently patting my back, hoping he can pound the sorrow from my soul and the demons from my home.

I honestly don't know where I'd be without him. I couldn't have survived the past six months of torturous hell without him and my Uncle Ray's family.

Eventually, my flooding tears subside and my hysterical hiccups fade. Together we move from the conference room and make our way through the sheriff's department to one of the detectives' rooms where Marcum shares an office with three other major case detectives. I sit opposite him, kicking my feet up on the edge of his desk, and pick up the latest framed picture. I smile at the toothless little baby boy staring back at me. Marcum's grandson, born the same day Carrie officially went missing.

"Six-month pictures," Marcum explains. "Makes no sense to me," he shrugs. "Why do Brent and Stephanie want to pay a photographer every single month for pictures when they can just take a Kodak themselves?"

I snort. Normally, I'd reply back with a smartass comment, but I agree with him. I rub my swollen eyes, then stretch my arms high above my head, trying to ease the tension from my muscles.

Softly chuckling, he mumbles more to himself than me. "Do your parents even know who you really are?"

It has to be a rhetorical question. We both already know the answer is no. I guess being the family man that he is, he can't understand coming from parents who are so disconnected from their child.

Knowing me better than I know myself, he reaches in his bottom drawer and tosses a protein bar at me. "Eat lunch?"

"Of course not," I say with a smile as I take it from him.

He walks to a small fridge in the corner of the room to grab me a bottle of water. "So, I wasn't kidding when I said that we're stuck. No new tips have come in to us, the University police, or the FBI in the past month. The lab rechecked all of the evidence from the SUV to make sure they didn't miss anything." He sighs heavily, sweeping his arm through the air. "And nothing."

I gulp a large swallow of water, toss my wrapper in the trash, and then hold my hands across the desk, palms up. Marcum grunts and does the same thing he has done multiple times a week since my sister went missing. He pulls the large, copied stack of evidence photos from the same third desk drawer as always and slaps them in my hand. And for the hundredth time, I carefully study the pictures of my sister's expensive-ass SUV, willing myself to have an 'Aha Moment'.

I close my eyes and picture everything that I remember from the last time I rode with her—the day she drove me to Uncle Ray and

Aunt Teresa's house for the cruise. I open my eyes and slowly and methodically flip through the pictures, looking for any clues. Any small remnant that might tell us what happened to Carrie, who took her, who has her. The pictures show the same scenes, over and over. The doors are closed and locked. On the passenger's seat is her purse and powered-off cell phone. A few receipts are stacked in the corner slit of the console. A large Styrofoam cup with watered-down Diet Coke sits in the cup holder. The sunglass clip snuggly holds her Ray-Bans, and the glove box contains no significant papers, other than her insurance card and tag registration.

"And the restaurant, where her car was found, had closed how long ago?"

I know the answer. Marcum knows I know the answer, but he still repeats the same thing he's said to me multiple times. That's just the kind of man he is.

"Over five years. And the owners no longer live here. They're in Florida. Just saving the land and the building in case their kids wanna do something with it one day."

I nod. "Right." I sit back in the chair and look around. "Where's Leary today?"

"Field trip with his kid." Marcum laughs. "I remember those days."

I bite my lip. I *don't* remember those days. My father never went on one single field trip with me. My mother did, but she never did it to spend time with me. She just did it because the other moms were going, and it afforded her an avenue to gossip and play the over-doting mother card.

I tilt my head at the picture that shows all of the receipts found in her car. As always, two particular receipts annoyingly tug at the periphery of my mind. Travis Boys Gas and Country Mart. Both receipts show where she bought gas, filling her tank. One's dated for the day she was last seen by friends. The next day—the day after buying this gas—she was supposed to go to Dakota's apartment for a cookout and didn't show. That's when they knew something was wrong. The other receipt is dated eleven days prior to that. It's not shocking to me that Carrie saved her receipt. She typically saved all of her receipts until she could reconcile them with the monthly credit card statement or bank statement. It's just one of the many life lessons she was teaching me.

Lessons that should come from parents.

Lessons like balancing your checkbook, doing your own laundry, properly cleaning your house, and mowing the yard.

I tap the image with my pointer finger and make a clicking sound with my tongue. "You checked how many months of our checking account statements and credit card statements?"

Our meaning mine and Carrie's joint account.

"About three months before she disappeared. You still fixated on those gas station receipts?"

Tossing it on the desk, I stand and walk to the window, passing by Detective Colson. He's distracted on the phone, so I use the opportunity to aggravate him by turning the framed picture of Sparky, his golden retriever, upside down. Colson is anal-retentive and extremely protective of his desk, so everyone within a ten-mile radius of the station makes a special effort to annoy him on a daily basis.

Detective Peele, Colson's partner, tosses me a dirty look. He doesn't hide the fact that he thinks Marcum and I have grown too close, that Marcum lets me know too much about the investigation.

I ignore him. And avoid him. Like a hooker running away from Sunday School.

The lights from the Christmas tree on the plaza sparkle against the midday sun. Christmas was last week, so we still have three weeks before they take down the decorations, storing them for another year. "It still doesn't make any sense to me. Why travel to the whole other side of the county just to go to one particular gas station?" I hold up my hand before Marcum can respond. "And yes, I know they are the only station in all of Central Alabama that carries Slayton's Southern Blackberry Tea," I say with a completely bitchy, sarcastic attitude.

"That's right. And apparently, your sister isn't the only one who travels to that shit-hole area for that special drink. I told you we watched ten different tapes from ten different days when Carrie went there. I bet a dozen people buy that drink each day. Tried it myself. It was damn good. I'm not willing to drive thirty minutes for it, but it was good sweet tea. They've got good fried chicken too," he says with a rub of his belly. "Plus, their gas is a good five cents cheaper per gallon than here in town."

I raise my eyebrows, pinning him with a stare. He holds his own hands up in surrender, almost mimicking me. "I know, I know. Carrie isn't penny pinching on her gas savings, but still." He heaves a loud sigh and tugs on his belt.

I make my way back over to his desk and sit down. "And you saw her on camera?"

"You know I did, Ella. She always came out with that drink. Sometimes she bought gas, sometimes she didn't. Sometimes she bought something to eat, sometimes she didn't. But she always had that drink. Nothing unusual. I've heard of people driving all the way down to Gulf Shores just to eat a good seafood lunch and then turning right back around to come home."

I shake my head. "If this $4 gourmet drink has such a hold on my sister, why not buy more than one at a time? Why not buy everything the gas station has so you don't have to go back there, over and over? Like you said, it's not in the best area."

Marcum shrugs his shoulders. "Ella, she's still a kid. Kids don't always think of the big picture."

"I just don't get it. She goes to the gas station, always uses the ATM, and then pays for her stuff with cash. Why not just use the credit card? She buys gas from there on the credit card."

"That's not unusual, honey. Sometimes, people prefer to pay cash in a seedy place. Then, you don't have to worry about a cashier stealing your credit card number. I actually saw tons of people using that ATM machine on the videos." He scratches his jaw. "The gas pumps have card machines built in. She wasn't handing her card over to anyone to buy gas outside the store. That's safer."

Unable to think anymore, I let Marcum walk me to my car. He nods at nothing in particular. "So, they're serious about leaving town and going on vacation?"

I wish I could say they were kidding, but they weren't.

I snort in disgust. Ironic that Addison will be rearranging his surgery schedule so he can cart his wife off to some tropical island. I wonder what he'll have to give Addison to make up for it? It's common knowledge that Addison, my father's personal assistant, is one of his many mistresses.

Marcum shakes his head in disbelief. "Well, I'll send a uniform by your place a couple of times a night just to check on things."

"You don't have to do that."

His words are simple. "I know."

I open the door to my own expensive-ass SUV and climb in.

Chapter 2

Ella

I sigh and bounce my head against the steering wheel when I park in the driveway and see Kristie's Mercedes sitting there. Not that I truly mind her being at my house, I mean, Carrie gave her a key for a reason. But... it's just that I want some alone time to think about what comes next for me. For Carrie.

Kristie has always spent a lot of time with us—sleepovers, dinners, homework—but since Carrie went missing, she's been at the house far more than normal. If she's not at school or work, she's typically here. It's a little weird having her here because she was always closer to Carrie than me. Her mom died when she was six years old, so it's just her and her dad, who happens to be the orthopedic surgeon at my father's surgical practice. Dr. Phillip Vann. In fact, he's the surgeon who operated on Carrie's knee two years ago when she fell off her bike during a cycling race. With him working so much, we got used to Kristie showing up unannounced at odd times. She's never come right out and said it, but I don't think she likes being alone.

In her second year of college, Kristie's older than me, but younger than Carrie. She also works at the surgical practice part time, acting as her dad's personal assistant. Not to mention, she's in training to be the head office manager one day. She's the closest thing I have to a friend—now that Carrie is gone.

Well, she and Hudson. If anyone can classify Hudson as a true friend, that is.

I make my way into the house, tossing my purse and phone on the granite kitchen counter and grabbing a bottle of water from the fridge. Kristie is sitting on the living room floor with papers spread in every direction around her. Settling on the plush couch, I hug a pillow tightly to my chest. "What are you doing?"

"Studying the medication logs. Dad is teaching me about that."

I nod, taking a long swallow of my drink.

"So, how'd the meeting with the police go?"

"Not good. They're done. Well, not really, but they are at a standstill until more tips come in. And no tips *are* coming in. Nothing. It's completely stagnant."

She turns to me, studying my reaction. Her thick auburn hair is pulled back in a ponytail, and her pale skin has a dewy glow, dotted with pale red freckles. Sometimes she wears too much makeup. I like it when her freckles show. She's pretty, but like me, she doesn't really date. I don't date because I haven't met anyone whom I really *want* to date. I think Kristie doesn't date because her father doesn't let her. Having lost his wife so many years ago, he can be a little overprotective. He's charming and handsome and powerful, just like my own father, but at least he appears to take an interest in his daughter's life. Dad has never shown one ounce of interest in me, and the only activity that he and Carrie happen to share is a love of biking, which coincidently, Phillip introduced to my sister. Not our father.

She leans her head back against the loveseat, closing her eyes. She must be worn out between school and work. She's always dozing off whenever she comes over. "And how do you feel about all that?" she asks in a sleepy whisper.

I rub my temples, squeezing the frustration from my brain. I'm pissed. Really pissed. Of course, I'd never say that. Why? Because I have to be more politically correct. More regal. More polite. I roll my shoulders back and sit up straight. "Someone out there knows what happened to my sister, and they're keeping the information all to themselves."

I press my lips into a thin line.

Because I sure as hell know my sister didn't—and wouldn't—leave me all alone.

I can't believe I'm doing this. Am I really doing this?

I close my eyes and slowly replay what I know. Unsettled with the stall in Carrie's case, I quickly ordained myself as an amateur sleuth. I made a timeline of everything I knew from the week of Carrie's disappearance and the days immediately following, which is hard since I was on vacation with Uncle Ray, Aunt Teresa, and Holt most of the time. I talked with her ex-boyfriend, Caleb. They had broken up about a month and a half before she went missing. I talked with some of her friends—Hannah, Catie, and Dakota, who all share an apartment near the university campus.

I even tried to talk with Mom and Dad upon their return from Bermuda a week and a half ago, but they were both completely and utterly distracted, as per the norm. Dad with rescheduled patients for surgery and rescheduled mistresses for sex, and Mom with rescheduled pseudo-friends for tennis and rescheduled rich bitches for wine tasting. Trying to talk to them and get anywhere is like trying to wrangle a herd of alley cats in heat.

Each night, after finishing my homework, I studied one small aspect of the case. I printed off our bank and credit card statements for the past two years and combed through them so precisely it felt like I was memorizing the entire first act of *Romeo and Juliet*. Last night I isolated Carrie's change in spending habits. I feel like I've hit on something very important, but I just can't pinpoint the significance, though.

About fourteen months ago is when things changed. Which would have been about eight months before she disappeared. That's when Carrie started driving all the way across the county to shop at this one particular gas station.

And then six months before she vanished is when she disabled the GPS tracking system in her car. That was one of the first things that Marcum and Leary did. They tried to obtain all of the GPS data from her SUV. But it had been manually disabled. This was also around the time she started turning off her cell phone for large stretches of time, rendering that form of GPS untraceable as well. There was no answer for any of that. And it wasn't like any of us knew that she'd done that as we weren't in the habit of following her every move.

It didn't take me long to realize that I needed answers. *Real answers.*

I was banging on the girls'—Hannah, Catie, and Dakota's—apartment door before school this morning, begging and pleading for any information. They claimed not to know anything, but I have a distinct feeling that they're hiding something. I went to Caleb's apartment next, and he finally confirmed my suspicions. Something was—*something is*—going on at the gas station. He wouldn't divulge more than that, but his eyes did hold a new pain I hadn't noticed before.

And then he shut the door, telling me to go to school.

But only after begging me to drop it. Begging me to let this go and just live my life.

Of course, he knew I wouldn't. That's probably why he shut the door... because revisiting past demons first thing in the morning is obviously a hard pill for him to swallow.

I tap my fingers on the steering wheel and glare at the overhead signage reflecting in the rearview mirror.

Travis Boys Gas and Country Mart.

The warm January sun of the late afternoon has me quickly breaking into a sweat as I sit in the driver's seat. Typical Alabama winter. It was forty-five yesterday, and today the high is sixty-eight.

And... now, I'm fixating on the weather in a pitiful attempt to talk myself out of something monumentally stupid.

Chapter 3

Ella

Here I still sit, twenty minutes later, building up the courage to step inside the gas station that may hold secrets to the whereabouts of my big sister. Acid churns in my stomach like the swells of stormy ocean waves, and my temples throb with pressure. With one last deep breath, I tightly grasp my phone and my paisley wristlet in my right hand and step from my vehicle, locking the door behind me. There's nothing unusual about the outside of the station. You can tell it's been remodeled within the past few years, and there are eight gas pumps divided into two lanes. One pump is currently occupied by a black sedan where a gentleman patiently fills his tank.

I slowly walk from the side of the station, where I parked, to the front door, searching the spattering of surrounding buildings. Across the street is a dollar store and a fast-food restaurant, and on the same side of the street, just down a small alleyway is a body shop. Harlan's Garage and Automotive. I'm about to head into the station when something catches my eye at the body shop.

Rather, *someone* catches my eye.

A tall, muscular man leans over a car, working beneath the hood. He's wearing boots, blue jeans, and a stark white T-shirt, which contrasts nicely with his unseasonably tanned skin. His shoulders and upper back are broad and his waist is trim. I can see the muscles that run the length of his arms flex and pull as he grabs something from the vehicle's engine, looks at it, and puts it back. There's a ballcap on his head so I can't really make out the color of his hair, but I'm pretty sure it's brown. Maybe dirty blond.

He reaches around to the rounded globes of his firm backside and tugs a white hand towel from his back pocket. He wipes his hands and then tucks the rag back into place. An unusual, soft tingle rolls from my belly down to my groin and ends up in a pool in my toes.

I shake my head, clearing my lust-fueled thoughts. I better head inside before he turns around and completely shatters the illusion.

Not to be judgmental, but based on the track record of people from this part of town, he most likely has only three teeth in his head, an eye patch, and a tattoo of a snake on his face. At least that's what the guy looked like who was dumpster diving at the fast-food restaurant earlier.

The door emits a soft, electronic chime as I push it open. The smell of fried food and Clorox overwhelms my senses. A woman with bright red hair buys a bag of chips and an apple juice, while a little boy with equally bright red hair tugs at her pants leg. They finish their transaction, and I step to the side, making room for them to pass, and watch them walk to the waiting black sedan.

There's one guy standing at the register. He looks to be in his mid-twenties. His light brown hair is a little on the greasy side and a little on the long side. He's tall and thin with nice bone structure and big brown eyes. Maybe, he'd be handsome if he weren't so... skanky.

I can't tell if he uses drugs or drinks and smokes too much, but something is definitely going on with him. Something has eaten away at his boyish good looks and healthy stature.

He eyes me suspiciously so I quickly smile and politely nod, walking away before my monstrous nerves get the best of me. I meander down the aisles, aimlessly picking up concessions here and there in an attempt to disguise my investigation of the store. I surface on the drink aisle and freeze mid-step. Slayton's Southern Blackberry Tea offensively stares back at me from the glass refrigerator door. I grab the bottle from the cooler with shaky hand and make my way back to the register.

"How you doing? That'll be all?" The man's voice is scratchy and his tone disinterested, but interestingly enough, there's a pulse between us.

A hum. Like he's dying to say something but doesn't.

Needing an excuse to stay longer, I add food to my order. "Can I get a fried chicken breast too, please?"

"To go?"

I glance over my left shoulder to see a row of dining booths lined against the window. "For here."

He says nothing as he places a large, golden fried piece of chicken on a paper plate and calculates my total. "That'll be $7.56."

I hand him a ten-dollar bill, and he flips it over, studying it. He smiles, flashing his smoke-stained teeth. Handing me the change, he points, "Napkins on the table."

My voice wavers slightly. "Thank you."

I feel his eyes on me as I cross the store, and it feels like a thousand fire ants are crawling across my bare skin. Itching. Burning.

Damn skeeving me out.

In perfect timing, the door chimes, announcing the arrival of a new customer, and the cashier's attention is diverted elsewhere. I sit at the first booth on the side that faces the register. I want to see everything this guy does. I scoot to the right, partially hiding myself behind a four-foot-tall cardboard cutout hailing the greatness of a new candy bar flavor. I open the glass bottle and take a small swig of the drink.

Surprisingly, *it is* very good.

Excellent, actually. But I still wouldn't drive thirty minutes one way for it.

I tear off a small piece of chicken skin and quietly chew, watching the transaction at the register with one eye.

Huh. Marcum's right. The chicken's not half bad.

I eat slowly and do my best to nonchalantly observe all of my surroundings, absorbing each and every detail. I'm on my fourth bite of chicken when my attention peaks to high-alert. An attractive woman, dressed in an expensive, fine-tailored navy-blue pantsuit with stylish nude pumps, heads to the counter with a bottle of Slayton's Southern Blackberry Tea clutched in her perfectly manicured hand. I quickly chew and swallow, nearly choking, so I can hear the interaction without interference from my own loud mouth.

She places the bottle on the counter and slides a folded bill across the stained Formica. The cashier smirks. "That'll be it?"

"Yes. Could you place my drink in a paper bag, please?"

His smirk grows to shit-eatin' status, and he grunts. "Let me grab one from the back." He takes the money and tea with him as he disappears behind the interior doorway with the 'Employees Only' sign hanging above the doorframe. The woman impatiently taps her foot against the tile floor.

Tap. Tap. Tap.

She nervously glances out the glass door. I suppose she's checking on her vehicle.

Suddenly, the cashier's greasy head pops from the abyss, and he places a small brown paper bag on the countertop. "That'll be $4.31." He unfolds the bill. "Out of five." His fingers make nimble work of the register, and it pops open, where he makes her change.

She bolts from the store as soon as the coins are in her hand, causing him to chuckle under his breath.

My mind swirls in deep concentration. What the hell was that all about? That was weird.

I spend the next hour at the gas station. When my chicken breast is nothing more than a pile of bones, I buy a bottle of water and a candy bar, just to give me something else to do without raising suspicion for not leaving. Not that I really need to worry about that; the cashier decides not to pay me any more attention. I'm just a fly on the wall. And for that, I am thankful. Because his gaze irks me. And makes me want to gouge his eyeballs out with a coat hanger.

The visit does prove interesting, though.

Three more people come into the store to buy the same tea. A complete and total variety of people. One middle-aged man who looks like a factory worker who has just gotten off shift. One teenage girl wearing a shirt that is two sizes too small with a skirt that barely covers her cellulite-covered butt cheeks. And one young guy in his twenties, with a pock-scarred face, who looks completely strung out and paranoid.

Each transaction is just as odd as the first, with the cashier leaving the counter to grab a paper bag from the back supply room. If people like those dang paper bags so much, why not keep them under the register?

I climb into my SUV, just as the parking lot lights buzz to life underneath the darkened night sky. They hum like mosquitoes in the summer. The garage door is still open at the body shop across the way. In the shadows, a body leans against the doorframe, studying me. My heart flitters in my chest, like a hummingbird racing around the garden.

I quickly lock my doors.

I turn my radio off and drive in silence.

Think. Think. Think.

Why does Carrie go there? Why does Carrie drive all the way out there for gas? For tea?

Maybe she's secretly dating someone who works there. Not the guy who was working there today, obviously. But maybe someone like the guy across the street at the body shop...assuming his front side looks as good as his back side.

Maybe there's some big corporate conspiracy. Maybe that company puts some sort of addictive additive in their drink, and Carrie needs it, like a smoker needs nicotine or a caffeine addict needs a cup of coffee.

Think. Think. Think.

And then it happens. A small iota of an idea grabs the corner of my mind. It tugs annoyingly at my subconscious, twisting and turning reality into a distorted vision of horror.

That can't be right.

My mind is playing tricks on me.

It has to be. It just has to be.

I increase my speed as my heart thunders in my chest, and I find myself racing for answers.

And racing back to Caleb's apartment as fast as my $100,000 vehicle can legally carry me.

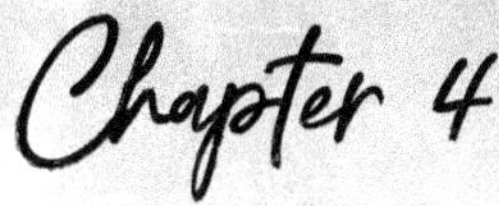

Chapter 4

Ella

Caleb barely has the apartment door open before my loud words push against him violently. "Why does my sister go to that craphole gas station!"

It takes Caleb a few seconds to recover. Dressed in gym shorts and a T-shirt with a beer bottle in hand, he glances self-consciously over his shoulder to the group of friends scattered around his living room, playing video games. The muscle in his jaw twitches. "Ella, I already told you. I don't know."

His eyes shift back and forth as he stares at the concrete threshold, and then he takes a long swig of his beer, avoiding eye contact at all costs.

My head cocks to the side, deep in concentration. "But you have an idea?" That comment sparks some interest.

Eventually, he sighs, shifting his body to the side so I can enter his second-story apartment. He nods to the back balcony door, indicating the need for some privacy. I recognize several of the guys in his living room, not only from the times that I hung out here with Carrie, but from the searches that we did for her right after she went missing. As I approach, a handful of them catcall to me, inviting me to join the play on the newest and latest video game.

"Not now." Caleb's firm tone leaves nothing for debate, and they quickly turn their attention away from us.

I take a seat in one of the chairs on the back balcony.

"Just a second. I'll be right back." Caleb returns a few moments later and passes a bottle of water and a blanket to me before taking the seat next to mine. He's holding a long-sleeve shirt in his hand and quickly pulls it over his head, adding an extra layer to fight against the cooler temperature of the night.

Settling into the chair, he twists the lid off his fresh beer bottle and tosses the cap into a small trash can stashed in the corner. Neither of us speak; we just stare in silence, looking out through the black metal slats of his balcony railing.

"So, you have an idea of why she goes to that gas station? Why she drives thirty minutes when there are fifteen gas stations less than five minutes from our house?"

Caleb's solemn face is sobering. He's always been so jovial and happy. I just knew that one day he would be my brother-in-law. I knew it the minute I saw him and Carrie together. They met the week she started college, in her American History class. He was basically a member of my and Carrie's little nuclear family. Until he and Carrie stopped dating.

Completely cold turkey.

They stopped calling one another, stopped seeing one another, stopped... everything. Carrie refused to talk about it. Even to me. I thought she just needed time, so I didn't pressure her.

Why rush? We had all the time in the world.

Until we didn't.

He nods and takes a long, deep drink from his bottle. I mindlessly run my fingertips around the back of my neck and finger the raised edges of my scar, patiently waiting.

"Carrie's a drug addict, Ella."

My heart stops. My breathing stops.

Drug activity became my educated hypothesis upon observing the gas station cashier and patrons all afternoon, but I refused to believe that Carrie was directly involved in that. The whole ride back into town, I marinated on a myriad of possibilities, no matter how far-fetched.

Maybe Carrie somehow got roped into being an informant for the police and she goes to the gas station to keep tabs on the comings and goings of criminals. Maybe she got recruited by an overzealous reporter to act as some undercover spy to detail what happens in the drug underworld. Hannah is a journalism major, I think, so it's completely plausible.

But all of my fantasies dissolve into a bitter pile of acid with Caleb's one simple statement.

"Wh—what?" My voice is raspy and dry.

He shakes his head and quickly downs the rest of his beer, anger and frustration consuming his every feature. He raises his arm over his head and throws the beer bottle from the second-story balcony like he's pitching in the last inning of the World Series. A small scream rushes my lips as I rise forward in my seat, just in time to see the brown bottle crash into the open mouth of a large dumpster below. The explosive shatter echoes through the night, and I sigh, just glad Caleb didn't hit some straggling pedestrian or animal.

"A drug addict. She's addicted to drugs. Prescription drugs. Well, not *legal* prescriptions," he clarifies.

"I don't understand. Carrie doesn't do drugs."

Caleb glances over and looks at me with complete and utter sympathy. He stares at me like I'm nothing more than a naïve adolescent with 'sunshine and rainbows' syndrome.

He should know better. Carrie should have taught him better.

I stopped believing in sunshine and rainbows a long time ago.

"She does. You name it, she does it. Oxy, Vicodin, Percocet. Hell, even fucking Ritalin."

I shake my head in disbelief. "It can't be. I would know. I would see the signs. We're together *all* the time." It hurts to even talk. It feels like I just drank hot tar. "How? When?"

"After her surgery."

My mind churns. About a year and a half before she vanished, Carrie had a terrible fall from her bicycle and completely shredded her knee. She broke her patella and tore her ACL and had to have surgery with extensive physical therapy afterward. The surgery that Phillip did. Carrie, Phillip, and Dad had been out riding together with their normal cycling club when it happened.

"She got addicted to the pain medication and she can't stop." He tosses his hands in the air, not sure what tense to use. "Couldn't stop." He sighs deeply. "She wouldn't stop."

I find myself rubbing my scar again, lost in thought. I quickly pull my hands into my lap. Carrie's always trying to break me of that bad habit. I'm surprised I even realized I was doing it.

"You have to be mistaken, Caleb. She had pain killers after surgery, sure, but she stopped taking them all within a month after surgery."

"You're wrong. That's when the doctor stopped prescribing them. That's not when she stopped taking them."

I simmer on his words, letting them seep into my subconscious. Is that right? Is my sister a druggie? "Carrie doesn't act like a drug addict. She doesn't look all strung out and dirty and nasty. She takes care of me."

Caleb stares at nothing in particular. "Of course, she doesn't look like an addict." He closes his eyes and sighs softly. "She's fucking gorgeous." His voice cracks with emotion, and I find myself involuntarily consoling him.

I give his forearm a gentle squeeze, giving him just a moment before I pepper him with questions. "I don't understand. How'd she get them? She'd never ask Dad, and no one else at the practice would risk their medical license for that kind of stuff. There's like...a thousand forms to sign where you promise not to go against doctor's orders on your meds."

"At first, I wasn't sure where she got them. Or if she got them at all. I'd see her taking one, and she'd just say, 'Oh, I had a few left in the bottle.' That went on for months. I think her addiction started slow. Like only getting high once or twice a week. But, that one bottle was like a clown pulling scarves out of his sleeve. It just kept going and going. One night, I found a stash of pills in her purse. She had them in that tin mint container." He points to me. "What's the one you hate?"

"Altoids."

"Yeah, that's it. Anyway, I confronted her about them. She told me that she was still having pain so she got some pills from a friend. She promised she wouldn't do it again. A few months later, I walked in on her buying pills from one of my fraternity brothers. I beat the shit out of him and told Carrie that she had to stop or I would go to your parents. Everything was good after that, or so I thought. I thought I had her back. But I was wrong. She just got better at hiding it."

He stops and doesn't say anything, but I can tell there's more to the story, so I don't interrupt. Eventually, he starts again. "There's more, Ella." He shakes his head. "She's not just a user, she's a dealer too."

"What!"

"That's why I broke up with her. I found out she was selling."

"Selling? Selling to who?"

"Just some people at school," he says with a shrug. "I'm not sure who all it was, but I do know at least to Catie, Hannah, and Dakota."

"What! Are you serious?"

"Yep. That's how I found out. Catie apparently couldn't pay one day so she made a pass at me. Said she'd sleep with me in exchange for me stealing some Oxy and Ritalin from Carrie."

"Are you kidding?"

He drags his hand over his face. "I wish I was."

My body feels like it's on fire. A burning, scorching mess of confusion, anger, and denial. I put the cool water bottle against my sizzling forehead and rub it around. "And the gas station is where she can get drugs?"

"I'm not for sure, but I think it is. She never let me ride out there with her, but I saw receipts in her vehicle from gas and stuff. Whenever I asked her about it, she always made up a different excuse of why she went out there."

I close my eyes and lean my head back against the wooden slats of the chair. "I don't see how I could've missed all this." It's Caleb's turn to comfort me now. He reaches over and gives my knee a reassuring squeeze.

"I know you hate it when I talk about you being young, but it's the truth, Ella. You were what, one month away from turning sixteen when she had her surgery? You were a kid. You're not supposed to watch over your older sister. That's what parents are for. It's just shitty luck that you have a mom who's more interested in the next piece of jewelry she can buy, and a dad who's more interested in the next piece of cunt he can screw." Caleb doesn't hide the utter disgust in his voice. He's always been protective of Carrie and me, and I've always loved him for that.

"Why didn't you tell anyone about this, Caleb? Why not tell me or Detective Marcum, at least. He needs to bring Catie, Hannah, and Dakota in. He needs to question them."

Caleb chuckles cynically. "He'll never get anything from them. They'll deny everything. They don't wanna be known as the crack whores they really are."

"But still, why not tell Marcum about Carrie's addiction?"

"You know what happens when people find out that the missing person they're looking for is a drug addict. They stop looking. It's automatically assumed that they went away on some bender. That they just walked away from life because they wanted to. You think Carrie's face would've been plastered across every news outlet in America if they knew she popped pills like they came out of a PEZ dispenser? Hell no! My girl would've been tossed to the back page of the newspaper. Keeping this secret is the only way I can make sure that every single person in the lower forty-eight knows what Caroline Hill looks like."

I chew my bottom lip. He's got a point. Not that I agree with it, but it's probably true.

He lowers his head between his hands. "We were kids too. Me and Carrie. I thought I could do it alone. I thought I could save her just by loving her. She's the love of my life. Still is. But there's no way I can compete with addiction."

Chapter 5

Ella

Friday night.

Friday night and I'm back in my car outside of the gas station.

I played my life with Carrie over and over on a loop in my scattered brain all last night and all day today. I googled the symptoms of prescription addiction. I pinpointed every time she acted euphoric. Every time she acted depressed. Every time she was sick with a headache or nausea. I focused on every time she dozed off for a nap during the day. I thought about every time she rubbed or touched her face. I fixated on every all-nighter she pulled to study for a test. I concentrated on the ten pounds she lost in the last few months before she disappeared.

I should have paid more attention.

I failed my sister.

I'm a fucking failure.

I debated telling Marcum what I found out. It would be so easy. Easy to pass the buck. Easy to pass the responsibility. But I just couldn't bring myself to do it.

I'm stubborn. And I'm foolish. Like a mouse eating food from a mousetrap. I ignore the risk for the reward.

I'm not sure this situation has a reward… but I guess I'll find out soon enough.

The dollar store and fast-food restaurant are busy tonight. The gas station too. I watch as the light inside the garage next door turns off. A few minutes later, an old truck drives away from the back door. Grabbing my wristlet, I zip my phone into the middle pocket and head into my destiny.

I take a deep breath and straighten my spine the second I see him walking over to my table. Lifting my chin in the air, I study him. His hair is covered with a red ballcap, and he scratches at a scab on the side of his nose. His face is a contradiction. Swollen, yet gaunt.

A new cashier just came in so he must be off duty now. Sliding into the opposite side of my booth, he picks up a piece of chicken I didn't eat and pops it into his mouth. "So, you wanna tell me why you've been parked in my gas station, watching me for the past two hours?" He waggles his eyebrows. "You like what you see?"

Like what I see? I'd be more turned on watching a colonoscopy. "Your gas station? You own it?"

He laughs, rubbing his tongue across his stained teeth. He pulls a cigarette from the pocket of his shirt and twists it around in his hand. "Nah, who wants all that pressure. I just work here."

"You mean you work here and sell here." I can't believe I just said that. My heart feels like it's being powered by a stampede of wild mustangs.

His eyes narrow and he looks me up and down, slowly, like an oscillating fan moving back and forth. "What do you think you know about it? You work for the police?"

"No."

"You know if I ask you, you have to tell me the truth. Police entrapment and all that."

What a dumbass. He's watched too many movies. "I said I'm not police."

"Well, if you're looking to make a deal, this isn't the way to do it.

Whoever sent you here should've given you full instructions. You've only been doing half of it. Buying fried chicken ain't the other half."

Well, I guess he just confirmed my suspicion that the sweet tea has something to do with it. That must be the 'half' I'm getting right.

"She doesn't know I'm here," I say.

He smells his cigarette. "And who is *she*?"

"My sister. Her name is Caroline. Carrie."

His eyes grow wide as saucers. "No shit?" He vehemently shakes his head, "I don't know anything about her going missing. The cops were here. I gave them the videotapes of the store. I answered all of their questions."

"Yes, but did they ask the right questions?"

That comment strikes him as funny and his cackle fills the distance between us. "You're kind of a bitch. You know that?"

"So, I've been told." It's true. I've been told that more than once.

He grunts, flipping the cigarette back and forth between his fingers. "Everyone calls me Trash."

I roll my shoulders back, "Ella."

"So why are you really here, Ella?" His tongue flicks out to lick his cigarette.

He's not even lit the damn thing, and he's treating it like a long-lost lover.

"I know my sister was using. And I know my sister was selling. It all leads back here. I'm not trying to get anyone into any trouble. I'm just trying to find out what happened to Carrie. Does someone know where she is?"

He studies my face for sincerity, and for the first time, I notice that his pupils are small and constricted. "Well, I don't know where she is."

"What about your friends? Business associates? Would they know where she is?"

"Business associates?" He laughs. "I'm not pushing Mary Kay, sweetheart."

I wanna punch him.

When I don't say anything else, he sighs dramatically. "Look, I'm late for a party. If you promise not to cause any problems, you can come. Ask around. Just be careful what you say. Don't act like a rat. That shit will get you in trouble." He swings his skinny body from the booth and pushes the door open. "You coming?"

Mouse meet trap.

I hope the measly piece of cheese is worth it.

Chapter 6

Crutch

She's rich.

How do I know?

You can just tell.

Her leather knee-high boots for one. The soles are flat. The girls around here wear stripper heels, even on their boots. Her leggings look like cream-colored pants and not ripped jeans. Even her hair looks expensive. Like maple syrup, golden brown mixed with shiny light colors.

She didn't see me when she came outside. I'm sitting in the shadows of the back porch with only the light from my laptop screen shining on my face. Standing at the deck railing, she looks out at what should be a patch of trees and forest. But it's nothing but stumps. Trash had the trees cut down a few months ago for more drug money. Apparently, his habit has now surpassed his legal—and illegal—income.

Sighing deeply, her shoulders relax, and she slumps forward. Leaning far over the railing, she pours the liquid from her beer bottle, emptying it on the ground.

And... now I know she has a great ass.

"Not a fan of beer?"

My words startle her, and she yelps, quickly spinning around. It takes her a moment to regain her composure. I'm sure it does seem odd to see someone on a computer, in the dark, outside, when a party is raging just inside the trailer doors.

And... now I know she's fucking gorgeous.

She stiffens her spine and lifts her pouty little nose in the air. "Not a fan of lowered inhibitions."

I don't think I've ever seen someone with such good posture.

"What about you?" She dips her chin at me. "Not a fan of parties?"

I take a swig of my own beer. "Not a fan of escaping reality."

She opens her mouth and then closes it, thinking about and accepting my answer, without prying more.

"I've not seen you here before."

"That's because I've not been here before." She doesn't elaborate.

And... now I know she's kind of a bitch.

"Invited or crashing?"

"Trash invited me."

Disappointment courses through my body, deflating it like a popped balloon. So, she's one of *those*. Pill-popping, little rich girl, ready to piss off Daddy by banging a junkie from the wrong side of the tracks. "I see." Turning back to my laptop screen, I do my best to ignore her.

Which is very hard to do. I mean, she's really fucking gorgeous.

My silence aggravates her and she takes some tentative steps in my direction. "So, you come to parties here often?"

"I'm not the person to see for pills."

She pins me with her eyes, forcing me to look away from my homework. "I'm not here for pills."

Her hair hangs straight like a curtain, falling around her ample breasts. Not that I can see her ample breasts; her shirt doesn't show any cleavage.

I've offended her. She didn't like me insinuating that she was here to score drugs. I quickly save my document and flip the lid of my laptop closed, gently laying it on the railing beside me. "What's your name?"

"Everyone calls me Ella."

"Why does everyone call you that? Is that not your name?"

She breathes deeply.

It must suck, standing like a statue all the time.

"My name is Luella. But no one calls me that. It's just Ella."

"Luella." I work the word over my tongue. It stirs a weird feeling in my stomach. "Alright, Lulu, it is."

She snorts, not realizing that I will never call her Ella now.

"What about you? What's your name?"

I smirk, taking another pull of my beer. "Everyone calls me Crutch."

Her eyes flare, immediately ready to give me a dose of my own medicine. "Why does everyone call you that? Is that not your name?"

"My name is Ryland. But no one calls me that. It's just Crutch."

"Ryland." The second she says my name, my dick jumps in my jeans, and I quickly shove my bottle down in front of my crotch. "Alright, Ry, it is."

I can't help it. I laugh. I twist the chair beside me in her direction. "Have a seat, Lulu, and you can tell me why you're really here."

She tries not to smile. Really, she does. And then, she tries to hide it behind her glossy hair. But I see it nonetheless.

She sits down in the cheap lawn chair, folding the wrist wallet against her hand and picking at the label on her empty beer bottle.

"Here," I reach down beside me to the bottle of water I haven't opened yet. "Seal's not open. Want it?"

Nodding, she takes the bottle from me and her fingers brush against mine. Her touch burns my skin. She's even more beautiful up close. If her hair is maple syrup, then her eyes are honey. Light brown, circled with a dark brown, almost black color. Her skin is olive toned and she has a small freckle above the right side of her upper lip.

A lip that would look great around my—

"So, do you know a lot of people here?"

"I do. Unfortunately. Why are you here? You're definitely not the normal kind of girl who comes to these parties."

She twists open the lid, making sure the cap breaks. "What's that supposed to mean?" She takes a long drink, watching me though squinted eyes.

"You're not gonna make me say it, are you, Lulu? I think you're too smart to pretend you don't see the differences between you and the other girls you met inside."

I'm rewarded with that pointy little nose lifting back up in the air. "I'm looking for my sister."

"Who's your sister?"

"Caroline Hill. Carrie Hill."

The breath rushes from my lungs. "No shit? You're Carrie's sister?"

She eagerly pushes her body forward. Her eyelids sparkle with color. She probably spends more money each month on makeup than I spend on food and gas.

"You know her? You've met my sister?"

I nod. "I only met her once at a party here. I don't come all the time, though, like some people. Most of the time I saw her going into the gas station. I work at the body shop across the parking lot."

She collapses back against the chair, trying to hide the shock from her face. She doesn't hide it very well, though, because she still looks like she stuck her tongue in an electric socket. Reaching up, she rubs the back of her neck. "You're the guy from the gar—"

A shrill cry interrupts our conversation. "Crutch! There you are. I've been looking all over for you."

It's not like my brother owns a seven-bedroom mansion; this is a seven-hundred-square-foot mobile home. How hard did she really have to search?

"Hi, Amber." I look past Amber, her jet-black hair, and visible red lace bra and nod to the friend trailing behind her, stumbling in high bliss. "Mandy."

Lulu immediately hides the emotion on her face, squaring her shoulders.

Amber leans against the deck railing, jutting her leg out in front of her like a model posing for a photo shoot. Well, attempting to pose like a model for a photo shoot. It's hard to do when you're three sheets to the wind. She raises her cigarette to her lip right as a small gust of wind blows ash on her chest. Flicking it away, she stomps on it, kicking it across the wooden porch.

"What have you been up to? We missed you last weekend." Her purr sounds more like a growl.

Mandy nods, enjoying the feel of the movement against her drugged-out brain.

I take a pull of my beer. "I'm sure you did." I make it a point to never sleep with anyone from my side of town. I never have sex with someone who knows me, my family, or where I come from. So, she may have missed me, but she didn't *miss* me.

She fake pouts. "Of course, I did. It's not a party unless you're here. Don't you know you make everything better," she says, lowering her voice a decibel.

Lulu rolls her eyes.

She may try to hide her smile, but she makes no attempt to hide this. It's a blatant, over-exaggerated movement, complete with a head roll.

I can't help it. For the second time, Lulu has me laughing out loud.

Her eyes flicker to me and she purses her lips in a straight line.

Finally, Amber pays attention to the girl sitting beside me. She snorts, "Who are you?"

"I'm Ella."

Amber quickly dismisses her, sizing her up as no competition.

She's wrong. Lulu should be the competition for every girl.

"Put away your homework, Crutch, and come inside. We can grab a drink and talk."

"I have a few things to finish up. I'll be in soon."

Amber rubs her thumb over her lip. "Promise?"

I just shrug.

Accepting that as an affirmative answer, Amber and Mandy snake past us into the trailer.

I don't say anything, waiting on Lulu to make the first move. I have no idea how she is going to react, and I'm sitting on damn pins and needles, eager to see.

"Well, your friends seem... eager to please."

I chuckle. "I guess so." I finish the last of my beer. "And I never said they were my friends."

Her eyes flicker over to my closed laptop. "Homework?" she questions, picking up on Amber's comment.

I just shrug again. "It's nothing."

Staring at me, Lulu narrows her eyes, considering my words. Her tongue darts out to lick her lips before she switches topics. "So, you know my sister?"

"Not well. Like I said, I only met her once at a party here. I'm sorry she's missing. I actually joined some of the search parties when they were looking for her in the woods by the restaurant where her car was found. We didn't find anything."

She slowly nods. "Thank you for your help." She takes another small sip of her water. "So, you saw her at the gas station? Did she go there a lot?"

"More than a girl like her should've." If I stare hard enough, I'm sure I can see the wheels of Lulu's brain turning, twisting, spitting out ideas. "What do you know about the gas station?"

She takes a deep breath. "I know it's where people go to buy drugs. I know that my sister went there to buy drugs." She clears her throat. "And she apparently sold drugs too."

"Holy shit." I lift the ballcap from my head and drag my fingers through my hair. "Carrie started pushing?"

"Huh?"

"Pushing drugs for the dealer."

"Oh. I guess. Who's the dealer? Trash? He was selling drugs at the gas station yesterday and today."

I narrow my eyes. "You were at the gas station yesterday and today?" I sigh, dawning with realization. "The Infiniti SUV. That was you?"

She nods.

I glanced up from my work when the expensive SUV pulled across the street. The second I saw one long leg climb from the front seat, I went back to my work, underneath the hood of an old station wagon. As the drug business grew, more and more clientele came searching for their next high. Clientele with a lot of money to spend.

"So, you didn't know about Carrie using or selling until now?" I ask.

"No." Her shoulders stay square, her spine stays firmly straight, but her eyes fall to the floor. Her heart is breaking, and for some strange reason, it fucking breaks mine too.

"I'm sorry you had to find that out. Some secrets are best left buried."

She doesn't like that answer. "How can you say that? These drugs? This gas station? I'm sure it has something to do with why she went missing. It's the puzzle piece we've all been looking for. Someone here has to know what happened to my sister."

"Lulu, the police already came out here. Questioned Trash and the owner of the station. Something about ATM charges."

"Yes, but that was before they knew about the drugs."

I fling forward in my seat. Reaching across the distance between us, I squeeze her leg. Her own hand flies to her mouth, and she stares at my hand, splayed across her lower thigh, just above the knee. My mouth grows dry and my brain fogs.

I toss those feelings away like yesterday's dirt. "What do you mean that was *before* they knew about the drugs. Did you tell the police that drugs are being dealt at the gas station?"

She doesn't answer.

Begrudgingly, I remove my hand.

She lowers her fingertips from her mouth and answers. "No. Not yet."

Finally, I can breathe again. "Good." I sit back in my seat. "You can't."

"I *can't*? What do you mean, I *can't*? That's illegal activity. You know the police kind of frown against that."

If the situation weren't so serious, I would find her sarcasm cute.

"What are you doing, Lulu? Playing some kind of amateur detective? This isn't a TV show. This is dangerous shit. My brother isn't the dealer. He's a pusher, just like Carrie. The dealer is a bad guy. I mean, really bad. And if he's that bad, who knows what the hell the supplier is like. You go around ratting to the police, that shit will get you into trouble. The dead kind of trouble."

She cocks her head to the side. "Trash is your brother?"

And, there it is.

The look.

The look that always happens when someone finds out who my brother is. Who my parents are. The kind of look that says, 'Oh, I thought you might have been different. I guess I was wrong'.

I don't know what to say. So, I don't say anything.

She stands from the chair. "Well, I'm sorry that your brother is involved with this, but I plan on finding my sister. And if that means telling the police about this drug business, then so be it."

She starts walking toward the sliding glass door that leads to the raging party inside. I jump from my seat, grabbing her arm and spinning her around. I don't mean to grab her so hard. I don't mean to spin her around so hard. It just happens. And regardless of my intent, I get to reap the unexpected reward. Her body stumbles into mine, knocking me sideways. I wrap my hands around her waist, steadying us.

I didn't realize she was so tall. The top of her head comes to my chin. And I'm six-foot-four.

My fingers squeeze her hips as she slowly raises her head to look into my eyes. Her breasts rub against my chest, and I pray she can't feel the rock-hard erection that has suddenly sprung to life in my jeans.

Or maybe, I do hope she feels it.

The words get stuck. I have too much to say and not enough brain power to say it. I clear my throat. "What are you doing? Where are you going?"

"I'm gonna question your friends."

"They're not my friends."

She pulls from my grasp and heads inside to join the party. "Then it shouldn't matter to you what happens to them."

It doesn't.

But for some strange reason, it matters what happens to her.

Chapter 7

Crutch

Working on my Western Civ paper after that was a moot point. I packed my computer bag, stored it in my truck, and I've been watching Lulu like a creep from the corner of the living room for the past thirty minutes.

She doesn't really fit in. And you can tell she hates small talk. Even more than that, you can tell she doesn't have the patience to talk to stupid people. Which actually plays out nicely—nearly everyone here is high or drunk, rendering even the smart ones a little moronic.

Amber gave up on her quest of bagging me and currently has her tongue down the throat of some guy with a tattoo on his forehead of two people fucking and some kind of chain connecting his nose ring to his earring. When I turn my eyes back to Lulu, she's gone. I don't see her anywhere, and a small fire of panic swirls into my throat.

My brother's loud, cough-filled laugh draws my attention, and when he shifts to the side, I see Lulu standing beside him, talking to another guy and girl. The second my brother's arm snakes around her shoulder, I find myself pushing through the crowd.

Why?

Who the hell knows?

Do I plan on giving my dumbass brother a bloody nose simply for putting his arm around a girl? A girl I don't know. A girl I don't care about. A girl who could have him thrown in jail.

Oddly, I think the answer to all the above is yes. *Hell yes,* to be more precise.

"Look at this girl, y'all. My new friend, Ella. Didn't I tell you she had the best fucking legs you've ever seen. Miles long." He turns to her, rubbing his nose against her earlobe. "I bet you look great in shorts."

I'm gonna kill him.

Lulu's straight spine stiffens even more. "You're right, Trash. Your parties are great. I'll be right back. Just need to use the ladies' room." She sneaks out from under his arm right when I'm within reaching distance. Catching my eye, she smirks and quickly darts into the hallway.

That little minx.

I don't make it past my brother before he's wrapping his arms around me for a hug. "Bro! I'm so glad you came inside. You need to stop being a pussy and doing homework all the time. You need to get some actual pussy." Laughing, he stumbles, sloshing beer on my shirt.

Please. I've had more pussy in the past three months than he's had in the past three years.

"Here, I have something for you." He shoves a little plastic bag with three pills inside—blue, white, and pink—into the pocket of my long-sleeve T-shirt. "I know you never take, but you've been so stressed out lately. It's my gift to you. Late Christmas present."

I don't remember my brother ever getting me a Christmas present.

Knowing he's too messed up to even remember this conversation, I just nod my head and turn down the hall. There she is. Standing in front of the bathroom door, she's talking to Christina, one of the hardcore girls.

I went to high school with Christina. She's two years older than me. She used to be smart. Wasn't that bad to look at. Now, she looks terrible. Absolutely terrible. She just got released from jail a couple of weeks ago. I don't even know what she was in for this last time. She's already had three kids by three different guys, and all three have been taken away by Child Protective Services. Skin and bones, she shakes just standing there. Touching her face, she picks at an imaginary spot on her chin, scratching a scab that's already been picked a hundred times over.

The only thing surprising about Christina is that she still carries a camera around her neck. She was really big into photography back in high school. I'm actually surprised she hasn't pawned the camera for drug money, because Lord knows she's sold anything and every-thing she can for her next high—including herself from what I've been told.

She stares at Lulu with sunken eyes.

"So, my sister used to come to these parties. I was out of town for a long time, so I wasn't able to come with her. But she had planned to bring me. She wanted me to get in the game."

Get in the game? She *has* been watching too many TV shows.

She reaches up again, rubbing the back of her neck. "You know, the pill game. She went missing. So, I'm just trying to pick up where she left off. You know, meet the needs of my friends. Hey, maybe you know her. Carrie? Carrie Hill?"

She's so bad at this. She might as well be wearing a neon sign that says 'Narc'.

Right then, some people from the living room cheer, and a hush of whispers travel through the crowd. "Trey! Bout time you showed up."

Fuck me.

Time to go.

I walk down the hall and grab Lulu's elbow. Firmly. Bending my head, I place my lips across the ridge of ear. "You need to get out of here. Now."

It could be my imagination, but I think she shivers.

Pulling back, she opens her mouth to argue, but quickly pulls her bottom lip between her teeth when she sees the look on my face. Sensing the tension pouring from my body in huge, pounding waves, she nods.

One simple nod.

I slide my hand down her arm, taking her hand in mine. Before we can walk away, Christina snatches out, grabbing at Lulu's shoulder.

"Hey! Cops are looking for that missing girl. You trying to bring cops around here?"

Lulu's eyes widen.

"No, Christina, she was just kidding. Here." I grab the baggie from my pocket and shove it in her hand. The Holy Trinity packet in front of her consumes all of her thoughts and desires, and she quickly loses interest in us, or why we're there.

Ignoring Lulu's piercing glare, I tug her behind me. Stopping at the edge of the living room, I take stock of my surroundings, spying Trey on the other side, next to the kitchen. Tucking Lulu against my opposite side, I wrap my arm around her, shielding her from view, and guide her across the room and out the front door. I make sure we're halfway down the dirt driveway, behind some cars, before I let her go.

She immediately puts distance between us and then slaps her hands on her hips. It's the first time I've seen her slouch and cock her leg out to the side. "What was that?"

I turn the ballcap around backward on my head. The lights of the trailer are behind us, so the only thing lighting Lulu's face and body is the full moon of the winter night.

So fucking gorgeous.

Trash was right. She has the longest legs I've ever seen.

"You weren't exactly being discreet in there. I told you those people get crazy when they think about cops coming around. That guy who just came in? Trey? He's the dealer, the middleman between the supplier and the pushers. At least, that's what these losers call it—it's like a drug pyramid scheme. Anyway, he's the one I told you about. He *will* kill you if he thinks you're a narc."

"You're just saying that."

"I'm not! He's killed before, Lulu. He only served four years because of a plea deal. It was technically ruled self-defense, and he got the actual time on a possession charge. But all of us around here know it wasn't really self-defense. He murdered a guy."

She swallows. Placing her hands at her side, she pulls back her shoulders and lifts her head. A statue again.

I sigh, tossing my hands in the air. "You can't question these people, Lulu. I know you want to. You have a right to. But you can't. The normal rules of nature—the normal rules of society—don't apply out here. These people are fiercely protective of their addiction. They'll do anything to keep it safe. No one is gonna talk to you. No one is gonna give you any information at all. Even if they know something, they won't tell you."

She doesn't answer.

I kick the ground with the toe of my boot. "You need to leave. You need to get out of here."

Eventually, she nods. I take a quick look around searching for her vehicle. I'm about to ask her where she parked when she walks right past me, heading back in the direction of the front door. "Where are you going? I thought I just told you—"

"I'm going to get your brother."

Harsher words have never been spoken.

"He brought me. My car's not here. It's at the gas station. He has to drive me back."

Red flashes behind my eyelids. "You rode with Trash? You let him drive you? Are you damn crazy? Never, ever ride in a vehicle with any of those people behind the wheel." I throw my hand in the direction of the mobile home. "You understand me? Never."

She just stares.

"Promise me."

She nods. One simple nod.

This nodding and staring shit is driving me mad.

She unzips her wrist wallet and pulls out her phone. I laugh when I see her pecking around on the screen. "You're not gonna get an Uber out this way, babe."

Her head jerks from the screen.

I can't decide if she likes being called 'babe' or not.

"Come on, I'll drive you," I say. With slow, trepid steps, she follows me over to my old truck. I open the passenger-side door, but she doesn't move to get in. "It's a 1970 Ford F-250 Crew Cab. It may not look like what you're used to, but I promise it's perfectly safe. I've spent years working on it."

That comment sparks more emotion on her face than me telling her that Trey could kill her. She doesn't like me insinuating that she's too rich to ride in my truck.

"That's not it. You just told me to never get in a car with any of those people. But you were drinking too. You had pills in your pocket."

"You're right. I was drinking beer. But I don't take pills. My brother stuffed them in my pocket."

She thins her lips when I don't elaborate. "Well, do you plan on telling me how much you had to drink tonight?"

I bend down, sinking to her eye level. "Not enough to forget about meeting you."

I leave the door open and walk to the driver's side, climbing behind the wheel. The truck purrs to life, rumbling in the night like a low thunder, before she climbs in and slams the door. For the first several minutes, she stares out the window. Her reflection against the dark glass mesmerizes me. She doesn't know I'm looking at her. And her face is finally soft. Relaxed. She chews against her bottom lip in thought and rubs the back of her neck.

Why does she keep rubbing her neck? Maybe she pulled a muscle?

Eventually, I break the silence. "Go ahead and ask me. I know you want to."

She turns to me, studying my profile. "What?"

"Don't make me say it, Lulu. And don't beat around the bush. I like you when you get to the point."

I do like her. So help me, I like her.

"Did you kidnap my sister?"

"No."

"Did you hurt my sister?"

"No."

"Do you know where she is?

"No."

"Do you know if anyone kidnapped her or hurt her?"

"If I knew something like that, I would've gone to the police. It may seem like I'm trying to hide something, with the drug business and all of that, but I'm just being realistic. If one of those people knows something, it will come out sooner or later. When they're older. More scared. Less scared. More sober. Less sober. But nobody is gonna talk now. All you're gonna do with your questions is build brick walls. And it will take a very long time to tear them down."

Her next question catches me completely off guard.

"Did you sleep with my sister?"

I nearly run off the road. "What?"

"Did you have sex with Carrie?"

"Why would you ask that? What would make you think that?"

She adjusts the air vent blowing on her. "Those girls insinuated you are promiscuous. Carrie and her boyfriend broke up before she went missing."

"Promiscuous? Are you turning me into an after-school special?"

"Are you avoiding the question?"

"I didn't sleep with Carrie. No." She exhales, loud enough for me to hear. I hate the next words that come from my mouth. Why? I don't know. "But we did kiss."

I side glance at her. Her jaw tightens and she's stiff as a board.

Is kissing me really that horrible of a thought?

"I didn't take advantage of her, if that's what you're thinking. I make it a point to never get involved with anyone from my brother's parties. Carrie seemed different, though. Smart, kind, flirtatious. She kissed me. And I didn't stop it. At first, that is. As soon as I realized she was under the influence, I left."

She refuses to look at me.

We ride in silence, eventually pulling up at the gas station. I park next to her SUV and fully expect her to jump from my truck so fast she leaves sparks in her wake. But she doesn't. She doesn't even reach for the door handle.

She's drowning in thought.

Drowning in memories.

I'm about to get myself into trouble.

So much fucking trouble.

"There's a place I wanna show you? You feel up to it?"

Chapter 8

Ella

Why the hell did I say yes?

Why the hell am I alone in a truck driving to who-knows-where with a complete stranger?

I have no idea.

When he asked if he could take me someplace, my lips wouldn't form any other word than yes. I tried to say no. Really, I did. But my brain couldn't make me utter that one simple syllable. My heart was leading the show, and for some reason my heart said yes.

Maybe it's because he is a link to Carrie. He knows her. His lips have been on her lips. And somehow that makes us share a common bond in some way.

Or maybe it's because my stupid teenage hormones want his lips on my lips.

I try to watch him, without him watching me. He's the best-looking guy I think I've ever met in person. I was caught completely unprepared when he surprised me on the back porch of the trailer. And I was completely and utterly floored when I found out that he's the same guy I saw at the body shop.

His skin is perfectly flawed, with small white scars on his hands and forearms from his job. His light brown hair is styled short and his green eyes are so pale, they almost look translucent. Clean shaven with a firm, square jaw, everything about him screams masculinity. Yells it. From the bottom of its lungs. And he's tall. Very tall. Rolling muscles stretch across his shoulders, back, and chest. And let's not even talk about how good he fills out a pair of jeans.

He doesn't look like any of the other people who were at the party. And that's a good thing.

In fact, he doesn't look like any of the other people in this world. And that's probably why those girls at the party were hitting on him.

He casually reaches up, removes his baseball hat, and tosses it in the back seat. I twist in my seat, paying attention to the back of his pickup truck for the first time. Despite being so old, his truck is lovingly cared for. Clean. The front seat is a bench seat, so all that separates us is a small section of patterned, brown cloth. The back seat catches me by surprise. It's clean too, don't get me wrong, but it's packed with stuff. Folded blankets and pillows, two large duffle bags, and a computer bag are all on the seat. Two big coolers sit on the floorboard.

"Are you in the middle of moving?"

One side of his mouth tilts up. "You'll see."

He suddenly turns off the road onto a gravel and dirt-packed driveway that can only be seen because of two blue reflector lights on either side.

Well, this can't be good.

Panic flutters around my chest like a moth racing to reach the flame. Did I just willingly agree to my own kidnapping?

Did I just become another face on the nightly news? A haunting split-screen image of the two missing Hill sisters plays in my mind. Look what happens, America, when your perfect little sweethearts mix with the wrong company.

I clear my throat, making sure my vocal cords are free of phlegm for when I have to scream. No way I'm going down without a fight. I even move my fingers toward the door handle. He's not driving too fast, I could probably jump and not completely incapacitate myself.

Discreetly glancing at him, I'm surprised when an eerie calm washes over me. Something tells me he's not an ax-wielding murderer or a kidnapping psychopath. And I'm hoping it's not just his extraordinary good looks giving me that vibe.

Catching my eye, a low chuckle rumbles deep in his chest. "You can take your hand off the door handle, Lulu. I'm not a murdering maniac. There really is a place I wanna show you. And I promise when it's time to leave—later tonight—you will be in one piece with your virtue fully intact."

I don't acknowledge his admission, but I do breathe an internal sigh of relief. We drive for about a quarter of a mile through the wooded trees when we come up on a clearing. His headlights shine brightly on the camp in front of us.

And that's just what it is. A camp.

Immediately in front of us, there's a huge concrete pad decorated with mismatched pieces of outdoor furniture—some regular lawn chairs, a couple of Adirondack chairs, and a wicker love seat with a bright red cushion. There are some wooden cable spools masquerading as tables. Right in the middle is a firepit. I lean forward, clamping my fingers on the dashboard to get a better look. Something shimmers just beyond the concrete pad. "Is that a lake?"

"Pond."

I shift to look at him, watching in awe as he runs his fingers over his mouth. Butterflies soar from my stomach to my groin. Unable to accept the heat growing in my body, I quickly turn back to stare out the windshield. To the right of the concrete pad is a really big tent. Like a tent you sleep in when camping. (Not that I've ever been camping.) There are several large, outdoor resin storage containers, both next to the tent and to the left of the concrete pad. Solar lamps protrude from the ground around the site, providing small slivers of light that allow me to see what the headlights don't illuminate.

"Ry, do you live here?" It's the first time I've called him by that nickname since I announced its existence on the back porch of the trailer.

The second he hears the name leave my lips he sucks a hiss of air between his teeth. That small noise throws me off balance, making me feel things I don't want to feel. Not about him. Not about a stranger.

I quickly sit up straight and square my shoulders.

He snorts underneath his breath. "Wait here. I'll be right back." He hops out of the running truck—never answering my actual question—and I follow his movements as he walks through the streams of light. He grabs something from one of the storage containers before jogging back. Leaning through the open driver-side door, he turns off the truck engine, shrouding everything around us in darkness. He turns on the switch to the battery-operated lantern in his hand and it puts out a surprising amount of light.

"Come out this way." He reaches across the bench seat, holding out his hand.

I shouldn't take it.

I know I shouldn't.

So, I do. I always do what I shouldn't.

His calloused fingers wrap around mine, and together we guide my body across the seat and out the driver-side door. He walks me across the gravel and leads me to the concrete pad. The night air has turned cooler, but I can't feel it. All I feel is the strength of his hand around mine. Driving me slowly crazy. Deliciously crazy.

It feels so damn nice. I've never held hands with a guy before. Well, unless you count school dances where I had to hold hands with Hudson because our parents had to take pictures of us dancing together.

"Are you cold?"

"A little." Can he tell I'm lying?

He immediately drops my hand and heads over to the firepit. I watch him grab sticks and a fire starter from a metal bucket. A few seconds later, a fire crackles to life. Setting the lantern on a side table, he steps out of the way, watching me, waiting for me to react.

"Thank you." I can feel the chill now, now that his body isn't connected to mine anymore.

I slowly walk around the concrete patio, checking out the furniture. I steal a few glances at him, and he looks completely and totally amused. Eventually, he sits down in a chair, spreading his legs wide in front of him, giving me unrestricted time and access to snoop around his space.

His obviously private space, based on the way everything looks so well-cared for.

There's a worn wooden dock that juts out over the pond. There's no noise. The bugs are lying dormant for the winter. But I bet the summer months are a symphony of cicadas and crickets. I meander around to the large tent, accidentally knocking over one of the small solar lamps with my foot. I stumble over myself to right it, embarrassment leaking from me like rain through a splintered window.

Still, Ry says nothing.

I shouldn't be snooping. I shouldn't even be here.

But I can't help myself. I'm drawn to this place for some odd reason.

Drawn to him.

Unzipping the tent, I peek inside. It's tall enough to stand in. There's a blow-up mattress on the floor and some blankets, sheets, and pillows neatly folded in the corner. Doesn't everything get wet when it rains? The tent must be waterproof. I take a step back and notice that it's sitting on a large pad of brick pavers, protecting it from the actual dirt of the wooded ground, as well as the potential of standing water during a rainstorm.

I open one of the storage containers. It's filled to the brim. Flashlights, lanterns, fire starters, tarps, towels, gallons of sealed, purified water. I walk to the other side of the campsite. I don't open the storage containers on that side, assuming they hold the same necessities as the other one. There's a walkway into the woods, lit by some of the solar lamps.

Eventually, I make my way back to the firepit. I start to sit in one of the Adirondack chairs, but quickly rethink my decision. That reclines too far back. I need to sit upright in case I need to make a quick getaway.

I mean, maybe—just maybe—Ry *is* a chainsaw murderer, despite what I feel and despite what he said. Not that I saw evidence of any tools of the trade while I was snooping, but you never know.

My seating debacle amuses him, and he hides his smile with his fingertips. Which really pisses me off. One, I don't want him to laugh at me. Two, I really like it when he smiles. Number two pisses me off more, I think.

Trying to control the situation, I break the silence. "You don't live with your brother?"

"Hell no. I only go there when I have to. The last thing I need is to be caught in the middle of the shitstorm Trash calls life."

"So, you live here?"

He shrugs. The movement of his strong shoulders mesmerizes me. "About half the time, yeah."

"And the other half?"

"Harlan has a room at the garage. Small bathroom. Kitchen. I stay there. But I don't want him to feel like I'm taking advantage of him. Plus, he has poker nights with his buddies on Tuesday and Friday nights. And he and his grandson work on cars Saturday night. I give them their space."

"What about your parents? Why not stay with them? Or rent some place of your own?"

He clears his throat, shuffling in his chair. "Let's just say that my parents make Trash's shitshow look like a kids' cartoon."

He doesn't answer the rent your own place question. Maybe he thinks I'm being nosy. I guess I should stop asking questions. I chew my lip in thought. Instead, I ignore my good sense. I always do. "Why were you at the party tonight, then? If you only go to his house when you have to? Was the party a 'have to' kind of thing?"

"Wi-Fi."

"Huh?"

"I needed his Wi-Fi to work on a paper."

Well, that's not the answer I was expecting. "Why not use your phone? Turn on your hotspot?"

"I don't have a phone."

Well, that answer is even more shocking. "You don't have a cell phone?"

"Lulu, I'm living in a tent. You think I have money for a cell phone and a data plan? All of my money goes toward gas, food, tuition. It's not like Harlan is paying me a massive salary. He gives me a room, and he gives me this." He waves his hands around him.

"What do you mean?"

"This land belonged to my grandfather." He turns away, studying the glow of the moonlight reflecting on the pond. His profile is so handsome, it takes my breath away, drying my throat, making me feel like a dehydrated castaway searching for an oasis. "He was supposed to build his dream house here. But my grandma got sick, and he needed money. Harlan bought the land so it wouldn't go to some stranger. When my grandpa died, Harlan tried to give the land back to me, but I wouldn't let him. So, I defer some of my wages. We count it as a monthly payment. One day, I'll be someone. I'll have something to show for this crap life. Then I'll buy it back and build my dream house."

One part of that horribly sad story sticks out to me. Sticks out like a sore thumb. "You are someone."

"Huh?" He turns back to face me.

"You said one day you'll be someone. You *are* someone."

Ry's stare is so intense it grabs the soul from my body and shakes it. Violently. Fiercely. Passionately.

Breaking the tension, I point out the obvious. "That's what coffee shops are for."

"Excuse me?"

"Free Wi-Fi. Buy a cup of coffee and you can have hours of internet usage."

He smirks. "I guess you're right. I've just never seen myself as much of a coffeehouse kind of guy."

Glancing around, I point behind me. "What's up the pathway?"

"Restroom."

I swallow. Loudly.

That really makes him laugh. He leans forward, stoking the fire with a long metal rod. "Trust me, you don't wanna piss where you sleep and eat."

No. No, I would not want to do that.

Suddenly, my phone chimes with an incoming text message. Apologizing, I quickly grab it from my wallet and scan the message from Kristie, wanting to know where I am. Apparently, she's sleeping on my couch tonight. Again.

Turning his wrist to look at his watch, he sighs. "It's late. You should be getting home." He grabs a large metal lid and snuffs the fire. We stand, together, watching the red edges of the embers slowly fade to black.

He holds the lantern to the side, casting some light in my direction as we walk. "Watch your step on the—"

His warning falls on deaf ears because my foot is already slipping off the small lift of the concrete patio, causing me to trip forward. Ry's arm snatches out to grab me. Quickly rounding my side, he pulls my body against his. His large frame stops my momentum.

And then it fucking stops my heart.

I'm pressed against him. His arm snakes around my waist. I slowly lift my head. I'm just going to say thank you. That's all I'm gonna do.

So, why is my heart racing? Why are my hands grabbing the sides of his muscular hips? Why are my lips parting?

He looks at me. I mean, he *looks at me*.

Kiss me, I silently plead with him. I say the prayer a thousand times in my head in the span of one second.

His head bends. His lips are so close to mine. My eyes close. His perfectly sculpted mouth nearly joins with mine.

Achingly so close.

And then… he steps away.

My eyes flash open and I watch him drag his hand across his face. He groans, clearing his throat. "You should leave."

I do my best to pretend those words don't hurt me as I turn to walk back to his truck.

We don't talk on the drive back to the gas station to get my car. Not one single word.

When we pull up, he places the truck into park, idling the engine. Staring out the window, I reach for the door handle, but his words freeze me in position. "I meant what I said about not pursuing questions and answers with this part of Carrie's life. It will lead to nothing but trouble, pain, and heartache."

I scoff. "And that's your professional opinion? Please give me more. I aim to please."

"I'm serious, Lulu." He taps his fingers on the steering wheel. "Don't take this the wrong way, but I hope we never see each other again."

How am I supposed to take that except for exactly how he meant it?

I open the door and climb out, not looking back at him. I can't stand the thought of looking at him. Why? Because I'm angry, sad, disappointed, and frustrated. All at the same time.

"What did you mean? Earlier at the party, you said you weren't a fan of escaping reality. Why?"

The melancholy in his sigh is tangible. "Because reality reminds you where you belong. Enjoy your life, Lulu."

I slam the door.

And I hope I break the damn thing.

Chapter 9

Crutch

Kill me now.

I can't believe I'm about to do this.

The next thing you know, I'll be getting a nose ring, wearing a cardigan, and asking someone to go to the art museum with me.

I stare up at the neon sign of the pretentious coffeehouse, silently cursing my life. And silently cursing the girl who made me rethink my decision to come here. It's not like I hadn't thought about it before, but I guess it took Lulu calling me out to finally make me dive outside of my comfort zone and come here. Hoisting the computer bag on my shoulder, I begrudgingly open the door.

Even at night, the line snakes around the front of the store, and the back is filled with tables and people. People reading, people working on computers, people softly chatting. At least it seems like everyone is minding their own business. I make note that several people have empty cups in front of them. So, I guess they don't kick you out once you're finished downing their fancy drinks. Good. That's what I was hoping for.

The girl behind the counter is pretty. Brunette. Knit cap on her head. When she finally focuses on me, her body language changes and she leans forward against the counter.

Of course, she does.

I can never decide if being good-looking is a blessing or a curse.

"What can I get you?"

"Large coffee. Regular." I grab the wallet from my back pocket.

"Our house brew today is the Hazelnut Smokehouse. Is that okay?"

Are you serious? "Uhhh, sure."

Licking her lips, she rings me up. "That'll be $4.71."

"What! For plain coffee? Are you serving gold dust in the damn thing?" I'm not joking. This is fucking absurd.

Of course, she thinks I'm joking and laughs hysterically while making change for my $5 bill. My hard earned $5 bill.

"I know, right? I had to cut back to only one a day. Why don't you find a seat? I'll bring it to you when it's ready."

I grunt, pocketing the coins and mumbling thanks.

One day, I'll spend $5 on a cup of coffee and not even think twice about it. One day.

My eyes flicker around the tables, trying to find the best place to work. Every table has someone at it. These people make me nervous. I feel like they're judging me while they're not even looking at me.

And that's when it happens.

The dream and nightmare that I fought all night long after driving Lulu to her car last night collide in a tsunami. Engulfing me. Drowning me.

"So, you *do* have some common sense. Decided a coffee shop is a better place to work than a pill party, huh?"

Slowly, I spin around to face her.

I meant it when I said I hope we never see each other again. But for some reason, an exhale of relief pours from my lungs when I see her standing there, straight back, stiff shoulders, little chin pointed in the air. She has her hair pulled back tonight, halfway up and halfway down. Her designer jeans and sweater form fit to every curve and long line. But what looks even better is the little smirk cutting across her face.

"Someone pointed out the free Wi-Fi. Thought I'd give it a try."

Her eyes travel the length of my body. "Well, all the tables are full. You can sit with me, if you'd like." She points to a small table in the back corner.

She doesn't wait for my response. She simply turns on her heels and walks away.

And me, being the idiot that I am, I follow her.

I pull out my computer and notes, and she pretends to read in a book, flicking her ink pen against her notebook. I quickly glance at the cover. *Jane Eyre.* I read that book. Years ago.

"Lulu, just how old are you?"

She peers at me over the pages of her paperback. She thinks about lying. She really does. I can see the lie swirling around behind her gorgeous honey eyes like a tornado. Eventually, she slaps her book down on the table. "Seventeen. Why?"

I lean back in my chair and scrub my hand across my face. I nearly kissed a seventeen-year-old kid. Correction: I really *wanted* to kiss a seventeen-year-old kid. "Holy shit, Lulu. You went to a drunken, drug party, acting like damn Sherlock Holmes, and you're a junior in high school? Are you crazy?"

Well, that was the wrong thing to say.

She reaches across the table and slams the lid of my laptop closed. "I'm a senior, if you must know. I'll be eighteen next month. And don't presume to know anything about me, Ry. I'm more of an adult than most forty-year-old women out there. My mother included. You don't want people to treat you like the guy from the wrong side of the tracks. So, don't treat me like some inept, whiny, princess child."

I didn't tell her that.

But she knows.

She can *see* me.

And now, she's even more beautiful than she was.

"Well, there you are," a high-pitched voice interrupts us, "hiding in the corner. Here's your coffee. And some cream and sugar. But, in my opinion, it's already sweet enough." The cashier girl licks a fake drop of coffee from her fingertip.

I glance over at Lulu. She rolls her eyes and picks up her book.

"Thanks so much..." my voice trails off.

"Peyton. My name is Peyton."

"Peyton. Thanks for the coffee."

"My shift is over at eleven. If you want to get to know one another, give me a call. I wrote my number on the napkin." Peyton flashes a wink and walks away.

Lulu's eye roll, this time, is so dramatic I nearly spit my coffee all over the table, laughing.

Her nose scrunches in annoyance. "What?"

"You're jealous."

"Excuse me?"

"You get jealous when girls hit on me."

"Are you high right now? I have no idea what you're talking about." She writes something in her notebook, pretending it's very important.

"You know exactly what I'm talking about. You roll your eyes. Maybe, you don't realize you're doing it. But it's a moot point. The fact remains that you're totally jealous."

And I love it. I love that this gorgeous, stubborn, strong woman rolls her eyes. For me.

Correction: I love that this gorgeous, stubborn, strong seventeen-year-old *kid* rolls her eyes.

I'm a fucking sicko.

"I did not roll my eyes."

"Of course, you did."

"Well, maybe, I did. But come on, she's flirting with you and I'm sitting right here." She points at her own lap. "Right across the table. For all she knows, I'm your girlfriend." As soon as the words leave her mouth, she blushes.

She blushes, but she doesn't look away. She stares at me, eye to eye. I get the feeling that Lulu never looks away.

Standing up from the table, I walk to the nearest trash can and toss the napkin—and Peyton's number—inside.

Ignoring Lulu's gaze and the seductive way she nibbles on her lower lip, I open my laptop, connect to the Wi-Fi, and try my best to do my homework.

Hours. It feels like damn hours.

How can anyone get any work done in here? People are constantly ordering coffee, the blender is constantly blending, and I feel like these strangers are watching my every move.

She places her bookmark in her book, closes her notebook, and puts the cap on her ink pen. "If you sigh or grunt one more time, I'm gonna lose my mind."

I glance up from my screen. "What are you talking about?"

"I think it's pretty obvious that this has been the worst thirty minutes of your life."

Shit. It's only been thirty minutes?

She rubs the back of her neck again. "You're miserable here. Let's go back to the homestead. You can use my hotspot."

I lift my eyebrows.

"My *phone* hotspot. You know what I mean."

I take the last drink of my coffee. Surprisingly, it wasn't too bad. I actually liked it. "The homestead?"

"Makes sense to call it that. It aligns with your long-term goals."

I have to be dreaming. It almost sounded like pride in her words. Pride and confidence that I can make something of my life. Be something better. The only ones who have ever spoken to me that way were my grandparents and Harlan.

"But I can call it a campsite, if you prefer? Tent in the woods? Hideout from the FBI manhunt? Your call."

How did she get to be such a hard ass? My voice catches in my throat. "Homestead sounds nice."

Her whisper floats across the table, carried from her pink lips. "Homestead, it is. Let's go."

Chapter 10

Ella

I think I'm mentally unstable.

Like the purple-wigged old lady I see in the grocery store, wearing a nightgown and pushing a Cabbage Patch doll in a baby stroller. Last week, she opened up a jar of sardines on aisle four and tossed one in my face when I tried to squeeze past her. I'm talking that level of derangement, if not more.

That can be the only answer for why I offered to come back to Ry's homestead and let him use my hotspot.

I take a staggered breath and slide out of my SUV, dragging my backpack behind me. Ry wanted to drive me out to his place and then drive me back into town when we were finished with our homework. It made no sense. He started to argue about my safety, so I locked myself in my SUV and pulled up beside his truck, idling the engine, until he climbed in his vehicle and led the way.

He quickly places battery-operated lanterns on all of the side tables on the patio and lights a fire. I settle into one of the Adirondack chairs, deciding it would be more comfortable for reading than the chair I sat in last night. Plus, there's a lantern right beside it, shining brightly. By the time Ry sits down in the seat next to me, I've already turned my hotspot on. He must see it right away on his laptop wireless options because he softly says thank you for no other apparent reason.

We work in silence for a while; the only noise is the crackling of the fire and the clicking of his fingers on the keyboard of his computer. I'm handwriting the outline of my theme paper as I read. I hate those things. Despise them. It shouldn't even be classified as writing.

"I think symbolism is a bunch of crap. Don't you think that sometimes the author chooses to make the person's shirt red simply because it's the first color that pops in their head, and not because red symbolizes that this character represents the red devil that lives in all of us?"

He looks up from his keyboard. "Yep. I take it you're having to write a paper on the book's symbolism?"

"Yes, and it infuriates me."

"I felt the same way in high school."

"Ry, how old are you?"

"Twenty-one."

He must be in the same year of school as Carrie. She's only twenty, but she's always one of the youngest in her class because her birthday isn't until June. "So, you're a junior in college?"

"No, this is my last semester at the two-year community college."

I chew my lip, thinking of the math in my head.

His raspy chuckle stirs that lustful feeling low in my stomach. "Hell, Lulu, don't overthink it. I didn't fail a grade. I took a year off after high school to save money."

"Save money for what?"

He opens his mouth and then shuts it. He was going to make a smartass comment about me coming from money. I know he was. "Tuition and books and this computer."

"What about student loans?"

"I refuse to take student loans. I don't wanna start my life indebted for an education, an education I have to have because of some unwritten bullshit law that book experience is more valuable than real-life experience. Every job requires training. Book smarts don't account for much in my opinion."

Is that code for someone who has struggled in school? Someone who has made bad grades? That's surprising; Ry strikes me as a very intelligent person.

"You worked at the garage to save money?"

"I did. I started working there part time in high school. Harlan and my grandpa were best friends."

I study the shadow of his face. He's so damn good-looking, he drives me insane. "So, how often do you work?"

"My classes are Monday, Wednesday, and Friday, nine a.m. to two p.m. I work after that, and I work all day on Tuesday and Thursday. Sometimes, I work on Saturday morning before Harlan's grandson comes over." He rubs his fingers across his lips, watching me, studying me. "What about you? Do you have a job?"

"Of course, I do. It's a little thing called *finding my sister*."

He rolls his head back, eyeing the moon hanging in the sky. "Way to make a guy feel like an asshole."

Sometimes I really am a bitch. I try to hide my smile by biting the end of my ink pen.

He closes his laptop and sets it down beside him, staring at the fire. "So, tell me, what is the latest on Carrie?"

My mood swings to the opposite end of the spectrum, pulling me down into a deep hole of melancholy. I stack my book and notebook beside me on the side table and straighten my back. "Nothing. No new leads have come in. That's why I started looking at things, looking at the gas station. I noticed Carrie was driving all the way across the county to go to that gas station. She was using the ATM inside the store. Which didn't make sense because she used her credit card every place she went. And she was buying that certain drink, which was just weird—that blackberry sweet tea. So, I decided to stake it out. I confronted her ex-boyfriend and he finally told me that she was using drugs. And pushing them, like you called it."

All of a sudden, I realize I described my sister in the past tense. Guilt shrouds my heart and I wonder if I should correct myself.

"Stake it out? You realize how that makes you sound, right?" he asks, interrupting my disturbing thought.

I square my shoulders and grip the armrests of the chair. "How does it make me sound, Ry?"

"Like a Nancy Drew vigilante."

"And what would you do if it were your brother?"

"You have met my brother, right?"

I keep my comments to myself. It's one thing to speak ill of your own sibling, but a completely different thing to have someone else speak ill of them.

"No new leads?" he asks when I don't say anything. "All of the news stories haven't produced anything?"

"In the beginning they did. But I've learned more in the past couple of days than I have in the past six months. We really got lucky with the news coverage, but even the major news outlets are starting to lose interest. And they are tiring of my parents' antics and attitudes. At least we got what we did." I snort. "Another benefit of being a blonde-haired, blue-eyed girl—a white girl—who looks like a super model." Sad, but true. I wish every missing person got the kind of media attention Carrie did—no matter what they look like and no matter how much money they have in the bank.

He nods, agreeing. "Carrie is very beautiful."

And there you have it... Now, I'm jealous again of my kind, loving, older sister. My missing sister. No wonder he kissed her. He stopped because she was under the influence. What if she hadn't been? Would Ry have had sex with her? With my sister?

"Go ahead and ask me. I know you want to."

I raise my eyebrows.

"Don't beat around the bush, Lulu. I already told you I like you when you get to the point."

I give in to his demand without fighting. "Would you have slept with her? If she hadn't been under the influence, would you have had sex with my sister?"

His stare is so dark and intense it makes my heart race in my chest. My palms break into a cold sweat. I hate the feeling. And I also like it. Really like it. I feel more alive with Ry than I have since Carrie disappeared.

I feel more alive with him than I've ever felt in my entire life.

His voice cuts through the air like a knife. "I wish I could say no, but I can't. I don't know what would have happened. But I have never slept with any girl who has been drunk or high. And I don't ever plan to."

Well, that statement opens up the door to so many unanswered questions. Does he exclusively hang out with impaired women? How many girls has he slept with who haven't been drunk or high? Does he have a disease?

And shoveling a few feet deeper down this different rabbit hole, I wonder if he thinks I'm beautiful like Carrie? Does he wanna kiss me? Sleep with me? Touch me?

Accepting my silence, he stokes the fire and leans back in his seat.

I reach back, rubbing my scar in thought. Five minutes? Ten minutes? Who knows. I rub until my skin is raw. Slapping my hand in my lap, I ask him another question. "So, what are your plans after this school year?"

"I don't know. My degree will be in General Studies so, I guess, I've left the door open for a lot of stuff." He turns to me. "What about you?"

"I'm supposed to start at the University of Virginia. Architecture."

"You like architecture?" He can't hide the surprise in his voice.

Avoiding the question, I stand up. Embarrassment is better than talking about architecture and the future my parents have outlined for me. I loudly announce, "I need to use the restroom."

Ry leads me over to the lit pathway, reaching into one of the storage containers to hand me a roll of toilet paper.

I can't believe I'm about to pee in the woods.

Before I head back into camp, I pull out my phone to check the time, firing off a quick text message to Hudson, telling him that I won't be meeting everyone for the late movie.

Ry's still standing there when I walk back. I notice he placed a blanket on my chair, paying attention to the temperature drop that's happened over the past hour. "Wash your hands?" He holds up a gallon of the distilled bottled water and a pump bottle of hand soap. Laying my phone down on the top of a storage container, I hold out my hands while he squirts soap into my palms and then rinses the bubbles away with water. Right then, my phone beeps and lights up with a text message on my home screen.

Hudson: What do you mean you're not coming to the movie? What are you doing?

Ry sees it. And reads it. He doesn't even hide it.

Pulling open the doors to the storage container, he puts the stuff back where it belongs and secures it. I'm flapping my hands around to air dry them. He grabs the edge of his long-sleeve T-shirt from where he haphazardly half-tucked it into his belted jeans. "Here. Dry."

I know he has towels and paper towels. I saw them last night. So, why is he offering me his T-shirt?

Who cares? I sure as hell don't.

I twist my hands in the blue fabric, sucking my bottom lip between my teeth when my fingertips brush against the taut skin of his abdomen. The unread text message beeps again, and I quickly grab my phone.

"Movies? With the boyfriend?"

"I don't have a boyfriend." I shake my head. What an absurd notion. "I was supposed to meet some people for a late movie if I didn't have anything else to do."

"Friends?"

"They aren't my friends. They're just classmates."

He cocks his head to the side. "So, I go to parties with people who aren't my friends. And you? You go to the movies with people who aren't your friends."

"Sounds about right."

He opens his mouth, but is interrupted by the jarring ring of my cell phone.

Guess his sarcastic but spot-on reply will have to wait.

Chapter 11

Crutch

Sighing, she politely excuses herself, turning around to answer her phone. The tension in her shoulders is palpable. Based on that alone, I can already tell I don't like this Hudson douche.

I shouldn't eavesdrop on her side of the conversation. So, of course, I do.

"No, Hudson, I'm not coming to the movies tonight."

...

"That's not what I said. I said I would come if nothing else came up. Something else came up."

...

"I'm doing homework. Reading and working on the theme paper."

...

"I'm not at home."

...

"I'm not alone."

...

"Who am I with?"

She halfway turns, watching my movements out of the corner of her eye. Here it comes. The moment when a girl like *this* lies about being with a guy like *me*. It's part of the reason I never sleep with a girl who actually knows me, knows where I come from, knows who my family is. It's easier to be with a girl who only knows me as some guy she goes to college with. Some guy she met at the grocery store. Some guy she ran into at the mall, buying jeans.

Then, I can pretend. Pretend I'm someone normal. Pretend I'm some upper-middle-class college student. Worry free and living the young adult dream.

A girl like *this* never has to lie about a guy like *that*.

But Lulu isn't a 'girl like this'. I knew that the second my eyes cruised over that delicious backside of hers on the deck of my brother's mobile home. Even though I wanted to pretend she wasn't any different from the rich girls I typically screw, deep down, I knew she was.

"I'm with a friend, Hudson."

Her words strike me to my core. Like a bolt of lightning.

Spinning away from me, she whisper-yells into the phone, rage growing with every question she answers. "Yes, a guy. And no, you don't know him."

...

"Why in the world do you wanna know his life story? He's in college. He works at a body shop. He's nice and kind and interesting. And he's my friend. That's all you need to know. And just so you know, I wasn't even obligated to tell you that." She sighs loudly. "Now, enjoy the movie. I'll see you at school on Monday."

She's not ashamed of me.

I'm in trouble with this one. I know I am.

"Sorry about that." Walking over to her backpack, she silences her phone and slides it into her bag. Sitting down, she covers herself with the blanket I put out for her.

The phone call irritated her. Her back is stiff and her chin tilts up in the air.

"So where do you go to school, Lulu?"

"North and Camden Academy."

I whistle through my teeth. "The most expensive private school in the state?"

"That's the one."

"Well, do you like it?"

"It's a school. Walls, floors, desks. Didn't you just say that book smarts are overrated."

I nod.

"Where did you go to school?" she asks.

"Public school. Out here, everyone is zoned for East County."

She makes an odd face. "And you performed well there?"

I laugh. She's so damn funny. "You wanna know if there's a reason I think formal education is overrated. You wanna know if I'm smart or stupid. Do you think I'm stupid, Lulu?"

"No."

Of course, I know I'm stupid. I keep seeing her, don't I?

She pulls the blanket up around her neck, and I quickly toss some more wood on the fire to ward off her chill. A cold front is moving in tonight. She gifts me a soft smile in thanks. But it doesn't last long. Holding to her own, she digs in, "So answer the question, then. Did you perform well there?"

I lace my fingers behind my head. "Valedictorian."

"Seriously?" She can't hide the shock in her voice. "What did you score on the ACT?"

Normally, I wouldn't answer that question. That's nobody's business but mine. There's lots of reasons I'll enter a dick-measuring contest with someone, but an ACT score isn't one of them. But she's not asking to be competitive. She's asking out of genuine intrigue.

"33."

"Holy crap! A 33! That's wonderful, Ry. I only scored a 30. I'm so proud of you." Catching her intimate words, she blushes and then smiles. Smiles at me. Smiles for me. "I know you don't want student loans, but what about scholarships?"

I scoff. "Schools don't give scholarships to people like me. They give scholarships to people like you."

"What are you talking about?"

"Why the University of Virginia? I'm assuming they have a great architecture program, but why them? You have a full ride, don't you?"

She refuses to look down. That's not what Lulu does. But she doesn't answer. And that silence is answer enough.

"That's what I thought."

"Did you try? Did you apply for scholarships? I'm sure you did, but I have to ask," she says.

"Of course, I did, but I wasn't one of the favorite pets of the school guidance counselor. She gave me no information about scholarships. She didn't even reach out to the majority of the class for pre-graduation counseling. I did what I could on my own. I was awarded one scholarship for $1,000. That's it."

"It doesn't make sense. Why?"

She's so innocent. "Lulu, you don't even have to do a background check on me to find out my brother and parents have all been in jail. A simple Google search will give you that information. I'm not exactly a scholarship poster boy."

"That's terrible. It's not fair and it's terrible," she pouts.

Ignoring her comment, because how can I rebut it when I agree with it, I stand up and stretch, pulling my arms high above my head. My stomach must show because I catch her staring at my mid-section. Her heated gaze makes my dick pole vault in my pants.

Suddenly, I'm suffocating.

"Thirsty?"

She nods, following me to my truck with the blanket wrapped around her like a cape. Leaning in the back, I open the drink cooler and grab a bottle of water for her and a bottle of beer for me. Slamming the door, we lean against it. She downs half of her bottle in one fell swoop.

I'm an asshole. I should've offered her something to drink before now.

Taking a pull of my beer, I let the cool liquid coat my throat. Twisting the brown bottle back and forth in my hand makes me remember something. "When you dumped your beer, you said you weren't a fan of lowered inhibitions. What does that mean? Did something happen?"

"I've only drank one time. Last year, it was a Cinco de Mayo party, and I thought I would try the margaritas. I didn't really like the taste, but I liked the way it made my brain feel fuzzy. I didn't think so much. On the flip side, not thinking has its disadvantages. I did something I shouldn't have with someone I shouldn't have."

A vise clamps around my heart, squeezing it in a death grip. "You had sex with someone?" The Grim Reaper slices his scythe through my chest. Why does the thought of Lulu having sex with someone drive me insanely mad? The idea alone makes me feel unhinged.

"No, of course not. But I did kiss someone."

"Who?"

She nods her head in the direction of her chair. In the direction of the phone nestled in her backpack.

"That Hudson guy?" I ask.

She nods, taking another drink of her water.

My voice is scratchy. I sound like I ate a damn cactus. "Well, it's just kissing." Is this how she feels about me kissing Carrie? Does it hurt like this?

"It wasn't just any kiss. It was my first kiss. And now it's tainted. Forever."

I watch her fingers tear at the label on her bottle. If I thought I ate a damn cactus before, I'm not sure what the hell I just ate now. Glass? I have to clear my throat before words will even come out. "Well, just pretend your second kiss was your first kiss."

"I will. When it happens."

Fuck. Me.

I reach over and put my beer bottle in the bed of my truck, and slowly spin around, placing my body right in front of Lulu's. She bumps back against the closed truck door. Taking the water bottle from her hand, I lean over, setting it down next to mine. I'm so close, my chest brushes against her large breasts.

I don't pull back. I'm not giving her space. I can't. I need to be *in* her space.

I push the blanket from her shoulders.

I need to do something with my hands. If I don't control them, they will be everywhere. On her. In her.

I'm an asshole. But I'm not *that* kind of asshole.

I lift my arms and grip the roof of my truck so tightly I think I break my knuckles. And the whole time, her eyes never leave mine.

I love it that she doesn't shy away. Ever.

I hate it that she doesn't shy away. Ever.

When her trembling hands travel up and glide underneath my shirt, stroking the sides of my waist and ribcage, I nearly lose my shit.

Her whisper becomes the end of my life as I know it. "Ry."

Bending my head, I crash my lips to hers. Our kiss doesn't start softly. It doesn't start gently. Immediately, I part her lips with my tongue, thrusting into her mouth, exploring her, tasting her.

I've never had a kiss like this before. She matches me, stroke for stroke. Giving, taking. Making me new. Making me feel like I'm a better man. She pulls my body against hers, rubbing against me, moaning into the kiss.

We kiss until neither of us can breathe, function. Slowly, I pull my tongue from her mouth, leaving my lips resting against hers. Our hot breath mingles, carrying air from my lungs to hers, and back again.

And that's when I see it. When I feel it. Her body relaxes, her shoulders roll forward, and she sighs deeply, contently.

This is Lulu.

Lulu is a completely different person from the Ella everyone in her circle knows.

And Lulu is all mine.

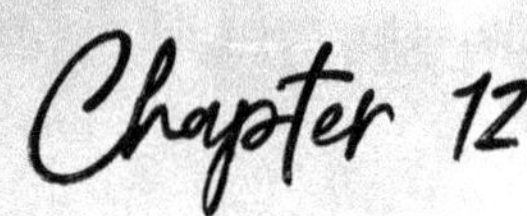

Ella

It's been less than forty-eight hours, and I haven't been able to get him out of my mind. I'm surprised I made it through the school day without cutting class to drive out here. If it weren't for a stupid math test, I probably would've.

And Ella Hill does *not* cut class.

Can you imagine what the school administrators would say? My classmates? My parents? Why being the talk of the town isn't what sweet little Ella Hill should be known for. Avoiding drama means I get to avoid my parents, and avoiding them works way better for me than pining after them with unrequited love.

Besides, why should I skip class? Ry and I parted with no promises. No plans to see each other again. No commitments of a relationship.

Sure, that kiss was... well, it was everything.

And sure, I'm almost positive I heard him whisper, 'My Lulu', against my swollen lips. But that doesn't mean anything, right?

And yet, here I am. About to show my hand. About to be the weaker link. I figure anger is the easiest way to follow through with this asinine plan, so that's what I choose.

I spot him—well, half of him—the second I walk through the bay of the garage. He's lying underneath a car on one of those rolling cots with just his legs poking out when I walk up. He knows I'm here. He senses me. I know he does because the clanking noise he was making when I pulled up has stopped.

I fold my arms across my chest. "You're gonna kiss me like *that*, and I don't even know your full name?"

He pushes out from underneath the car and shields his eyes from the bright, overhead lights. He has a grease stain streaked across his cheek. So freaking sexy. I shake my head to clear my thoughts.

Standing up, he leisurely grabs a towel from his back pocket and wipes his dirty hands. He takes a step toward me. "We kiss like *that*, and knowing my full name is your only concern?"

Well, of course, that isn't my only concern, but it became the most plausible reason for me to come here this evening. To see him again. And holy hell, did I want to see him again.

Anger, I remind myself, think anger.

We've already established I've been acting like a lunatic for the past day and a half, my brain completely monopolized with thoughts of him.

Five different times yesterday I found myself sitting in my vehicle, ready to trek all the way across the county to see him. To be near him. To kiss him again.

But I didn't.

Each time, I begrudgingly climbed out of my SUV and sulked back into the house. We ran into each other at the coffee shop randomly. Me, driving out to see him on purpose, that's a completely different situation. And it's not like I can wait on him to come see me. He doesn't know where I live. And that's assuming he even wants to see me again.

Ry tosses the rag to the side and steps even closer to me. Close enough that his body grazes mine. I freeze. I'm afraid that any slight movement will disconnect the tether pulling him to me.

Bending his head, he whispers against my earlobe. "Because my only concern is *when can we do it again.*"

Shivers run down the base of my spine, swirling deep into my stomach, wetting my panties. All these feelings are foreign. And wonderfully delightful.

Kiss me. Kiss me forever.

I pray he can read my thoughts.

My lips part...

And we're interrupted.

"Well, hello, there. Anything I can help you with, miss?"

I quickly step back from Ry, squaring my shoulders and standing straight. Not because I'm embarrassed to be next to him, but because I can't think when I'm that close to him. He eats away at my brain cells, like my own personal drug.

It's obvious that I'm more of a junkie than my sister.

One simple taste and I'm hooked.

Ry notices my change in demeanor and chuckles before turning away. His arm moves in front of him, and I can't help but wonder if he's adjusting an erection. That thought really makes me feel like a woman. Not a girl. But a woman.

Our intruder can only be Harlan. I don't have to think too hard about that because his mechanic's shirt does have 'Harlan' embroidered on it. He's a couple of inches shorter than me, with white hair and kind blue eyes.

"Hi, sir. I'm a friend of... Crutch." It takes me several seconds to actually remember the name everyone else calls him. "I just came here to visit him. I'm sorry; I didn't ask if he was allowed to have visitors at work. I hope it's okay."

He grunts. "How good of a friend are you if you can't remember his name?"

I glance over at Ry, who's leaning against the car with a very bemused look etched on his face. Evil bastard obviously likes it when I'm tongue tied and out of control.

"Well, I can't say aloud the name I usually call him in private. It's not suitable for the ears of elders."

Harlan doesn't smile.

Shit. I've gone too far. My parents would die if they heard that.

I'm about to profusely apologize when Harlan bursts out laughing and wrestles me into a hug.

I don't get hugged by adults often. My Uncle Ray and Aunt Teresa hug me. Detective Marcum hugs me on occasion. And the truth is… I secretly love hugs. Well, I love hugs when they come from the right people. And something tells me Harlan is the right kind of person.

"He didn't tell me you were so funny," Harlan says.

I glance over my shoulder, catching Ry in a rare moment of embarrassment. Pushing away from the car, he pretends to busy himself, but the only thing he can think to do is lift his baseball cap, fuss with his hair, and settle it back on his head.

He talked about me?

Harlan squeezes my shoulder. "The kid's just finishing. Come with me. I'll get you a cold drink while you wait." We walk through the garage and a small, cluttered office, winding around to a small kitchen. There's a fridge, microwave, and oven with a range. He motions for me to take a seat at the table and joins me after grabbing two Diet Cokes from the fridge.

"A friend of Crutch's, huh?" he asks.

"Yes, sir. We met just the other night."

"Well, he mentioned meeting a lady. He used the word friend too, but I gathered there might be more to the story."

"Oh." I take a sip of my drink, trying to stop myself from asking questions that I shouldn't. The stall tactic doesn't work, and the words come out of my big fat mouth without any hesitation. "So, does he have a lot of *friends* who visit him here?"

"No one has ever come to visit Crutch at work. Unless you count that worthless brother of his. And sometimes his parents will come, asking him for money. But no other ladies, if that's what you're trying to hint around about."

I point my chin in the air. "Yes, that's what I'm trying to ask about."

Harlan laughs. "No beating around the bush, huh?"

"Ry likes it when I get to the point."

"Ry? That's what you call him?"

"Yes, sir."

"And what's your name, honey?"

He doesn't get Lulu. No one but Ry gets that. "Ella. My name is Ella."

Harlan looks over my shoulder, and I swivel, following his gaze. Ry's standing in the doorway, watching us. His ballcap shades his face in the most delicious of ways. He's carnal and masculine and everything I never knew I wanted.

Or needed.

He smirks, enjoying the way I'm staring at him. "I'm gonna get a shower."

Harlan's voice catches my attention. "You have really good posture, you know that," he says, nodding at my ramrod straight back and shoulders.

Ry's laugh echoes down the hall.

"I say something funny?" Harlan doesn't wait for an answer. "Well, it's past my quitting time. I'll leave you two kids to it."

I politely stand, but Harlan shoos me away. "No need for the pleasantries, sweetie. Make yourself at home."

I take a few more sips of my soda and meander my way through the rest of the building. Off the kitchen is a hallway. The door on the left is closed, and I hear running water. Bathroom.

The door on the right is closed too. So, of course, I open it.

It's a very small bedroom. Twin-size bed, neatly made, with a blue plaid quilt on it. A scratched-up chest of drawers with a small TV on the top. An end table with a lamp. Some men's boots and sneakers are neatly stacked in the corner.

I lightly run my fingers across the bed.

Ry's home that's not his home.

It's sad. But it's not sad. I don't know if I've ever met anyone so strong. So brave.

A wave of sorrow and worry knocks the breath from my lungs. I pray Carrie is that strong. That brave. So brave that she's surviving wherever she is. And if my deepest, darkest thoughts are true—the thoughts I've never spoken aloud to anyone—I pray that she *was* brave, *was* strong.

Before I know it, I find myself outside in the dark, staring across the large, asphalt parking lot at the lit gas station. Its lights are so bright, it completely overpowers the dollar store and fast-food restaurant across the street.

How many people in there right now are buying drugs? Is there anyone in there right now who knows what happened to my sister?

Because if I know anything, it's that someone knows something.

Chapter 13

Crutch

She's gone when I get out of the shower.

For a split second, my heart breaks in two, but then I see her car is still parked in one of the spots between the gas station and the garage. I walk outside into the cool night air, searching for her. If she's gone to the gas station, I'm gonna beat her ass.

Not literally, of course. Woe be to the man who lays a hand on My Lulu. She'd probably rip his balls straight from his body.

There she is.

Standing in the middle of the asphalt parking lot, watching the comings and goings of the gas station. She's absentmindedly rubbing the back of her neck again.

Maybe she slept wrong and has a crick.

She takes two steps forward.

"What the hell do you think you're doing, Lulu? Get your ass back over here."

She spins around, catching my voice on the wind. One long leg cocks to the side, and she crosses her arms against her chest. "Seriously? You're gonna call to me like I'm some dog and expect me to heel?"

Forty steps. It takes me forty steps to cross the distance between us. And she doesn't move one single inch.

She likes it. She likes me coming for her. Fighting for her.

I know she does. Because I like it too.

I stop mere inches from her. I reach out, wrap my fingers around her waist, and tug her against me. Her hips are soft yet firm. Her pupils dilate in anticipation, and it doesn't go unnoticed by me that she takes a deep breath, plumping her breasts between our bodies. I bend my head so she can hear me better against the sounds of the night. "You stray, looking for trouble. What else would you have me do? Besides, it looks like I'm the one who heeled to you."

"Is it time to kiss me again?" Her whisper sends a live electric current pulsing through my entire body.

Her eyelids grow heavy with want and her arms lift, ready to circle around my shoulders. Nimbly I pull from her grasp.

That does *not* make her happy. Hell, it doesn't make me happy either.

But I have to take my time with Lulu. I can't rush all of our kisses. Why? Because I'm on borrowed time. Hours? Days? Weeks? It won't be long until she realizes that I have nothing to offer. No plan. No future. No stability.

A loser.

A selfish loser who's willing to use desire to draw out the inevitable.

I shake my head. "Not yet."

"And just why not?"

"Because it's suppertime. Come on, I'll make you a sandwich." I grab her hand and drag her back in the garage.

"Lettuce, tomato, and cheese?"

Squaring her shoulders, she politely nods, but there's a little glint in her eye, telling me something not's right. I pause, freezing my hand over the sliced chicken sandwich. "Lulu," I warn.

She blinks and forces herself to shrug. "Sorry. I'm used to agreeing to everything in restaurants to make it easier. I don't like tomatoes, Ry."

"Okay. No big deal."

She pops a cheese cracker in her mouth. "I like tomato soup and ketchup, but I don't like tomatoes."

"Well, I like French fries and baked potatoes, but I can't stand hash browns, tater tots, or mashed potatoes."

She giggles. That simple noise makes my heart heroically swell like I just saved a drowning kitten or something.

"No mashed potatoes at Thanksgiving? How un-American."

"Well, I haven't had a true Thanksgiving meal in years. Not since before my grandma got sick." I set the sandwiches on the table and take a seat next to her. Maybe a little too close to her...and we start eating.

Our first meal together.

"That's terrible," she says. "Tell me what happened."

"Well, she was diagnosed with early onset Alzheimer's when I was a freshman in high school. The first year wasn't so bad. She just turned a little forgetful. 'Where's the car keys? Did I leave the stove on?' Then, it was like the dripping faucet turned into a fire hydrant. It got bad quick. Neither me nor Grandpa could safely take care of her. He found a great place for her. But it was private. No Medicare. They had other insurance, but it wasn't all that great either. So, my grandpa sold the land to get money. He visited her three times a day. The commute back and forth from town three times a day was wearing on him. A year later, he sold his house and moved into a small apartment near the nursing home. That's when I started staying here, at the garage. It was my senior year of high school, and I didn't wanna switch schools."

"You lived with your grandparents?" she asks.

"Yep. My mom's parents. Moved in with them when I was ten. Trash was in juvie for the first time. My grandparents tried to get custody of both of us numerous times. But my parents would clean up just long enough to convince Child Services that they had their shit together. They received food stamps and other welfare income for us. That's why they didn't want to give us up."

She has a dollop of mayonnaise on the side of her lip. Her napkin keeps missing it. I reach over with the pad of my thumb, wipe it, and suck the sweetness from my finger. Her tongue darts out to lick the skin I just touched.

It's so damn distracting, I have to clear my throat, giving myself a second to remember where I was. "Anyway, Trash was in juvie, and Grandpa showed up on the doorstep. Said my parents had two choices, they could let him take me and he wouldn't tell anyone, they could keep claiming me as a dependent and get all of my benefits. Or, they could keep me, and he would hire the best damn attorney in the state and fight until he had me and they had nothing. They shoved me out the door without even packing me a suitcase."

Tears moisten her eyes and she reaches over, wrapping her fingers across my calloused hand. Her nails are painted navy and her fingers are long and slender. I rub my thumb slowly back and forth across her smooth, olive skin.

"Don't feel sorry for me. Living with my grandparents gave me the best years of my life."

"And your grandpa passed?"

I nod, swallowing against the boulder lodged in my throat. "The end of my senior year. Massive stroke. Died alone in the apartment. The nursing home called me at the garage when he didn't show up to visit Grandma."

I look up at Lulu, mesmerized by the silent tears flowing from her eyes. Her mascara turns clumpy and her eyeliner streaks, paving a small black roadmap down her cheek. She pouts in anger. "Ugh. I hate crying in front of people."

She's so damn beautiful, it hurts.

She thinks my grandma is dead too. I don't correct her.

"My name is Ryland Joseph Crutchfield," I say, answering her question from when she first got to the garage. I push away from the table. Tugging on her arm, she yelps when I pull her from her chair, onto my lap.

"Now, Lulu. Now it's time to kiss you."

And so I do.

Chapter 14

Ella

I've been hiding in the shadows of the apartment corridor for nearly forty-five minutes now. I've texted and called Dakota, Catie, and Hannah over the past several days, ever since I found out the truth from Caleb, telling them that I need to speak with them. They keep putting me off.

No more. That ends today. Whoever comes home first is the lucky winner.

Five minutes later, Catie walks up the stairs. Her keys jingle in the lock and she smacks the gum in her mouth. Walking into the apartment, she flicks the door closed behind her, but not before I slam it open with my fist. It bounces off the wall with a loud bang.

Catie spins around, her hand covering her heart. She heaves a sigh of relief when she realizes it's me. "What the hell, Ella? You scared the shit out of me."

"Well, I could say the idea of you propositioning my sister's boyfriend with sex to get drugs scared the crap out of me too."

Her mouth falls open and her face burns bright red. Tossing her purse, backpack, and shopping bag on the kitchen counter, she starts shuffling through the mail, avoiding my gaze. "I have no idea what you're talking about."

"Don't lie, Catie. I know Carrie was using. And selling to you. My sister was obviously doing some bad things with some bad people and now she's missing. How could none of you think that is important information to give to the detectives? If just one of you had told the truth, maybe she would be here now, instead of who knows where?" I toss my hand around the room, mimicking the vast unknown.

She doesn't turn around, but I do hear her sniffle. She mumbles her response, "I don't know what Caleb has been telling you..."

"The truth. But only after I searched and found most of the answers myself. What if this drug business got her into trouble?"

She turns around, sniffling again. Strange how she can sniffle, but her eyes are bone dry. Is she fake crying? Is this bitch seriously fake crying right now.

"Are you going to the police? Are you gonna tell them we were all doing drugs?"

"Are you kidding me right now? That's what you're worried about? People finding out you're a junkie? You're more worried about your stupid reputation than my sister's well-being?"

Now tears do stream down her face. Selfish fear has her trembling in her fur-lined boots. Her cell phone starts to ring in her purse, but we both ignore it. "Please, Ella, you don't understand. No one can know. I'm not an addict or anything. I just do it occasionally to take the edge off. If my parents find out, they'll make me come home, leave school. What about graduating? I already have some companies looking at me."

I stand straight, breathing deeply through my nose, trying to calm my raging thoughts. I press my palms to my eyelids, pushing until my vision turns black with purple and yellow spots. Finally, I put my hands down and ask the question that's the root of it all. "If I tell Detective Marcum about the drugs, about Carrie, about you, about everything, will you come clean? Will you admit the truth and help me find my sister?"

She wipes the tears with the back of her manicured hand. "No. I'll never admit to drug use. I'll deny everything. Tell them I have no idea what you're talking about. So will the other girls. It will be you and

Caleb against us. And I'll tell everyone that Caleb made a pass at me and I turned him down. That's why he's making up this story now."

So, that's it. That's how it's gonna be.

Caleb is right. The girls will never tell the truth. They are more interested in their reputation. And their future. Which does nothing but pulverize Carrie's chance of a future if she's even still alive.

And Ry is right, the people involved with the gas station will never tell the truth, either. They are more concerned with their next high and protecting that Trey person. And whoever his supplier is.

I'm defeated. I feel like I've been trampled by a herd of stampeding rhinos. My weakened voice stretches the distance between us. "I just don't get it. How did you even get started in all this? I know Carrie had the bike accident, but what happened to you? To Hannah? To Dakota? Why on earth would you start using drugs?"

Catie scoffs, folding her arms across her chest. Seeing she's won this battle, she wants to drive the sword through my heart even more. "It's all Carrie's fault. She brought that shit into this apartment. Begged us to use with her. Told us how good we would feel. How we could all escape from reality. There's no one to blame but her."

I lose my mind. Literally.

I'm a wild heathen trapped in the body of a southern debutante.

I race across the room, shoving her out of the way. I blindly flail my arms, pushing mail and bags to the tile floor. A drinking glass flies off the counter and shatters. My fingers wrap around the strap of her purse, and Catie screams at me, trying to rip it from my hands.

I'm tall. Really tall. And Catie isn't. I use that to my advantage, shoving her and bumping her with my hips. She stumbles back and falls over the loveseat. I quickly turn her purse over, dumping all of the contents around me.

Her shout echoes in my ears, but I choose to ignore it. "What are you doing? Stop! What are you looking for?"

And then I see it.

It tumbled under the strap of her backpack. It's hiding from me. But I see it nonetheless. The small tin breath mint container. It's so offensive, it makes me want to throw up.

Carrie always has a tin of breath mints in her purse. Always. And she knows I'll never open it. I hate them. I hate the aftertaste. I hate the texture.

Gum. She always carries gum for me in her purse. Even though she hates gum.

I grab the container and turn to the kitchen sink. This makes Catie scream absolute bloody murder. It could be the loudest noise I've ever heard. "Stop!" She's standing now and races to the kitchen to stop me.

I flick open the lid and five little pills stare at me. Three white, one pink, and one blue. Her stash. I found her stash. She grabs me by the waist trying to pull me back, but I've already turned on the faucet and disposal. My hips bump across the handles of the cabinet drawers, bouncing one open. She reaches around to smack the tin from my hand, but I turn my shoulder, blocking her access. With one fluid flick of my wrist, I chop her little dreams into powered dust and wash them out to sea.

Or at least to the water treatment plant.

She immediately freezes in shock and we both watch the water swirl around and around in the stainless-steel sink. Eventually, I flip the switch to the disposal and turn off the faucet, covering the apartment in a deathly silence.

That is, until Ry's words leave my mouth. "You shouldn't need an escape from reality. Reality reminds you where you belong."

She turns to me with a look of pure evil etched on her face. "Fuck you, Ella."

I'm not prepared for her retaliation, not prepared for her shove. That's why I fall, why I stumble. My hand knocks into the side of the open drawer, right where the unfinished wood meets the finished wood, and my knuckles scrape. I fall on my butt, but make the mistake of grabbing the open drawer when trying to clamber back to my feet. That's when she slams my hand in the drawer.

Hard. Not as hard as it could have been. But still hard enough to bring tears to my eyes, making me bite my tongue in pain. The back of my hand bruises instantaneously.

Catie races to her bedroom, locking the door. Leaving me flopping on the kitchen floor like a dying fish.

And still no closer to finding out where my sister is than before I confronted Catie.

Chapter 15

Ella

I lift my eyes from the TV show I'm watching on my laptop to watch Ry walk away from the firepit and patio. He heads over to the tent. I stare until his body blurs with the edges of darkness and that delicious ass disappears. It's Harlan's poker night so I knew Ry would be at the homestead.

My excuse tonight was that I figured he needed to use my hotspot for homework. The truth is, I wanted to see him, wanted to be near him after my run-in with Catie.

He didn't say anything to mock me when I showed up unannounced. Just smiled and nodded.

And to my credit, he *has* been doing homework on his laptop.

And to my detriment, I am now apparently the kind of girl who shamelessly chases after a guy.

I always thought I'd want the guy to chase after me. I guess not. When did I become so pathetic? If Carrie were here, she'd know what to do. Or, maybe she'd be high, and she'd have no clue how to help me navigate these uncharted waters.

Next, I hear him rummaging around in one of the storage containers and then I hear him fiddling with something in his truck. I have no idea why he is flittering all over the place, acting like a lost hummingbird. Taking a deep breath, I try my best to focus on the show in front of me. I'm sitting on the wicker loveseat, and I pulled a side table in front of me so I could watch the show on my laptop.

My focus is interrupted a second later when Ry appears, hovering over me. "Scoot over," he orders.

I quickly make room for him, staring at the objects in his hands. He sits down and I immediately get butterflies in my stomach just from his proximity. He's wearing a gray hooded sweatshirt tonight with jeans that are a little bit tighter around his thighs than some of the other pairs he has.

He also hasn't shaved. The two-day scruff is a major turn-on, making him look older, more dangerous. More feral.

He reaches over, covering me with a thick quilt. And then he wraps one of his thin white garage towels around an ice-filled plastic bag. Grabbing my battered left hand, he tenderly touches my scrapes and bruises, studying my face for pain. Gently laying my hand in his lap—very near his crotch—he covers it with the ice pack. "Doesn't look like anything is broken."

I shake my head. "No, I don't think so."

"You plan on telling me what happened?"

"No."

"Well, I suggest you quickly modify your plans, then."

Sighing, I debate on telling a lie.

He cocks his head and squints his eyes. "And so help me, if you lie to me, Lulu, I'll flip my shit."

I snort. "Well, that's kind of what happened to me."

He raises his eyebrows.

"I flipped my crap," I admit.

I tell him about what happened with Catie just a few hours ago. He's not happy, that's for sure. He doesn't interrupt, but his jaw tenses and the muscle in it constantly twitches. It's actually pretty cute. A few times the tension has him squeezing my hand a little too hard. When he sees me wince, he eases up, realizing what he's unintentionally doing. Each time, he rubs his thumb in small circles against the back of my wrist, trying to soothe the bite of his grip.

When I'm finished, he swallows, bobbing his Adam's apple. He doesn't say anything.

"Aren't you gonna say something? Say I told you so."

"I may be an asshole, Lulu, but I try not to be petty. So, no, I'm not gonna tell you I told you so. I actually wish you would've proven me wrong. It's your sister we're talking about. Your *missing* sister. You want her home. And I want her home with you. I also wish her friends would prove my theory wrong. I wish her friends would stand up for her and do what's right. But they're addicts. And that's one thing I know about. I've lived with it my whole life. Their most fierce and loyal love is the addiction."

I try to discreetly shift closer to him. He smells like soap and firewood smoke. Chuckling under his breath, he wraps his free arm around me and pulls me against his side. He's not discreet. He's purpose driven.

Eventually my stiff shoulders and back begin to ache, and I sink down against him, resting my head in that perfect divot where his shoulder meets his chest. I pull my legs up beside me on the seat, making myself more comfortable.

He leans close to my ear, sending a rippling shiver down the base of my spine. "Why crime and murder shows?"

"Hmm?"

"We've watched TV together twice. Last night at the garage and tonight. Both times, it was crime documentaries. Why?"

I shrug. "Intrigue. Fascination. Research."

"Research?"

"Well, you didn't just become a great mechanic overnight, did you? You studied different makes and models. Learned the fine details of the process. It's pretty obvious that whatever happened to Carrie involves a crime. I need to study it. Learn about it. Grow from it. If I ever plan on finding her, I need to become proficient in the art."

He wants to chastise me. Order me to stop. Demand I stop looking for answers. But he doesn't. "Tell me about her. What was she like growing up? Tell me about what happened."

I reach around to the back of my neck, rubbing my scar while I think. How do you start? How do you begin to tell a story that's still being told? One whose epilogue is yet to be written?

"She's an amazing big sister. And I'm not just saying that, Ry. She really is. I know your parents are terrible parents. Mine are too, just in a different way. So, it was always me and Carrie. She's a big sister, best friend, and mother wrapped into one. Everything I learned, I learned from her. Well, her and our nanny, Janine. Janine was hired when I was five and Carrie was eight. She lived with us. She moved to Arizona to be with family when Carrie turned sixteen and could drive.

"Anyway, she's always been beautiful. Those big blue eyes, that blonde hair, that flawless skin. When we would play princess, I always wanted her to be the princess and me be the maid. That part just fit her. My Princess Carrie."

I pull my hand down, snuggling against him and relishing the feel of his hard body supporting mine. He removes the ice pack, setting it on the ground beside him, and he pulls the blanket closer around my body. I can't believe I'm letting all of my guards down around him. I never snuggle with anyone. Ever.

Except Carrie.

"We had a little system. Janine wouldn't teach us both something at the same time. She'd teach Carrie and then Carrie would have to teach me. She wanted us to always rely on one another. Lord knows, we can't rely on our parents for anything. Except money.

"Carrie taught me how to read, how to ride a bike, how to do a cartwheel. She showed me how to vacuum and do laundry and iron. She helped me with my homework and taught me how to cook. How to plants flowers and mow the grass."

I glance up at him and I'm surprised when I catch him staring at me, so intently. I shift my body, sitting up, and swinging my legs around to his lap so I can look at his face while I talk. Look into his pale green eyes. I can tell that he likes it when I look into his eyes. He repositions the blanket over us and holds my legs against his body, rubbing my shins as I talk. The touch of his skin burns through the fabric of my black leggings.

"Push mowing," I explain. "Not doing the riding lawn mower. My first time, I ran over a piece of metal. It flung out and hit her in the arm. She had to have ten stitches. I'm lucky it didn't poke her eye out or stab her in the head." I smile. "Janine took us out for pizza and ice cream after that."

I sigh. There are too many important memories to pluck from the air and pinpoint. Each and every one is special in its own place and time.

"She made friends so easily when we were growing up. She's so outgoing. Like almost annoyingly outgoing. And she always had a boyfriend. She'd refused to date anyone who wouldn't let me tag along. She knew I didn't really have friends. Why did I need friends when I had her?

"She met Caleb during her freshman year of college, and he became part of my and Carrie's everyday family. They are just meant for each other, you know? But he found out about the drug use and just couldn't handle it. He tried to stop her. He broke up with her when he found out she was pushing. She wouldn't talk to me about the breakup. She's never done that before. She talks to me about everything. I should've pressed more. I should've gotten to the bottom of it."

"You can't play the 'should've game', Lulu. It's a roulette wheel."

"I know. I wasn't even here when she went missing. I was on a cruise with my Uncle Ray, Aunt Teresa, and cousin, Holt. I wasn't supposed to go. Uncle Ray had bought it as a surprise Christmas present, but my older cousin, Raylee, was awarded a really prestigious summer internship at a company in Washington, DC. She's a year older than Carrie and is a senior at Florida State University. She couldn't pass up that opportunity. So, they had one extra ticket. I'm closer in age to Holt, so they thought he and I would have more fun together. He's a junior in high school this year."

I suck my bottom lip through my teeth. "She went missing Fourth of July weekend. She just turned twenty at the end of June. I was in the middle of the Caribbean when my sister disappeared. We didn't make it home until two days after the police report was filed. My sister was most likely fighting for her life and I was snorkeling on a coral reef. How do I live with that, Ry?"

He plants both hands on the side of my face. How can one's heart stop beating and race at the exact same time? I don't know, but that's what Ry does to mine. His hands lower from my face and run down my shoulders and arms until his fingers fold around my wrists. Lifting my hands, he wraps my arms around the back of his neck.

He doesn't have to tell me twice.

I pull him into my arms and snake my fingers through his hair, rubbing against the fuzzy new growth that's grown on his neck since his last haircut.

His gaze drifts to my mouth. The heat from his stare has me opening my lips and running my tongue across them, simply trying to cool down. It's a job that he obviously wants to do. His tongue flickers out and dances across my upper lip. Teasing me, he slides his tongue into my parted mouth, but retreats the second my own rises to meet his.

My panted breath creates an audible rhythm between our bodies. I'm growing impatient, and I force his neck down, begging for his face to come closer to mine. He pulls back, tsking me with a click of his tongue. Instead of kissing me, he just watches me. Mere centimeters from my face, he watches me. His pupils dilate with desire, driving me absolutely mad.

Just when I think I'm about to explode, he leans forward and sucks my bottom lip between his teeth. The second I moan into the night air, he consumes me.

I can't imagine there is another human on the face of this planet who kisses like Ryland Joseph Crutchfield. He kisses me like his whole purpose for living is to make me happy. To make me feel wanted. To make me feel desirable.

He kisses slow. He kisses fast. He kisses sloppy. He kisses neatly. His kisses aren't just an event occurring at this one precise moment. They're a multi-faceted, multi-dimensional, quantum leap across time and space. A full-fledged saga.

His kisses are a saga.

His tongue tangles with mine, pooling heat and fire in every fiber of my being. Each time I'm about to suffocate with my own need to pull him closer, he shifts his face, covering my jaw, neck, and earlobe with the same lavished attention. But he always comes back.

Always comes back to my mouth. To my lips. To my tongue.

I pray he always comes back.

To me.

Chapter 16

Crutch

One week.

I've known Luella Margaret Hill for exactly one week today. I've kissed Luella Margaret Hill three times. And I've wanted to kiss Luella Margaret Hill three-thousand times.

I didn't see her on Wednesday or Thursday, and I was moping around like a love-sick puppy. Neutered and pitiful, I couldn't even think straight.

She called me at the garage to say she had a student council meeting on Wednesday night and dinner with Detective Marcum and his wife on Thursday night. She asked if I wanted her to come to the homestead Friday night—tonight. I nearly jumped through the damn phone I was so excited.

But there are so many things wrong with this picture. It's like looking at a portrait of the Mona Lisa, only she's wearing a tube top and smoking from a bong.

First: Lulu's on student council. That's a sentence I never fathomed myself saying. I'm a man dating a high school student. I know that's over-simplifying it, but technically it's true. Lulu is right; she's more mature than almost anyone I know. But she's still seventeen. And that's part of the reason we have only kissed. Normally, I have sex as soon as the girl is willing and ready, *and* she makes the first move. But not with Lulu. Even if she were eighteen, it would be too soon. I'm only the second guy she's ever kissed. Which, by the way, still pisses me off. I should've been the first. And let's not forget that I made the first move. I kissed her. I started this chain reaction. But now, I'm no different than my brother's customers…I'm addicted. I can't do more than kiss her right now. Anything else, would lead to a new addiction. And neither of us need that. I'm already fighting a losing battle when it comes to keeping my lips off hers.

Second: I'm an asshole. That seems to be a recurring theme as of late. I'm making Lulu do all the work. She drives thirty minutes one way to see me. I don't even know where she lives. She's called me at the garage, obviously having looked up the phone number on the Internet since I didn't give it to her. I don't even have her cell number. That all ends tonight. Tonight, I get her number and her address. Plus, I know where she goes to school. I can be one of those guys who leaves a note for his girl on her windshield. Can't I? The thought is cheesy enough to make me want to throw up, but I vow to do that at some point. Leave a note; not throw up.

Third: I'm really selfish. When Lulu told me she had supper with Detective Marcum, one thing went through my head. *Please don't tell him about the drugs.* I'm not naïve enough to worry about my brother. He made his bed a long time ago. He can wallow in its filth all day long as far as I'm concerned. But Lulu is a different story. For once in my life, I'm terrified. Terrified of her getting hurt, of Trey finding out she told someone about his business and him coming after her. And I can only assume the supplier is a hundred times worse than Trey.

These spinning thoughts are interrupted when I hear her tires crunch down the driveway. Jumping out of her SUV, she tries not to smile when she sees me. Really, she does. She tries to hide behind her hair. She tries to bite her lip. But eventually she gives up, granting me the gift of her radiant smile.

I'm stepping off the patio to greet her when she thrusts a large white bag in my hand, catching me by surprise. "I brought dinner! Are you hungry?"

She doesn't wait for me to answer. Instead, she hurries over to one of the chairs and quickly pushes a table in front of her, setting her own bag down and pulling out Styrofoam containers.

"Hell, Lulu, I thought you were smiling because you were excited to see me, but I think you're more excited to eat."

"Of course, I'm excited to see you. I'm here, aren't I? But I haven't eaten all day and I'm starving. I had a phone call during lunch and missed the whole thing."

I grab a water and beer from the cooler in my truck. By the time I set the water bottle down beside her, she's tearing through a sandwich like a rabid animal. A very messy sandwich. Pulling a chair next to her, I chuckle, watching a large streak of grease slip between her fingers and run down her wrist. "Is that a Philly cheesesteak sandwich?"

She quickly wipes her hands—taking extra care with the healing bruise and scrape on her left hand—and takes a drink of water. "Mmm-hmm. Yours is too. I hope you like them."

"I do." When I don't unpack my bag, she glances over at me, shrugging her hands in question. "I didn't peg you for a Philly cheesesteak kind of girl."

"What did you peg me as?" She stuffs a bite that's too big into her mouth and tries to politely find a way to chew. She can't. She eventually covers her mouth with her hand so she can chew open-mouthed without me seeing the food.

"Salad. A chicken Caesar salad when you wanna get crazy."

"I *am* that kind of girl. That's what I order when I go out with my parents or with my classmates. That's what they expect a girl like me to order. So, I do."

I don't like that comment. I don't like it one bit at all. "I don't know how you do it. I know I couldn't. I couldn't pretend to be someone I'm not just to make others happy."

I guess that's a little bit of a lie. I actually pretend all the time. I pretend I'm not poor white trash with every woman I meet. Every woman except Lulu.

She puts her sandwich down, staring at me like I've gone stark-raving mad. "I don't do it for them."

"Who do you do it for?"

"I do it for me."

I furrow my brow. "You pretend to be a different person, pretend to act a certain way, and pretend to like certain things all for your own benefit?"

She nods.

"How? How does that benefit you?"

"Because they don't deserve to see the real me. None of them do."

Words choke in my throat, constricting my voice. "But I do?"

This time she doesn't try to hide her smile. "Of course, you do, Ry."

It's been a great night.

I've had Lulu tonight way more than I've had Ella. Each time we're together, I see more of the real her, and after her admission at dinner, I can't wait to see every part of the real Lulu. Learn everything about her. She's my new favorite subject, and I'm gonna become the most eager student there ever was. A damn Nobel Prize Laureate of what makes her laugh, what makes her cry, and what makes her angry.

And especially what makes her moan the same way she does when she's ready for me to kiss her.

It's official. I've apparently grown a vagina and become a love-struck woman in one week's time.

Actually, let's not call it love-struck. Let's call it 'like-struck'.

She's engrossed in another crime documentary and absent-mindedly reaches behind her and starts rubbing her neck again.

That's it. I'm taking her to a doctor.

"Lulu, scoot closer." We're sitting on the loveseat, and I reach around, pushing her hips closer to mine. Without getting her permission, I push her head forward and wrap her glossy hair around my fist.

"Ry?"

That's when I see it. A pink, puffy scar on the back of her neck. I reach out, brushing it with my calloused fingertips. When her body shudders, my dick jumps in my jeans. "You have a scar."

"Yes. How did you know? Was I touching it again?"

"Again?"

"I apparently do it a lot. Carrie is trying to break me of the habit."

"What happened?" Releasing her hair, I pull her back against my shoulder. Now that's she sitting right next to me, there's no need for her to move away.

Accepting the new position, she snuggles closer to my side. The winter air is mild tonight, and the fire alone provides just the right amount of warmth. "Carrie burnt me with a curling iron when we were little. We were playing beauty pageant and she was trying to curl my hair. Burnt my hair right off too. I had to get three inches cut off. My mom was furious. She actually made me wear a hairpiece for our Christmas card pictures."

"Tell me about them. Your parents."

"They're horrible people."

I open my mouth to placate her concern.

"Ry, don't. Some things in life can't be denied. This is one of those things. My parents are not nice people."

She grabs my hand and starts tracing my work scars with her fingertips. It makes the back of my throat tickle. It feels nice. Real nice.

"My dad came from a good household. Nice, hard-working, middle-class parents. I know he did because my Uncle Ray turned out to be such a nice guy. You would love him, by the way. But he always said that something was different about Dad. Like something boiling beneath the surface. This urge to think he was better than everyone around him, that the world owed him something because he was handsome and smart. You've heard of gold-digging women?

Well, I guess you could call my dad a gold-digging man. According to my Aunt Teresa, my dad's whole goal while at college was to find a rich girl to hook up with. He moved far away from home, went to the University of Texas.

"Well, guess who went there too? Miss Susan Oglesby. Debutante and granddaughter of a dead oil tycoon. Dad swept her off her feet. All Mom saw was a handsome, pre-med student who could one day give her the prestige she craved. All Dad saw was a good-looking, future-housewife set to inherit millions on her twenty-second birthday. They got married right after graduation and Dad had all of his medical school expenses paid by his young, rich, newlywed wife."

She frowns at a small scar on my thumb—one caused by a socket wrench—and plants a small kiss on it, trying to make it better, even though the injury is over two years old. "I guess it really made my grandmother angry, my mom's mom. Apparently, she thought my father was below the desired, old-money pedigree that my mother deserved. She disowned my mom. She lives in some fancy retirement village in Florida. I've never even met her.

"Anyway, Dad became a general surgeon, came back here, and used Mom's money to build his own practice. It's that huge building down by the river. Hill, Vann, and Weaver Surgical Arts and Concepts. My dad is the general surgeon, Phillip Vann is the orthopedic, and Mary Ann Weaver is the cardio-thoracic. They each have their own floor. There's a pharmacy there too, and a therapy place. So, now Dad makes his own millions. And Mom is his trophy-wife.

"His favorite hobby is what Carrie and I call sex-spin-the-wheel. He just spins the wheel to see which lucky mistress will have him in her bed that night. Mom's favorite hobby is what Carrie and I call jealousy-spin-the wheel. She just spins the wheel to see what lucky item she's gonna buy that day to try and make other people jealous. A car, an outfit, a diamond ring? The possibilities are endless."

She sits up straight, adjusting to look me in the eyes. I like it when she looks me in the eyes. "Do you know that I technically don't live with my parents?"

"Huh? What are you talking about?"

"Let's be real. My parents didn't really want kids. They just had us because that's what they were supposed to do. They actually couldn't stand having us around, making noise, playing, interrupting them. They built a whole other wing to the house, connected by a breezeway. A *long* breezeway. We—me and Carrie—have a kitchen, living room, two bedrooms, two bathrooms, and a laundry room. Separate entrance, separate driveway."

She fakes an English accent and tosses her hand in the air, faking high elegance. "The Children's Wing." She giggles at herself. "Anyway, that's when they hired Janine. We needed someone to live with us. Carrie and I had one room, and Janine had the other. And that's when I stopped trying. At five years old, I knew it was pointless to win my parents' love. I was their *thing*. Their pretty little daughter to dress up and show off only when the need arose, but nothing more. So, that's what they get. I give them what they want and keep the real stuff in here." She points to her heart.

Her eyes cloud with thought and her brow furrows. "They made everything about Carrie's disappearance about them. I don't know if you've watched any of the interviews they did, but they're painful. They've used my sister's case to give them some sort of celebrity status. The last time they went to New York City to do the circuit of news shows, they actually requested a fully stocked dressing room, a Presidential suite at the Plaza, and a personal driver."

I don't know what to say to that. Except they sound like exquisitely perfect douchebags.

She shakes her head, clearing her eyes. "Ry, you mentioned marshmallows? Can we cook them?"

When she told me that she had never had campfire s'mores before, I nearly fell out of my chair. I stopped at the dollar store after leaving work today and bought graham crackers, marshmallows, and chocolate bars.

I stare at her, watching her innocent eyes widen in delight when I nod. She shouldn't be here. She shouldn't be with me. She's too good. Too perfect. I need to tell her to leave. Right now.

That's what I *need* to do.

So, what do I do?

I make a s'more for My Lulu. Because we all know I do what I shouldn't.

Chapter 17

Ella

"I still don't understand why you drove out here if we are just gonna drive back into town so you can show me where you live." Ry lifts the ballcap from his head, scratches above his ear, and tugs it back down, bending the bill around his eyes.

Today's another mild day. And more importantly, another Saturday that I'm getting to spend with Ry—it's been a month of Saturdays from when we first met. They say a cold front is coming through tonight, but the Alabama sun is blazing down on us right now. He's wearing a pale-yellow, long-sleeve shirt with the sleeves pushed up his forearms. I love it when he shows his forearms. It is most definitely the sexiest part of him.

After his ass. And his eyes. And his hands. And his broad shoulders. And the firm sides of his ribcage that I rub when we kiss. I haven't seen him without his shirt, but I bet he looks mouth-watering.

I need cold water. Now. On my crotch.

"Lulu, are you listening to me?"

"Of course, I'm listening. First of all, I knew we would be coming back to this side of town afterward. You may wanna see my place, but I can't imagine you wanting to hang out there. When Janine left, Mom hired a decorator from one of those TV shows on HGTV. So, everything looks a little too fake 'comfy and homey'," I say with air quotes. "Plus, you said you were working on your truck this morning. I didn't know if you wanted to give the truck a siesta for the rest of the day." I run my hands across the hood of his well-used, well-loved truck, and dangle my car keys in front of him.

His eyes light up like a Christmas tree. "No shit? You'd let me drive your car?"

I snort. "Why wouldn't I let you drive my car? And before you go getting paranoid thinking I don't wanna be seen in your truck in my neighborhood, you should know that I would drive down the middle of the richest street in the world with you and that truck. But I saw the way you looked at those stupid controls and gadgets last night when you walked me to the car and buckled me in. I just thought it would be a nice gesture."

He leans over and plants a soft kiss on my lips. I immediately shift closer, trying to wrap my arms around his shoulders. He nimbly escapes my grasp, plucking the car keys from my fingers.

He jogs across the parking lot, unlocking my SUV and hollering at me before climbing in. "Come on, Lulu. What are you waiting for?"

Harlan's laughing so hard he can barely stand.

I love to hear him laugh. "Well, Harlan, I guess that means it's time to leave. I'm sorry your grandson couldn't come see you today. You said he has the flu?"

"Yeah, whole family has a touch of it. I talked to my son last night. He and my granddaughter are doing better. But the boy and his momma still have a fever."

"Well, I hope they get better real soon. Do you need anything from town?"

"I'm good, sweetie. You kids go have fun."

There was a large wrecker dropping off a car for service when I got here this morning. It was blocking the area I normally park in so I had to park in the middle of the lot, closest to the gas station.

The damn gas station of my nightmares.

I'm still thinking of a safe way to find out more about the drug business and what that may have to do with my sister. Of course, I haven't discussed any of this with Ry; he's made his viewpoint pretty freakin' clear.

I'm nearly to my vehicle when a guy rounds the other side of the dumpster, stepping in my way. It startles me and takes me a few seconds to register that Trash is standing in front of me. "Trash."

"Well, look who it is. Sweet little Ella."

I'm five-foot-ten, shithead. There's nothing little about me.

"I thought that was your car. I've seen it here a couple of times, but you haven't come inside. Why are you watching the station?"

He takes a step closer to me. His eyes appear more bloodshot than normal, and he reeks of stale booze and cigarette smoke. With a small hint of body odor. Despite wanting to put distance between the two of us, I don't take a step back. That's not what I do.

"She's not watching the gas station. She's here to see me." Ry's voice catches me off guard as he climbs out of the driver's side of my SUV and slams the door. Loudly.

Walking over, he stands next to me, folding his arms across his broad, muscular chest. Trash can't hide his surprise. He doubles over in laughter, grabbing his stomach. Ry takes a small step forward, angling himself in front of me.

"Oh, shit! You're banging the missing girl's sister. So, that's why I haven't seen you around lately. She does know that you and Carrie," Trash looks into my eyes and makes an obscene gesture with his hands, "nearly fuc—"

Ry interrupts him. "She knows."

Trash is making my blood boil. My blood pressure is rising like I'm cooking my body in a damn pressure cooker. I'm almost on the verge of whistling.

"So, y'all have been seeing each other since the night of my party?" He reaches into his pocket and pulls out a cigarette, quickly lighting it. Each drag makes his hollow cheeks sink in even farther. "Just call me Cupid."

I wanna call him many things. And none of those names have anything to do with a flying, chubby baby.

"Did you need something, Trash? We were just heading out." There's a bite in Ry's voice. I heard that same bite the night he pulled me out of the trailer and warned me about Trey.

"I see that. And she's letting you drive that expensive car? I guess you really are a good piece of ass, huh, Crutch." Again, he doubles over, laughing at his crude joke.

"Don't you have some blackberry tea to sell, Trash?" I lace my voice with as much sarcasm as I can muster. "I heard there was a four-car accident on the highway last night. Maybe some new customers will head your way in a couple of months after they get hooked on pain pills. Do you give them a discount if they can show a surgery scar?"

Ry's head snaps around and he firmly but gently grabs my elbow, pulling me against him. He hisses my name between his teeth like a snake. "Lulu. Go get in the car. Now."

I straighten my shoulders and point my chin in the air. "I'm fine right where I am."

Trash narrows his eyes. "I knew you had spunk, Ella, but you keep surprising me every time we see each other. You know, Trey likes feisty women. Says they make good pushers."

Ry's built like a brick wall. That's the only reason I'm not attacking Trash's face like a wild alley cat. Besides, I know it's a moot point to even try. At some point, Ry's fingers meandered their way to my back side, and his fingertips are holding onto the belt loop of my jeans. Even if I tried to spring forward, I wouldn't get very far. And I'd probably look like a moron in the process.

Ry clears his throat, drawing attention back to himself. "Trash, you're coming off a high. You need to turn around and leave before you say something that you're gonna regret. Something that's really gonna piss me off."

"But I'm your brother."

"And that's the only reason you're not lying flat on your ass right now."

Trash spits on the ground. Stomping on his cigarette, he walks away. He's halfway to the door of the gas station when he turns around and hollers back at his brother. "Was I right? Do her legs look as great as I imagined? What about when they're wrapped around you, Crutch?"

Uh-oh...

Ry takes off like a bat out of hell with me trailing after him. It's fine for me to beat the crap out of Trash, but I don't want Ry to do it. What if Ry gets in trouble? In trouble because of me?

Fortunately, a minivan comes to the rescue.

By now, Trash is standing at the door to the gas station when the minivan at Pump 1 opens its doors and two young kids jump out. They race around one another, playing a quick game of tag and talking about what kind of candy they want to buy inside. Ry immediately stops his pursuit. Trash knows he won't do anything now. Smirking, he opens the door and slips inside.

Ry's shaking in anger, clenching his fists. The motion flexes the tendons in his arms. Laying my forehead between his shoulder blades, I slowly trace my fingers across his back, trying to scratch the tension from his muscles. Eventually, he sighs. Turning around, he wraps me in a hug.

Ry always hugs me before I leave him. Adding him to the small list of people who hug me was epic. It's almost better than kissing him. *Almost.*

I love the way his large frame covers my body, wrapping around me like a blanket. Plus, he *really* hugs. Firm and hard. Not just loose arms and lazy body. He always squeezes me, making me rise to my tiptoes.

"I'm sorry about that. It happens with Ritalin for some reason. When he's coming off a Ritalin high, he's a different person. Mean."

I don't say it's okay. Because it's not. Nothing about Trash is okay. Apparently, nothing about Carrie was okay, either.

"Come on. Harlan said he didn't need anything from town, but let's get him something anyway. Cheer him up since he can't see his grandson today. Chocolate cake is his favorite, right?"

Chapter 18

Crutch

So, being rich is one thing.

But having *this* much money? That's a completely different thing.

"So, that oil tycoon great-grandfather you mentioned? His last name wouldn't happen to be Exxon, would it?"

She laughs, slapping a hand across my chest before jumping out of the passenger's side of her SUV. I follow her, staring at the monstrosity of the house in front of me. I swear it would take up half a city block. We parked in the driveway on the left side of the house. Lulu's side of the house. There's a completely different driveway on the right side of the house, but you can't even see it from here. The house is that big.

Massive pecan trees line the yard, closest to the road, and the front of the house is immaculately groomed with shrubs and blooming winter flowers, accenting the red brick and regal white columns. Before heading inside, Lulu walks me around back, opening an ornate, wrought iron fence. There's an infinity pool with a hot tub and a waterfall. The kind of pool that you can't see the bottom of—where the water looks like a black opaque blanket glittering in the sun. Patio furniture decorates the porch. Matching patio furniture. Expensive patio furniture.

"So, this is the outside. I spend most of the summer out here. Mom never swims. It would mess up her hair and makeup. So instead, she uses the tanning booth in the gym on her side of the house."

When we go inside the Children's Wing, I can see exactly what she was talking about. It looks comfy, don't get me wrong, but it also looks forced. Everything is decorated in varying shades of white, gray, and navy. The gray marble floors, the white granite countertops, the overstuffed navy sofa with furry white blankets strategically draped over each corner. The TV is bigger than my tent.

It looks like a perfect model house and not an actual *home.*

I know I want a home one day. A perfectly imperfect place for me and my family.

Says the kid who's homeless. So, who am I to judge where Lulu lives, but this place isn't a home.

Carrie's bedroom is decorated in navy and white. The bed's neatly made, but there are some clothes tossed on the floor near the full-length mirror and some shoes laying under the chair of the corner desk.

"I put everything back the way it was." Lulu rubs the scar on her neck. "When I got home from the cruise, the police had searched her room. Mom had a maid come in and clean everything up afterward. But Carrie always leaves those Crocs under her desk chair. She wears them in the house like house shoes. She can't stand walking around barefoot. The marble is too cold on her feet. And those clothes," she points to the ones on the floor, "they were laying on the floor the last time I was here, before I left for the cruise." She loudly swallows, her throat making a strange little noise. "I guess I feel a little less alone when I see those shoes and clothes. Like, she'll be back in just a day or two, you know?"

My heart fucking collapses in my chest.

Walking across the hallway, she walks me into her bedroom. The midday sun filters through the wooden blinds, streaking her white and gray comforter in light. Gray and white, gray and white.

Her room looks like the rest of the house. Neat as a pin. Professionally decorated, even down to the pictures of her and Carrie nestled in the ribbon of a picture board.

"Your mom decorate in here too?"

"Yeah, why?"

"*My* Lulu doesn't really strike me as a gray and white kind of girl."

She bites her lip, trying to hide her smile. "*Your* Lulu isn't." She points to the darkened bathroom on the opposite side of her bedroom. "Bathroom is through there if you need to use it."

Giving her hip a little squeeze, I head into the bathroom while she goes to get something to drink. Her bathroom is bigger than most people's apartments. There's a large tile shower, a claw-foot garden tub, and a large marble vanity covered in baskets of neatly stocked cosmetics and jewelry. I peek into one, filled to the brim with necklaces. Just looking at the necklaces makes me smile.

Lulu stopped wearing long necklaces. At my suggestion, might I add. I hate when they get caught between us when we are kissing.

Those damn beads can easily bruise a man's chest. And since my kissing of Lulu ramped up like a drag racer on nitro after our first week together, I was bruised. A lot.

Back in the kitchen, Lulu's on her laptop. "Sorry, I just needed to plug in for a quick second. I had to email that history assignment."

"So, how do you get to the other side of the house?"

She walks me back down the hallway, and at the very end, there's a simple white door. She opens it, and I stare down the long marble hallway, leading to the Big House. It strangely feels like a pathway leading to death row. "Through there."

"Lulu, this is weird, right? Most houses don't have this. It's like your parents live in a completely different land."

"Yep, told you it was a very long hallway. Over there is the land where hopes and dreams go to die."

"Are they home right now?"

"Not that I know of. I sometimes go for days without seeing my parents. But my dad usually works on Saturday mornings and then plays golf with friends. Or plays doctor with one of his mistresses. Mom usually sleeps off her wine hangover until lunch and then has afternoon brunch at the country club."

She doesn't ask if I want to meet her parents and I don't press the issue. I've never met a girl's parents before. Why the hell would I want to start now?

Besides, like I've told myself a thousand times, this thing with Lulu is temporary. Very temporary. I don't need her parents to point out the fact that I'm a deadbeat and cause me to lose Lulu any quicker than I already am.

It's inevitable.

And I really want to fight off the inevitable for as long as I can.

We're walking out the door when a Mercedes pulls into the driveway. Lulu murmurs under her breath, standing taller and holding back her shoulders. A girl with red hair climbs out, hauling a big-ass purse behind her.

"Hey, Ella, where are you going? I thought we were gonna hang out and watch a movie."

"Kristie, what are you talking about? We did that Tuesday night. Remember? We ate pizza and watched *Titanic*."

The girl takes the large black sunglasses off her face and rubs her forehead. "Oh, right. I'm sorry. Things have just been crazy between work and school." She finally looks over, noticing me. "Oh, hello."

"Kristie, this is Crutch. Crutch, this is Kristie Vann. Her father, Phillip, is the orthopedic surgeon in practice with my dad. Kristie goes to the university. She's a year younger than you and Carrie. She's a sophomore. But she also works in her father's office."

I hold out my hand. It takes her a few minutes to shake it because she's rubbing imaginary circles on the ruddy skin of her puffy cheeks. Her pupils are small pinpoints. She quickly pulls away when she sees me studying her eyes. Interesting...

She clears her throat. "So, you're the person who has been monopolizing our little Ella?"

Our? She should know that Lulu belongs to me not her. Plus, I'm pretty sure Lulu would hate being called little.

"How did the two of you meet again?"

I keep my mouth shut. I'm not sure what all Lulu has told Kristie about me, so it's best if I keep my mouth shut. All I know is that the words 'drugs, Carrie, and Trey' had better stay trapped inside Lulu's own beautiful mouth.

"Remember, I told you we met at the coffee shop. Crutch is finishing his last year at the community college. He works as a mechanic."

There she goes again. If she's embarrassed by me, she hides it well.

Kristie licks her lips a few times, nodding her head. "That's right. Nice to meet you. Ella, Dad is having some painting done in our kitchen this afternoon. Fine if I hang out here for a while?"

She wants to say no. I know she does. But this is Ella we're talking about. Not Lulu. "Of course, Kristie. Make yourself at home."

Once we're backing out of her driveway, I ask Lulu about Kristie. "So, this is the girl who spends a lot of time at your house? The one who just shows up uninvited?"

"Well, I don't really know if you can call it uninvited. Carrie gave her a key to our house."

"You let her stay in Carrie's room?"

She gasps in horror. "Of course not. If she stays the night, she either sleeps on the couch or with me, in my bed." She sighs. "I don't know why I let it irritate me. She's not a bad person. She's shy and meek. Friendly, though."

"Yeah, she seems nice."

Now I just have to find the right time to tell Lulu that this 'nice' girl was just high off her ass.

Chapter 19

Crutch

She's studying the bakery case like the answer to world peace lies in the red velvet on display.

"Lulu, they have food here. Do you want something to eat? I'm hungry."

"Yeah, sure. I'll take the soup and sandwich combo. Tomato soup and chicken salad sandwich." She quickly goes back to ignoring me, asking the bakery attendant a question about the icing on the chocolate cake.

I head over to the register and pick up a menu, browsing to see what I want. A college-age girl walks from the back to stand behind the register. "What can I get for you today, sir?" Her posture and attitude completely change when she looks up from the machine and sees me standing there.

Uh-oh. I know that look.

Her smile flashes, showing her white teeth, and she immediately stands tall, pulling the kitchen apron lower on her body, exposing the small amount of cleavage poking out from her V-neck T-shirt. "We have a special on the potato soup bowl today. Tell me, have you been here before?"

She's really pretty. Normally, the kind of girl I'd be fucking in my truck a few hours from now.

I rub my hand over my jaw. The stubble scratches my fingers. I need to remember to shave tomorrow. "No, this is my first time."

And of course, it's just my luck, I had to use a sexual innuendo.

She giggles. Lowering her voice an octave, she says, "Well, we need to make this first visit extra special so you'll have a reason to come back and try *other* things on the menu."

Of course, Lulu walks up right when the girl is saying this. In no time flat, Lulu's eyes roll back in her head. Each time this happens, her eye roll gets more dramatic. One day her head might actually fall off.

"Did you pick something out?" I ask her.

Swallowing her pride, she politely looks at the cashier. "We'd like the chocolate cake on the second shelf, please. The chocolate and vanilla cake with chocolate frosting."

I add to the order. "And we'll take two orders of the soup and sandwich combo. Both with tomato soup and a chicken salad sandwich."

She looks into my eyes. "For here?"

I nod and she quickly gives us the total. I reach into my back pocket to grab my wallet as Lulu starts to dig through her purse. "Here, let me get this. It was my idea to get a cake for Harlan."

I firmly put my hands on hers, stopping her movement. "Lulu." My warning gives no room for debate. Sure, the total made my heart stop for a second, but I've still got some nuts attached to my body. No way I'm letting her pay for this.

Taking the cake box with us, we head over to a two-person table. I fix us each a drink while she grabs the napkins and utensils. Sitting down, Lulu opens her mouth to start a conversation, when we are suddenly interrupted by a loud, nasally voice.

"Ella, darling. It's been so long since I've seen that gorgeous face of yours. I nearly forgot what it looked like."

Lulu immediately stands, stiffening her back, squaring her shoulders. Trying to be the gentleman, I stand as well.

"Mrs. Plott. It's nice to see you too. Pleasant weather, isn't it? Hard to believe tomorrow will be thirty degrees cooler."

Weather. Why do rich people wanna talk about weather?

"Yes, I know. What can you do? The woes of living in the South." Lulu softly chuckles.

The lady's gaze travels over to me. A total cougar, her eyes dilate in appreciation. Fondling the pearls on her neck, she looks back at Lulu. "Aren't you going to introduce me to your friend?"

"Of course, how rude of me. Mrs. Plott, this is Ryland Crutchfield." Lulu stares into my eyes. Taking a deep breath, she turns back to the woman. "Ryland is my boyfriend."

Her what?

The woman's mouth gapes open in shock.

"Ryland, this is Mrs. Noreen Plott. Her son, Hudson, and I are classmates."

"Oh dear, you're more than that. You two have been friends since you were in preschool." She reaches across the table, and I shake her hand.

She's one of those women who doesn't really shake your hand, though. She simply holds her hand on top of mine, like she's the queen waiting for me to kiss her knuckles.

"Hudson didn't mention you had a boyfriend. Neither has your mother. I just left her at the country club."

Lulu nods. "Yes, ma'am. You know me. Quiet as a mouse about some things."

Ella may be. But My Lulu is louder than a tomcat in heat.

And growing louder every day. Finding more of her voice. Becoming more of who she really is.

The rich girl people say is a bitch is really just a feisty, spunky woman trying to break free of the cage she's been trapped in.

"Well, I'd better head out. I just came in to buy some of those gluten-free, high-protein muffins that Hudson likes so much. I'm sure you've noticed how much he has been working out lately."

"I suppose so." She leaves it at that as they say goodbye, and she walks away, leaving a trail of overwhelming perfume burning the insides of my nostrils. We both sit back down, and I lean back in my chair, spreading my legs wide in front of me. Lulu takes a large gulp of her drink.

"Boyfriend, huh?"

She looks down at her hands, fidgeting. And then she remembers who she is and she stares deeply into my eyes with her head held high.

"Well, Ry, it's been a month. We've been seeing each other nearly every single day since we met. I feel that is the most logical title."

I tilt my head, watching her. "Go ahead and ask me. I know you want to."

"What?"

"Don't beat around the bush, Lulu. I like you when you get to the point."

I'm an asshole. This is something the guy should do. Not the girl.

She licks her lips and clears her throat. One hand reaches around to the back of her neck, fingering her scar. "Ry, do you wanna be my boyfriend?"

Right then, the pretty cashier delivers our food to the table. People have a real knack for interrupting us at pivotal moments.

She's removed the black kitchen apron and applied fresh lipstick. Crossing her legs over one another as she stands there, propping her hand on the back of my chair, she says, "I had the chef do a full chicken salad sandwich instead of just a half. Like I said, we have to make this first visit special."

Lulu's eye roll drives me completely over the edge. I was already teetering, about to fall. About to fall so hard I don't think I'll ever be able to get back up. Ever be able to walk again.

And that head swivel and eye roll is what do me in.

Pushing back from the table, I stand. Grabbing Lulu, I pull her from her seat and swing her into my arms. And in the middle of the bakery on the rich side of town, I kiss her.

Holy shit, do I ever kiss her.

And I know it's way better than that chocolate cake she just ordered.

Chapter 20

Ella

Harlan and I sit in the small kitchen finishing our slices of chocolate cake while Ry changes the oil in my SUV. He nearly had a heart attack earlier when he glanced at the windshield sticker and saw I was past due on my oil change.

"Ella, I appreciate this. It was very thoughtful."

I toss the paper plates and utensils in the trash, box the cake, and place it in the fridge. "It's no big deal, Harlan. We just thought it would be something nice. Ry actually paid for it."

"That boy doesn't need to be spending his money on me. He already does enough as it is."

I wipe the crumbs from the table. "What do you mean?"

"Don't get me wrong, my son is great. He would do anything at all for me. But he lives in town. Works fifty to sixty hours a week at his office job, so I feel bad asking him for help with things around the garage or the house. All I have to do is mention something in passing, and before I know it, Crutch has already handled it. Already fixed it for me." He leans over and pats my hand. "You're really good for him, Ella. I've never seen him happier. He thinks he's poor, white trash. Hopefully, you'll be able to convince him otherwise."

He grunts, rising from the table. "Well, it's time for me to call it a night. Leave you kids to it. Don't let him go to the land tonight.

Cold front has already started to come through, and it's freezing outside. Make him stay here tonight."

"Yes, sir."

I meander out to the garage floor. Sitting in the rolling chair I've claimed as my own over the past month, I watch Ry as he works. The comfortable silence engulfs us like the steam from a hot shower.

Time to splash some cold water on things.

"I have something for you."

Walking around the side of my vehicle, he bends down in front of me, framing both of his hands on the armrests of the chair. Brushing his lips against mine, he growls low, "I've got something for you too."

The timbre of his voice sends shivers across my body, and I squirm in my chair, fighting the urge to touch myself. Which I never used to actually do, but find myself doing all the time now, when we aren't together.

Chuckling, he stands upright and spins my chair in circles as he walks away.

I lick my lips. "Anyway, as I was saying, I have something for you. But I'm not gonna give it to you until you promise that you'll accept it."

"Is there a reason that I wouldn't accept it?"

"Yes, you being a butthole is the reason."

He slams the hood to my vehicle, laughing uncontrollably. "Lulu, do you ever cuss? I've not heard you utter one single curse word in the time we've known each other."

"Cursing is not expected of me, so I don't do it. If you want me to break that habit too, it may take a little bit of time. And don't change the subject. We're talking about me giving you a present. It's rude to turn down a present, so you have to promise to accept it."

"I'm not gonna promise that. Tell me what the present is and then we can discuss it."

Unhappily grunting, I root around in my purse for the old cell phone I grabbed earlier at my house. Standing tall, I walk over to him, holding it hostage behind my back. "Hold out your hand and close your eyes." He does as he's told. I slap the cell phone in his hand and race to the other side of the garage, taking sentry behind his tall rolling tool box.

He stares at his hand like I just gifted him a dog turd. "A smart phone?"

"Yes, and before you say anything, I didn't buy it. It's my old phone. It has wireless and can be used as a hotspot. It's all under mine and Carrie's family plan, so it only cost an extra $10 per month to keep the phone line activated. Unlimited data so you don't have to worry about going over on minutes or data."

He holds the phone out to me, waggling it in my direction. "No, I'm not accepting a phone from you. It's too much. If I want a phone, I can buy it myself. Come take this back."

"No."

"No?"

"You heard me. Why can you give me something, and I can't give you anything?"

"Lulu, that's the point. I'm a loser. I haven't given you anything."

I gasp like he's just physically slapped me. I narrow my eyes and stare at him over the top of the tool box. "Ryland Joseph Crutchfield, I don't ever wanna hear those words come from your mouth again. There's so much wrong with that statement I don't even know where to begin."

He doesn't say anything. He just clutches the phone, turning his knuckles white.

"Let's look at what's in front of us," I say pointing to my car. "How much are you gonna charge me for the oil change?"

"What?" He shakes his head in confusion. "Nothing."

"Exactly. That oil change and tire rotation usually costs me $200. I know that synthetic oil's not free. Who's paying Harlan for that? You, right?"

The muscles in his jaw work back and forth. His translucent green eyes are set on fire, making his beauty even more breathtaking than normal.

"That's what I thought. And you're saying you can't trade out with me? Mine only costs $10 a month." I emerge from my hiding place and close the distance between us.

I'm standing just a foot away from him. All he has to do is reach out and touch me. Reach out and pull me against him. One small tug. It wouldn't take much for him to crash my body into his.

"I'm not trying to keep tabs on you. I just wanna talk to you, Ry. When I'm away from you, I wanna hear your voice. Sure, we can talk on the garage line, but what about when you're at the homestead? We can text or talk or just say hi to each other. Won't that be nice?"

His features start to soften, and I can tell it's time for me to bring my argument to its pinnacle. I had hoped I wouldn't have to bring this up, but who was I kidding. I knew getting him to accept any gift like this was going to take convincing. "What about all those nights I drive home by myself? If something happens to me, I'll be able to call you on the cell phone." I bat my eyelashes at him. "Don't you want me to be safe, Ry?" I take one small, baby step forward, inching my shoe along the floor. "And what about the nights we can't be together? When you're all alone and thinking of me, just like I think about you? Maybe—just maybe—I could send you some pictures to keep you company." I cock my hip to the side and shift my torso so the neck of my loose sweater falls down my shoulder, showcasing my pink lace bra strap.

And with that, his fingers snatch out, grabbing the front waistband of my jeans. I tumble against him and he wraps me in his arms. Sweeping his tongue into my mouth, he kisses me with so much fervor and passion, it makes me feel like we've been lovers for a thousand years. Connected from the beginning of time. When we finally break away, we're both panting and gasping for air.

"That's not fair, Lulu. You're manipulating me. After all this time, you're telling me you don't play our game fair? You don't play by the rules?"

I lean up and bite his lower lip. "Game on."

It's so cold our breath makes fog every time we speak. "I can't believe how cold it's turned in just a few hours."

Ry leans past me, into my car, and turns the heater up as far as it will go. He drove it out of the garage bay a couple of minutes ago, and it's idling in the parking lot, waiting on me to drive home.

He softly kisses my lips. "Today was a good day. I got a phone, some chocolate cake, and a girlfriend." He sighs in contentment. "That was some really good chocolate cake."

Laughing, I slap his arm, and then use the opportunity to snake my hands up his shoulders and around his neck. I tug on his hair just the way he likes, the harder the better.

My whisper gets caught in my throat. "Tell me something."

"Tell you something? Tell you what?"

"Tell me something no one else knows."

He shakes his head. He's about to tell me no. I know he is. But then he changes his mind. How can he deny me such a simple request? A perfectly complex, yet simple request. He closes his eyes, thinking.

"I stole something once. It was before I lived with my grandparents. My parents had been on a bender and hadn't really fed me anything for a few days. I was with my dad in the grocery store. He was buying beer. All of this food was just calling to me. I was so hungry, people in Idaho could probably hear my stomach growling. I took a candy bar. Just grabbed it and put it in my shorts. When I was walking out the door, I looked back and saw the cashier. She knew I took the candy bar. I just kept waiting on her to stop me, to call out. She didn't, though. She just smiled. I spent the next several weeks terrified that I was gonna go to jail. My mom and dad had both already spent time in jail by then, and I knew it was a place I didn't wanna be.

"The summer before my senior year of high school, I saw that same cashier at the nursing home when Grandpa and me were visiting Grandma. I saw her talking to some nurses when we walked by. I heard them whispering about her mother, saying she would be passing at any minute. It was the end. When Grandpa was with Grandma, I went back to see her. I bought a candy bar at the vending machine and went into the room with the cashier and her mom."

Ry tilts his head to the side, his vision clouds with memories. "She looked up at me. With these tears streaming down her face. She noticed the candy bar in my hand and just smiled. She remembered me. Just like I remembered her. I gave her the candy bar and just sat with her. Neither of us said a word. Three hours and fourteen minutes later, her mother took her last breath. She died. The lady wiped her tears, took the candy bar from the table and walked out the door."

He turns his focus back to me, rubbing his hands up the outside of my thighs. He doesn't touch my legs often, but when he does, he lights my insides on fire. "And I never saw her again."

This man. Who is this man in front of me?

Technically, I knew it the first second I saw him on the back porch of that trailer, but now, I can actually admit it to myself. I love him.

I'm in love with him.

My compass. My rock. My calm before the storm.

And... my raging hurricane in the middle of the ocean.

"You wanna tell me where that came from, Lulu? What made you ask that?"

"It's something Carrie and I used to do."

"So, someday you'll tell me something you've never told anyone else?"

My frozen lips reach up to find his warmth. "All you have to do is ask."

Chapter 21

Ella

The sound of her acrylic nails tapping on the granite kitchen island is about to drive me to the brink of utter insanity. How the universe thinks the two of us fit together like mother and daughter is beyond me.

"How could you embarrass me like that, Ella? You made me seem like a complete imbecile. A mother who doesn't even know her own child."

Well, you don't know me. What do you expect me to say?

"And then to tell a lie on top of it all," she continues.

"It's not a lie. I do have a boyfriend, Mom." I stuff my laptop in my backpack and zip it.

"How can you have a boyfriend? You always said you were too busy to date."

"No, I said I was too busy to date the boys you tried to fix me up with. Including Hudson."

She fans herself with her hand and straightens a pillow on the couch. "I just don't know what's gotten into you lately. What will your father say? We don't even know this boy, where he's from, his pedigree..."

Well, his detailed pedigree may be found at the county jail, depending on the day you look.

"He's good to me. Really good. Isn't that what's important?" I fling my backpack over my shoulder and grab my purse. "Mom, I'm heading out."

"Where are you off to now?"

"I'm going to see Detective Marcum. I'm going to check on things."

And then, she remembers she has a daughter who's missing. She wipes at her eyes and sniffles. "Oh, my sweet Caroline. I've been praying for her so hard as of late. I just feel her presence reaching out to me." Straightening the diamond tennis bracelet on her wrist, she nods in my direction before walking down the hall. "Be careful, my darling. I don't know what I would do if something happened to you too."

I do. Collect the insurance money and take a relaxing trip to Fiji.

After covering every square inch of Colson's desk in yellow sticky notes, I plop down in front of Marcum, flinging my feet up on the chair next to me.

Detective Leary groans, cursing under his breath. "Son of a bitch, why does this copy machine mess up every single thing I copy." Grabbing a large stack of papers, he stalks out of the room.

As he's passing me, I smile up at him. "Ever heard of user error?"

He smirks, flicking me on the earlobe.

Marcum studies the yellow blob that is now Colson's desk. "You know he's gonna blame me for this? Say I have no control over you."

"I *am* quite the unruly girl." I hold out my hands, awaiting the stack of evidence pictures.

They seem different now. Every image holds a different meaning. Deeper. Hidden. I'm trying to piece together Carrie's secret life. Secrets she kept from me. Secrets I should have known.

Marcum leans back in his chair and flicks his ink pen against his chin. "You seem different. What's up with you lately?"

"Nothing. What are you talking about?"

He shrugs, being nonchalant. He's playing detective with me now. Waiting on me to make the first move.

I'm learning more from him than I am the crime shows I keep watching.

I then realize something. If Carrie kept her pills in the tin mint container—like Catie—why wasn't one in her purse. It wasn't in the evidence log, and it wasn't in the purse itself. Not in the car, either.

Someone must've taken it.

A random junkie? Trash? Trey? The supplier?

The person who took my sister?

I snuggle deeper in the blanket, mesmerized by the show on my laptop. Ry's been working tonight, engrossed in the homework on his own laptop. The firepit crackles, drawing his attention. Stoking the fire, he stands and stretches his arms high above his head. The hem of his long-sleeve black T-shirt rides up, giving me a small glimpse of his boxer briefs. He touches something on the left side of his chest, studying his T-shirt. Grabbing a lantern, he walks away, toward his truck. "I'll be right back."

I sit up and watch. What's he doing? He just got us fresh drinks a little bit ago. I follow him, carefully watching my step in the dark. Quietly, I tiptoe across the dead leaves and crunchy gravel. Ry's standing in the open doorway of his truck, pulling a fresh T-shirt out of one of his duffle bags. Grabbing his collar, he yanks his shirt over his head, gifting me the sight of his bare back. A large lump forms in the back of my throat. His broad shoulders look even better than I imagined. Every small movement has the firm lines of his lower back flexing, begging to be touched.

And then he spins around.

He freezes when he sees me. He stands there, watching me watch him.

Desire floods my heart, flows into my stomach, and sinks down into my groin. Tingles build between my legs, and I rub my thighs together, begging the tension to release. These feelings. I want these feelings more and more, every day. Touching myself, thinking of Ry. I haven't been able to bring myself to orgasm yet, but I want to. I want to, so badly. And trust me, I've been trying—a lot.

The muscles of his waist taper into a V, riding low beneath the waistband of his jeans. A six pack of abs ripple across his midsection. His pectorals jump under the perusal of my eyes, bringing a peak to his brown nipples.

But something else catches my attention. A small crease of blood on his upper left chest.

Worry replaces lust, and I race to him. "Ry, you're hurt."

I tenderly reach out, touching the skin around the two-inch long cut. Immediately, his skin breaks out in goose bumps and breath hisses between his teeth. He does the same thing when I slide my hands underneath his shirt when we're making out. Feeling his body is one thing. And seeing it is something completely different. Combine the two into one, and my mind can't even form the words to describe the level of perfection.

The cut is long, but not deep. More of a scrape than anything else. "What happened?"

"Bent over the hood of an old car today. It scratched me. It's nothing. I was just changing because my shirt had some blood on it."

Without thinking, my fingertips circle around his chest. You'd think I'd never seen a guy's chest before. Not like this I haven't. Never a guy like this. Never a guy this handsome. Never a guy I call my own. I graze his right nipple, and his hand clamps down on my wrist.

"Don't."

"Don't what?"

His grip prevents me from rubbing my hand down his rippling abs like I want to, but it doesn't prevent me from flattening my palm against his chest and feeling his thundering heartbeat. It must match my own. He bends closer to me, sliding his hand up the side of my hip.

I moan. I need him to kiss me. So, I moan.

In one microsecond, he releases my hand, grabs my butt, and lifts me up into his arms. Obviously, I've never been carried by a guy before, but I instinctively wrap my legs around his waist and smash my lips to his. Kicking the truck door closed with his foot, he maneuvers to the back, lowering the tailgate with one hand. The back of the truck has quickly become one of our favorite kissing spots in the past few weeks. I sit on the tailgate, and he stands in front of me between my legs. This time is no different.

Except this time Ry doesn't have his shirt on.

And I'm running my hands over every square inch of naked real estate he's given me.

His hands tangle in my hair, pulling my neck back, showering me in kisses and licks and nibbles.

And… something else is different this time.

Ry's hands are always on my face, on my back, in my hair, or on my thighs above my knees. Occasionally, he'll rub my hips, caressing the curve of my body around to my ass. But tonight, his left hand leaves my face, traces my collarbone, and falls to my right breast.

Oh. My. Gosh.

He gently rubs his hand over my fleshy mound. My nipple strains against the fabric of my bra and shirt, becoming painfully tender and swollen. Eventually, his light strokes become soft massages as he explores me, explores both of my breasts. Learning my size, my heaviness. Learning the touches and caresses that make me arch my back and moan even more.

The hard ridge of his erection rubs against the inside of my thigh, and I think that may be the sexiest thing I've ever felt in my entire life. Ry *always* has an erection when we're kissing, and it *always* drives me crazy.

Pushing him back, I grab the hem of my shirt, wanting—needing—it off my body. Needing to feel his skin on my skin. But Ry pulls away, gently wrapping his fingers over mine and pulling my shirt back down.

As always, we find ourselves panting and grunting, racing to catch our breath. I stare into his eyes. I see the same desire I have. The same want. The same need. "Why did you stop me?"

"There's no rush, Lulu. We have time. Time to take it slow."

Swallowing, I nod. It's not the first time that's happened. It happened once when I tried to take his shirt off, and it happened once when I pulled his hands up to my ass, wanting him to grab me, to touch me.

I can't help but think it has something to do with my age.

Well, he better prepare himself. Because two days from now, that'll be a moot point. He'll need another excuse.

Chapter 22

Crutch

I really hated taking the phone from her. Despised it.

But when I hear her voice, late at night, after a long day of work and school, I think maybe it wasn't such a bad idea.

"So how was the study group?"

She scoffs. "How do you think it was?"

"That much fun, huh?"

"I don't see how anyone could think studying in groups is a productive way to spend time. Studying is a solo activity. Study groups are just a way to gossip and waste time while pretending to be effective."

I hear her rustling around, the sounds of her body moving beneath the sheets of her bed causes my body to instantly react. Adjusting myself, I try to focus and have a somewhat civilized conversation. "Well, you study with me."

"We don't study *with* each other, Ry. We study *next to* each other."

"And your classmate, Hudson, was there?" I try to sound as lighthearted as possible, but the question still comes out with a healthy dose of bitter sarcasm. There's just something about that little douche that pisses me off. And I've never even met him.

"Yes. And of course, he had to ask all sorts of questions about my new boyfriend. I think he's more obsessed with you than I am." Her laugh makes the back of my throat tickle.

If she's obsessed, then I'm fucking captivated. Imprisoned. Held hostage. Tortured.

I think last night proved that. I nearly went too far. She touched my chest, and I couldn't even think straight. And then I couldn't keep my damn hands off her. I wanted to rip that shirt right off her body, wanted nothing more than to roll my tongue across her breast.

But I stopped myself.

I refuse to do anything more than just kissing—and maybe a little heavy petting, you know, over the clothes, middle-school-style—until she's legal in the eyes of the law. I guess, really, I'm just using her age as an excuse to force myself to slow down.

Because when I'm with her? I feel like a damn jet engine flying through the atmosphere at six-hundred miles per hour.

I don't know when she will turn eighteen, but I don't know how much longer I can wait before touching her. I thought she said her birthday was this month.

I make a mental note to ask her. But that's not the question I called to ask tonight.

"So, I hear, there's this little thing called Valentine's Day tomorrow. Now, I'm not much on tradition, but I'm pretty sure the boyfriend is supposed to do something for the girlfriend. What do you say? Feel like doing something special?"

Now, I've just got to figure out what the hell to do to make it special. Since I'm an asshole, I haven't planned anything yet.

"Oh Ry, that's an amazing offer. I didn't think you realized it was almost Valentine's Day."

"I do own a calendar, Lulu. It's not like I built a sun dial and counted out the months."

She giggles. "Well, I'd love to. But... I already have plans."

Well, that knocks the wind right out of my lungs. Red anger and green jealousy color my eyes. My fist grips the phone so damn hard, my finger slips, bleeping the number four in our ears. "Excuse me?"

"Not like that, you idiot. I have plans with my parents."

My brow furrows. "You have Valentine's Day plans with your parents?"

She's quiet for a moment. "Not Valentine's Day plans. Ummm... birthday plans."

Holy shit.

"Lulu, I swear on all that's holy, if you turned eighteen and didn't tell me, I'll flip my shit."

She ignores my question. "What time is it?"

Frustrated, I turn my wrist to check my watch. "Ten minutes after midnight."

"Then, I turn eighteen now. Today's my birthday, Ry. I was born on Valentine's Day."

Holy shit. *She's legal.*

My mouth is as dry as cotton. My brain swirls with an emotional fog so thick, I can't even think straight. I'm excited. And incredibly sad. She didn't say anything. "Why didn't you tell me?"

She sighs. "I didn't want you to feel obligated to buy me a present."

I rub my hands over my face. And there you have it. The pitfalls of dating a poor, homeless man. Why doesn't she leave me? Why doesn't she find someone better? Someone like this Hudson guy. He can probably buy her what she deserves for her birthday. Some diamond earrings or some bullshit like that.

She needs to leave me.

Oh God, please don't let her leave me.

"I was gonna tell you. Just not tomorrow—I mean, today. I was gonna wait until Saturday."

Doesn't she realize how bad I would feel if I missed her birthday. Doesn't she realize that I may not be able to buy her the sun, but I'd at least like to be given the opportunity to capture it for her.

"Ry, say something."

I lower my voice, speaking slowly and clearly. "Don't do that again, Lulu. Don't hide something from me and take away my choices. Buying something for you wouldn't be an obligation. And who in the world said presents have to be bought. A true gift is given. Freely and willingly. Don't take away my options and say it's for my benefit." I pace across the garage and grab a water from the fridge. "Do we understand each other?"

"Yes."

I open it and drink half the bottle in one swallow. "So, what are your plans with your parents?"

"They always take me out to eat for my birthday and then shower me with an expensive, last-minute present that has absolutely no thought put into it whatsoever."

"Last minute?"

"My parents usually forget my birthday, until at least midday when Carrie calls to remind them. And then Dad will have his assistant throw something together. You know, nothing says 'Happy Birthday' like asking your mistress to buy a present for your daughter. But I'm pretty sure he lets her get something for herself too, so she's probably been counting down the days, eagerly awaiting Dad slapping the credit card in her hand. Last time I saw her, she was wearing the exact same pair of white gold and emerald earrings they gave me for my fifteenth birthday."

Talk about fucked up. "Your birthday is on Valentine's Day, and they can't remember that?"

"It's okay. I'm used to it."

Well, screw that. And screw them.

Me: How is dinner with the parents going?

Lulu: Really good. Thanks.

In the time we've known each other, I've heard Lulu describe her parents in many ways, and 'really good' has never been one of them.

Me: Where did they take you?

Lulu: I'll call you in a while.

Lulu's avoiding my questions and being evasive.

She's not at dinner. If she was, she would tell me more about it. She wouldn't leave me hanging like this. I sigh in frustration. Here we are. Two completely different sets of parents, and both of them shitheads.

Looks like Lulu is getting her present from me early.

"Lulu, if you make me knock on this door one more time, I'm gonna bust it down."

She opens the door and my fucking heart breaks in two.

You can tell she's been crying. Her expertly applied eye makeup is a little smudged, her caramel eyes are red, and her nose is pink and splotchy from blowing it. She's dressed up tonight—high-heel ankle boots, tight black dress pants, and a beautiful red shirt. Red for Valentine's Day, I guess. Her hair is in this weird braid thing, hanging over one side of her shoulder. It's weird, but really pretty.

But what hurts the most is that Ella answers the door. Not Lulu.

Her back is stiff, her shoulders are square, and her head is tilted high in the air. She walks away, leaving me to close the door. Sitting on her couch, she crosses her legs, and turns down the volume on the TV. I look over my shoulder to see one of her crime shows playing.

"What happened with the birthday dinner?"

She takes a deep breath. For a moment she avoids eye contact, but then faces me, boring her blank stare into my eyes. I like it much better when Lulu stares at me. Fire and passion and anger and happiness gleam in Lulu's eyes. Ella is nothing but politeness, resignation, and controlled defiance.

"I waited. They always walk over and get me when my father gets home from work. Tonight, they never came." She purses her lips together. "My sister is missing. There was no phone call to remind them. So, they obviously forgot."

"Why don't we just walk across to the Big House, find them, and confront them? I'll come with you."

"They're not home."

"How do you know they're not home? You already checked?"

She grabs her phone off the coffee table, clicks on something, and tosses it across to me. I catch it with one hand. "Didn't have to. That's the truly disgusting thing about social media. I know where they are and what they are doing without much effort."

Glancing down at the phone, I see a smiling picture of Lulu's parents, sitting at a dining table decorated with candles, shining crystal, and red roses. You can tell it's a table for four, but you can't see who the other couple is with them. The menu laying in front of them is embossed with the name of the most expensive and most exclusive restaurant in a four-county radius. The caption to the photo reads, *"Valentine's Day on a Friday night? Reservations are no problem when your husband (and love of your life) is a real-life superhero. Saving lives and still making my heart swoon, even after all these years."*

It's even got a hashtag with it. #hothusbandsurgeon

I wanna throw up.

I toss the phone on the matching loveseat so I don't have to look at the vile picture anymore.

Sitting right next to Lulu, she stiffens even more. Her body actually leans to the side, avoiding direct contact with me. I don't even think she's aware she's doing it. It must be some sort of habit. A coping mechanism. Like her scar. Nearly the whole time I've been here, she's been rubbing the scar on the back of her neck.

I can't stand the thought of losing My Lulu.

I kick my leg out and push the coffee table away from us. Swinging down in front of her, on my knees, I haphazardly fling her one leg off the other, uncrossing them, and yank her forward so she's gripping my waist with her thighs. Good thing I'm fast because I'm not giving her a chance to react. I pull her head down, crashing her mouth onto mine. I suck on her bottom lip and tease her with my tongue.

Now, I know for sure that she's been crying; I taste the salt of her tears on her lips.

For a few seconds, it's like kissing a zombie. I whisper against her, pouring my breath into her lungs. "They don't matter, Lulu. It's just me and you. Me and you."

And she gives in. I know the exact moment she releases and becomes her true self again. She does that little moan that she always does when she's ready for me to kiss her.

And I do. I kiss her to not only heal her heart, but mine as well.

Minutes pass before we pull away from each other. She stares at me, with her Lulu eyes, and quickly wipes an errant tear, trying to catch it before I see it.

I run my hands up her arms. "Tell me something. Something no one else knows."

She bites her lip, hiding the sad smile of her soul. "When I was little, I would lie in bed at night and pray that I was adopted. I wished that Uncle Ray and Aunt Teresa were my parents. Or Janine. Or my teachers. Even the postal lady. She always had the kindest smile. Anyone but my parents. I wanted parents who would play with me, pay attention to me. In first grade, there was this girl who said that every night after dinner, she and her parents and her brother would play a game together. Old Maid. Or Crazy Eights. Or Uno. I wanted that, you know? A simple card game. Fifteen minutes. I wanted fifteen minutes of my parents' time. I just wanted parents who loved me." She swallows loudly, choking her sob back down to the pit of her stomach. "I want parents who love me."

Fuck them. I don't say these things to her but try to convey the feelings with my actions as I kiss her breathless.

I love you, Lulu.

It's me. I'm the one who loves you.

Chapter 23

Ella

"I'm excited. When did you plan this?"

"I told you it was supposed to be for tomorrow night when we saw each other, but it's perfect now. We can celebrate Valentine's Day and your birthday on the actual day." Ry looks at the clock on the dashboard of the truck. "Well, as long as we do it in the next three hours before the clock strikes midnight."

I look out my window, studying the road, judging how far we are from the homestead. I'm distracted by my reflection playing against the darkened window and run my fingers over my hair. "It's called a French Dutch into a fishtail braid. I can't do it. Carrie can. She always did my braids for me. I paid for this. I went to the salon and had this done today for my birthday, so it would look nice for dinner with my parents." I turn to look at Ry. "That's stupid, isn't it?"

Reaching across the seat, he wraps his hand around mine, squeezing tightly. "You're beautiful, Lulu. Your hair is gorgeous. I can't imagine you looking any different tonight. You're perfect."

Turning onto the driveway, Ry stops halfway down the path. "Alright, you stay here."

"What?!"

"I have everything laid out, but it will take me a few minutes to get it ready. You have to wait here." He jumps out of the truck. "And

I'm starving, if you take a bite of my cheeseburger, I'm gonna murder you." Slamming the door, he jogs off into the darkness.

On cue, I look down at the bag filled with our cheeseburgers and cheese fries and my stomach growls. Crossing my arms over my chest, I try not to starve to death.

Ry's 'few minutes' turns into fifteen minutes, and I start to worry. I'm about to slide over behind the wheel and haul ass down to the homestead when I see his muscular body jog back into focus. He jumps back in the truck, with a wide smile on his face.

He holds out a bandana. "Here, put this on."

"Seriously? If you were gonna blindfold me, you could've driven down to the site instead of leaving me up here, worrying about you and any ax-murdering psychopaths in the woods."

"Psychopaths stay away for Valentine's Day. Too much pressure. Performance anxiety."

Ignoring his stupid joke, I fold the navy-blue bandana around my eyes. I don't have to worry about it messing up my eye makeup. I cried most of it off earlier.

Once we're parked, he comes around to the passenger's side to help me. Scooping me into his arms, I wriggle, trying to force myself back to the ground. "Ry, have you lost your mind? I'm too big for you to carry. Put me down. Now." I guess it feels different when you're not in the throes of passion... because I sure wasn't thinking about my size when he picked me up the other night. That was the last thing on my mind.

"You're tall, Lulu, not heavy. There's a difference between tall and heavy."

I hear him reach around and grab the bag with our food. I can decipher enough about his movements to know that he's taking me down to the pond. My suspicion is confirmed when he sets me down and my boots clank against the wood of the small dock. Ry doesn't remove his hand from my back. Slowly, his thumb circles against the soft fabric of my shirt. I'm glad it's mild tonight. If I had a jacket on, I wouldn't be able to feel his hand.

"Alright, you can take the bandana off."

I do.

And my heart explodes in my chest.

The pond glows with the soft beautiful light of dozens and dozens of floating water lanterns. It's one of the most beautiful things I've ever seen. The calm waters ripple back and forth, twinkling the soft flames into the night sky. Like a million fireflies. Like a million shooting stars. Like a million kisses from Ry.

"It's gorgeous. Absolutely breathtaking."

"You like it?"

"I love it."

What I want to say is I love you.

He nods, accepting my compliment. Spinning me around, he shows me the rest of the dock. It's piled high with tons and tons of blankets and pillows. One of the small tables is set up and Ry's laptop is perched on top of it. Our food bag is over to the side, and he has already set out a beer for him and water for me.

"A picnic?"

"Do you want your Valentine's Day gift first or your birthday gift first?"

He got me two gifts? "Valentine's Day."

"Good choice." He plops down on the blankets and pats the comfy area beside him. "Sit. I have something for us to watch."

I lift an eyebrow. "Ry, I have no doubt that some people think watching porn on Valentine's Day is a romantic thing to do, but I'm not sure I'm one of those people."

He tugs my arm, pulling me down next to him. "I always knew you were a prude." He leans over and nibbles the side of my ear. His hot whisper sends an electric current pulsing down my spine. "One day I'll get you worked up enough, you'll be begging me to watch porn." He kisses along the side of my neck, sending waves of desire crashing through my emotion-stricken body.

"You don't play fair."

He pulls away, resting on his elbows. His growl drives me crazy. "Game on."

I'm not sure what kind of face I make, but the bastard thinks it's hilarious. "It's not porn. You said you always wanted to watch *Singin' in the Rain*. So, here you go," he waves his arm at his laptop. "I downloaded it. And you better enjoy it. I hope this is the only time in my entire life I have to watch a musical."

He remembered. I mentioned it just one time in passing. But he remembered.

It was several weeks ago, when we were saying goodnight by the open door of my vehicle. Raindrops starting falling, coating everything around us in a cold mist. When we were little, Carrie and I would slap our feet in the rain puddles, pretending we were tap dancers. When we got older, we always talked about watching *Singin' in the Rain* but never did.

I told that story to Ry. A short and simple fifteen-second story. And he remembered.

We eat our dinner and watch our movie. Our food has turned cold, but we are both so hungry it doesn't matter. It tastes phenomenal. Best birthday meal I've ever had. More importantly, Ry holds me close during the entire movie. He pays attention, engrossed just like me. He'd never in a million years admit to liking it, but I think he does. Almost as much as me.

When the movie is over, we lay on the dock, watching the lanterns as they float. "I haven't forgotten today's other big event. Are you ready for your birthday present now?"

"Yes."

Jumping from the dock and grabbing a battery lantern, he walks over to his truck. Not wanting to be left behind again, I follow him. He reaches into the glove box and pulls something out. He tries to block my view with his body. Peering over his shoulder, I'm mesmerized by what I see before he slams the compartment closed. He shuts it quick. Real quick. He doesn't want me to see what's in there.

Not fast enough, though. Condoms.

There are condoms in his glove box.

Shutting the truck door, he walks around to the back, lowers the tailgate, and lifts me up, sitting me on the edge.

"So, I debated about giving this to you. It's gonna fire you up. But you have to promise me to be smart about this. Don't do anything about this right now. Or for the foreseeable future. Do you hear me? Tell me you hear me."

I narrow my eyes, wondering what in the world he's talking about. When I don't answer quickly enough, he squeezes my knee with his hand. "Fine. I agree. I hear you."

He mumbles under his breath and begrudgingly holds out his hand.

It's a picture.

Of my sister.

My gasp is loud and frightening. Running my fingers over the photo, I study my sister's image. She's so damn gorgeous. My whole life I've been envious and proud of her beauty, all at the same time.

My words are defeated, crushed by visual evidence. "She's beautiful. Even high, she's still beautiful." And you can definitely tell she's high. She's sitting on a couch I don't recognize, with her head tilted to the side, her eyes closed, and a euphoric glow on her face. Wearing shorts and a tank top, she's holding her hands in front of her and doing this weird twitching thing with her fingers.

I glance at the date in the bottom corner. I know that date. I've memorized so many of them over the past few weeks of my investigation. It was two-and-a-half weeks before she went missing. "She turned her phone off on this date. I have a record of all the times she did that to her phone." Next to the date are some letters—like an abbreviation that's part of the digital timestamp. I'm not sure what they mean.

"Is this Trash's house? I don't remember seeing this couch there."

Ry shakes his head. "No, that picture was taken at Trey's mobile home. He lives about a mile up the road from Trash."

"You've been to his house? I thought you said to stay away from him."

"I've been there a few times, and none of them by choice." He bends down, stares into my eyes, and points his finger in my face, like a parent scolding an unruly child. "And I do mean it, Lulu. You stay the hell away from there."

"Why did you go there?"

"My brother. Trash overdosed once. I had to get him and rush him to the hospital. A couple of other times he had bad trips, and I had to go get him, calm him down. The crew doesn't party at Trey's much. They mostly go to my brother's house. The times I've been there, the crowd was small. The timing may revolve around when deliveries come from the supplier."

"So, Carrie was probably there that night, picking up stuff to sell. I guess she had to try her own product." The disgusting sarcasm coats my tongue like a fungus. "Quality control."

"Don't be like that. Carrie was different. *Is* different. She just got in too deep with something that was supposed to help her. It ended up consuming her."

"Where'd you get this picture?"

Please don't tell me you've had it this whole time.

"I haven't been to Trash's in a long time. Since I started using your hotspot," he winks at me. "But I had to go over there the other day to get a lawnmower part. My stupid ass father needed help fixing his, and of course, I agreed to help. Anyway, Christina was there, and she was flipping through this huge stack of pictures she had just developed. I saw this one. She gave it to me."

"Christina?"

"The woman you were talking to outside of the bathroom that night at the party. She had a camera hanging around her neck?"

Realization dawns in my brain. "That's right." I shake my head in confusion. "That doesn't make any sense. If Trash and Trey and everybody is so afraid of someone ratting on them, why on earth would they let someone take pictures of any part of their crime scene? It's evidence."

"Trey is more lenient on Christina than most. They're fucking. In fact, there's a good chance he's the father of the last kid she had, but no one knows that for sure. Taking pictures makes her happy, so he lets her. She's not allowed to take pictures of the drugs or any-thing illegal, and she knows that."

I look back down at the photo. Sure enough, there are no little pills sitting on the coffee table in front of the couch. There's not even a beer bottle in the picture.

"There's something else."

My heart skips a beat. "Ry, I don't know if I can handle anything else."

He hands me a note. It's in his own handwriting. "It's the code for how people buy drugs at the gas station."

My head snaps up, soaking in his words like a sponge. "What?"

"I'm sure you already know that when a person buys that sweet tea and asks for a paper bag, that's code for 'they wanna buy'. Well, they place the order with the money they use. A $1 bill folded on the outside means they want to buy Ritalin. A $5 bill folded on the out-side means they want to buy Vicodin. A $10 bill is Percocet. A $20 bill is Oxy, and a $20 bill with three pennies with it means the Holy Trinity—Oxy, Soma, and Xanax. Folded inside has to be the exact money for how much the person wants to buy."

Holy shit.

Holy. Shit.

"How do you know this? When did you find out?"

"I've known it. For quite some time."

Anger flares up in my chest. "You've known about this? And you didn't tell me?"

"No. I told you I didn't want you asking questions about this. Getting yourself into trouble."

"Then why tell me now?"

He shrugs, running his hand over his jaw. I like it when he does that. It's super sexy.

I shake my head, ridding myself of that thought. No, I'm mad at him right now. Not horny.

"Because keeping it from you started to feel like a lie. I'm not sure why, but it just did."

"How did you first find out about the code? Did you watch people in the gas station? Did you monitor it?"

"Slow down there, Sally Sleuth. It wasn't anything that dramatic. Trash told me a long time ago. Back when he was trying to get me to push. He wanted me to come work at the gas station with him."

My hand covers my mouth in shock. "I'm so sorry. I can't believe he would try to drag his own brother into that life."

"Why not? He dragged your sister into it, didn't he?"

I guess I've never thought of it that way. I look at her face, tracing her features with my fingertip. "I guess so."

"I hope I made the right decision. It's definitely not the most conventional birthday gift." He snorts. "I probably should've just done a card and a balloon."

I tuck the picture and note in the corner of the truck bed so they won't get lost. Grabbing his forearms, I pull him closer to me. I curl my finger, begging him to come even closer. When he does, I plant my lips on the ridge of his ear. "I hate balloons."

His chuckle vibrates low in his chest. Grabbing my wrist, he looks at my watch, checking the time. "Well, Lulu. You have three minutes left, and then your eighteenth birthday will be gone forever. Any last birthday wishes?"

Kiss me. Kiss me forever.

But I don't have to say the words.

All I have to do is moan and he makes my unspoken wish come true.

Chapter 24

Ella

R y kisses with his whole body and not just his lips. It's part of the reason I can never get enough of him.

Never, ever, ever.

His tongue sweeps across mine and his hands graze up my stomach, nearing my breast when he suddenly breaks away, leaving me dazed and empty. "Give me just a minute." He walks several paces away from me, and I watch the movement of his back and shoulders as he adjusts the massive erection straining against his jeans.

"Does it hurt?"

Taking a deep breath, he spins back around. "Does what hurt?"

The sight of him makes my mouth dry. I nod my head at his crotch.

He furrows his brow. "My dick? Does my dick hurt?"

I grunt. He knows what I'm talking about. He's just being difficult. Just being Ry. "Having an erection and knowing there's no immediate relief. Ummm...release."

I'm not sure of the proper word.

He smirks, tugging his mouth into a sly little smile. "Oh, I'll have release. I always have release. The second your car pulls out of this driveway, I'll have my fist wrapped around myself, thinking of you." He props his hands on his waist and tilts his head. "Never mind, I drove you here tonight. Let me rephrase that. The second I drop you back at your house, I'll pull over on the side of the road and have my fist wrapped around me, thinking of you."

My face flushes red and my body grows hot. "You do that?"

He laughs. "Of course, I do that, Lulu. I'm a guy." He takes a step toward me. "You're telling me that you don't? You don't touch yourself and think of me?"

I don't avoid his gaze. Because that's not what I do. But I do know that my face must look like I just dived into a plate full of ketchup. Bright red. I can feel it.

His laugh is lower now. "Good. I'm glad to hear it."

"There are condoms in your glove box."

He swallows. "Yes."

"Do you use them?"

"When I have sex, I do."

Sucker punch. Holy shit, that hurt. The thought of him with another woman makes me sick. Physically sick. "Oh. And do you do that often?"

"Not since I met you." He holds up his hands, showing me his palms. "These calluses aren't just from working on cars."

"So, you haven't had sex with anyone since you met me?"

"I just said that, didn't I?"

"What about before you met me? Did you have a lot of sex then?"

"I did."

I can't breathe. That sucker punch cracked a rib. I lift my chin, refusing to show how much that answer affected me. "How many girls have you slept with?"

He folds his arms across his broad chest. "Why? Why are you asking me that question?"

"Because I've decided that I'm going to have sex with you. Not tonight, of course. But one day, we'll have sex. So, I think I have a right to know how many women you've been with. It's a responsible and reasonable question."

I am so bad at this, but he knows by now that I'm nothing if not forthcoming.

He rubs his hand over his jaw. "You've decided, huh? You know, Lulu, losing your virginity is a very big deal. It's not something to take lightly."

"Who said I was a virgin?"

He rolls his eyes. "Are you serious right now? Come on."

I wave my hands around in the air. "Fine. Fine. Point taken. But you're still avoiding the question."

"Because I don't wanna answer it."

"That many, huh?" I bite my bottom lip in thought. He said he never sleeps with a girl who's high, but that doesn't mean he doesn't sleep with drug addicts who happen not to be high at that particular moment. Has he had sex with that Christina girl? She looked really nasty.

"Go ahead and ask me. I know you want to."

He's right. He's always right. So, I do. I ask.

And he doesn't like the question.

"I don't have sex with drug addicts, no. And I try to make it a point not to have sex with ugly girls."

"Ry, this isn't funny. I'm being serious."

He throws his hands up in the air. "Me too, Lulu. You wanna know my life's sexual history? Fine! I was a virgin until after I graduated high school. Why, you ask? Because I make it a point to never have sex with a girl who knows where I come from. Who knows my past. Who knows my family.

"I'll meet a girl at college or at the bar and have sex in my truck. Sex at her place. Hell, I've even had sex in a public bathroom. I've never gone on more than a handful of dates with someone because that would have them getting too close. And even then, it's not actual dating. It's just fucking.

"I prefer to meet a strange girl, have some fun, and she'll never know that I come from filthy white trash. She'll never know that I don't have a home. That I sleep in either a twin bed in the middle of a body shop or a blow-up mattress in a tent in the woods. She'll never know that, most days, I shower at least two or three times because I'm terrified of physically looking like the white trash I am."

He's pacing. Breathing hard. Clenching his fists.

All of that hurt. Every single word. That broken rib just pierced my heart. I hate to think of him with other women. I hate to think that his body has been inside of someone else's body. A body that's not mine.

More importantly, I hate what he thinks of himself.

Ry is my world. My person. My soulmate. My one true love.

I wish he could see himself the way I see him.

He stops stomping around and stares at me. "Well? What do you have to say?"

"I hope you've been tested for STDs because I need to know you're clean for when we have sex."

He bends back, screaming into the night sky. "You drive me fucking mad, woman. I tell you all of that, and that's all you have to say? And yes, by the way, my cock is absolutely 100% perfect. Condoms do their job."

I scoff. "That's not all I have to say, but it's the only practical thing to say right now. I could tell you what a wonderful person you are and how none of those things you think about yourself are remotely true, but you wouldn't believe me. It would go in one ear and out the other. I could tell you how I'm terrified that you won't wanna have sex with me because I know who you are and where you come from. I could tell you that the thought of you being inside of another woman makes me wanna throw up because the only person you're supposed to be inside of *is me*. I could tell you that I'm terrified that you'll grow tired of waiting for me and go find someone else to have sex with. I could tell you that I'm terrified of leaving here tonight and not feeling your body on top of mine. Feeling what I want. Feeling what I need. Because I feel like I'm about to die without it."

He's giving me a headache. I grab the tie securing my braid and work my fingers through my hair, shaking everything loose until a pile of waves fall around my shoulders. "So, tell me what you want me to say. Tell me, Ry, and I'll say it."

For several long minutes we stare at one another. He's watching me, studying me. Looking at me like I'm a flower blooming in the middle of the night. Looking at me like I'm the most precious thing he's ever seen.

And I love it.

"Tell me what happens when you orgasm, Lulu. Do you cry out? Do you shake?"

I don't know how he hears me. I can barely hear my own whisper. "That's never happened. You know I'm a virgin."

"You don't need to have sex to have an orgasm. What happens when you touch yourself and think of me?"

"It feels good. Really good. But I can't bring myself that far. It doesn't happen for me."

Ry crosses the distance between us, closing the chasm that nearly broke us apart. Stepping between my legs, he bends down, brushing his lips against mine. I wrap myself around him, my arms, my legs. I press his new erection against me.

"Go ahead and ask me," he presses. "I know you want to."

"Are you gonna have sex with me tonight?"

"No, you're not ready." He leans back and looks into my eyes. "Do you trust me?"

"You know I do."

He kisses me long and deep, leaving my body swirling in a desire thick as molasses. Fire burns my skin, butterflies dance in my stomach, and need pulses through my core. Unwrapping himself from my legs, he unzips my ankle boots, placing them on the other side of the truck bed. He laughs when he sees my socks—black with pink hearts.

"It's for Valentine's Day," I say.

He nods, stuffing them inside of my shoes.

I shiver when his hands grab the waistband of my black ankle pants. If the feeling of his fingers on my stomach leaves me this affected, what's going to happen when he does whatever he's about to do? Nodding for me to lift my butt, he pulls my pants down and takes a step back, admiring my body.

He struggles to clear his throat. "I've never seen your legs. It's winter. You're always in pants."

Self-conscious, I rub my palms up and down my thighs.

His hands quickly replace mine, massaging me like he's trying to warm my body. "Are you cold?"

I shake my head, too consumed to speak. When he grazes the sensitive skin on the inside of my thigh, my head lobs back in ecstasy. He stares at my satin panties. It feels like an entire lifetime passes before he grabs them, slowly sliding them down my body. My bare ass is on the cold bed of the truck, and the temperature difference between it and my scorching skin shocks me. Ry lifts my panties to his face. Turning the cotton gusset outward, he shows me the stream of milky white desire made by my body's arousal. His tongue lashes out, tasting it. Licking it clean.

Oh my gosh.

Tossing my panties to the side, he grabs my discarded pants and rolls them into a ball. "Use this as a pillow so you don't hurt your head. Lie down."

I do as I'm told.

My heart's beating so fast I think I'm having a heart attack. He takes my legs and bends them, placing the bottoms of my feet on the edge of the tailgate. My body shakes in anticipation.

I close my eyes.

And Ry buries his head between my thighs… definitely making this the best birthday I've ever had.

Chapter 25

Crutch

I have a new purpose in life. A new reason for living.

Bringing Lulu to orgasm. Making her scream. That's my new purpose. And I could do it all day, every day, from here to eternity.

Lulu's loud when she orgasms. Really loud. I thought the little moan she gives when she's ready to be kissed was hot. Hearing her cries when she comes all over my face or my fingers is a completely different story.

I'm addicted. I'm an addict.

I can't keep my mouth off her. I can't keep my fingers out of her. The days have been a blur of normal life, rushing through the motions, counting down the minutes until she shows up at the garage or at the homestead.

I don't know how I don't have lock jaw. I also don't know how she can even walk.

"Ry, are you listening to me?"

I glance up, watching Lulu draw her straw through the whip cream of her frozen coffee drink.

Laughing, I remove the ballcap from my head and run my fingers through my hair. "No. No, I'm not listening."

She narrows her eyes. "And just why not?"

I lean close. Anticipating a secret, she does the exact same thing.

"Because I'm daydreaming of throwing you across this table and ripping the panties from your body. With my teeth."

She doesn't shy away. That's not My Lulu. But she does blush. "Well, I definitely don't see how that would complete your psychology homework."

"No, but it sure as hell would be a lot more fun."

Tossing her straw wrapper at me, she turns back to her own chemistry homework.

Another cold front has come through. This one harsh, making the homestead too cold for us to hang out at, even with blankets and a roaring fire. That's why this Saturday finds us at the coffee shop. At the same table we sat at last time. The same cashier was working as last time too. Lulu quickly reminded me her name was Peyton. She was also quick to roll her eyes when Peyton offered to fix me the same house coffee as last time because I obviously made an impression on her.

It tastes good this time too. Maybe I *could* be one of those douchebags who buys fancy coffee every day. When I have money, and when I'm somebody, that is.

We spend hours huddled around the small table, working, talking, laughing. Refilling our drinks when they get low. Lulu always jumps up before me, feeling bad that I paid for the first round. We're in the middle of a very serious conversation about our favorite colors—Lulu is very passionate about green—when we're interrupted.

"I usually only see you talking this much when you're trying to give me a headache."

She jumps up from the table and wraps her arms around the man. She's not stiff. She's not standing like a statue. She's acting like Lulu and not like Ella.

She's completely and totally comfortable around... a police detective. Detective Marcum. I know him from Carrie's case, obviously. He came over to the body shop when he was questioning everyone at the gas station. He asked if I knew anything. Of course, I told him no. Because I don't. I don't know what happened to Carrie.

But I also knew him from before then.

Years ago, he was the detective working on a case of fraudulent checks and property theft. Yep. Dear old Dad broke into a house and stole some checks and electronics. Not just anyone's house. It was his boss at the time. He fired Dad for missing too much work and Dad thought he would get even. I remember Marcum coming to my grandparents' house to ask us questions.

He knows my immediate family tree. A tree that sucks the life nutrients out of the soil around it. You don't need weed killer, you just need my father, mother, and brother in the vicinity.

Their familiar whispers sprout a tinge of jealousy. But not for long. Lulu swings to me. "Marcum, this is Ryland Crutchfield." She looks back at him, smiling, whispering. "My boyfriend."

He's caught completely off guard. His eyes grow round and his mouth opens in surprise. "And when were you planning on telling me this, Ella?"

She raises her eyebrows. "Now, Marcum. I'm telling you now."

I rise from the table, offering my hand. Marcum shakes and furrows his brow, trying to recall how he knows me. "Crutchfield. Oh. Are you related—"

I interrupt him. "Yes, sir. Unfortunately, that's me. Whoever you're thinking of—my father, my mother, my brother. They've all been in jail."

He nods, slowly, analyzing my face. Trying to see how much of their shit has rubbed off on me. Normally, I don't get nervous. But he makes me nervous. Without looking I hold my fingers out to my side, begging for a connection with Lulu. I don't have to wait long. Her fingers quickly wrap around mine, and we discreetly hold hands behind our legs as we stand.

Not discreetly enough. Marcum sees. Well, I guess I should expect that. They don't give detective badges to just anyone.

"You know, son, if we were all judged by the actions of our families, there wouldn't be any good people in this world."

He called me son. Just like Harlan. Just like my grandpa.

"Ella, can I talk with you in private for a minute?"

She holds her head high and squares her shoulders. "Anything you have to say to me, you can say in front of him."

Marcum's eyes flicker back and forth between the two of us. He snorts on a chuckle. "Tuck your tail feathers back in place. I was just gonna tell you something about the case."

Her shoulders slag back into a comfortable place. "You should've led with that."

He ignores her comment, used to it. Grabbing a chair from the table behind us, he motions for us all to sit down. "We received two anonymous tips over the past two weeks. One sighting in a small town near Phoenix. The other in Nashville. Locals already checked on the Phoenix one. It was nothing. We haven't been able to discredit the Nashville one yet. Someone said they saw Carrie working at a flower shop downtown. Flower shop has been closed for the past few days, some kind of renovation, and the owner has been out of town. It's supposed to open back up this coming week. I'll let you know what they find out."

Lulu shakes her head. "Not her. Carrie wouldn't work with flowers. Pollen makes her eyes water. She hates it when her eyeliner runs."

Marcum nods. "Plus..."

Lulu stares into his eyes. "Plus, she would never leave me, willingly. Alone. With *them.*"

"Speaking of, I called them earlier this week to tell them about the leads. They never called me back."

She shrugs. "Didn't you see Dad's interview in the newspaper about doing the gallbladder removal for the president of the university? And Mom had some kind of tennis club function. So, you see, their priorities are found much higher on the social ladder than worrying about their missing daughter."

He clears his throat, taking a drink of his coffee. "Well, I called Ray and told him. I didn't wanna distract you from the trip presentation. He said you're supposed to go over to his house for dinner tonight. He said he would tell you then. You can just tell him we ran into each other."

Dinner tonight? Why didn't she tell me? I thought we had the whole day and night together. And what trip presentation? Apparently, Lulu isn't telling me shit.

"Thanks, Marcum." She flicks her eyes over to me. "I hadn't told him about the family dinner yet. Now you've given him time to try and back out."

Laughing, Marcum slaps me on the shoulder, taking me by surprise. "Take it from me, son, if going to a dinner will make Ella happy, then do it. She knows how to aggravate the hell out of you if you don't give her what she wants."

So, he does know Lulu. Not just Ella.

"I have to go get Nancy. She's in the hair and makeup store. The kids have a date night tonight so we get to watch Nate." His smile jumps to ten miles wide.

Lulu tells him to send her regards to the woman named Nancy, and he walks out the door, bundling up against the cold.

She picks up her pencil and immediately goes back to doing her homework.

"Are you kidding me?" I pluck the pencil from her hand and hold it hostage in front of me. "What dinner? What trip? And who is Nancy?"

"Nancy is his wife. His son and daughter-in-law must be having a night out so they are getting to watch their grandson. He was born the same day Carrie went missing."

"You haven't told Marcum about the drugs?"

"Of course, I haven't. You told me not to. So, I didn't."

I nod. She's so amazing.

"Now, what's this about a family dinner? And what trip?"

This is the family Lulu and Carrie should've been born into.

Hell, this is the family *I* should've been born into.

Ray and Teresa are the quintessential parents—kind, loving, funny, concerned. Their modest home is comfortable and well-taken care of. Their daughter, Raylee, is home visiting from Florida State University. Their son, Holt, stayed for dinner but then went out with friends. I guess he's some superstar football player. You wouldn't know it from meeting him—he's a pretty chill young guy—but it's hard to ignore the trophies and framed newspaper articles spread across the living room. He's a big guy too. Leaner than me, though, and not quite as tall, just about an inch shorter.

More importantly, Lulu is completely comfortable. Completely herself.

Today's been a great day. No interruptions from people who make Lulu prickle, who make her stand at attention like a clothes hanger is attached to her back, pulling her upright.

Raylee boxes up the board game we all just finished playing as Lulu snuggles next to me on the couch, unabashedly laying her hand across my thigh. I can't believe I just had a family game night.

Me.

The kid who used to turn his mom on her side so she wouldn't choke on her own vomit during the night. The kid who saved all the pennies in his piggy bank for when his dad would need bail money. The kid who refused to tell his older brother when he was getting bullied at school for being poor because he was afraid that his brother would kill someone. Literally.

"Crutch, are you sure I can't get you any dessert?" Teresa lingers at her chair, awaiting my answer before sitting down.

"No, ma'am. I'm absolutely stuffed. I haven't had homemade lasagna in years. My grandma used to make it."

She smiles, switching topics. "I remember seeing you. At one of the searches for Carrie. When we were looking in the woods, near where her car was abandoned."

I nod, squeezing Lulu's fingers. If she doesn't stop rubbing my leg, I'm gonna embarrass myself with a huge boner.

Raylee plops down on the opposite end of the couch. "I don't remember seeing you. And I would've definitely remembered seeing you." Her eyebrows waggle underneath her bangs.

"Raylee!" Teresa chastises.

She tosses her hands in the air. "What? Are we seriously supposed to pretend he isn't one of the hottest guys to ever walk the face of the planet? He should be happy. It's a compliment."

Damn good thing I don't blush.

Lulu doesn't roll her eyes; she just laughs.

Ray walks into the room, two fresh beers in his hand. "And I suppose I'm one of those guys too. Right, sweetie?"

Raylee snorts. "Yes, Father."

Leaning across the coffee table, Ray dangles a beer in front of me. "Ella said you are twenty-one?"

"Yes, sir." I eagerly grab the beer from his fingers. It's a craft beer. Expensive.

Lulu sighs. "I wish I could've been more involved with the searches."

"The public relations stuff was important too, Ella. It was the beginning. Getting Carrie's information out there was vital. Your parents needed you by their side." Teresa's just trying to placate Lulu's frustration. I think we all know her parents could've handled the spotlight just fine, all by themselves. But they needed Lulu there to fully portray the perfect, nuclear southern American family.

"How did you know Carrie, Crutch?"

I freeze. Taking a large gulp of beer, I stall for time. What am I supposed to say?

Lulu answers for me. "The body shop he works at is across the parking lot from that one gas station on the other side of the county. When Marcum and Leary went out there to question the employees, they walked across and talked to Ryland and Harlan."

"Well, that's really good of you, son. Every warm body helps."

He called me son. Just like Harlan. Just like my grandpa. And now just like Marcum.

Raylee kicks Lulu with her feet. "How did your trip presentation go?"

I completely forgot about the trip thing that Marcum mentioned. I was too consumed with thoughts of meeting Lulu's family.

"It went really well. The vote was seven yes and three no."

"That's great. Congratulations."

I clear my throat and nudge Lulu's side.

She giggles, taking my breath away. She glances around at her family. "I haven't told him anything about it."

They all nod, knowing a secret I don't know. And I don't like it.

"Back when Carrie was a senior in high school, she tried to convince them to do something really special for the senior trip at the end of the year. She wanted them to do something civic related. Do something for charity, for the greater good. Not just the same old trip for getting drunk and partying. Student council voted her down.

"I thought trying the same thing would be something nice to do. For Carrie.

"So, our senior trip will be a two-week trip to Puerto Rico. The first week, we will be partnering with a charity organization to buy and distribute water filters to those in need of clean drinking water. The last hurricane still has the infrastructure messed up. We'll also help with a school and park remodel. The second week, we'll do the normal senior trip thing. We'll stay at an all-inclusive resort on the coast. Get some sun. Play in the water. Let those who party, party."

I discreetly rub the side of her hip with my thumb. "You did that? You convinced a bunch of self-centered, rich kids to give back? To spend part of their senior trip doing charity work? That's amazing. You're amazing."

She shrugs off my compliment, reaching for her glass of water on the coffee table. "It's no big deal. Most of them are just doing it to pad their future resumé."

"Well, I'm proud of you. Regardless of everyone else's intentions, I know what your intentions are."

She leans against me, staring into my eyes. Her brown eyes shimmer like honey in the sun. She winks at me, teasing me. She loves to tease me. "By the way, guess I should mention that I'll be taking a two-week trip in May?"

I'm just excited that she thinks she'll still want to be with me come May.

Color me surprised, but trying to keep this thing with Lulu as 'temporary' isn't working out too well for me. I'm like the poor, pitiful dog from the pound, instantly attached to the pretty lady who took me home.

Woof.

Chapter 26

Crutch

I did mention she's a tease, right?

A complete and total tease.

It's my fault, though. Because I'm a fucking idiot.

When we got to Lulu's house after our dinner with Ray and Teresa, we decided to watch a movie. Lulu paid almost $10 to rent one of the new action movies for us to watch. Twenty minutes in, she reached over, pulling my head down to hers, wanting me to kiss her.

And... I pulled away.

"Lulu, you just paid ten bucks for this movie. We can kiss afterward. Don't waste money."

I will never forget my sheer stupidity for as long as I live. What man turns down a woman who wants to make out? I mean, those very words could be the death of me. Because I'm about to die right now. Literally.

She promptly obeyed my words, sliding to the opposite end of the couch. After a few minutes, she left the room without saying a word, returning a short time later in a completely different outfit than the leggings and sweater she was wearing.

I glance over at her long legs as she props them up on the edge of the coffee table. She's wearing really short cotton shorts and a tank top. The straps over her shoulders are no bigger than a piece of string, and she obviously has no bra on. The plump curve of her breasts is driving me to the brink of delirium, and her pebbled nipples have my dick springing to life in my jeans.

Despite my latest run of stripping Lulu from her pants and panties whenever we're together, I haven't actually seen her without her shirt or bra. Never laid eyes on her naked chest.

Why?

Sensory overload.

She's too perfect. I have to focus on one thing at a time with her or I'll be too overwhelmed. And I've been quite content focusing on her perfect little pussy as of late. And trust me, it's perfect in every single way.

But now all that's standing between me and her chest is a thin piece of baby-blue fabric, and I think it might be time for me to acquaint myself with a new part of her body.

"Why'd you change clothes?"

"Got a little hot." She reaches up, rubbing the back of her neck.

"Hmm." I reach across the couch cushion and hook my pinky around hers. "Come closer."

She yanks her hand from mine. "Shh." She points to the TV. "I'm watching the movie. We can talk afterward. Don't want to waste money."

That little minx has no clue what's happening on that screen. How do I know? The hitch in her breath. The uneven swallow of her throat as she pretends to ignore my stare. The way she nonchalantly rubs her thighs together.

Reaching behind me, I grab the collar of my shirt and pull it over my head. I toss it across to the loveseat and settle back against the comfortable couch cushions.

Her head snaps over to mine. "What are you doing?"

"You're right. It's a little warm in here."

This time she doesn't ignore me. But she's definitely not looking at my face. Her eyes roam over my torso, widening in pleasure, soaking up every last detail. Despite her best efforts, she hasn't seen me shirtless since that one night.

Why?

That same damn sensory overload.

There's no way I would be able to pleasure her if she were touching me. Rubbing my chest, teasing my abdomen with her teeth. Just the thought of it makes me wanna come.

And as I've already said, bringing her to orgasm is my new addiction. I'm not ready to give that up for my own pleasure.

Squaring her shoulders and lifting that stubborn nose in the air, she eventually clears her throat and turns her attention back to the movie. We both spend the next five minutes pretending to watch car chases and gun fights.

Finally, Lulu stands. "I need to refill my drink." She makes a very extravagant show of bending forward to lift her glass from the coffee table. When she does, her cotton shorts ride up, revealing the thin strip of white skin underneath her ass cheek. She's wearing black lace panties.

I can't stand it. She wins.

Snatching out, I grab her waist and spin her around in front of me. Her plastic water cup flings across the room, scattering ice cubes everywhere.

I'm not sure how it happened after that. Either I tugged her onto my lap, or she eagerly jumped onto my lap. Either way, she's straddling me now.

And that's all that matters.

Her chest heaves underneath my chin. All I would have to do is reach out with my tongue—just a little bit—and her nipple could be in my mouth in a split second. The thin strap of her top dangles from her left shoulder. In a nano-second, I could grab it with my teeth, exposing the fullness of her breast.

But I can't do either of those things. Because I'm currently consumed with the feel of her tight little crotch being lined up perfectly with my rock-hard erection. My fingers grip her hips so tightly, fusing her body to mine, I'm probably bruising her.

I'm twenty-one years old. I should be too young to know what perfection feels like. Too young to know that nothing better exists in the world.

But somehow, I know. Me and Lulu... This is as good as it gets.

Her hair falls forward, tickling my own bare skin. She reaches around and traces the faint white scar from the cut I had on my chest a few short weeks ago. Her fingers shake as she caresses both hands across my own peaked nipples and down the hard ridges of my abdomen. My eyes close and my head automatically falls back.

I'm definitely not having sex with Lulu. Not tonight. She's not ready.

But I'm definitely gonna have to jack off five-thousand times to get rid of this rush.

Her fingers trace my collarbone. "I thought you wanted to watch the movie?"

I lick my lips. "Nope."

She does the same, mimicking me. "You said you did."

"Because I'm a fucking idiot."

Her giggle sends tingles across my body. "You took your shirt off."

"Yep."

"But you wouldn't take if off for me all the other nights? When I wanted you to? When I wanted to look at you and touch your skin?" Her whisper is heady, thick with desire.

She's killing me. "Nope."

"Why not?"

"Because I'm a fucking idiot."

"You took it off tonight. You're playing our game. And you're not playing fair."

I growl. "Game on." I press her body even tighter into mine, rubbing the hard seam of my jeans into her sensitive skin. The skin I know is throbbing to be touched. The skin that's leaking her tasty, warm desire all in the crotch of her panties.

Her back arches, and she moans. *My moan.* Telling me she wants to be kissed. *Really kissed.*

We crash into each other, unable to function for one more minute if our lips aren't tasting each other. Her tongue plunges into my mouth, searching for me, calling to me. I bite her lip and quickly suckle away the pain. I reach up with both hands, slowly pushing the straps of her top, lower and lower. I have to see her. I need to see her.

And then there's a knock at the door.

Holy shit. I have never wanted to break something so much in all of my damn, miserable life.

Lulu pulls away. Her lips are swollen, her eyes glazed over. She looks like a disheveled sex goddess.

We both quiet, trying to listen for sounds above the panted breaths heaving from our lungs. Sure enough, there's another knock, followed by what sounds like stumbling.

"Ella, it's me. It's Kristie. Your car is here. You told me I have to knock if you're home instead of just using my key." You can tell her words are slurred. Is she high again?

"Are you kidding me right now?" I'm not talking to anyone in particular.

Lulu seems just as flabbergasted as me, mumbling unintelligible words underneath her breath. She crawls off my lap, and the pressure from her body that was providing a small modicum of relief to my raging hard-on is gone. Painfully gone. Very painfully gone.

Raking her hands over her shirt to smooth it, she gasps when her hands brush her own massively erect nipples.

Note to self: My Lulu has very sensitive nipples.

She grabs my shirt from the loveseat and wriggles it over her head. Seeing her in my shirt nearly rips the beating heart from my chest. Shaking my head to clear my thoughts, I toss my hands in the air. "What am I supposed to do without a shirt?"

She smirks, "It's not your top half you should be concerned with." She nods at my lap and tosses me a pillow so I can cover myself.

We can hear Kristie struggling to get a key in the lock. The second Lulu opens the door, she staggers in, stumbling over her own feet. She snatches out, folding Lulu in a hug.

Lulu likes to be hugged. I know she does. You can see it on her face. But she only likes to be hugged by people she deems worthy.

And I can see that Kristie doesn't necessarily fall into that category. She falls just short on the Lulu meter.

Lulu pushes Kristie away, attempting to stand her upright. When she coughs in Lulu's direction, Lulu's eyes widen and she starts coughing herself. "Oh my god, Kristie, did you drink the whole bar? I hope you didn't drive here like that."

So...not high this time.

Drunk.

Kristie waves a hand in the air and meanders over to the loveseat, flopping down. She's wearing a really low-cut shirt, an extremely short skirt, and fuck-me stilettos. I'm surprised she doesn't have hypothermia. No doubt, she was definitely on the prowl tonight dressed like that. Since she's here with us, that must mean she didn't find what she was looking for.

Lulu steps around the corner, pulling the sleeves of my shirt over her hands. Her back stiffens when she realizes what Kristie's wearing. "Kristie, I've never seen you in clothes like that. You look..."

Kristie laughs, loud and boisterous. "Hot?"

Lulu purses her lips together. "I was gonna say cold."

I slide my hand over my mouth, trying to politely cover my laugh. Lulu's damn funny when she wants to be.

"Well, I was just trying to get a date, Ella. I didn't feel so bad about not dating because you weren't dating, either. But then," she waves a hand over in my direction, "you started dating."

"It's not a competition, Kristie. You'll date when the right person comes along. You don't have to go searching for it. It's not something you find at the bottom of a shot glass. Look at me, happenstance brought me and Crutch together. And look at Carrie and Caleb. They met in class. Just a normal day in class."

Kristie flings an arm over her eyes. "Ugh, Carrie." She sniffles and starts to cry.

Lulu and I look at each other. "Better get her some water."

I follow Lulu over to the kitchen. Grabbing some paper towels, I clean up the spilled water and melting ice cubes from earlier while

Lulu plays nurse to Kristie. I sit back down on the couch and lower the volume on the forgotten movie. Dabbing the mascara from her eyes, Kristie asks Lulu for some aspirin.

Lulu disappears into her bedroom and comes back out, shaking an empty bottle. "I'll be right back. I'll walk over to the Big House and get some."

I sit up, "Do you need me to go with you?"

"No, it's fine. Stay here with Kristie. I'll be right back."

Great. Just great. I don't really want to be left alone with her for some reason.

The moment the hallway door closes, Kristie seems to invigorate. Uh-oh.

"I'm sorry to barge in. I hope I didn't interrupt anything too special."

You did. You interrupted my life. My moment with Lulu. I shake my head. "No. We were just watching a movie."

Her eyes slowly roam over my body. "So, do you always watch movies shirtless?" It's not her words that concern me, but her actions. She slowly uncrosses her legs and opens them wide, flashing me a glimpse of some red satin panties.

I jump up like my ass is on fire. Wishing I had a shirt. And wishing my jeans didn't sag slightly at the hips, flashing my black boxer briefs. I walk into the kitchen, reaching in the fridge to grab a soda. As soon as I turn back around, Kristie is in my personal space. Way too damn close for comfort. She twists her red hair around her fingertips.

Her eyes narrow, and her gaze follows the curve of my shoulders. She takes another step closer, close enough for me to smell her. Vodka. Cheap vodka was her drink of choice tonight.

"Ella is still a child. If you're just looking for someone pure, you can have me. My cherry's never been popped." Her pink fingernails scrape across my belt buckle. "I can even offer a preview. A blow job doesn't count as sex so you'd be doing nothing wrong." Her voice lowers to a whisper, making my jaw clench in anger. "I will blow your mind."

I grab her hand. A lot harder than I intend to. She pulls from my grasp and massages her palm. "Get your hands off me." I walk around the kitchen island and stare at the closed hallway door. She follows me like a little puppy. "You're supposed to be her friend, right? And you're hitting on her boyfriend? That's plain shitty. I'm hers. No one else's. And she's not a child. She's the most mature person I've ever met." I lean down to her level, growling in her face. "You were high the first time I met you. If you ever show up here high again, there will be hell to pay. You keep that shit away from my girl."

Kristie's mouth gapes open and she starts to drunk hiccup. I leave her standing there and walk back over to the couch, fighting the urge to let her and my sudden pissed-off mood ruin the day and night I just had with Lulu.

My tension eases a fraction when I hear Lulu open the hallway door. She shakes two aspirin from a fresh bottle into Kristie's hand and ushers her into the bedroom. "Go lie down, Kristie. I'll be in soon."

I'm perched on the edge of the couch, my elbows on my knees and my hands clasped in front of my face. Squeezing around me, Lulu sits on the coffee table, between my legs.

Pulling my hands away from my face, she stares into my eyes. "What? What's wrong?"

Kristie is a sleaze, that's what's wrong. "I don't like this situation. She's taking advantage of you. Showing up here all hours of the day and night."

She bites her lip. "We grew up with her, Ry. What am I supposed to do? Carrie felt bad for her. Growing up without a mother, being secluded by her overprotective father."

I reach out, running my hands up the sides of her thighs. She shivers underneath my touch. "You grew up without a mother too, Lulu."

She chokes on her whisper. "It's different. And you know that."

I do know it. I grew up without a mother too.

Gripping her legs, I tug her closer to me. It doesn't matter when I touch Lulu, where I touch Lulu, her legs are always smooth. My hands glide across her like melted butter. Bending my forehead against hers, I close my eyes.

Her breath whispers across my eyelids. "Tell me something. Something no one else knows."

"Before I go to sleep, I read. I'm afraid of looking stupid so I read the classics. Dickens, Hemingway, Fitzgerald. I didn't read *Jane Eyre* for school. It wasn't on our required reading list. I read it for me. So, someday, when someone asks if I read it, I can say yes."

She gently kisses my eyelids, my nose, the side of my mouth before scooting back. Grabbing the hem of my shirt, she tugs it over her head. Her own tank top catches in the material and rises above her belly button, gifting me a small glance of her bronzed skin and flat stomach.

She holds the shirt out to me, pulling it back when I reach for it. Her innocent eyes grow wide. "Ask me."

Holy hell. Has anyone ever had so much power over someone? She holds the key to my life in her hand.

"Tell me something. Something no one else knows."

"It makes my heart beat faster knowing that you'll be smelling me on your ride home. Smelling me on your shirt. Thinking of me."

This time the moan is mine.

Kiss me, Lulu. Kiss me forever.

Chapter 27

Ella

I want to take off running, but I don't.

The second I see him, leaning against his old truck, parked next to my SUV in the school parking lot, I want to take off in a wild sprint, toss my arms around him, and never let go. But I don't. These people are watching. It's not what's expected of me. I would have too many questions to answer.

I don't mind answering the questions. Really, I don't. But I like having something that's just mine.

And Ry is mine.

As I walk across the asphalt, soaking in the early spring sun, I can feel it. The glare of every single girl who goes to this pretentious-as-hell high school watching the sexy stranger. Silently pleading that he is some secret cousin of mine, meaning he is free for the taking. Holt has visited me at school a few times, and the female classmates who saw him bugged me for days for his phone number and contact information. Now, they're wondering who this sex pot is.

He's smiling when I reach him. Grabbing the heavy backpack from my shoulder, he smirks. "What are you about to do, Lulu? I know that look."

I glance around. I was right. Every single person with a vagina is staring at my man. Hell, even some of the guys are staring too.

Back off bitches, he's mine.

Snaking my arms around his neck, I pull Ry down for a kiss. He doesn't need more of an invitation. He thrusts into my mouth, kissing me with passion and fervor, digging his fingers into my waist. We haven't seen each other in two days. He had a mid-semester exam Wednesday night. And last night I had to attend a country club function with my parents. They needed their token daughter.

Eventually pulling away, he starts laughing. "I knew that would happen. Girls should make you jealous all the time. A man could get used to a welcome like that."

"What in the world are you talking about?"

He waves his hand around at our distant audience. "You just rolled your eyes at a whole high school of girls, Lulu."

I pout. "I don't roll my eyes."

"Whatever you say." Folding his arm against the small of my back, he waits for me to unlock my door and then puts my backpack in the back seat. I toss my purse onto the driver's seat.

"What are you doing here? Shouldn't you be at work?" A split second of horror streaks across my heart. "Is Harlan okay?"

"Harlan's fine. He let me have the afternoon off. There's something I want—"

Ry's rudely interrupted by a member of the distant audience who decided not to stay so distant.

Hudson's voice is prickly and filled with bitterness. "So, now I see why you canceled on the trip. You're still seeing this guy, Ella."

Ry peers around me, seeing Hudson for the first time. He makes a move to place himself between me and Hudson, but not before whispering his words of concern to me. "You canceled the charity trip? Why?"

I shake my head. "No, not that trip. It—"

It doesn't matter. Hudson once again interrupts. "Our trip to Miami Beach. Spring Break is next week, and we're supposed to be leaving for Miami tomorrow, but Ella backed out on me."

Our trip. Hudson's making it sound like a lover's getaway and not the large group trip it's supposed to be. I take a step forward, but

Ry doesn't like it. His fingers twitch out to my side, grazing my thigh, begging me not to leave the sanctuary of his shadow.

So, I don't.

"Hudson, you know I never really wanted to go on that trip. And I didn't *just* back out, I told you three weeks ago that I wouldn't be going. You'll still have twenty other people there to keep you company."

Half the senior class decided to go to Miami Beach, and the other half to New York City. The trips weren't scheduled through the school so no chaperones would be needed. Just a big pile of eighteen-year-olds headed off to party by themselves. My father had Addison book my flight to Miami Beach simply because that's where Hudson was going. His parents paid for a huge rental house. Three weeks ago, I canceled the flight without telling my parents.

"You used to never cancel plans with your friends, Ella."

I shouldn't engage him. Really, I shouldn't. But we all know I end up doing the things I shouldn't do. Even more so now after meeting Ry. "Hudson, we're all getting older, living our own lives. That's no one's fault. It's just the way the world works. I don't wanna go to Miami. So, I'm not. It's as simple as that."

"Well, you'd still be going if it weren't for him. I wouldn't call that simple. I thought you two were just having a fling. Aren't you done by now?"

Uh-oh.

Ry's fist clenches at his side and he takes two steps toward Hudson. "What the fuck did you say?"

There's no comparison. No fair match. Hudson is my height. In fact, he usually wears lifts in his dress shoes if he knows he's going to be dancing or posing for pictures with me. He's cute, don't get me wrong. And most girls in school would line up to date him, but he's always made it pretty clear that he was holding out for me. Waiting on me to jump from the 'friend zone' into the 'relationship zone'.

Never gonna happen. Never. Ever.

I've made that clear on more than one occasion. Especially after the drunken margarita kiss.

Ry's growl and threatening size give Hudson pause and he takes a small step back. Fighting isn't really something boys at my school do. How can you fight when you're wearing jeans that cost $300 and the latest, most expensive smart watch?

Ry shouldn't need any more confidence; he's built like a brick shithouse. But still, he takes advantage of Hudson's small sidestep, closing even more distance between them. "You should know Lu—" he breaks off, not wanting to share his nickname with the crap bag in front of him. "Ella isn't the kind of girl who has flings. Insinuating that she is makes you a liar. And we don't deal too kindly with liars where I come from." He flicks his chin in the air. "So, tell me, Hudson. Are you a liar? Or just an asshole who can't respect the woman's wishes? It seems to me she made them pretty clear. And she wishes to be nowhere near you this Spring Break."

One of his friends, Matt, tugs him on the shoulder. "C'mon, man. Let it go."

Puffing out his chest, Hudson makes the right call and decides to walk away. "I just hate to see you missing out on fun with your friends, Ella."

But they're not my friends. So, I'm more than willing to take that gamble and miss out on whatever activities their pea-size brains deem 'fun'. As they walk away, Thomas, a Grade-A-Douche, leans against Hudson and whisper-yells, "Yeah, she's totally not worth it."

Pure luck and heavenly grace are on my side. It's the only explanation for why my reflexes are so fast. I reach out, grabbing Ry's waist and holding him against me with all of my strength, using all of my muscles. I'm no match for him either. He walks several paces, treating me like I'm no more than a feather on his back. "Ry, stop. Please. Please, don't do this. It's what they want."

I jump off his back and race to his front, planting my hands on his chest. That stops him.

Looking down at my hands, he takes a deep breath, trying to release the pounds and pounds of tension sitting on his shoulders. I stare up into his eyes. He seems taller today because my shoes are completely flat. It was warm enough for shorts and a long-sleeve sweater so I have flat sandals on my feet. His translucent green eyes flare, setting my heart aflutter.

"Ask me," I demand.

Shaking his head, he snorts. "Tell me something. Something no one else knows."

"You know you told me that you never hear me say a curse word?"

He nods.

I lean in, waiting on him to do the same, waiting to share my secret with him. "In my head, I cuss all the time. I'm like a fucking sailor."

Catching him completely off guard, he bursts out laughing. Lifting me into one of his all-encompassing hugs, I quickly wrap my legs around his waist and he carries me back to the cars.

"Yours or mine?" he asks, standing between our two vehicles.

"Where are we going?"

"It's a surprise."

"Yours!" I shout. He sets me in his truck. Leaning across to my SUV, he rifles through my purse, grabs my wristlet wallet with my car key and phone tucked neatly inside, slams the door, and locks it.

When he starts driving, I slide across the bench seat, planting myself right next to him. "I love surprises."

"And I love a safe Lulu. Scoot back over and put on your seatbelt."

We're both deathly quiet for the rest of the ride.

Because did Ry just say that he loves me?

Chapter 28

Ella

I stare out the window at the large brick building with its rows of windows and a seating area planted in the middle of a small flower garden. I've never been here, but the sign tells me that we're parked outside of the premier nursing home in the county. Well, in all of the surrounding counties too.

The nursing home where Ry said his grandmother lived, back when she was battling her illness.

Wait. Did Ry ever *actually* tell me his grandma passed away?

He opens my door, holding his hand out to me. "Ry? Why are we here?"

He smiles sadly. "There's someone I'd like you to meet."

I instantly know… his grandmother isn't dead; he just let me think that she was. Of course, I just assumed and never asked him outright.

His grip on my hand tightens when we walk through the door. Despite their best efforts to disguise the scent, the smell of disinfectant and cafeteria food wafts through the air.

A middle-aged woman with short brown hair quickly notices Ry. "There you are, Crutch. We were wondering when you would make it back out here."

They call him Crutch? Reading my thoughts, he leans over and whispers. "They got used to Grandpa always calling me that." He reaches for a sign-in sheet and signs both of our names.

"You brought a guest with you today." She smiles, flickering her eyes between the two of us. "I need to make a copy of your driver's license, honey."

I reach into my wallet and hand her my ID. She copies it and slides it back across the counter. "She's been in a good mood today. You picked a good time." The nurse looks at the clock on the wall. "She should be sitting on her patio right now. It's been warm enough the past couple of days for her to go outside."

Ry leads me down a corridor, politely nodding to the workers and patients. Several of them know him. Nerves circle in my stomach, creating a tornado of acid rising into my throat. We stop outside of Room 14. The door is open, and Ry quietly makes his way inside. I can't help but feel like I'm invading someone's personal space, someone's sanctuary.

The room is neat and tidy. The hospital bed is made. The wall behind the bed has all the same stuff as a regular hospital—plugs, oxygen hookups, a call button. There's a dresser with framed photographs spread across the top and a small sitting area with two comfortable chairs positioned around a television. There are two closed doors. One must be a closet and one must be a bathroom. Making his way across the room, Ry stops at the sliding glass door and looks out.

I can now see that the back side of the brick building has an arch to it. Each of the rooms has a small square patio space that opens up to a middle courtyard. Several people are sitting outside on their personal porches, enjoying the sunshine. Some of the patients also have visitors sitting with them. Two nurses wander from patio to patio, keeping a constant check on everyone.

I can feel the nervous tension radiating from him. It's a tangible heat, raising my body temperature. It doesn't take a genius to know what we're about to go through is going to be hard. I don't know much about Alzheimer's, but... we're in a nursing home. I guess that fact alone makes things pretty self-explanatory. I rub my hand up his back, sliding my fingers along his spine and across the broad muscles of his shoulder. "Ry? It's okay. You're ready. I'm ready. We can do this."

His shaky breath nearly crumbles my resolve.

He opens the sliding glass door, and we step out into the afternoon. She's sitting in a wheelchair, covered with a thick blanket. Her short white hair billows in the breeze. She's thin. And she looks many years older than she actually is. But I can see her in there. The person she used to be. Vibrant, young, loving, beautiful.

How can I see it?

Because of the way Ry looks at her. The love on his face, the admiration. It tells me she was those things and so much more.

It's an agape love. A love that's more than just the word.

"Michael? Is that you?"

He nods for me to take the open seat next to Grandma. I quietly do as I'm told, and he kneels between the two of us.

"No, Grandma, it's me. Crutch. Grandpa's not here."

She smiles and nods, but you can tell that it doesn't register. She doesn't know who he is right now.

"You look really good today. I'm glad that it finally warmed up so you could sit outside and enjoy the garden. I know it's not the same as your orange roses from home, but it's still nice."

She turns her face to the sun, ignoring Ry's attempt at conversation.

"There's someone really important I want you to meet, Grandma. This is Luella. She's..." his voice tapers off as he stares into my eyes for a moment, before turning his attention back to her. "Well, she's mine." He reaches out and rubs her hand. "Just like Grandpa was yours. Lulu's mine."

Oh my god. Shatter my heart. Toss my future hopes and dreams into a burn barrel because nothing else matters in this world except Ry. My Ry.

"It's really nice to meet you," I say. I'm not sure what to do, so I just do what I feel like. I reach out and rub her other hand, slowly tracing my fingers across the wrinkles and protruding veins.

"That tickles. Betsy knows how to tickle the best."

He clears his throat and directs his next comment to me. "Betsy is her older sister. Lives somewhere in Oregon now. I haven't seen her since I was in middle school."

"My older sister would always tickle me too," I say. "She'd tickle me until I couldn't breathe. It drove me crazy. I hated it. And I loved it."

She repeats my words. "Hated it. Loved it."

"Grandma, is there anything you need? Are you thirsty? Are you hungry?"

One of the nurses circles around to us. "Crutch, it's so good to see you." He stands up, giving the woman a hug. She's older than us, but still young. You can tell she finds him attractive, but she doesn't ogle him the way most young women do. I'm pleased to see a wedding ring on her finger.

"Yeah, it's been a while."

He doesn't offer any other explanation, and I feel bad. Have I been occupying too much of his time? Has he not been able to visit with his grandmother because of me? Have I been selfishly monopolizing all his free time?

"Claire, this is Ella, my girlfriend. Claire is one of Grandma's nurses."

I make a move to stand up, but Grandma grabs my hand, clutching it tight.

Claire chuckles. "Uh-oh. Looks like you've made a friend."

"How bad has it gotten?" he asks Claire. "She looks thinner. She remembered Grandpa's name when I got here, thought I was him. That's a good sign, isn't it? I mean, that she remembered him today?"

Claire shakes her head, tugging him by the elbow. "You know my rules, Crutch."

He looks over at me. "I'll be right back. Are you okay here?"

I nod. "I'm fine. Go talk."

I watch as Ry and Claire walk toward the middle of the courtyard and stop. They talk for several minutes. Ry's emotions seem to be all over the place. One minute he's gesturing angrily with his fingers, and the next, he's dragging his hands through his hair with a distraught look on his face. Eventually, they break apart, and he walks in the opposite direction from me.

Claire wanders back over, smiling professionally. "She really likes apple juice. I sent him to the cafeteria for some juice."

"Oh, okay." I think I see Grandma shiver so I wrap the blanket more snugly around her.

"He's never brought anyone to visit her before."

"He hasn't?"

Claire shakes her head and uses a Kleenex to wipe some moisture from underneath Grandma's nose. "No, you must be very special to him."

He's very special to me.

"I made him walk away because I don't talk about my patients' conditions in front of them. I hated when my parents would talk about me like I wasn't in the room. Like if I got in trouble or something? I can't help but think they," she nods her head at Grandma, "feel the same way."

I nod. "That makes sense. I was in the hospital once with bronchitis. I was very young, but I still remember it. And you're right, I hated when people talked about me while I was lying right there in a hospital bed."

"I saw the look on your face when Crutch mentioned he hadn't been out here to visit in a while. I've been here for five years already so I've gotten pretty good at reading people. Just so you know, you haven't prevented him from coming out here. You're not the reason. Crutch is a masculine guy, macho. Believe it or not, they take stuff like this the hardest. They are fixers. And this is something they can't fix. They're completely and totally helpless with this disease. It's easier on their hearts if they avoid it. Easier on their souls. But you have nothing to worry about. She's getting the very best care here. She doesn't know if he comes to visit once a day or once a year. All that matters is she knows that he cares. Which she does. She knows."

Claire stops talking when she sees Ry walking back up. She gently pats him on the shoulder. "Holler if you need me."

Kneeling back on the ground, he pops a straw in the juice box. "You okay?"

I grab his hand. "Of course, I'm okay. Your two best girls were just counting down the seconds until you returned." I playfully wink.

Ry smiles. "You hear that, Grandma? My two best girls. What do you think of that?" She mumbles something. "Here, I got your favorite—apple juice. Let's show Lulu how you drink out of a straw."

Like a toddler, Grandma slowly sips from the straw. When juice dribbles down her chin, Ry wipes it with the sleeve of his shirt.

We sit and visit for another thirty minutes. Talking and receiving no feedback. Asking questions and receiving answers that make no sense. And finally playing along to a childhood memory of Grandma going to the park. Or at least, that's what we think she's talking about.

When we get back out to the truck, Ry doesn't open the doors. He lowers the tailgate and together we sit, studying the sun as it lowers behind the nursing home, shading it in streaks of pink and orange and red.

"I'm sorry I assumed your grandmother had passed away. I'm glad to know she's alive."

He turns to me. "Is she?"

"Huh?"

"Is she alive? She can't chew her food because she forgets how to do it so they blend her food. She can't even use the restroom properly. My grandma has to wear diapers. And she hasn't remembered my name in years." He rubs his hand over his face. "Is that being alive, Lulu?"

I scoot closer to him. "I don't know the answer to that. And that's because the answer is different for everyone. Some people wouldn't wanna live that way. And some people wanna stay on this earth until the very last minute possible. The fact remains that no one with Alzheimer's has ever miraculously been cured and told everyone else what actually happened to them when they were lost in their own minds, lost in their own thoughts, locked in their own memories. Maybe she knows you and hears everything; she just can't verbalize it. Or physically show it." I shrug, sighing. "At least, that's my thoughts on the matter."

Ry jumps off the truck and walks around to the side, shielding himself from view. I don't follow him. He needs a few minutes of space, and I graciously give him that. Eventually, he comes back around. His eyes are a little red, but he would never in a million years admit to crying.

Suffocating.

My love for him is suffocating me like a fucking pillow over my head.

He leans against the tailgate, trapping me between his arms. His muscles flex and his jaw twitches. He is breathtakingly handsome when he's vulnerable. A shooting star that I can't believe fell within my reach.

"I guess that wasn't much of a fun surprise, huh?"

I slide my arms around his shoulders, tugging him closer with my legs. "It was one of the best afternoons of my life. You gave me something special today, Ry. You gave me your trust. I'd call that a pretty good surprise."

He bends down and gently kisses my lips. When he pulls away, he caresses the side of my face with his hands, tracing the curve of my jaw, the circle of my cheek, and slant of my nose. He runs his fingers through my hair, causing a tickle in the back of my throat. Lifting a strand to his face, he inhales deeply, smelling the remaining scent of my coconut shampoo.

Content with his perusal of my body, he lifts me by the waist and sets me on the ground, slamming the tailgate closed. "Come on. I told Harlan we would pick up dinner and eat with him before his poker buddies show up."

Chapter 29

Ella

Ry's taking a shower while Harlan and I finish eating. Ry eats double what we eat and still finishes before us at every meal.

"So, he really took you out there today, huh?"

"Yeah. I was shocked in the beginning simply because I had assumed that she passed away."

"He's never taken anyone else out there. I went a couple of times with Michael, but Crutch doesn't want me to go. He wants me to remember Dottie as the vibrant young woman I always knew."

"What about his parents? Trash? Do they ever go to visit?"

He takes the last bite of his cheeseburger. "They can't. They're not allowed to."

I furrow my brow, dragging a French fry through a mountain of ketchup. "What do you mean? They're family."

"They can't visit without Crutch's permission. He's got power of attorney. He can designate who's allowed to visit and who isn't. And Crutch would rather eat razor blades than let those lowlifes around her."

"He's Grandma's power of attorney? Not his mother?"

"Hell no. She would take everything she could get from Dottie and dump her in the lowest-cost facility she could find. You know something terrible like what you see on those hidden camera news investigations."

"But Ry's so young to be in charge of all of those major decisions."

"He's an honorable boy. Best thing Michael ever did was draft a will the second Dottie got sick. He had everything figured out to protect both Dottie and Crutch. I was named temporary power of attorney for a few months after Michael's death. As soon as Crutch turned nineteen, everything turned over to him. He's a remarkable young man. I'm proud to call him my own. Although, he did go against Michael's wishes in one aspect, and I've never really forgiven him for that."

I lean forward, engrossed in learning more about Ry. I do feel like I'm doing something a little forbidden, though—talking about him behind his back. I cast a look over my shoulder and quietly listen. When I hear the shower still running, I turn back to Harlan. "What happened? What did he do?"

Harlan leans back and stretches his arms behind his head. "It's more of what he didn't do—college. I mean, he's gone to the community college, but he was supposed to go to the big university. He got in, but he was real pissed he didn't get a scholarship. He said the school guidance counselor is supposed to help with things like that, but I know her and her family. Stuck-up little thing who thinks Crutch is like the rest of his family. But a scholarship was a moot point, Michael had set aside money for college. He planned ahead.

"When he sold me the land, it was to help offset the future expense of the nursing home and care for Dottie. But when he moved to the apartment in town and sold his house out here, that money was earmarked for Crutch's education. Specifically."

My mouth gapes open in shock. I stumble over my words. "Huh? Why didn't he go to the university then? Why miss out on school for a whole year to save up money for a two-year college? Instead of going to a four-year school immediately?"

"He's scared the money will run out, and Dottie will still be living. Still be in need of care. Some people with Alzheimer's, especially early onset like Dottie, can live for fifteen, twenty years. He couldn't bear to spend that money for school, knowing that someday, ten years from now, he may need it to care for her.

"Michael was in the service—Marines. Since he was activated during a wartime classification, the VA will pick up and pay some nursing home benefits to the surviving spouse once their assets get below a certain point. If the money from the land sale started to run low, the VA benefits and Medicare would still provide a nice place for Dottie. It just wouldn't be the place she is now. She's in the best place in the damn state. Crutch wasn't willing to take that chance. He hasn't spent one dime of the money from the sale of the house. He's saving it all in case he needs it for her."

I rub my temples with my fingers, trying to make room in my brain for this explosive new information.

Harlan stands up, tossing the last of his trash. "Welp, I'm gonna head outside and smoke a cigar before the boys get here for poker." He stops at my chair, flicking me on the shoulder. "Come on, honey, stand up. Give this old man a hug."

In a zombie-like state, I do as I'm told, quickly resting my chin against Harlan's chubby shoulder. He smells like grease, deodorant, and sweet chewing tobacco. "Now don't go feeling sorry for the boy. This was all his choice. It's how he wants to do things. You have to respect his wishes. Family means more to him than some piece of paper with a degree written on it. Shows a shitload of character in my book." He pats my head. "And he doesn't wanna be less in your eyes. You're the first girl to ever treat him like a real equal. He wants to be the kind of man you deserve."

I pull away, dabbing at the moisture in my eyes. "*I'm* the one who doesn't deserve *him*, Harlan."

True story.

And what the hell am I supposed to do with these feelings? Because how can love uplift you and cripple you at the exact same time?

Chapter 30

Crutch

I'm an asshole.

And now, I'm a lunatic asshole.

I thought about it the entire drive back into town. I thought about it the entire time we kissed goodnight, leaning against her car in the school parking lot.

I was halfway home before I turned around.

And now, here I am, banging on her door in the middle of the night, like a straight-up lunatic. But I couldn't wait another second, let alone wait until a reasonable hour. I want her with me. I *need* her with me. Now.

I hear rustling on the other side of the door. "Open up, Lulu. It's me."

She gasps. And doesn't say anything.

I take a step back. Maybe I'm too close to the door and she can't see me through the peephole. She should always check the peephole.

But still, the door doesn't swing wide open.

What the hell?

"Lulu, I hear you. Open the door."

"No."

I take another step back and look at the door like it's a talking spaceship. Like the word 'no' just came from the mahogany wood and not her mouth.

I lick my lips, not enjoying the joke. Where's serious Lulu when you need her? "What do you mean no?"

"I mean no. I'm not letting you in."

"And just why the hell not?"

"Because." There's more noise on the other side of the door, and it sounds like she bumps into a piece of furniture. Her whisper is louder than she intends for it to be. "Ouch, crap."

My heart starts drumming in my chest at a faster beat. I don't like this joke. My back starts to sweat, and my shirt instantly sticks to me. "That's enough. Open the door, I need to talk to you. It's important."

"No, Ry. Go home. We can talk tomorrow. It's late."

Something's wrong. Something has to be *really* wrong. Is someone in there with her? Is someone hurting her?

My heart is beating so loudly now, I can hear it reverberate against my eardrums. "Lulu, you are starting to freak me out. I'm about to flip my shit, and I swear on all that's holy, I will break down this damn door to get to you. Open. The. Fucking. Door."

She grunts. Pissed. Frustrated. Hearing that actually calms me. Pissed Lulu can't be Scared Lulu. Can't be a Lulu who's being held captive by some mass murderer on the other side of the door.

"I can't let you in because I'm ready for bed. I've already washed my face. I have no makeup, no cute clothes, and my hair is messed up."

I was not expecting that answer.

What am I supposed to do with that answer?

I do what I probably shouldn't. I always do what I probably shouldn't.

I burst out laughing. I laugh so hard I give myself a stitch in my side.

"Ryland Joseph Crutchfield, so help me, if you don't stop laughing, *I am gonna flip my crap.* And it will make your outburst seem tame."

I rub my hands over my eyes. "Are you serious, Lulu? You won't let me in the house because you don't have mascara on? I thought someone was in there trying to kill you."

"Why would someone be in here? It's the middle of the night."

I throw my hands up in the air. "Precisely."

"Well, like I said, you'll just have to wait until tomorrow when we see each other. Well, I guess I mean later today, since it's so late."

"I don't care that you don't have makeup on. Or normal clothes." I chuckle. "In fact, all clothes are overrated. Strip down. Open the door. I need to tell you something."

"You may not care, but I do."

"Why?"

"I'll ruin the illusion."

I lean against the door. "What illusion?"

She does the same. The door thumps against the sag of her body. "Of being pretty."

Holy. Shit.

Did My Lulu just say that?

"What in the world are you talking about?"

"Ry, look at you. You know what you look like. Women basically throw their panties at you all day long. You've only seen me with makeup and nice clothes and fixed hair. Girls look different without that stuff. What if you think I don't look pretty? I mean, guys hit on me, but guys hit on anything, right? It doesn't necessarily mean I'm beautiful. Carrie is the pretty one, not me."

The thought of other guys hitting on her sends me into a spiral of rage. Before spinning too far down, I try to focus on the problem in front of me. Or, rather, the problem behind the thick wooden door. "Lulu, I can't believe that you would even fathom the possibility of me not being attracted to you. It's... it's... impossible. I can't even think of the words to describe how unrealistic that comment is. You're the most beautiful girl I've ever laid eyes on, the most beautiful woman. Makeup. No makeup. Burned and scarred and disfigured... in my mind, in my heart, in my eyes, you're the only thing of beauty in a world filled with ugly."

Slowly, the door creaks open, one centimeter at a time. I rush inside, eager to have her in my arms. I slam the door closed with my foot. She's standing in the shadows so I can't even fully see her, but then she takes a step back. Her whole body is illuminated from the lamp on the side table between the couch and loveseat.

I try to swallow, but nothing happens. My throat is paralyzed with awe.

This is her. This is My Lulu.

Her glossy, golden brown hair is piled high on her head in a messy bun. Strands poke out in every direction. Her face is clean, washed fresh. Fucking perfection. Her honey and amber-colored eyes look brighter and darker all at the same time, driving me insane with the need to study them. The black ring around her iris shines like black diamonds. She's wearing a hot pink sweatshirt, over an oversized T-shirt. The hem of the T-shirt grazes the tops of her thighs. The thighs I can't get enough of. The thighs I lick with my tongue when I'm getting ready to go down on her, getting her ready to scream my name.

My gaze makes her nervous. She reaches around, fondling the scar on her neck.

"Oh, Lulu." I hope she can hear it in my voice. Because I'm a pussy and can't talk.

She does. She hears it. I know she does. Because she blushes and licks her lips.

I bite my own lip, raking my eyes over her again and again. "You're beautiful."

She holds her head up high, staring deeply into my eyes. "Thank you."

I'm not sure how long I stare at her, but it's probably long enough to make most people uncomfortable. But most people don't have a Lulu to look at.

"What did you have to tell me?"

"Stay with me this week. It's Spring Break. Neither of us have school. I still have work, but we can be together all day and all night. Stay with me."

She tilts her head and raises her eyebrows. She smirks. I knew her sassiness couldn't stay gone for that long. "That sounds like a statement when it should be a question."

She's busting my balls at a time like this?

"Will you stay the week with me, Lulu?"

She pretends to think. She pretends to mull it over. I know she's going to say yes, but she still makes me sweat it. After an eternity, she takes a deep breath. "Yes."

"Perfect. Go pack your shit. I'll wait."

Now it's her time to burst out laughing. "Ry, it's after two in the morning. This can't wait until tomorrow?"

I close the distance between us, wrapping my hand around the back of her neck and threading my fingers through the tangle of hair escaping from her bun. "Do you wanna wait, Lulu?"

Well, that had more sexual connotation than I meant for it to, but hell, if she doesn't swell her chest out, making my erection ache.

"No." Her fingers graze across the top of my jeans, barely whispering across my scorching hot skin. "But it's late. Let's stay here tonight. I'll pack up tomorrow and follow you. That way, I'll have my car in case I need to come back to town for something."

It's settled then. We're going to stay the night together. We're going to stay the week together.

When I was little, I wanted to go to Disney World. I wanted to go so bad my little heart actually ached with longing. I eventually outgrew it, but the lingering wish stayed with me for years. That's how I feel now. A lingering wish is finally coming true. And I'm not even talking about sex. I'm talking about having a life with someone.

Albeit just for a week.

"Come on." Grabbing my hand, she pulls me behind her, into her bedroom. I pretend not to notice the tremble of her hand. Her comforter and sheets are already turned down, indicating that she was, in fact, in bed, or about to go to bed. I know because Lulu always makes her bed each morning. That's what Carrie taught her to do, so that's what she does. "Do you need a toothbrush?"

"I have one in the truck. I can go get it."

"Don't be silly. I have extra. You might as well keep one here." She reaches into a drawer and grabs a handful of toothbrushes. She must buy in bulk. Tossing back the pinks and purples, she gives me a blue one, and we stand together at her sink, brushing our teeth.

When finished, she untangles her hair and starts to brush it. I meander across the threshold and stare at her bed. "Which side do you sleep on?"

"I sleep in the middle, usually, so I guess it doesn't matter. What about you?"

I chuckle. "As you know, I either sleep on a twin bed or a blow-up mattress, so I'm pretty much in the middle too."

"Well then, you choose."

I slip out of my boots and socks. I tug off my T-shirt and toss it on the chair in the corner of her room. My belt buckle clangs together as I pull it from my belt loops. I plop down on the bed.

Sweet mother of pearl.

This bed is like laying in a swimming pool of clouds and cotton. The sheets smell like lavender and Lulu. One day I *will* have a bed like this. I'll have sheets that smell like lavender. And I'll be the one who gives it to Lulu. Not the other way around.

I prop up on my elbows and watch her as she emerges from the bathroom. She's nervous. But she holds her head high, never breaking my gaze. In fact, her eyes widen in appreciation of the view, making my own nipples hard. She likes me being in her bed.

Well, get damn used to it, woman.

She pulls the sweatshirt over her head. When she does, her T-shirt gets hung in the bottom of the sweatshirt band and it rumples upward, revealing her light blue cotton panties. She's left standing there in that big, oversized T-shirt.

It takes me a second to read the writing on the front.

A fraternity.

Lulu's wearing some other man's T-shirt.

I sit up straighter. "Whose fraternity T-shirt is that?"

She looks down at her ample chest. "Oh, it's Caleb's. He gave Carrie and me a bunch of extra T-shirts from his fraternity. The big ones that were leftover. Those guys all want skinny shirts to show off their muscles. Or lack thereof."

I shake my head. Over my dead body will she wear another man's clothes. I don't care if he is like a brother to her. "Screw that. I'll be right back." I jump out of bed, not even bothering with my boots. That's the good thing about not really having a house. You always have bags packed with clothes.

When I walk back in the bedroom, she's still standing in the same spot. I toss one of my clean T-shirts from the body shop at her as I jump back on the bed. She smiles and lifts it to her nose, inhaling deeply. "Mmm."

She stops my cold heart, cracking it open a little more. Damn if her every move doesn't rip emotions from my locked vault, forcing them into broad daylight.

"I take it you don't like me wearing another guy's shirt?"

"Nope."

She turns to head back into the bathroom to change, but then stops. She looks at the T-shirt in her hand and then her own body. Spinning back around, she lays my shirt on the bed and slowly lifts Caleb's shirt from her body. Her arms lift high in the air, elongating her torso. She tosses it over her shoulder and stands there for a moment in nothing but her skimpy, light blue panties.

Has anyone ever died from a dick explosion?

Because it's about to happen to me.

My Lulu may have a perfect little pussy, but her breasts sure are giving it a run for its money. They are large but not too large. Perfect handful size. The creamy skin matches down below. Together, they are three shades lighter than the rest of her bronzed body. Not that I can see her promised land now. But trust me, I have it memorized.

Her nipples are hard and erect, pointing in the air, like beacons of hope. Beacons of light, calling to me. The heavy slope of her breast angles against her torso in the most gorgeous of ways. Her stomach is flat with a slight curve to her love handles and hips, making me want to grab her and bite her.

And then... there's her legs. My dumbass brother was right. Lulu's legs are the fantasy of my wet dreams.

She grabs my gifted nightshirt off the bed and slowly slides it over her body. Turning off the lamp on her newfound side of the bed, she climbs onto the plush mattress. Folding her arms underneath her pillow, she stares at me. A small light filters in from the hallway, lighting her profile like an angel.

I'm worthless. I'm ruined for all of eternity.

Mimicking her movement, I lie down on my pillow. We're so close our breath whispers across each other's faces. I slowly graze my hand up her thigh, relishing every inch of her smooth velvety skin. My fingers settle against her hip, slowly kneading the plump skin where the curve of her ass starts.

My words are thick. "Go ahead and ask me. I know you want to."

"What?"

"Don't beat around the bush, Lulu. I like you when you get to the point."

"Are you gonna have sex with me tonight?"

I can't believe I'm saying this. "No. Not tonight. You're not ready."

"How do you know I'm not ready?"

"Because I'm not ready."

She gasps at the honesty of my words. And then she leans over and kisses me. She kisses me so intimately that I nearly forget those words because all I want to do is roll her over and slide into her until I'm buried to the hilt.

But I don't. Because I'm *really* not ready. I don't know if I'll ever be ready. Making love to Lulu will end in the complete and total consumption of my soul. I won't even be a person anymore. I'll just be a part of Lulu's DNA.

"Are you really gonna sleep in your blue jeans?"

I look down at my own crotch. It's like I'm trying to sleep with a sword between the two of us. She immediately giggles and blushes.

"I think my blue jeans are protecting us both tonight."

She reaches over and tugs the elastic band of the red boxer briefs that peek out from the top of my jeans. It snaps against my abdomen, humming the already sensitive area. I push against her, non-verbally telling her to roll over. She quickly complies, and I pull the thick sheet and down comforter over our bodies.

I'm spooning with Luella Margaret Hill. Little Miss Prim and Proper. Bitchy rich girl with the missing sister.

And I've never been damn happier.

Chapter 31

Ella

Three nights. Three nights I've slept with Ry.

Actually slept.

Don't get me wrong, there's been orgasms. Mind-blowing, earth-shattering orgasms. But no sex.

Ry was right. I'm still not ready. Hell, I still haven't even seen his cock yet.

Something I plan to remedy real soon.

The warm Spring Break weather has held steady, and the forecast says it will keep for the rest of the week. That means we should be able to keep sleeping at the homestead. He told me that we'll sleep at the garage or drive back to my house if the temperature dips down too cold. I wasn't sure how I would like sleeping on a blow-up mattress in a tent in the woods. But it's nice. Especially since Ry made me pack the goose down comforter from my bed and the lavender sheet spray.

The one thing I miss is my shower. We shower at the body shop. Although, Ry is a neat freak and keeps everything spotless, it's small. And there's no ledge for me to hike my leg on when shaving. Yesterday, I cut the back of my knee with my razor when I slipped, and he had to play doctor with salve and a Band-Aid.

Plus, I always pop a breaker with my blow dryer. But Ry knows better than to ask me to go without my fixed hair and makeup. It's hard to stop that routine. When you're always told that you have to look perfect, that you have to look completely polished and present-able, it's a hard habit to break. Mom wouldn't even let Carrie and me run to the grocery store for a loaf of bread without full makeup.

Ry says he doesn't mind me taking forty-five minutes in the morning to shower and get ready, because at night I take it all off for him. He says it's like a butterfly breaking free of her cocoon.

Walking back through the garage from the kitchenette, I hol-ler to the boys. "I'm gonna go get us some fresh snacks. There's not much in the cupboard. I'll be back soon."

Ry is hidden underneath the hood of a vehicle, but that state-ment quickly garners his attention. "Go to the dollar store."

I pretend to busy myself, grabbing my wristlet. "The gas station is just right here."

He pulls the white towel from his back pocket, wiping the grease from his hands. His warning is low and deathly serious. "Lulu."

I flicker my eyes over to the customer waiting in the corner of the garage, playing a game on his phone. Whatever Ry is fixing isn't going to take long, so the guy opted to just wait. I use the spectator to my advantage. Speed walking into the sunshine, I wave over my shoulder. "Don't worry. It's fine."

He definitely doesn't like that.

The gas station is crowded today, but it is the lunch hour, so some people are probably just buying fried chicken.

Some people are also probably buying other things.

The doorbell chimes when I walk in, and Trash's eyes instantly meet mine. He smirks, flashing me a glimpse of his cigarette-stained teeth. He's seen me over at the garage numerous times since our last run-in, but he has kept his distance. He may be more afraid of Ry than he is of that Trey guy. Although, I doubt it. I grab a small basket by the door and wander the aisles, grabbing some chips that Harlan likes, some protein bars that Ry likes, and some sour candy that I like. I stock up on some bottled water and sodas, pausing when I get to the specialty drink area.

Slayton's Southern Blackberry Tea stares at me. Mocking me. Mocking my sister.

I'm not sure exactly when I decide to buy drugs. I would like to say it was a spur-of-the-moment decision, but the fact remains, I've been thinking about it since Ry gave me the 'cheat sheet' for my birthday. Opening the cooler, I grab the bottle, holding it tightly in my hand. I have to wait on two people to check out in front of me. Trash starts laughing when it's my turn at the counter. I'm not exactly sure what the hell he finds so funny.

I guess it's me.

"You slumming it again, princess?"

"You're sorely mistaken if you think keeping company with your brother is in any shape, form, or fashion 'slumming it'." The words taste like bitterweed coming out of my mouth.

"Egh, at least it's kept him out of my hair for a while. He's always been a buzzkill." He shrugs. "I keep him around for the ladies. When he turns them down, they seek comfort in the arms of the next best thing."

It's pretty obvious he thinks he's the next best thing.

The woman standing in line behind me snorts. Just like me, she probably considers a bridge troll a better hook-up than Trash.

He finishes ringing everything in my basket and leans over the counter, nodding at the drink in my hand. "That too?"

I lift the tea bottle in the air. "I'll be checking out with this one separately." That comment piques his interest.

I pay for the groceries with my credit card. Shoving the plastic bags to the side of the counter, I set the drink in between us. Condensation rolls onto the Formica. I reach into my wallet and grab the money I carefully folded.

I guess it's hard to propose my actions are spur of the moment, when I folded my money weeks ago in case the situation ever presented itself.

Sliding it across to Trash, I choke on my words. My throat makes a weird gargling sound like I'm trying not to swallow mouthwash. "I'll take that in a paper bag, please."

Did I really just say please? At least I'm polite when I buy drugs.

Trash studies the $20 bill folded in front of him. Before he grabs it, I lay three pennies across the top. Eyes shining, he grabs my drink and money, walking quickly to the backroom. "Let me just grab one from the back." He's so excited, he's practically skipping.

Douche.

He returns just a few seconds later with only the $20 cover bill in his hand. The rest of the money that was folded inside is gone. He quickly makes change and hands the bag to me. "Enjoy. I think you're gonna love it. I'm sure I'll see you back real soon."

Gathering the bags in my hand, I make my way to the door, side-sweeping my view from one end of the store to the other. What if the lady behind me is an undercover cop? What if those cameras are a live feed to Trey and he sees that I just bought drugs? What if Trash planted a bomb in my paper bag instead of drugs?

I lift up the small brown bag. It just looks like someone's lunch bag. I put it to my ear. I don't hear anything suspicious.

The door chimes again, when I butt it with my hip to walk out. Trash's voice follows me outside. "Hey, Ella. I was right about your legs."

I don't even turn around to look at him. I run-walk back over to the garage, my heart slapping against my ribcage in adrenaline. The knowledge I did something wrong is floating in my head like seaweed in the ocean, clogging my thoughts.

Ry's finished the customer's car, and he's already slid underneath another one. His boots slap against the floor as he rolls his body and the creeper into a better position. Harlan is chatting with the guy at the register in the far corner.

"I'm back. I'll put everything away." I rush into the small kitchen, quickly tossing the groceries into the cabinets and fridge. Quietly racing into Ry's small bedroom, I lock the door. Leaning against it, I take a few deep breaths, trying to calm myself. Sitting on his bed, I lay the paper bag in front of me. Grabbing his pillow, I clutch it against my chest.

Was Carrie this nervous the first time she bought drugs?

When 'normal' people have a major surgery, they take pain pills. When those pain pills run out, they stop taking them. What makes a person cross over the invisible threshold? What makes them think they need more pain pills? What breaks the border between 'normal medical patient' and 'drug user'? And what made Carrie the latter versus the former? Was she always meant to be an addict? Is it in her body's chemistry?

What about me? If I took one pill, could I stop? Or would I be an addict too?

Flopping the pillow on my lap, I reach into the bag. My fingers grab the drink first. I lay it on Ry's quilt. At first, I don't feel the small plastic bag and I think Trash has played a horrible trick on me.

And then I feel it.

I lay it on the bed next to the tea bottle.

I can't touch it. It burns my fingertips like a hot iron.

I stare at the small pills—white, pink, and blue. Ry called it the Holy Trinity, before. Oxy, Soma, and Xanax. Nothing seems holy about it. In fact, I feel like I'm staring at the Devil himself. I sniffle, trying to keep the tears in my eyes. It's a completely moot point, my eyes are apparently operating under direct order from my stupid, stupid brain.

I cry and I cry and I cry, silently praying that Ry and Harlan don't hear me. I don't see any tissues, so I reach in the top drawer of the small nightstand next to me. Grabbing a pair of Ry's clean boxer briefs, I wipe my runny nose and try to dry my falling tears.

And then Ry walks in.

I guess the door doesn't actually lock.

And I'm too sad to even be shocked.

He stares at me, his eyes roaming back and forth between me and the pill baggie. I'm surprised I can even hear his whisper. It's quiet. Like a feather blowing on the wind. "What the fuck is going on?" When I don't answer, his voice grows louder. "You bought pills?"

I nod, rubbing the crotch of his underwear across my face.

He takes a step toward me, clenching and unclenching his fist in anger. His jaw tightens. "Why? Why would you buy pills, Lulu? Please tell me you weren't thinking about taking them."

What. The. Hell.

I square my shoulders and lift my chin. "You're being obtuse. Of course, I wouldn't take these pills. These pills took my sister away from me. These pills ruined your chance at a childhood. They're vile and repulsive."

In less than a second, he's on the bed, pulling me onto his lap, cradling me. I don't even mind that he smells like sweat and oil and Harlan's tobacco. "Then why? Why buy them? Why have them here?"

I shrug. "Lots of reasons. I wanted to see how easy it was. I wanted to know what Carrie felt like the first time she came here and bought these dumb things. I wanted to look at them. To try and figure out what makes Carrie so different from me." I raise my head and look into his haunted pale green eyes. "Am I really different from her, Ry? If I took those pills right now, would I become an addict like Carrie? Why does it happen for some people and not others? Why couldn't she avoid it? Why couldn't she resist it?"

He strokes my hair, trying to place my body into a patterned rhythm, allowing the repetitive motion to calm me. Eventually my tears subside, leaving my eyelids swollen and raw.

His voice soothes my rattled nerves. "I don't know the answers. If you and I took those drugs right now, we might both be fine. Or I may become an addict and not you. Or vice-versa. I have no idea. All I know is that you and I are strong enough not to tempt those fates."

Tugging my chin, he places his lips on mine. Not kissing me, but just connecting. I love it when he does this. When he acts like he can't function in the world unless he tethers himself to me.

His breath smells like toothpaste.

I can't believe I just cried in front of him. And I'm not even embarrassed.

Running his hand down my back and over the roundness of my ass, he eventually pulls away and smiles. "Have you been blowing your nose in my underwear?"

I look down at the crumpled boxer briefs in my hand. "Yes. Yes, I have."

His laugh is contagious, making me giggle. He tugs me from the bed. "Come on."

"Where are we going?"

"We're gonna flush those pills down the toilet and get you something to drink. Your body is burning up; you need to cool down. And we're definitely gonna throw my underwear in the washing machine."

Once he gets me settled at the small kitchen table, he hands me a bottle of water and a package of crackers. "Eat. Drink." He leans forward, kissing me on the crown of my head.

He turns away, but not before I see the kind smile on his face disappear. His jaw twitches, and he twists his neck to both sides, stretching it. A low growl rumbles from his chest as he turns the corner, leaving the room.

Worry escalates in my heart. "Where are you going?"

"I'm gonna kill my piece of shit brother for selling drugs to my girl."

Chapter 32

Ella

Three punches.

It could've been way worse.

Harlan and I were only a step behind Ry, but he still landed a solid three punches on his brother before we pulled him off. Not that we *actually* pulled Ry off his brother. Ry is stronger than ten of me and Harlan put together. He just stopped fighting because he was worried about one of us getting hurt instead. And of course, Trash is too thin and weak from partying to be any sort of match for Ry. Fortunately, the gas station was empty except for one guy over by the slushie machine. And he looked like a regular, if you catch my drift.

Apparently, I'm more of a bitch than I previously thought because my heart actually got all warm and fuzzy when I saw Trash's bloody nose and blackening eye.

Hours have gone by since then. The body shop closed for the night and Harlan went home. Ry is currently in the shower, and I am responding to a text message from Kristie. She's texting to say she is going to stay at my house tonight. Again. She's taking full advantage of my 'vacation' with Ry to escape from her father's controlling hand.

My attention is quickly diverted when a gray car, with a damaged front end, parks next to Ry's truck. A brown-headed woman in extremely tight jeans and a T-shirt that is two sizes too small walks over to the open bay of the garage.

I stand to my feet, straightening my spine. "May I help you?"

Her voice is scratchy. "Is Crutch here?"

"He's occupied right now. I'm sorry, ma'am, but the body shop has closed for the day. I'll be happy to take your name and phone number so Harlan or Crutch can call you when the shop re-opens in the morning."

She takes a step closer to me, sizing me up. Immediately, I lift my chin, doing the same to her. She's petite. Probably only an inch or two over five feet. Her hair needs a washing, her face needs a scrubbing, and her stomach needs some of that gas station fried chicken. Other than that, she's pretty. Her age is hard to read. Thirties? Forties? Maybe, this side of the county has it right. Maybe grunge and whore-chic is the next big thing, and I'm the one who's missing out.

"You work here? Harlan hire someone new?"

"I just help out on occasion, ma'am." I pick up my phone, quickly opening the note section. "So, I'll be happy to relay your request for some vehicle work or maintenance. I can take the information right here. Name?"

"I don't need my car worked on. I need to speak with my son."

I look into her eyes. Her green eyes. Eyes that should be vibrant and nearly transparent. But they look dead. Void of life. My heart drops to the bottom of my shoes. "Your son?"

She doesn't have to answer. Ry protectively snags his hand around my waist, pushing my body behind his. "Hello, Mom."

"There's my boy." She reaches out, standing on her tiptoes, trying to wrap him in an awkward hug. He flicks his head to the side, trying to avoid her kiss. She misses his cheek and pecks him on the neck instead.

"What are you doing here?"

"I just wanted to come check on you."

I peep around Ry's massive shoulders. "If this is about the fight, I'm sorry, ma'am. It was completely my fault."

"Luella," Ry warns.

Uh-oh. I don't think I can even recall a time when Ry has used my true, given name. And that worries me. I quickly decide that obeying his intended warning is the smartest thing to do. I clamp my mouth shut. It's really hard, but I do it anyway.

Besides, I really need to stop calling her ma'am. She's a terrible mother. And a terrible daughter. She shouldn't have 'ma'am' status in my book.

"What fight? Did you get into a fight?"

"It's nothing. Just a disagreement with your other son," he answers.

She cackles, reaching around to her back pocket to grab a cigarette. "That's good. Brothers are supposed to tussle every now and then."

Ry plucks the cigarette from her mouth before she can light it, breaking it in half. "I tell you every single time you come here that there's no smoking in the garage." His body is so damn tense, it looks like his muscles might actually break.

She runs her tongue across her teeth, biting back what she really wants to say. My phone pings with another text message from Kristie, drawing her unwanted gaze to me. She looks at the positions of our bodies, immediately realizing that we are more than mere co-workers. "Aren't you gonna introduce me to your little friend."

I'm not little.

"Cindy Crutchfield, this is Luella Hill."

Cindy spreads her arms through the air. "And Luella is your...?" She pauses, wanting Ry to fill in the blanks.

"Luella is my business." His tone leaves nothing up for discussion.

She grunts. Tiring of this standoff, she begins meandering through the garage. Sidestepping us, she heads for the kitchen. "I'm just gonna grab a quick drink."

Leaning his head back, he sighs in frustration. In anger. I slide my hand up his spine. He's never felt so rigid before. We take a few steps to follow her when we are both caught off guard by the sound of a car door slamming shut. Spinning around, we see a tall, lanky man walking across the parking lot. He must've been on the passenger's side of the car, hidden by the shadows of the near dark sky.

Ry curses under his breath.

He's about two inches shorter than Ry. Ry's height must come from his father's side of the family. His hair is dark brown with gray around the edges. Wrinkles frame his face—wrinkles from drinking too hard, partying too hard, living too hard. Thin arms and thin legs. Beer belly.

Just like his wife, and just like his other son, you can catch glimpses of what might have been. Glimpses of the handsome, distinguished man underneath it all. Underneath the pile of shit.

"Crutch, your Momma come in here?"

"You know she did, so why ask the question?"

He points his finger at Ry. "Don't be such a smartass."

"Then don't ask such dumbass questions."

His father laughs. Ry doesn't.

His dad sniffles, twitching his nose like he has an itch. He seems a little jumpy.

His mom's voice calls to us from the other room. "Larry, I'm back here getting a drink."

Tucking my hand in Ry's back pocket, I follow him and his father through the garage. Cindy's in the kitchen alright. She's already opened half the food I bought today and is guzzling a soda. Larry immediately grabs one of Ry's beers from the fridge and dips his hand into the chip bag, dropping crumbs everywhere.

Ry sucks in a breath. He hates it. He likes things to be clean. It makes *him* feel clean. He draws their attention, loudly clearing his throat. "To what do we owe the pleasure?"

His dad wipes his hands on his T-shirt. "Well, you know we hate to do this, but payday isn't until Friday, and I was wondering if we could borrow a little bit of money. I have to fix the lawnmower."

"Try again. I already fixed that lawnmower for you. Don't you remember? Fixed it and changed the oil and the blades so it would be all ready for you this spring."

Larry's mouth drops open. Nope. He doesn't remember.

Cindy snickers, laughing at Larry's failed attempt to get money. Not liking that, Larry spins around and slaps her arm. Hard. Really hard. The soda flies from her hand and spills all over the tile floor. I'm shocked. But it doesn't faze Cindy in the least little bit. She just opens a fresh pack of peanut butter crackers.

Ry and I spent hours scrubbing that grout for Harlan just the other weekend. He mentioned it needed to be done, and Ry wanted to surprise him. I race to the countertop, grab the paper towels, and bend to clean up the mess.

And for the first time, Larry really notices me. "Well, look at that. You know, Trash did mention you had a new bed bunny at your side. What a pretty little thing she is."

I'm yanked back to my feet before I can process what's happening. Wrapping his arms around me, Ry pulls me into his grip so my toes aren't touching the floor anymore. I guess he's concerned I won't walk fast enough. Striding down the short hallway, he deposits me at the bedroom door. Cradling my face in both of his hands, his voice is so serious, it injects fear straight into my veins. A direct IV shot. "Shut this door. Lock it with the chain, not the doorknob. Doorknob is broken. Don't open it for anyone but me. Do *not* come back out here. Do you understand?"

I can't think. I need to touch my scar.

"Lulu, do you understand?"

I nod. He shuts the door, and I immediately search the side frame for the chain and lock it. My heart rattles through my chest like a derailing freight train.

On the other side, Ry yells at his father. "If you ever look at her that way again, I'll cut your fucking eyes out. Do you understand?"

Cindy's scratchy voice rises to a shrill. "Don't you dare speak to your father like that."

"I'll speak to him however I damn well please. This is my place of business. Harlan told you not to come back here—more than once."

Larry coughs and laughs. How can he find this funny? "Why are you so bent out of shape about a girl? She's hot. You can't blame a man for looking. I'm fifty, I'm not dead."

Ry lowers his voice. "Just tell me what you are doing here. The lawnmower is obviously fine. What do you need money for this time?

To pay a loan shark? You borrow from the wrong people again, Dad? To buy drugs? What's your venom of choice this week, Mom? You sticking with Trash's Oxy or you back on a crack kick with that guy down south?"

There's a loud slap. Deafening. Oh my god, she just slapped her son. My fingers fumble with the chain, trying to unlock it.

But I stop. Ry wants me to stay here.

Screw it.

Silently, I slip out of the small bedroom. Ry is perched like a cobra ready to strike. He's so focused in his anger he doesn't see me. Not until I slide my hand into his, gripping it tightly. His knuckle has a cut on it from his earlier fight. His head turns toward mine. His cheek is marked with an ugly pink welp. His beautiful cheek. His beautiful face.

I stiffen my spine and square my shoulders. "Next to the dollar store, they are building a new car wash."

Larry scoffs. Tossing his empty beer bottle across the room, it barrels into the trash can like a basketball and shatters. "Yeah, so."

"The construction crew left a bunch of old aluminum poles by the side of the road at the end of work today. Sign says they're free. You can sell the aluminum at the recycling plant in town if you need money. Because we won't be giving you any. And *we* won't be so hospitable the next time you come asking. I think it's time that you both leave."

Pleased with the immediate promise of money, and not concerned at all with my threat, Larry leaves. I suppose he's rushing out to make sure the poles are still by the side of the road.

Cindy doesn't leave quite so quietly. She stops right in front us and narrows her eyes. She points a finger in Ry's face. "Just when did *you*," she then moves her finger between the two of us, "become a *we*?"

I toss my chin in the air. "The second we met. Now leave."

Chapter 33

Crutch

I'm gonna kill her.

I know for a fact that when I got in the shower, my shorts, T-shirt, and boxer briefs were all laying on the countertop.

Now, only my boxer briefs remain.

"Lulu, what did you do with my clothes?"

"Huh? What did you say?"

I raise my voice a little louder. "Where did you put my clothes? My shirt? My shorts?"

"I can't hear you. Come out of the bathroom if you need to talk."

That little minx. She's been trying to get me out of my shorts more than usual these past few days. Just like normal, I keep putting it off. I'm drowning in my own jizz, but I'm too afraid to take it further.

Of course, I can't be too mad at her after what happened Monday night with my parents. She stood up for me. She made me feel like I was worth something. She didn't treat me any differently after meeting my repulsive parents.

She put ice on my cheek. Hugged me. Kissed me.

Loved me.

It was such a foreign concept but one that made me feel super human.

Sliding on my underwear, I open the bathroom door and stalk across to the bedroom. She's sitting on the bed, with my pillow hugged against her lap. I think I see my blue T-shirt hiding behind her back. Her eyes widen and she ogles every small detail of my body. Once. Twice. Three times.

I love it when she checks me out.

Reluctantly, she forces her gaze back to my face. "What were you yelling about?"

I fold my arms across my chest. "My clothes. What did you do to my clothes?"

"Does it matter? Aren't clothes overrated?" She blinks, trying to look innocent as she throws my own words back at me.

The second she licks her lips, my dick hardens. I need to get this situation under control. Fucking stat. Turning my back to her, I reach in the small dresser for another pair of shorts. She's quicker than me, though.

How'd she get so quick?

Her arm snakes around my waist and her fingertips brush against my cock. It jumps like I just received an electrical shot directly to my groin. Knocking her hand away, I shift to the side. "No."

She giggles. "No?" She tries to reach around me again.

The feel of her touch roaming across my wet skin makes me dizzy. "Stop it, Lulu." My tone is much harsher than I intend.

So harsh she gasps. "Ry, why don't you want me touch you? I know I'm not experienced, but..." Her voice trails off, unsure how to finish the sentence.

Quickly pulling on my shorts, I spin around. She's upset. And it rips the heart from my chest. She's rubbing the scar on the back of her neck, chewing on her lusciously pink bottom lip.

"That's what you think? You think I don't want you to touch me?"

She sighs. She wants to hide. She wants to run away, but that's not My Lulu. Instead, she takes a step in my direction, looking deep into my eyes. "Yes. Because I try. Over and over. And you won't let me. What else am I supposed to think?"

I shake my head. "All I want in life is to be touched by you. Twenty-four hours a day I dream about having your hand wrapped around me. I fantasize about having your mouth on me. It's *you*. I always want everything you have to offer, Lulu. Everything you have to give."

She likes the honesty of my words. Her lips curve into a small, sad smile. "Then why not let me?"

I run my hand over my face, scratching my three-day growth. "Because I would become obsessed. I know I would. The second you cross that line with me, Lulu, there will be no going back. When it comes to you, I'm an addict. The feel of your skin on mine. The sensation of your hot mouth sucking my cum from my body? It would be a never-ending obsession. And I'm not prepared to be one of those dickwads who expects a hand job or blow job from his girlfriend every single time they have five minutes alone together. I'm an asshole, but I don't wanna be *that* kind of an asshole."

She blushes, whether from anger or whether from my graphic words, I'm not quite sure. "But it's okay for you to have your fingers in me, to have your mouth on me? To have my wetness dripping from your chin?"

My dick is painfully hard right now. So. Damn. Painful. "Yes," I croak.

She points a finger in my face. "You're not playing our game fair, Ry." She puffs out her chest in defiance.

The chest I finally spent hours last night exploring. My initial thoughts were right. Her nipples are extremely sensitive. And perfect in every single way. I tilt my head to the side. "So?"

Wrong word to say.

"I can't touch you? Fine. Then, you can't touch me."

"Excuse me?"

"Your hands aren't allowed on my body until my hands are allowed on your body."

"You're kidding."

She leans forward, preparing to tell me a secret. Her whispered response sends a chill up my spine. "Game on."

Two days.

Two whole days with no kissing. No touching. No tasting.

She hasn't even let me 'accidentally' bump into her while we've been working at the body shop.

Why? Because I'm a fucking idiot.

Here it is Friday night and I'm nursing a beer, my bruised ego, and my swollen dick, in front of the laptop, watching one of Lulu's crime shows, with the firepit crackling in the background, spewing heat into the unseasonably warm spring night.

I'm pouting. There's really no other word for it.

We aren't even sitting in the loveseat together like normal. She's in one chair, and I'm in another. I glance over at her. She doesn't even act troubled by all of this. She's just watching the show and picking at the label on her water bottle.

I grunt. Standing from the chair, I stretch my arms high above my head. It's a planned move. Lulu loves it when I do this. My shirt rides up, showing my waist and the band of my boxer briefs. Except this time, she doesn't gawk. Not even a peep. I mumble, "I'm getting another beer. Need anything?"

"I'm good. Thanks."

Taking a long swig from my fresh beer, I'm walking back up to the patio when her phone rings. She jumps, startled by the jarring noise. Her jaw tenses. Based on experience, that means it's either her mom, her dad, Kristie, or Hudson. She smiles when her aunt or uncle calls. She smiles when her cousins, Holt or Raylee, call. Hell, she even smiles when Detective Marcum calls.

"Hi, Mom."

After several moments, she closes her eyes and rubs her temple. "No, Mom. I'm not in Miami. I left you two voicemails last weekend and even texted you. I also talked to Dad on Monday. He said he would tell you. I stayed here. I'm spending the week camping with Ryland."

...

She sits up straight, stiffening her spine. Uh-oh, this should be interesting. She tosses a glance over her left shoulder, presumably checking for me. She doesn't see me, though; I'm standing behind her right side. She hisses into the phone. "Yes, Mom. He's still a *thing*. And by the way, this *thing* is pretty real. So, you better get used to it."

...

She blows a raspberry. "Nothing is wrong with me. I've always been stubborn and combative, I just kept it buried beneath the surface."

...

"But I'm getting tired, Mom. I always do what you want me to do simply because it makes life easier. I act proper and polite, but only to those who come from lives like ours. Everyone else gets the cold shoulder. I wear the clothes you approve of because you believe the world judges a book by its cover. I picked my college major on what you and Dad deemed appropriate for our pedigree and station in life. I even eat the food you think I should. Heaven forbid, I gain ten pounds and go up a size."

...

"No, Mom. He's not a bad influence. He's the best person I know." She sighs in frustration. "Don't you get tired of it too, Mom? Don't you just wanna pull the curtain down and show someone the 'real' you? What about Carrie? Maybe if she had let more people into her authentic life, she wouldn't be missing right now. Don't we owe it to Carrie to be genuine and honest?"

...

"How about we talk Sunday night when I get home. We could have dinner, talk, hang out."

...

She bobs her head up and down, tsking her tongue. "Of course, you do. Do you even remember that we have a meeting with Marcum and Leary next Wednesday? They're supposed to discuss the latest testing methods the state lab got approved for and see if we think sending any more samples from the vehicle evidence would be beneficial."

...

"Of course, I'll handle it."

...

"No, we're not staying in some chic cabin with a waitstaff. We're sleeping in a tent, Mom."

...

"For him, I'd spend the rest of my life sleeping in a cardboard box if I had to."

...

"It's sad you can't understand that. Maybe that's where you and Dad went wrong."

...

She pulls the phone away from her ear and stares at it blankly. She mumbles to herself, "She hung up on me."

Huffing, she tosses the phone on a side table and stands up. Turning around, she sees me. Knowing I've been spying on her, she gets a little nervous; she rubs the back of her neck.

"What did she want?"

"She asked me to go to some distillery in Miami and buy five bottles of some ridiculously priced specialty rum to bring home."

"You're underage. How the hell does she expect you to buy liquor?"

Lulu shrugs.

"Why can't she meet with the detectives? Is she going somewhere?"

"Yep. Girls' trip to a wellness spa in Arizona."

I nod. What can you say about that? Her mom goes on so many trips she probably has her own TSA check-in line. Her own beverage cart. A drop-down oxygen mask plated in gold.

And what the fuck is a *wellness* spa? Trust me, it will take more than a one-week trip to make Lulu's mom 'well'.

"Excuse me, I'll be right back."

I watch as Lulu disappears into the tent. I'll give her a few minutes to clear her mind, and then I'll go to her. I have no choice. I'll always go to her. The way she talked about me to her mom? The things she said?

She said everything that I feel. And one of these days, I will grow big enough balls to actually tell her. Tell her that I love her. That I can't stand the thought of living one second of my life without her.

But what does that mean? Because what kind of life can someone like me give her?

She emerges from the tent with a blanket wrapped around her. I guess she got cold, although, it's a mild and pleasant night. I love the spring time, the months before the mosquitos of summer come out to feast. Instead of walking to the patio, she walks down to the old wooden dock and stares at the small waves in the pond. Tossing my now empty beer bottle in the trash, I walk down to join her. I don't say anything. Sometimes, Lulu likes to just think.

After a minute or two, it suddenly becomes my turn to think.

When she drops the blanket from her shoulders, I think real hard.

I think about how important this game of ours really is.

She's wearing one of those tank tops with the straps that are so thin they barely qualify as straps. No bra. Her nipples are peaked and calling my name. Screaming it. From the damn rooftops.

Her long legs glitter underneath the moonlight, and her white lace panties cover every part I long to touch, long to lick, long to taste.

Adding pure torment to my tortured libido, a breeze blows around us, sending the sweet scent of her shampoo and her arousal into the air.

She's good. Little minx is a damn good game player.

Slowly, I tug my shirt overhead, tossing it over into the grass. Next, I kick off my flip flops. The night around us stills. Lulu freezes, stops breathing. The zipper on my shorts is so deafening in the silence, it makes me cringe. My boxer briefs are pulled tight around the massive erection that's stealing all of the blood from my body. I don't give her time to look. I don't give her time to study. I grab her ass, hauling her into my arms. Immediately, she wraps her legs around my waist. Her eyes widen in desire and delight. I carry my girl into the comfort of our tent, with our lavender-scented sheets and crisp down comforter.

"You win, Lulu. Game over."

Chapter 34

Crutch

I'm thankful Lulu doesn't have experience.

My only prayer is that she will think three minutes is a very long time. Because I'll be lucky to make it that long without blowing my load.

Her kisses are wild and hungry tonight, driving me into a depth of longing that I've never felt before. Her moans are louder, her body hotter, swollen and tender. She slides her legs down, and I hold on tightly to her waist, making sure her feet are steady. We're standing at the edge of the blow-up mattress, and I don't want her to trip.

"Ry, it's time. I'm gonna wrap my hand around you. And I'm gonna put my mouth on you. And I want you to lead me. Tell me. Show me what you like. Show me how to make you feel as good as you make me feel."

Kill me now.

Lulu has gotten more and more verbal with each and every orgasm I've given her. Moaning, screaming, writhing. And dirty talk. Each time gets a little dirtier. And I fucking love it.

Without any hesitation whatsoever, she sinks to her knees. Grabbing the band of my boxer briefs, she tugs them down, taking gentle care to lift them over my bobbing erection. She gasps, staring at my body in stunned silence. She doesn't even untangle my underwear from my feet. I have to step out of them and kick them to the side.

Looking down at her, she's the most gorgeous creature I've ever seen. That I'll ever see. I push the hair away from her face. It flows down her back like a stream of maple syrup. "Have you seen a naked man before?"

"In pictures."

"Never in person?"

"Of course not, Ry."

I'm impatient to know more. "Well, what do you think?"

Her awed whisper makes me want to weep, cry like a freaking baby. "You're gorgeous. It's—*your dick*—is sexy. Powerful. Big. Huge. I'm completely astonished to think that one day it will be inside of me. Am I big enough for you to fit? It's all forbidden and perfect. Don't you think together, we'll be perfect?" She glances up at me, her eyelids heavy with lust.

Did I mention I'm ready to die?

Kill. Me. Now.

She lifts her hand in the air, fingers twitching. "I can't wait anymore."

Grabbing her hand, I show her. I show her what I like. And I talk to her. I tell her that I'm just like her, that sometimes I want a gentle touch. And other times, I need it harder, rougher. I slide her hand over my slit, spreading my pre-cum over my cock. I pump myself slowly and then faster, telling her how both rhythms feel good for different kinds of pleasure. I show her how hard she can grab my balls before causing pain.

Then, I leave her to her own devices. And as with everything else in life, Lulu is a quick learner. A complete natural. My body is already drenched in sweat and my quads are twitching. I can't make it much longer. She's taking me over the edge. The edge I want to jump right over and fall from. My mouth is dry, the words barely escaping. "Lulu, I'm so close."

Immediately, she yanks her hand away from my body. Oh, shit. I scared her. The lava boiling in my body simmers, shouting in pain for an eruption. "Lulu, I'm sorry. I shouldn't have pushed you. I've got to finish this, though. I can go outside and finish myself."

"No!" Her hands wrap around my thighs, locking me into place. "Ryland Joseph Crutchfield, don't even think about it. You didn't push me. I just don't want your first orgasm from me to be from my hand. I want it to be from my mouth. Just like the one you gave me."

KILL. ME. NOW.

"How do I do it?"

I'm surprised the English language is still a part of my vocabulary. I'm not even sure how I spit the words out, but I do. "Lick me, Lulu. That's how to start."

She absorbs my every word, follows my every request, moves her body every direction, as I gently guide her head. She works her mouth over my length, taking me as deep as she can, sucking my soul from existence. A couple of times, her teeth scrape against my sensitive skin. It doesn't bother me. I admire her. I'm not gonna lie; I'm pretty damn big. And giving me a blow job can't be easy. Many girls have said as much.

The sounds she makes when she's sucking my cock should be a criminal act in the lower forty-eight. Those sounds are maddening, fascinating, intriguing. Too damn alluring for my own good.

My legs begin to shake uncontrollably, my stomach muscles vibrate with need, and my ass clenches in preparation of an earth-shattering release. I massage her head with my fingertips.

Holy shit. It's never felt this good.

Never. Ever. Ever. Ever.

My growl is low, rumbling in my chest. "Lulu, it's time. It's okay; you can stop if you want."

But she doesn't back away. She doesn't stop. She doesn't leave her position.

My orgasm steals the breath from my lungs, steals the thoughts from my mind, and steals the love from heart. Hot spurts of desire flow from my body, and Lulu swallows every last drop. Pumping me dry. Leaving me fresh, new, and spotless. And I'm not just talking about my dick. Has she cleansed me of my impurities? Can I one day be the man she deserves? Give her a life worth living? Give her more than a crappy tent?

She untangles herself from my body and rubs her jaw with her hand. "You taste clean and salty. Is that what I taste like?" She looks up at me. Her lips are bee-stung, and her face is flush from exertion. "Did I do okay? Did you like it?"

Tugging her from the floor, I ravish her in a kiss. I taste the salt of my body on her tongue and it makes me kiss her even harder. She wraps her arms around my neck, bending my body close to hers. I'm still pretty hard, and she knows it. When my cock rubs against her stomach, she groans. I sweep her into my arms and lie her down on the mattress. Hooking my fingers in her panties, I slowly drag them down. Settling between her mile-long legs, I bury my face in her soaking wet pussy. I barely do anything at all, and she's coming all over my face. Making me hard as a damn rock again. Like concrete. Like steel.

Instead of wiping my face with my hand, I slowly climb over her body. My lips and chin are dripping with her juices. "Kiss me, Lulu. Lick my chin." She immediately does as she's told. "That's what you taste like. You taste like My Lulu and it's my favorite flavor in the whole wide world."

She blushes. When she takes a deep breath, her pussy rises to meet me. I quickly roll to the side before my animalistic behavior has me doing something we're both not ready for. Instead, I trace her thighs with my fingers, working my way to her clit, driving her to the brink of another orgasm. My finger delves into her, gently teasing. Reaching between her legs, she grabs my hand, pushing me a little deeper.

Her words are loud. Very loud. "More. Deeper. Go deeper, Ry. Use another finger. I want two fingers."

I always use my pinky finger inside of her. That's all that will fit without any force. And that only works, I'm assuming, because of her use of tampons. Not to mention, I've got giant hands. I kiss her eyelids, forcing her to open her eyes. "Lulu, I can't. Not without hurting you. I feel too much pressure inside of you, too much resistance. If I do more, I'll..." my voice trails off, worried about the best way to describe what I want to say. "If I do more, I'll pop you, break you."

She nods. "I know. I want you to do it. Now."

My jaw twitches. In excitement. In wonder. In concern. "What? Why?"

"I know it will hurt the first time we have sex. Especially after seeing your size tonight. But I want it to be as pleasurable as possible. I wanna make myself ready so I can focus solely on the joy of the experience. Don't you want me to be ready for you?"

"Of course, I do. But there's no going back once this is done. You understand that, right?" My passionate words feel thick as molasses on my tongue. "Once I bury my fingers inside you, once I stretch you, and claim the deepest parts of your pussy for myself, there's no going back. I'd be your first. I'd be the one who marked you. For all eternity."

She tugs me to her lips, kissing me until I'm so dizzy I don't even know what direction is up and what direction is down. Her low and sultry whisper hums in my brain, fogging my every sense. "Break me. Claim me. Mark me as yours."

Fuck. Me.

I reach behind me, grabbing a small blanket that's easy to wash. "Lift up. Put this underneath you."

"Why? Will I bleed that much?"

"I'm not sure. I would think so."

"You don't know? You've never done this before?"

No, I've never finger-fucked a virgin before. At least not that I know of. I mean, I guess it could've happened. But unfortunately, I've not been a super-concerned or super-attentive lover with the women of my past. I did get super concerned when that one girl from the college bookstore wanted to shit on me, but other than that, I typically did the deed without much foreplay and got the hell out of dodge. Diplomatically, I choose to keep some of those horrid thoughts and memories to myself.

I lean close to her face, studying her every feature, absorbing it all, committing it to memory. "You're the only girl I will ever mark, Lulu. Never before you. Never after you."

A tear falls from the corner of her eye. I plunge my tongue into her mouth. She gives back, clawing at my shoulders with her fingernails. I don't give her time to prepare. I don't warn her. I don't give her time to dwell on it. I immediately plunge two of my fingers into her darkest depth, twisting and pushing when I feel resistance. She tenses and cries out. I swallow her cries with my mouth.

Pulling my fingers out, I perform the same motion over and over. Sweeping into her with a twisting movement, trying to stretch her to the far sides, to the breaking point. Pressing deep into her, I wanna make the painful part as quick as possible. I'm ready for the pleasure. I'm ready to explore the hidden parts of her. Find the spots that make her go wild and buck against me. The spots that make her beg for more.

After a very long time, her body relaxes, and her frozen kisses melt. I'm so damn relieved that her kisses aren't angry. She's tasting and biting like a lover showering me with thanks.

Slowly, I pull my fingers from her body and lift them between us. Under the soft glow from one of the battery-operated lanterns, we look in fascination at what is before us. My fingers are stained pink with her blood. Some fine strings of bright red circle my nails and my knuckles. But more importantly, the white cream of her desire coats me from fingertip to palm.

"Did it hurt? Do you hurt? It might take a while before you can tell me what feels good inside of you. I want to find the spots that make you scream my name."

She nods, biting her lip. "It hurt. Not a normal kind of hurt, but a burning sensation. A tearing. I'm sorry I bled on you."

I kiss her neck. "I'm not sorry."

"Let's not wait to start finding what makes me feel good." She pushes my hand down her trembling body, sliding my fingertips against her engorged clit. "Make me scream your name."

And scream my name she does. It takes a while. We go slow. Very slow so as not to hurt her more than she already is. There are some areas that are too tender for me touch right now. There are other areas that, after some time and healing, we know will have her jumping from the cliff. But there are two spots, for now, that get the job done.

And trust me, my name has never sounded so damn good.

Unable to leave me in what she imagines is an extremely painful state, she jacks me off again, quickly switching to a blow job the second I tell her I'm about to come all over the place. It's the most euphoric form of déjà vu I've ever experienced.

Eventually, we clean ourselves with washcloths and fresh water from the gallon jugs. She digs through one of her bathroom bags, grabbing what she calls a panty liner, and puts it and a simple pair of black cotton panties on her sore and thoroughly loved bottom half. I gather my discarded clothes from beside the pond and place them in my dirty clothes bag along with the bloody blanket. I'll toss them in the washer when we go to the garage to shower tomorrow.

After snuffing the fire in the firepit, we crawl our exhausted bodies back into the tent. She snuggles into the lavender-scented sheets as I grab the book we've been reading this week. Every night before bed, I've read aloud from Hemingway's *A Farewell to Arms*. After just one chapter, I toss the book to the side and turn off the lantern.

Lulu's body wraps around mine, encasing me in her heat. In her warmth. In her love.

She traces the ridges of my six-pack and then slowly counts my ribs. "Tell me something." She leans over and kisses my chest. "Something no one else knows."

I think. "All of my best days are with you." Simple, but true.

"Ask me," she demands.

I kiss the top of her head. "Tell me something. Something no one else knows."

"I think my sister is dead."

I jerk, lifting my head from my pillow to look at her profile in the dark. "What? Why would you think that? There's still hope."

"One night on the cruise, I woke up out of a dead sleep. I couldn't breathe. My heart was beating so fast in my chest, I thought I was dying. It has never felt that way before. It's like I was drowning in agony, suffocating in anxiety. Holt was in the same room as me. It scared him to death. My aunt and uncle had to call the ship's physician to the room because I couldn't even move. Fortunately, by the time he got to the room, my symptoms had eased up. Panic attack. He said I had a panic attack."

She runs her fingertips back and forth across my collarbone. "Come to find out, it was the same night Carrie went missing. I don't feel her, Ry. In my heart, there's already a hole. A missing piece. I know she's gone. I can just feel it."

Her hot and silent tears fall onto my chest and race down my side, puddling between our connected bodies.

"So, what does this mean?"

"It means I'm looking for a murderer."

Chapter 35

Ella

I have a new purpose in life. A new reason for living.

Bringing Ry to orgasm. Making him scream. That's my new purpose. And I could do it all day, every day from here to eternity.

Ry's loud when he orgasms. Really loud. He says he has to be loud to keep an even pace with me.

I don't know about that.

Those are things I'm thinking about on this Saturday afternoon as I sit on the patio, sketching a rudimentary drawing of a house. I shift in my chair, trying to make my bottom half a little bit more comfortable. Last night's adventure left me sore, so Ry hasn't been able to lavish attention on me like he's used to. That's quite okay; I'm more than eager to make up lost time focusing on him.

It's definitely the first time in my eighteen years I woke a guy up in the morning by sticking my hand down his underwear. Of course, Ry is the only guy who's ever spent the night sleeping next to me, so I haven't been afforded the opportunity of fondling someone's morning wood before, but I know in my heart that it's one of my new favorite pastimes.

Spring is in full force now, and the grass around the homestead needed mowing. When we went to shower this morning, Ry loaded up a push mower and weed-eater from the garage, and he has been doing yard work most of the day. Without his shirt. Sweat pouring down his muscles. Ballcap shading his brilliantly translucent green eyes. And that's why, twenty minutes ago, I just finished giving him a blow job. He was too damn sexy to resist.

He's sitting in a chair opposite me right now, drinking bottled water to cool down. I steal a glance at him. He's watching me, rubbing two fingers against his chin in thought.

It's illegal. Inhuman. No one has the right to look that good.

He clears his throat. "What are you doing?"

I smirk. "Nothing."

"*Nothing* means you're sitting there, twiddling your thumbs. You're not doing *nothing*; you're obviously doing *something*."

"I'm just sketching."

"Sketching? Like drawing?" He doesn't wait on me to answer. Instead, he walks over, standing behind me. "Lulu, that's amazing. You didn't tell me you could draw."

"I can't *really* draw. I can only do buildings. I can't draw people, landscapes, nothing. I don't know why buildings come easy to me. They just do."

"Is this why your parents want you to become an architect?"

"Well, that, and they determined it to be a money-making profession. They want me to get every degree known to mankind and open my own firm one day."

Knowing that's not what I want, Ry doesn't even comment on it. "Whose house is that? Is that a pond out front?"

I always do what I shouldn't do. Always.

I shouldn't have started this drawing. And I definitely shouldn't be opening my mouth to tell him about this drawing.

I flick the pencil back and forth on the page and lift my chin in the air. "Well, that's our house."

"Excuse me?"

I try to crawl out of the big pile of shit I just jumped in. "Well, I've just been spending so much time out here lately, and you talk about living here, building a house like Grandpa wanted. I just thought I would draw something. For fun."

His features darken, but I can't exactly read his expression because his ballcap is pulled too low.

Lifting my feet, he sits next to me on the loveseat, settling my legs between his. He wraps his arm around me and pulls me closer. "So, do I get to know what our house is gonna look like, or is it supposed to be a surprise? You're the one who likes surprises. Not me." He points to the drawing. "Our front porch faces the pond?"

My heart bursts open, pouring all the love I have for this man into my body. Filling every cell. Filling every organ. Filling every fiber. I'm drunk on pure happiness. This is what life is supposed to feel like. I don't need the love of my parents. I don't need the camaraderie of friends. I just need him.

"Yeah. I've always been attracted to front porches more so than back porches. It's like looking at the future instead of the past. And I love the historic old farmhouse look." I point out all the details on my drawing. "White wood siding. Green shutters. Stone veneer around the front door and around the crawl space. I want a crawl space and not a slab, because I wanna walk up a set of stone and wood steps to get to the wraparound porch. And I want it to wrap completely around the entire house, except the left side here, where the garage will be. Front porch swing. Rockers. Dining table. We can sit on the porch to eat our supper, watching the sun set over the pond. And hydrangeas all in the front flowerbeds."

"Pretty damn nice, Lulu. What about the inside?"

I flip to the finished sketch of the downstairs. "First floor. Open concept for the kitchen and living room. Huge living room on the right side when you walk in the front door. Kitchen on the left. Next to it a mud room where you come in from the garage. Laundry room next to the mudroom. Then you walk down the middle hallway, there will be a half bath on the right, and then a large office on the right. That can be your office. The left will have a corresponding room, just larger. It will have a full bath connected to it."

"So, you're saying it's a bedroom."

I shake my head. "No. I was thinking it could be a joint office and... rec room, maybe."

I am so stupid.

He catches the trepidation in my voice and holds onto it like a kite blowing in the wind. "A rec room for whom?"

"People." I fidget with my fingers, squaring my shoulders.

He chuckles. Bastard likes to see me nervous.

Rubbing his fingers over his tanned lips, he bites back another laugh. "Are you talking about small, little people? The kind who don't like to eat their vegetables and who believe Santa Claus is real?"

I scowl. "Fine. Yes. Children. This can be a joint office and play-room. The kids can play while I work. And then, when we get too old to climb the stairs to our bedroom, this room can easily become our master bedroom since it will already have a full bathroom connected to it."

I fold the notebook and toss it on the side table. "It was just for fun. There's no need to freak out about it."

"Did I say I was freaking out?"

I turn to him, narrowing my eyes. I still can't see his and it's annoying the hell out me. I flick the bill of his hat with my fingers, popping it higher on his head so I can look at him. He definitely looks amused. But he doesn't look like he's freaking out. I guess that's a good thing. At least, he's taking this all in good humor.

I am too. At least that's what I'm telling myself. But the truth is, that's what I want. Every last bit of it. Four bedrooms upstairs. Each and every room filled with little humans made from him and me.

I guess he's still waiting on an answer, because he eggs me on. "Well?"

"No. Not freaking out." I untangle my body from his and jump up. Grabbing his water bottle, I quickly down the rest of it.

Suddenly, he's standing behind me, whispering against my neck, sending shivers down my spine. His bare skin rubs against my shoulder blades. "Did you pack your tennis shoes?"

"Yeah, why?"

"Come on, there's something I need to show you."

The trail was hidden between some trees behind the tent. That's why I never paid attention to it before. Fifteen minutes after dragging me into the woods, we emerge into a small green meadow.

And I hear something.

Water.

"Ry, is that a river?"

"Creek." He smiles widely, tugging me through the thick green grass. Slowly, the grass starts to thin, the rippling sound of water gets louder, and there's a reflection in the sunlight ahead of us. Like a mirage for the thirsty man who's lost in the desert.

It's gorgeous. This section of the creek is large and rocky. Not large enough to swim in, but definitely large enough to wade in. Big enough to play in. It winds past us into a dense wood that would be hell to hike. Wildflowers are scattered here and there, decorating our beautiful little scene in pinks and yellows and purples.

Ry drops the backpack from his shoulders and spreads a blanket out on the side of the bank. Immediately, I take off my socks and shoes, walking into the rippling current. The water is cold, but not freezing. It's too shallow to truly get freezing, only coming up to our knees. I step on something squishy and squeal.

Walking out to join me, Ry howls in laughter and I promptly splash him in the face. "Why didn't you tell me this was out here?"

He shrugs. "Just waiting for the right time, I guess."

We walk along the creek, skipping rocks and talking. Eventually, we drag our water-splattered bodies to the blanket and lie drying in the sun. We watch the passing clouds through the tree branches, enjoying one another's company in complete, comfortable silence.

Ry reaches out, tracing his fingertips across my hand. "I can't believe Spring Break is nearly over."

"I know. One more day." One more day, and then I'm back to living in the dungeon I call my house. One more day, and then I'm back at school, having to smile and grit my teeth while everyone around me spends the next week talking about how drunk they got or who they hooked up with on vacation. One more day of my perfect life on the homestead, sleeping in a tent, peeing in the woods, and showering in a stall no bigger than a thimble.

Who knew all of that could be so perfect?

He sighs. "What about this place? Should our house be out here, closer to the creek?"

I turn on my side and study his chiseled profile, his square jaw, his flawless complexion, the dark freckle by the corner of his eye. "No. The house stays where it is. This place is just ours. Hidden. Secret."

Leaning over, I kiss him.

And I let him know that I'm no longer sore.

Chapter 36

Ella

"I really appreciate you kids staying late tonight." Harlan squeezes me in one last hug before heading out the door.

"Harlan, it's just a normal Friday night. You act like we gave up Super Bowl tickets to stay and watch the garage tonight."

Ry reaches up, grabbing the frame of the garage bay. His shirt rides up, granting me a quick glimpse of his green boxer briefs and the muscular V that dips low beneath the band of his jeans and belt buckle.

Harlan catches me staring at Ry, and I blush.

He chuckles. "May not be the Super Bowl, but some kind of scoring may be going on tonight."

My scream echoes across the parking lot. "Harlan! And to think I was gonna say you looked nice all dressed up."

He puffs his chest out and runs his hands over the buttons of his shirt, taking my back-handed compliment at face value. "Thank you, Ella. Crutch, take care of our girl."

He smirks, lowering his hands and pulling a white towel from his back pocket. "I always do."

Harlan canceled his poker game tonight to go to a party at his son's house. Today is his daughter-in-law's birthday, and there is a huge surprise party for her. Ry and I agreed to watch the body shop.

A customer is supposed to drop a vehicle off for service sometime between seven and eight tonight on their way out of town for vacation.

Once we're alone, I sit back down in what has become my designated rolling chair, the chair where I spend most of my free time at the garage, watching Ry and Harlan work on cars. Over the weeks, Harlan has taught me how to work the register, order parts, and stock inventory. I like helping out where I can. But my main goal right now is to quickly finish my Advanced Biology homework so it's not hanging over me all weekend.

Ry leans down, pressing on the arms of my chair, locking my body into place. His growl is possessive and hungry, and it stirs a hot need low in my belly. "You're staying this weekend, right?"

I tilt my head. "That was the deal, wasn't it?"

He stands up, distemper quickly shadowing his face. "Right, the deal."

I purse my lips. "Ryland Joseph Crutchfield, put on your big girl panties and stop complaining. You think I'm looking forward to it? The thought of you being by my side is the only way I can muster the idea of attending this function."

Grabbing the laptop from my hand, he carefully lays it on the small table beside me. With me, he's not so careful. And damn, I love it. He forcefully yanks me from the chair, slamming my body against his. He grabs my ass with both hands. An electric shot of desire courses from my head to my toes. "I prefer not to wear women's underwear. I find them constrictive. So how about you wear no panties at all tomorrow, and I'll stop complaining."

"How about you stop complaining and I'll *think* about wearing no panties tomorrow."

He grunts. "You drive a hard bargain."

"It's all part of our game, isn't it?"

He gently kisses the tip of my nose. "Game on." Releasing me, leaving me wanting, he disappears into the bathroom for a shower.

Fifteen minutes later, he walks back out to join me, drinking a beer. His hair is still damp, and he's wearing cargo shorts and a mint green Harlan's Garage and Automotive shirt. His clothes and skin are always so clean. For someone who works with grease all day, every day, you've never met someone with as good of hygiene as Ry.

"After the customer comes, do you wanna go get something to eat? Or do you want me make something here? I've got stuff for sandwiches or—"

Ry is cut off by the ringing of his cell phone. The cell phone I gave him. We both look at one another. I'm sitting right in front of him, and we both know I'm not calling. Ry doesn't really have anyone else who calls him on the cell phone besides me—well, except for Harlan and the nursing home. He refuses to give the number to Trash or his parents. Digging the phone from his pocket, he answers.

"Hey, Harlan. You okay? You forget something?"

Finished with my school work, I close the laptop and stand, twisting the knots from my back, listening to his one-sided conversation.

"Okay. It happened where?"

...

"And you're sure you're okay?"

Worry circles my heart when I hear Ry ask that question, and I cross the distance between us, trying to listen in on the phone call. Beer still in hand, Ry wraps his arm around my waist. The cold bottle makes a wet mark on my stomach.

"Well, I can bring the wrecker, come get you, and take you to the party. You were planning on staying the night with your son, anyway, right?"

...

"Lulu can wait here for the customer. I'm sure she won't mind."

...

"No, the customer is a female. I wouldn't leave Lulu here if it were a male. But this is Scott Turner's sister. I met her once before. Married with kids."

...

"Okay. Sit tight. I'm on my way."

He barely hangs up before I pounce on him in curiosity. Tossing the half drank beer in the trash, he walks over to the wall to grab the wrecker keys from their hanging perch. "Harlan hit a deer. Front end of his truck is completely wrecked. I'm gonna go get him, take him to the party. Are you okay to wait for the customer?"

"Of course. Absolutely. She's just dropping off, right? No paperwork I need to give her? Nothing to ring up?"

"That's right. Just a drop and go. I already have all her contact information, so we are good there."

"And Harlan's okay?"

"He sounds perfectly fine, but I'll let you know once I get there and check on him."

"Okay. Be safe." I lean up on my toes, and Ry wraps me in a hug. One of his all-encompassing, full-body hugs.

Heaving me into his arms, my feet dangle in the air, leaving the toes of my sandals scraping against the concrete floor. He plants a quick peck on my mouth before setting me down. "Since I have to go to town, I'll just pick us up some food. Preference?"

I smile wickedly and clap my hands in front of me. "Yes."

He rolls his eyes and shakes his head. Grabbing his ballcap on the way out of the garage, he yanks it backward on his head, hollering behind him. "Two Philly cheesesteaks coming right up."

About twenty minutes after he leaves, Ry texts to let me know that Harlan is fine, and about ten minutes after that, the customer comes to drop off her car. Grabbing the keys to her black sedan, I watch in amusement as a minivan pulls into the parking lot to pick her up and honks the horn. Sighing deeply, she rolls her eyes. "Universal Studios. We're doing half the drive tonight. Three kids all under the age of eight. Pray for me."

Laughing, I stand, waving goodbye until they pull out onto the main road. I find her paperwork and tape the key to her folder, storing it in the drawer underneath the register. So, with nothing better to do, I turn on my laptop and start a crime show.

I know I should lower the large bay garage door, but I don't. It's nice outside tonight with a light breeze, so I decide to leave it open while I wait for Ry.

Once again, I always do what I shouldn't.

I'm absorbed in a documentary about blood splatter when a loud noise outside draws my attention. It sounded like someone throwing an aluminum can? Hitting the light post, maybe?

I ignore it, thinking it's probably just some underage drunk kid making a beer run to the gas station and they probably parked closer to our end of the parking lot to avoid the prying eyes of the gas station traffic.

But the noise happens again.

Being the dumbass that I am, I get up to investigate.

And that's when I see someone leaning against the back of my SUV. It's hard to make out much in the dark, but the thin frame tells me that it's probably a teenager. Younger than me, maybe. Stiffening my spine and squaring my shoulders, I take a few steps in that direction. "We're closed. This is private property. Not part of the gas station. So, you need to move on, okay?"

The kid is smoking a cigarette and he completely ignores me.

Rude little shit.

I walk in the direction of my car. "Hey, come on. Time to head out, buddy."

Stomping on the cigarette, he shifts underneath the glow of the lamp post, and I see that my first impression was quite wrong. Very wrong. Really wrong.

This is no kid.

This is Trey.

I freeze in my tracks. I don't have to worry about ruining our proper introduction, though. Trey does all the work for me. Crossing the distance between us, he reaches out his wiry hand. "I don't think we've had the pleasure of formally meeting. I'm Trey Holland."

I stare at his hand, feeling like I'm about to be sick.

Eventually he snatches it back. "Didn't anyone ever teach you that it's rude not to shake someone's extended hand?"

I snap my body into position and lift my chin. "Didn't anyone ever teach you that it's rude to sneak up on someone. At night. On property that's not yours. Uninvited."

"I didn't know I needed an invitation to visit a friend. I was looking for Crutch."

There's no point in lying. We both know that if Ry were here, he'd already be standing outside, right between the two of us. Teeth bared. Fists clenched. "He'll be back any minute. He's on a run with the wrecker."

"Pity. Been too long since I've seen him. We've missed having him at the parties lately."

"You don't really strike me as friends."

A smidge taller than me, he's definitely more put together than Trash. I can only conclude he must use way less of his own product than Trash does. His clothes are clean, and his face doesn't have any sores on it. But his frame is still thin. And he has bluish circles underneath his eyes. "Oh, but we are."

I fold my arms across my chest. "I'll be sure to add you to our Christmas card list this year."

He snorts. "Heard you were a bitch. Now, I see it's true."

I don't dignify him with a response. And that irks him.

"I also heard you were asking some questions. Questions about me and my business. Anything you care to ask me? Cut out the middle man."

"I *was* asking questions. Everyone who knows me knows that I've been asking questions about my missing sister. It's no secret she came out to this part of the county on occasion before she disappeared. The police were even here questioning people at the gas station. They have her on camera, buying gas, making purchases. What kind of sister would I be if I didn't do my own due diligence?"

"Well, just so you know, we are very protective of our own out here. Someone might interpret your questions wrong. Think you're trying to pin your sister's decision to run away on us less fortunate folks. I can't be held responsible for what someone might do if they think you're trying to hurt us, hurt our simple way of life out here."

I narrow my eyes. "Is that a threat?"

At least he attempts to act contrite. "Of course not. I'm just saying people seem really protective of me for some reason."

"Gee, I wonder why? And why on earth would you say my sister ran away? There's no truth behind that whatsoever."

"Really? I could have sworn that's what I heard. So, what are *you* doing? You've been spending a lot of time out on this side of the county lately. A little far away from home, aren't we?"

"Where I spend my time should be of no concern to you."

He lights another cigarette. "True. But you're obviously trying to escape from something. Or someone." He tilts his head back, blowing smoke into the sky. "You can play house with Crutch all you want, but it doesn't change one damn thing. He's one of us, and you are one of *you*. You think money and status and social hierarchy have no bearing on your relationship with him? Think again. He'll always be the poor boy with no prospects and no future. And that will be the one thing that will tear the two of you apart. One day you'll see. He will always choose his own miserable, pitiful life over the rich, make-believe world you live in."

Liar. Pathetic stupid liar. Nothing will tear Ry away from me. My jaw clenches so hard, pain erupts through my temples, stabbing me like an ice pick to the brain. "How dare you? You know nothing—"

He completely interrupts me. "Trash said you made a special trip to the gas station the other day. Bought some of that Blackberry Tea that sells so well. How'd you like it?"

"How do you think I liked it? Do I look like one of your normal 'tea drinkers'?"

"You look like some of them. Take your sister, for instance. Man, she was a beautiful piece of ass."

Pure hatred seeps through my skin like sweat on a hot day. I can think of nothing else except beating the smile off his pasty face until he's left with nothing but a mouth full of blood and broken teeth. I lower my arms and bounce on my foot, ready to body slam his ass to the ground, when I hear the tell-tale hum of the wrecker, slowing down, preparing to make the turn into the large parking lot. The hiss of the air brakes is unmistakable. I glance at the road, trying to get an idea of how much time I have.

By the time I turn my attention back to Trey, he's gone. Scanning the area around me, I spy him walking past the gas pumps, getting ready to head into the gas station. Laughing, he gives me a mock salute.

I salute him back. With one very important finger.

Ry turns the wrecker in front of me, severing my immediate war with Trey, the drug dealer. I back against the wall of the building, giving Ry a wide berth to back Harlan's mangled truck into the garage bay. He was right, the whole front end is wrecked.

Swinging the door open, Ry jumps down, depositing a bag of food into my hand. "You wanna get dinner laid out? I'll unhook this and be right in."

In the kitchen, my mind can barely focus as I set the table with plates and utensils. Normally, when cheesesteaks are involved, I start eating right away. I don't even wait for Ry. But tonight, my appetite lays in ruins beneath the bile rising in my throat. Five minutes. Ten minutes. I just sit there. Playing the movie in my head. The movie where I get to make Trey pay for every bad thing he has done. To me and my family. To every person he's ever gotten hooked on drugs. To that poor Christina girl who sleeps with him, not thinking she deserves any better.

In some scenes I send him to jail. Others, I kill him. I'm not sure which ending would satisfy me the most.

"I can't believe you actually waited on me. That's a first." Ry washes his hands in the kitchen sink, talking to me over his shoulder. "Hey, was somebody here?"

"Huh? What?"

He sits down next to me, planting a quick kiss on my cheek before unwrapping his sandwich. "I was asking if someone was here. There's some beer cans over by the lamp post, next to your vehicle."

I lick my lips, focusing on the food in front of me. "Huh. Must've been some kid."

I knew I was going to lie before the words ever crossed my lips. Why? Because I don't need the man I love going to jail for murder. And I have no doubt that if Ry found out Trey came here—came to confirm that he knows all about my little investigation—that Ry would make the movie I was just playing in my head look like a G-rated cartoon.

He will stop at nothing to protect me. I know that as fact.

So, see? Trey was completely wrong.

Nothing will ever tear the two of us apart. Me and Ry, we are forever.

Chapter 37

Crutch

$56.

Why do stupid khaki pants cost so much? They're not even cargo pants.

Lulu thinks I look dead sexy in my jeans, and they only cost $20 a pop. And I sure as hell wear them way more than I ever plan on wearing these pants.

But we had a deal. Lulu stays the weekend with me, if I go with her to this dumb annual charity brunch her parents are having at their house.

Lulu crawled out of the tent this morning, wearing the sleep shirt I gave her and hot pink cotton panties, and it hit me—I would crawl over glass, dig through a mountain of dog shit, and attend a hundred different charity galas, if it meant she would be by my side. Talk about love. I've got it bad. And if there were a cure, I don't think I would take it.

I'm the addict turning down help. The junkie running from the intervention.

We drove back into town this morning in her car, stopping at the mall to buy these pants. Of course, I refused to let Lulu pay, and then I had a panic attack the whole time I was in the shower thinking about the cost versus utilization rate. Now, I'm sitting here, waiting on Lulu to get ready, flipping through the channels on her big screen TV. She refused to shower in Carrie's shower, so she didn't start getting ready until I was dressed.

Well, to be fair, I dressed, then I *undressed*, and then I dressed again. Instantly, I'm drawn back to just an hour ago when her hand was wrapped around me, while at the same time my fingers plunged into her milky core, dragging a screaming orgasm from her perfect little mouth.

There's a jiggle on the front door, and I quickly grab a pillow, covering the lingering effects of my daydream.

Kristie.

Yay.

"Oh! I thought y'all would already be over in the Big House for the party."

"I'm just waiting on her to finish getting ready. She'll be done any minute." Erection suddenly dead, I toss the pillow to the side and sit up, clasping my hands between my knees. "I thought she told you to knock and not use the key."

Something about her really rubs me the wrong way. Well, let me rephrase that. Something—besides the fact that I've seen her drunk, seen her high, and seen her red panties as she offered me a blow job—really rubs me the wrong way. It's something...else. Something more.

She twirls her auburn hair around her fingers, and I try to look at her objectively, without my biases clouding my vision. She's cute. She definitely cakes on the makeup, but still, she's cute. She should get her act together and maybe she would find someone to be with. It's weird that she wants to spend all her free time hanging out at the house of her younger high school friend.

Not that I'm one to talk. I just had my fingers shoved inside of said high school friend.

She peeks down the hallway, checking for Lulu, and then sits on the loveseat. "Look, I'm really sorry about hitting on you that night. I was drunk. I know that's no excuse, but you have to know that I normally don't act like that. Carrie and Ella are the closest thing I have to family, to sisters. I would never jeopardize that." She sits back, straightening the collar on her dress. "And yes, I should have knocked. I just thought y'all would be at the party already. It won't happen again. You have my word."

She seems genuine. What choice do I have but to take her at her word. It's not like I can judge someone for getting drunk. I mean, DUI should be my father's middle name. And hopefully the getting high thing was just a one-time deal. I nod. Accepting my absolution, she sighs and smiles.

The sweetest voice interrupts us. "Okay, I'm ready."

I turn my head, sighing in my own absolution when I see Lulu standing there in a flowy, pink dress and high-heel sandals. The sleeveless dress has a high neckline, fully covering her ample chest, but it falls to mid-thigh, showcasing her amazingly perfect legs and the tan that's easily baked her skin in the time she spends outdoors with me. As she struggles to put on a tight white sweater—she keeps missing the arm holes—I jump up, helping her.

Perfect. She's just damn perfect. Not even caring that Kristie is staring at us, I bend down, gently kissing my girl's mouth. I don't have to bend far; those heels make her even taller. Her lips are sticky with some kind of lip gloss. She giggles when I pull away, quickly brushing her thumb across my mouth, wiping it clean.

I whisper against the shell of her ear. She loves it when I do that. "You're damn gorgeous."

She grabs my neck, holding me in place, and whispering against the shell of my own ear. Hell, I love it when she does that. "You clean up fairly nice yourself. And you rolled your sleeves up to your elbows." Her free hand brushes across my skin. "You know your forearms drive me crazy."

"You know your everything drives me crazy." I mean it. I really do.

Eventually she pulls away. "Kristie, you look nice. Is your dad already here?"

Kristie bites her lip, fidgeting with a ring on her finger. "Yeah, I think he got here about thirty minutes ago."

"Well, I guess we better get this over with, huh?"

I grab the remote and turn off the TV. "So, tell me one more time, this whole benefit is to raise money for your school? The richest private school in the state? *That school*?'"

She purses her lips. "Yes."

"How is that a charity function?"

"Well, the school operates a charitable foundation. It does some good things, don't get me wrong. In fact, it's helping with some of the travel expenses for the two-week graduation trip. But most of the time, it supports self-centered activities disguised as charitable events." She taps her heel, thinking. It clanks against the marble floor. "There was the benefit to raise money for the new gym, when the one we had was only five years old. There was the benefit to establish a teacher surplus fund with the intention of those monies being earmarked for higher education learning for the teachers who wanted to get their master's or doctorate degrees. But in fact, most of it was used to buy new cars as a sign-on bonus for teachers they hired after they fired a bunch of old teachers for not fully representing the qualities of our school—meaning the teachers were modest and not into social climbing and giving out A's like candy."

"Calm down. You're getting me so excited. I may never wanna leave this party." I roll my shoulders, trying to loosen the tension.

Kristie opens the back-hallway door and walks down the long corridor, heading into the Big House. We give her time, watching as she disappears, so the two of us can make the journey alone. This breezeway feels more haunted than Carrie's bedroom. Like walking through this hallway and into the lifeless, loveless mansion of Lulu's parents will suck the eternal soul from our bodies. She feels it too. She reaches behind her neck, rubbing her scar. Her heels echo all around us as she places one foot in front of the other. And I watch in speechless awe as each step drags My Lulu away, replacing her with Ella Hill.

We walk down the hallway, eventually passing the threshold into the Big House. We pass designer-decorated rooms on both the left and right. Guest rooms, guest bathrooms, something that looks like a home theater room. There's a room with wrapping paper and ribbons hanging on the wall and what looks like covered Christmas trees standing in the corner. That room by itself is three times bigger than my bedroom at my grandparents' house.

The soft music of a piano and muffled noise of party-goers filter through the air, growing louder the closer we get. Lulu's back is so straight and stiff, a construction crew could use her as a leveler. At last, we reach the main living room. The room is massive, with vaulted ceilings, and one side of the room has a large staircase that winds up to the second floor. The wooden banister and railing are draped from bottom to top in garlands of fresh spring flowers. Tucked underneath the curve of the staircase is a grand piano, where someone sits, playing a classical song. The whole back wall of the room is comprised of huge glass doors. They are all standing wide open, allowing people the luxury of walking around the custom-built swimming pool, hot tub, and waterfall. I see people sitting outside. In the matching outdoor furniture.

If I thought Lulu's wing of the house was boring with its white and gray and navy, I was completely mistaken. This room brings a whole new meaning to that style. I can only assume that her mom frequently redecorates the living room, matching to whatever style may be on trend at that particular moment. The wall next to us is lined with white bookshelves, filled to the brim with books that look just as boring as all the people in this room. All hardcovers with non-descript gold lettering along the spine.

"Have your parents read all these books?"

Lulu looks over my shoulder. "The last thing they do in their free time is read for fun. In fact," she nods her head at a buxom blonde in a tight-fitting purple dress, "there's one of Dad's hobbies right now."

"Addison? The assistant?"

"No. This girl is a pharmaceutical rep."

"Ma'am," a waiter in a black bow tie stops in front of us, offering us a flute of orange juice.

We each take one, and I quickly drink it down, wetting my parched mouth. The tangy sweetness catches me by surprise. I'm too late to stop Lulu, she already has the glass tilted to her mouth. "Lulu, it's a Mimosa." Even though the champagne is mild, it still has Lulu scrunching her nose and grimacing. She covers her mouth to cough. Grabbing her glass, I set them both on the bookshelf.

"Your parents are letting the waitstaff serve alcohol to minors?"

"You know you make our relationship sound very scandalous when you call me a minor."

I wink. "Maybe I like scandal."

Lulu's gaze darts off to the side. Her jaw twitches. I turn to see a whirlwind of a woman sweeping in our direction. "Ella, sweetheart. I was growing concerned about your whereabouts. So many people have been asking for you. Come, mingle." She grabs Lulu by the arm, urging her to follow.

Lulu yanks her arm from her mom's grasp. "Mom, I'll be happy to mingle, after I introduce you to Ryland. Ryland, this is my mother, Susan."

Her mom looks different from the last time I saw her on the news, talking about Carrie. Even different from the picture Lulu showed me on her birthday. I can't quite place it though.

"Oh, my." Susan covers her mouth in exaggerated shock. The diamond ring on her finger is large enough to ice skate on. "I wasn't aware you'd be joining us."

"Yes. You were very aware. I told you twice." Lulu's voice is cold and stoic.

Susan leans over, fake whispering at her daughter. At least she's attempting to pretend for my benefit. "Does Hudson know about this?"

"*This* meaning Ryland attending this function. Or *this* meaning my relationship with Ryland? Because last time I checked, Hudson is not the chairman of the party planning committee, nor am I indebted to get permission from him on whom I date. And yes, he is very aware that Ryland and I are dating."

Susan narrows her eyes and wraps Lulu in a fake hug, invading her personal space. "I do not know what has gotten into you, young lady, but you will not embarrass me today. I do not ask much of you. The least you can do is represent this family with the dignity and grace that we taught you."

Pulling away, she straightens her already straight dress and turns her attention to me. "Ryland, it is a pleasure to meet you." She limply dangles her hand in front of me.

What the fuck? Does the woman think I'm deaf? Or is she just delusional?

Having no choice, I try to shake her hand as graciously as possible. "Pleasure is all mine."

You can tell the second she actually acknowledges my full presence. The second she actually looks at me like I'm a human being. How can you tell? Because her skin flushes. "Well, I can certainly see why my daughter is drawn to you. You are quite handsome." She giggles and plays with the strand of pearls draped across her neck. "Any friend of Ella's is a friend of mine."

You have got to be kidding me.

Fortunately, she's called away by someone before she embarrasses herself any further.

Sucking in a deep breath, Lulu doesn't look at me. "It's the nose."

"What?"

"You were trying to place what was different about her. She just had a nose job. She thought her nose looked too big in one of the camera interviews she did for Carrie, so she just had a nose job."

"Her daughter is still missing, and she decides to have elective surgery?"

She points her chin in the air, not answering my rhetorical question. "Time to mingle."

Chapter 38

Crutch

Ella's definitely the dominant personality here, don't get me wrong.

But My Lulu roars like a damn beast during some of the finer moments of this pathetic party.

She flits around from person to person, hands neatly folded in front of her body, politely chatting about the weather or the excitement of her high school career drawing to an end. She agrees with everything that everyone says.

One person comments that the champagne in the Mimosas is flat. Ella agrees. Another person comments that the champagne is too bubbly. Ella agrees. One person argues that the President will be re-elected come November. Ella agrees. Another person argues that the President will be defeated in a landslide. Ella agrees.

Agree. Agree. Agree.

She often stands in silence, like a statue, just blankly staring at those around her as they have a conversation. It drives me damn crazy, quickly reminding me of the night we met. All that standing and staring. It makes me wanna scream. Grab her and shake her until her ball-busting, spit-fire persona comes bursting forth for all the people to see.

It's *My Lulu* whom I love.

Yes, My Lulu can stare with the best of them. But she stares with a passion and a fury, a lust for life. With an intensity that could bring a grown man to his knees.

And a couple of times, I see her come out to play. And it has me laughing so damn hard, I nearly piss my pants.

She introduces me to everyone she talks to. Most of them graciously ignore me. But a few of them decide to test me. They need to make sure my bank account has a certain number of zeros at the end of it before they'll extend their pleasantries.

Like the man who asks what year I graduated from North and Camden Academy. She promptly informs him I am a graduate of East County. When his mouth opens in surprise, Lulu jumps in—not Ella, but Lulu. "That high school proved to be very beneficial. Learning how to handle a firearm for self-defense is really a life skill we should all have." She walks away before he can even process a retort.

Or like the woman who asks what university I'm attending. Lulu quickly tells her that I am about to graduate from the community college. When the lady begins to stutter over her insincere congratulations, Lulu—not Ella—pipes in. "Who needs a four-year degree nowadays, anyway. Everyone knows that $100 on the Internet will buy you fake transcripts from any Ivy League." She leans in close, sharing her secrets with the woman. "Just ask the governor."

Or my personal favorite, the classmate of Lulu's who asks where I work. When Lulu says I'm a mechanic, the girl turns beet red, looking apologetic. You can tell she thinks manual labor is something beneath her, like all the hard work of the world is magically done by invisible little elves and not real people—hard-working people with hopes, dreams, and families. Lulu touches her arm in sympathy. "Oh, but don't worry. We have really high hopes that the position at the plumbing company will open up. Everyone knows septic tanks are where the real money is. You get high bonuses once you pump a certain amount of feces."

All in all, it's going as well as can be expected. That is until I see Vanessa. Well, I think her name is Vanessa. Names weren't exactly at the top of my list when I was doing her from behind.

I told you I was an asshole.

We met at a bar last fall, when I went out with a couple of people from my computer science class after the mid-term exam. Vanessa was one of the bartenders on duty. She definitely wasn't drunk, so that made her fair game. And when she told me that her apartment was right behind the bar and that she wanted to have a night cap when she got off work, I eagerly agreed.

And now here she is. Standing behind a makeshift bar, serving vodka and cranberry juices to stuck-up rich people.

Coming from the restroom, I'm making my way over to Lulu, who happens to be standing one person back from the front of the bar line, when my eyes lock with my former one-night stand.

Fortunately, Lulu's not paying attention to the fuck-me smile plastered across Vanessa's face when she takes her position at the bar. "May I have an orange juice, please. Virgin. No champagne." Her head is bent and she's fiddling with the bracelet on her wrist. I'm turning to make my quick getaway when she notices me. "Ry, can you help me?"

Kill me now.

What choice do I have? My girl called to me. I tuck my tail between my legs and head to face my doom. "Yeah?"

"This bracelet came undone. Would you mind?"

Damn jewelry. Of course, the lock is intricate, and my fingers fumble over it several times before I can get it latched. This has taken too much time. And we all know I'm not lucky enough to get out of this situation unscathed.

"Hi." Vanessa's chipper voice rings in my ears.

I clear my throat. "Hi."

Distracted and staring at me the whole time, Vanessa hands the orange juice to Lulu. Not paying any sort of attention whatsoever, she splatters some of the juice across Lulu's hand. Never one to miss a beat, Lulu darts her eyes between the two of us. Thinking this is just some random girl trying to hit on me, she rolls her eyes and sighs. Normally I love jealous Lulu. It's still funny. Makes me laugh every time she does it.

Except this time.

This time it isn't so funny.

"Crutch, right?"

Lulu's head snaps in her direction. I mumble yes under my breath.

Vanessa makes a dramatic show of handing me a beer bottle and brushing her fingers against mine during the handoff. "And if I remember correctly, beer is your drink of choice, right?"

I turn the bottle around in my hand, studying the label like it holds a mysterious portal. A portal I can crawl right through and vanish from this deathtrap. "Thanks."

Putting her juice down on the bar table, Lulu reaches for a napkin to wipe her hand. The person behind her filters to the side, getting assistance from the other bar maid. Folding her hands across her chest, she stares at me with that same passion and fury that I liked just an hour ago. "Care to introduce me to your friend?"

I drink half my beer in one swallow. "Sure. Ella, this is... Vanessa."

Vanessa scowls. "Clarissa."

Oh, shit. Yep. Her name is Clarissa.

Lulu holds out her hand. "Clarissa, nice to meet you. I can only assume that you know Crutch in the same way that I know Crutch. Is that a safe assumption?"

The two of them study one another, sharing some kind of women's intuition. Damn witchcraft, if you ask me.

Clarissa purses her lips. "It appears so."

"Well, let me give the two of you some time to catch up. It must be nice to run into old friends." I reach out, trying to grab her, but the little minx is quick when she's angry.

"How could you forget my name?"

"I'm really sorry, Clarissa. I am. I was an asshole that night." Eagerly, I try to pinpoint Lulu's tall frame shuffling through the crowd of people.

I turn back to Clarissa. Say something. Hurry. I need to go after her.

Seeing the anxiety of my face and realizing that Lulu and I must be an item, she nods. "It's fine. You can go."

"Thank you. Again, I'm sorry."

Well, it seems like Clarissa is a much better person than me. Spying Lulu on the other side of the staircase, I watch as she speed-walks down the part of the hall I haven't ventured to yet. I jog through the crowd of people, trying to catch up to her.

I'm caught off guard when Kristie grabs my upper arm. "Is everything okay. Is Ella upset?"

I shake her off. "Everything is fine."

When I turn around, my eyes land on Hudson. He's standing next to the piano player talking with some of his friends. Asshat is staring at me like I just killed his dog. It takes all my strength not to flip him off as I continue on my mission to find Lulu.

This hallway is long, just like the other with several rooms. Right next to the living room is a huge kitchen. It takes up nearly the whole left side of the house. I pass another bedroom and bathroom on the right and a huge office. Eventually, I'm left with my final two doors. One on the left and one on the right. I open the door to the left, and it's the garage. Don't think she went in there. Steeling my nerves, I open the door on the right. It's a home gym.

A state-of-the-art home gym. One whole wall is nothing but mirrors with different weights and yoga stuff sitting in front of it. There's a big screen TV, a treadmill, a rowing machine, an elliptical machine, and one of those stationary bikes that's more expensive than most people's cars. And let's not forget about the tanning booth in the corner. Lulu is standing with her back to me. In front of her is a small fridge. She's drinking a bottle of water and rubbing the scar on the back of her neck.

I don't know what to say, so I don't say anything at all. I just close the door to the room and walk closer to her. She places the water bottle on top of the fridge, but she doesn't turn around to face me.

This can't be good. If she can't even stand to look at me right now, this most definitely can't be good.

"Your body has been inside of her body, hasn't it?"

I really don't like those words. Those words should be saved for Lulu. They're too intimate. Too personal. I wish she just asked me if we had sex. The word sex I can handle. I'm an adult. It happens. It's non-committal.

"Yes, but it was just sex."

"But isn't that what sex is? Your hard dick being placed inside of her open and wanting body?"

I'm dying. I can't even answer that.

"I wasn't lying when I said the thought of you being with someone else makes me wanna throw up," she says.

I need something to drink. Skirting around her, I grab the open bottle of water and down the rest of it. She spins away to avoid looking at me, but her plan doesn't work so well because now she's facing the mirrored wall, and her reflection is staring right back at me.

"You won't ever have to worry about picturing me with some other guy. There's no worry about bumping into some guy at the store who has seen the parts of me that you have, who has touched me the way that you have. Does that make you happy?"

There's no point in lying. So, I'm honest. Brutally honest. "Hell, yeah, it makes me happy. I mean, I wouldn't think less of you if I hadn't been the guy to give you all of these firsts, but I'd be lying if I didn't say that it makes me feel pretty damn special. I'm not as strong as you. I wouldn't be able to stand here and picture you with some other guy's mouth on you. Some other guy's hands on you." I grab her waist from behind and it makes her flinch. "Some other guy's cock inside of you. I would flip my shit. Not on you. On him. I would beat him until he was paralyzed from the pain. But that has nothing to do with what I feel about you or that I would think less of you. It's because I'm selfish. I refuse to share you with anyone."

"Now you know how I feel."

Kill. Me. Now.

"That girl did nothing wrong. And yet I want to claw her eyes out. Pull her hair out by the root. Scream at her for having something that's supposed to be saved for me. And me only."

"I'm sorry."

"How can you be sorry for something that happened before we even met? It's irrational for me to want an apology.

"But I still want to give it to you."

She snorts. "Ry, by your own admission, you've had sex with *a lot* of women. We're bound to run into some of them. I'm surprised it hasn't happened before now. I refuse to throw a hissy fit every time it happens. And I refuse to be coddled. You need to tell me I'm being stupid. You need to tell me I'm being unreasonable."

"Not about this you aren't. I shouldn't have tried to escape my reality with meaningless sex. But I can't change that now." I bury my nose in her hair, inhaling the sweet scent of her shampoo.

"Meaningless? You didn't even remember her name. That's more than just meaningless."

"I know."

"Where did you meet? When did you have sex with her?"

I let go of Lulu's waist and begin to pace around the gym. "I'm definitely not answering those questions for you."

She squares her shoulders and pins me with narrow eyes. "You most certainly are."

Fuck me. She's like a mind-controlling she-devil. "Fine! We met at a bar. Last fall. I went out with some people from class after midterms."

"Did you hit on her, or did she hit on you?"

"She hit on me first. She was the bartender. But I returned the volley pretty hard."

Lulu bites her lip. "She's attractive."

I stop pacing and run my hands over my face. "She is."

"Hmm."

"Go ahead and ask me. I know you want to."

She feigns innocence. "What?"

"Don't beat around the bush, Lulu. I like you when you get to the point."

She growls. "Is she prettier than me?"

"No one is prettier than you."

She scoffs, not believing my answer, but it's the truth. I swear on all that's holy, it's the complete and utter truth.

"What kind of sex did you have with her? What position?"

"Are you damn crazy, woman!" I throw my hands up in the air. "Why do you think I would remember that if I didn't even remember her name?"

She crosses the distance between us and pokes my chest with her finger. "You may not remember her name, Ry, but you can't tell me you don't remember that." She tilts her head, mocking me. "Think. Think real hard."

I lean forward, grazing my lips against hers. She doesn't move away. I'll take every small victory I can get at this point. "We went to her apartment, and I took her from behind. We didn't even kiss."

That makes her jump back. I took it too far. Why did I tell the truth? I should've lied. I should've lied to My Lulu.

She's breathing hard. Looking away, she quickly wipes a tear as it chases the curve of her cheek. Nothing in this world feels as bad as this, knowing I've made her cry. When Lulu cries it sucks the very soul from my heart. Plus, she told me she hates to cry in front of people, on more than one occasion.

Stiffening her spine and tipping that cute little chin up in the air, she takes a step closer to me. "And one day soon you'll take me like that. And our bodies will wipe all those memories from the face of the earth."

Sweeter words have never been spoken.

I reach out to her, pulling her body against mine. My whisper is raspy, filled with emotion. "Lulu."

Hugging me close, she grabs my hand and skims it across the skin of her inner thigh. Up. Up. Up. My heart drums in my chest.

Holy shit. "Lulu, where are your panties?"

"A deal's a deal."

I run my fingers through her wet folds, plunging two fingers deep inside. The two fingers that she's grown to love. She moans, letting me know she's ready to be kissed.

But she doesn't let me kiss her. She pulls her head away.

Tugging my hand from her crotch, she guides my fingers to my face where she wipes her juices all over my cheeks and chin.

It's a struggle to even form a cohesive string of syllables. "What are you doing?"

"Marking my territory. There's a whole world of Clarissas out there. And they need to know what's mine."

She walks away, leaving me stunned and fully erect.

Pausing at the door, she asks me one final question. "Tell me something. Something no one else knows."

I sigh. "You already marked me. The very second we met."

Chapter 39

Ella

I must admit, it's pretty hot.

Knowing that my scent is trapped all over him right now.

First of all, I can't believe I actually did that. Second of all, the bitches all over this room staring at my man like cats in heat better take notice.

I watch him from across the dining room. We came in here to get some food and he got stuck chatting with an alumni who actually owns several car dealerships in town. They're talking about muscle cars. He catches my eye and winks.

"There she is."

I turn, smiling, happy to put the face with the voice. "Ridge! What are you doing here?"

Ridge wraps me in a hug. I forgot he likes to hug too. And he's definitely gotten better at them. I haven't seen him in a couple of months, and you can tell he's grown taller, more muscular. He's probably the same height as Holt now, maybe an inch shorter.

He nods back at the kitchen. "Making some extra money. Dad's the caterer on this one."

"I should've known. Look how good the food looks. I've been trying to get in here all day to eat."

He replaces a plate of freshly cut cheese and fruit. "Been stuck doing the small-talk thing, huh?"

"Yes, and it's driving me crazy." I peer past him, looking into the kitchen where constant food prep is still going on. "Is Holt working this too? He didn't call or text me."

"No, he was afraid he'd run into Delaney."

I chuckle. "Smart move."

Delaney is a very snobby sophomore at my school. She's one of the girls who fawned all over Holt when she first saw him. He made the mistake of taking her out on a couple of dates. One too many dates.

I believe Holt's exact words were, 'Money don't take the crazy out of people'.

I think my own parents are a testament to that.

I study Ridge's handsome face, his strong jaw. He's really turning into a heartbreaker. He has always played second fiddle to Holt, but he's finally coming into his own. Shining his own star. I take a quick glance around the room and notice more than one set of eyes watching Ridge's every move as we speak. "Hey, you know to avoid all the girls at my school, right?"

He rolls his eyes. "Yes, Mom. I've been duly warned."

Ry catches me off guard, snaking his arm around my waist, possessively holding me next to him.

Hello pot, meet kettle.

His obvious jealousy makes me want to laugh. I best put an end to his torture. "Ryland, this is Ridge. Ridge is Holt's best friend. Ridge and his family live next door to Uncle Ray and Aunt Teresa. We all grew up together. And Ridge's dad is the best chef I've ever met." I wave my hand at all the food spread across the table. "Ridge, this is Ryland, my boyfriend."

"Yeah, Holt told me you had a guy. Nice to finally meet you." Ridge furrows his brow. "For some reason, I thought your name was something different."

"You can call me Crutch. Everyone does. It's a pleasure to meet you too. And the food looks great. Please give my compliments to your dad."

A soft whistle travels through the dining room. "That's my cue. I'll see you guys later."

Ridge heads back into the kitchen, leaving Ry confused.

"Their whole family does it. It started when the boys were little and Ridge would be over playing in the backyard with Holt. His dad hated to always scream for Ridge to come home so he started whistling. They do it now for everything. If they're in the store and can't find one another, they just walk through the aisles whistling."

"Hmm. Effective."

I tug on his shirt. "I'm starving. Let's get some food."

We're filling our plates when Ry knocks me with his elbow. "What's that?" He nods to the wall above the antique sideboard.

"I have no idea." It's obviously a framed portrait. A huge framed portrait. But it's covered in black velvet; you can't see what's underneath. "I guess a portrait based on the size."

"Like a family portrait?"

"Not a family portrait. Unless they photoshopped me in. Maybe it's dear old Mom and Dad. Riding white stallions, down streets of gold."

He chuckles. "Could be worth something one day. Like a Monet, maybe."

After we eat, we escape out to the pool. Most people from outside have made their way back inside for booze or food, and it gives us a little breathing room. It's also here that we see my father, whispering in a corner next to the waterfall with Addison. She's not very happy. She's probably upset that some of his other sexual conquests are here.

I guess that's the recurring theme for the day.

Except I don't see my mom and dad fighting for one another the way Ry and I always do. We will always fight to make it back to each other.

Ry clears his throat, making our presence known. Dad and Addison quickly change their behavior, trying to appear nothing more than professional. They should really take cues from Mom. She's a much better actor than either of them. Smiling, Addison circles around us, nodding and giving me a quick compliment on my dress.

"There's my darling daughter." He leans in, giving me a quick kiss on the cheek. "Addison was just telling me about some surgery additions for the upcoming week." He holds his hands up in the air, wiggling his fingers. "Everybody needs the good doctor." He laughs at his own joke.

Neither of us laugh with him. "Dad, I'd like for you to meet Ryland Crutchfield. Ryland, this is my father, Robert Hill."

Dad tsks me, quickly making the needed correction. "Dr. Robert Hill. Nice to meet you."

Ry politely shakes my father's hand. I watch as the muscle in his jaw twitches. "Pleasure is all mine, sir."

"So, what year did you graduate North and Camden? Are you related to Andrew Crutchfield who owns the newspaper?"

"No, Dad. Ryland is my boyfriend. Remember?"

"The mechanic." The shock makes his voice falter off key. He sounds like a screeching girl.

Good to see my father is filtering his comments for my benefit. I nervously fiddle with the side of my dress. Without looking, Ry reaches over and grabs my twittering fingers, wrapping them in his firm grasp. My father glances down, watching in stunned silence as we hold hands.

"Yes, sir. I work at Harlan's Garage and Automotive. If you ever need any work done, we're the best in the county. I'm also about to graduate from the community college."

My dad sniffles. "That's right, community college. And what are your plans after that? Ella will be attending the University of Virginia."

Ry glances at me, smiling. "Yes, I've seen some of her drawings. You should be very proud. I'm not sure what my plans are yet, sir. However, I have a feeling a lot of weekend road trips to Virginia will be in my future."

Not only does that statement warm my heart, but it makes my dad shit a golden brick. Which I totally love.

One of these days I'm gonna have to break down and tell Ry— and my dad— that my plans have recently changed.

"Robert! Susan is looking for you." Phillip, Kristie's dad, joins us, his signature tumbler of whiskey in his hand. After my father excuses himself, I introduce Phillip and Ry.

Phillip is at least a better actor than Dad. I'd say he's par on target with Mom. He smiles at Ry, but his eyes are beady and hard. He looks at Ry likes he's a thief, about to make a getaway with the family silver. "So, tell me how you two met. There has to be some type of story there."

I shake my head, deciding to give a little more sanitized version of the truth. The story of meeting in the coffeehouse is just lame. "No story, really. I went out to visit that gas station that Carrie went to a few times before she went missing. Remember, the detectives went to all the places Carrie went in the months leading up to her disappearance?" Phillip nods, swallowing down the warm brown liquor. "Well, Ryland works at the body shop right across the parking lot from the gas station. Us meeting was just happenstance, really."

Phillip nods, paying special attention to the closeness of our bodies. His stare is so intense, it actually weirds me out a little bit.

He shakes his glass back and forth. "Well, that is definitely interesting. And did you know Carrie, Ryland?"

I'm taken aback by the look on his face. He looks angry and annoyed. No wonder Kristie never dates. My parents are rude, but Phillip is just plain scary.

Fortunately, Ry and I are saved from this odd torment. A waiter steps out onto the patio, ringing a water glass, calling us all inside the dining room. The hosts—aka my parents—are assembling everyone for a small speech. Same as they do every single year. Anything to stand in the spotlight for even the briefest moment. It takes several minutes for everyone to filter in, and it doesn't go unnoticed by me that Phillip and Kristie seem to be exchanging harsh words over in the corner. I did see her flirting with some of the college guys earlier. I'm sure that went over as well as a vegetarian at a slaughterhouse.

Dad clears his throat. "Thank you all for coming. Another year has come and gone. It's so hard to believe. None of this would be possible without the hard work of my lovely wife. Susan," Dad holds his arms open wide, "come over here, darling."

Feigning modesty while the crowd politely claps, Mom shoos Dad away. Finally, laughing and forcing a blush to her face, she races to his side. "Robert," she pats his chest, "don't embarrass me."

He fake laughs. "Never. Never." Everyone else in the room fake laughs too. What the famous doctor does, everyone does.

"We are all so proud to be a part of the North and Camden Academy legacy. And what better way to leave a lasting mark on the world than through charity work. Giving the gift of time, kindness, love, and… money." Everyone claps and chuckles. Dad points at some old guy in the corner. "That's right, John. Don't think you can drink the champagne and eat the beef tenderloin without pulling out your checkbook before you leave." John smiles and nods, toasting Dad with his champagne flute.

"The North and Camden Academy Charitable Fund has done so many amazing things throughout the years. But I don't think anything has been as special to my heart as the work the charity will be doing in the months to come, work spearheaded by one of the loves of my life." Dad holds his hand out in my direction. "Ella, sweetheart, come and join your old, sentimental parents."

I wanna strangle him. He knows I hate to be in front of a large crowd like this. He barely showed any interest at all in the graduation charity trip. I did all of the research, all of the planning, and presented it to the student council and the charity foundation board all by myself. Now he wants to take credit. All because it serves the current agenda in front of him.

Not knowing what I'll do, Ry gently places his hand on the small of my back, providing silent encouragement, letting me know he's got my back. That whatever I do, he'll stand behind me.

What choice do I have?

Squaring my shoulders, stiffening my spine, and folding my hands in front of me, I join my parents at the front of the room.

"I don't think it's news to anyone that personal tragedy has over-whelmed our family this year." My father twitches his nose, and my mother dabs the corner of her eye, wiping away non-existent tears. Whispers of condolence and sympathy travel through the crowd. "But even in the hardest of times, human resilience and strength can triumph. Turning the darkest devastations into the smallest iota of hope—of devoted sacrifice—is what makes us all grow as people. Grow as a community. Grow as a foundation for our future genera-tions.

"We all know that annual tuition was set at $40,000 at the last fiscal meeting. I think we, in this room, can all consider ourselves lucky for having the resources and ability to provide the very best education to those we love. Our daughter's passion for sharing love with everyone around her is what led to this momentous occasion. Susan and I would like to officially announce our donation to the North and Camden Academy Charitable Fund to establish..." he pauses for dramatic effect, "the Caroline Hill Memorial Scholarship for the Underprivileged!"

And with a flourish, Mom pulls the black velvet from the large portrait on the wall.

What. The. Hell.

Admiring gasps and loud applause threaten to clog my ear-drums. My mouth falls open as I study the larger-than-life portrait. It's a black and white painting of Carrie outside by the pool. Dressed in a short cocktail dress, the picture captures the radiant glow of my sister as she laughs. Perfectly painted lips pull across her brilliantly white smile. Perfectly styled blonde hair sways gently in the breeze. Perfectly manicured nails reach up, fondling the diamond pendant dangling from her neck.

She's laughing at a story Uncle Ray told us. How do I know? Be-cause I'm standing right beside her, laughing myself. But I've been cropped out of the picture. I know the picture well. Holt took it. My parents weren't even here at the time. Carrie wanted to have a nice family dinner for Caleb's birthday. His parents came into town. Uncle Ray and Aunt Teresa came over. Uncle Ray grilled steaks. Aunt Teresa, me, Carrie, and Raylee cooked all the side dishes. My parents were at a medical conference somewhere. San Francisco, maybe? After Carrie went missing, Holt posted the picture to his social media accounts.

I don't care that I was cropped out of the picture. I don't care that my father didn't congratulate me or express accolades regarding my work on getting the graduation charity trip set up. I don't even really care that he's giving money to a scholarship fund so more kids can go to my school and become spoiled, entitled assholes.

What bothers me is that word. *Memorial.*

Do I think my sister is dead? Yes. Yes, I do. But I would never say that out loud to a room full of strangers.

To have my ignorant, self-absorbed parents stand up here and basically announce her death to everyone—and wrap it up in a pretty money bow—in their exclusive circle of rich pricks? That's a whole new low.

My father taps his hand in the air, asking the crowd to lower their volume. "To support the dreams of our daughter, Caroline, we have decided to pave the way for three bright young youths who might not have the opportunity to thrive without our support. Three scholarships for three young minds for the full four-year high school education. Susan and I are donating $480,000." My father bows, acting as if he is overcome with emotion. "Excuse me, our sweet Carrie is donating $480,000. To Carrie!" He raises his glass high in the air. Everyone else in the room does the same.

And then my father downs his drink. I focus on the glass, my vision blurring. Vodka and cranberry juice, maybe? Dad likes that drink.

People immediately begin to flock around Mom and Dad, and even me, showering us with compliments. Congratulating us on our generosity. I can't breathe. I can't think. I want to scream. I wanna scream at the top of my lungs. What's wrong with these people!

Suddenly, I'm being pulled from the crowd. It's such a whirlwind, I don't even know what's happening to me. I'm having chest pains. Nausea. Dizziness. An out-of-body experience.

Am I too young for a heart attack?

Oh no, am I about to have another panic attack? Like the night on the cruise when Carrie went missing? Please, no. I rub my sternum, checking for a heartbeat.

Before I realize it, I'm standing in the middle of my living room in my wing of the house. Far away from everyone else. Is that Ry talking to me?

I blink several times, trying to focus. Ry grabs both sides of my face. Bending close, he forces me to look into his eyes. His voice is firm. A constant calm in my storm. "Tell me what you want."

"I wanna go home. Take me home."

Scooping me into his arms, his hand grazes my bare ass. Loading me in the car, he drives me home.

Taking me from the mansion to our tent in the woods.

With him.

He's my home.

Chapter 40

Ella

April showers.

There is no such thing in Alabama. There's only April tornados. And that's what's in the forecast for today.

School dismissed at noon in anticipation of the impending storm. Everyone hoped the outlook would improve as the day went on, but no such luck. Ry texted this morning to say his Wednesday classes at the community college had already been canceled for the day as well. The second I jumped in my car I tried calling him.

No answer.

Then I tried the garage.

No answer.

I texted.

No answer.

For fifteen minutes I sat in my car, waiting on a return phone call, as everyone deserted the school parking lot. I quickly tired of the worry and dread filling my stomach.

That's why I'm currently driving across the county, racing against the weather, as the weatherman keeps repeating a real-time play by play, as the bad storm treks from Mississippi to Alabama. The wind whips, forcing me to grip the steering wheel with both hands. Dark clouds cover the sky, swirling like the brew in a witch's cauldron. I slam the car into park the second I pull into the parking lot at the body shop. The chain link gate is pulled closed and deadbolted. I know the garage is closed, all lights are out, but I still scream out for Harlan and Ry. I'm silently praying that Ry isn't in the woods trying to ride this out.

Climbing back into the SUV, I drive like a somewhat cautious maniac to the homestead. Aunt Teresa calls to make sure I'm coming over to their house. When I tell her that I'm getting Ry and heading back home to the storm shelter in the Big House, the worry in her voice does nothing to calm me. She's not one bit happy that I drove out here. Especially considering it puts me closer to the storm, closer to danger. The bad weather will hit the garage and homestead first before making its way to town. I hear Uncle Ray screaming on the other side on the phone. But what choice did I have?

Relief floods through me when I see Ry's truck, sitting in its normal spot, tailgate pointed at the campsite, just like normal. Except this isn't *just like normal*. The tent, with our blow-up mattress inside, is no longer in its normal spot. I look over at the truck bed, and I see the blue fabric neatly folded. Some of the chairs are in the back too—the ones that fold, at least. Ry is bent over one of the large storage bins. It looks like he's securing it to a tree. I've never paid attention to it before, but all of the storage bins back up against trees.

I jump out of the car and race to help him. The temperature has risen in just the past few minutes, casting a muggy heat over the earth, instantly making my skin sticky. Large drops of rain sprinkle from the sky, painting my shirt in a tie-dye look. The wind whips my hair in my mouth. I grab a hair tie from my wrist and wrangle it as I race to his side. "Ry!"

He has a pile of ratchet straps dangling over his shoulder, and he's still bent over, strapping one of the storage bins to the tree behind it. His eyes grow wide. He was so concentrated, so focused, he didn't even hear me pull up. You can tell he's torn. Torn between the urge to take a break and wrap me in his arms versus the urge to secure all of his possessions in place, trying his best to protect everything he owns from the storm.

In the end, practicality wins over emotion.

Tightening the strap, he yells over his shoulder. "Lulu, what the hell are you doing here? A storm is coming."

"You didn't answer your phone. I was worried."

Finishing with the bin, he stands up, wrapping me in his arms. "I'm sorry, it's in my truck." He pulls back and studies me. A large raindrop runs down his cheek. "Are you okay? I can't believe you drove out here. It's supposed to be bad. What were you thinking?"

The wind picks up and I have to raise my voice. "I was thinking of you. No one is at the shop. Where's Harlan?"

"His son came and picked him up about an hour ago. They have a basement at their house."

It starts raining harder. "I have to finish securing everything. Go home. I'll meet you at your house, Lulu. Your parents are probably worried."

"My parents aren't even here. Dad's a guest speaker at another medical conference. They're in Las Vegas. And I'm not leaving without you. Tell me how to help."

"Leave."

"No."

He drags a hand over his face, spreading rainwater in his facial hair. He hasn't shaved in a few days, and it makes him look dark and dangerous. He watches the darkening clouds, settling lower around us. "Fine. But we have to hurry. We've got to get the hell out of here. Stack the Adirondack chairs over by that tree. I'll come strap them down when I finish with these bins. And grab my computer bag before it starts pouring." He points over by the firepit.

I run around, and we each complete our assigned tasks with super-sonic speed. The barometric pressure is rising; I can feel it making my ears hurt. We make the homestead as secure as possible, trying to protect our home from damage. By the time we finish, it's pouring rain. We are both drenched from head to toe.

"I'll follow you. Drive safe, but hurry." He kisses me and slams the door to my car.

I can barely see what's happening around me. I carefully turn onto the main road, sitting forward in my seat to see through the rain. I turn up the volume on the radio as loud as it will go to hear the announcements of the weatherman over the pounding on my windshield. The wipers are flipping back and forth at the fastest speed. I can barely see the lights from Ry's truck behind me. The storm is close. Really close. A tornado has been confirmed on the ground, and based on the street names and highway numbers being announced on the radio, it's heading straight in our direction.

A burst of rain and wind pushes my vehicle across the middle line, scaring the crap out of me. I can't even see. My vision is blurry. It's definitely not safe for me to drive, so I yank the car over to the side of the road. I'm fumbling for my phone to call Ry when my driver-side door opens.

He's standing there in the pouring rain. "Move over!"

I scramble across the center console and fall backward into the passenger's seat. Ry jumps in. I turn in my seat. His truck is pulled over behind me. Half of everything he owns is in that truck right now. He can't leave it on the side of the road. "Ry, what about your truck!"

He grabs my face in his hands. "Fuck my truck! You're the only thing that's important."

I don't know how he drives so fast. In the flooding rain. In the tossing wind. The first few seconds frighten the shit out of me so I close my eyes. I listen carefully to the forecast instead. By the time we get into the city limits of town, the tornado sirens are blaring. The tornado is chasing us. Chasing us down every street, past every turn, clipping our heels.

I pray. I don't think I've ever prayed so hard in my life.

Well, except for my prayers for Carrie.

A shaky breath of relief pours from my body when Ry finally pulls the SUV into my driveway. Flinging ourselves from the car, we run into the house. Ry follows me down the long breezeway that connects us to the Big House. "The decoration room is a safe room! Tornado proof."

Ry pushes past me, grabbing my hand, making me run even faster. Hurling me into the room, he flips on the light and locks the door. He's not happy with what he sees. "Your dumbass mother is the only person I know whose storm room is covered in breakables, scissors, and large paper cutters."

We're both out of breath. Water drips all over the floor, puddling around us. "Sorry." I'm not really sure what else to say, so I just say that.

All of a sudden, the overhead light flickers and then goes out. The constant hum of electricity wafting through the house dies. It's so quiet. Too quiet. My heart thunders in my chest, bouncing a tennis ball against my eardrums. I grab the phone from my shorts and turn on the flashlight.

And then... the noise starts.

News reports are right. Tornados sound like a roaring train. Like a huge waterfall. Like a jetliner flying directly overhead.

Ry grabs my shoulders, pressing his body against mine. Not waiting for permission, his tongue delves into me, kissing away my fear. Kissing away my every worry.

The noise gets louder. Louder. Louder.

He tips my chin up. His whisper is raspy and deep. "You're the love of my fucking life."

I can't even respond. I'm not given the chance. And I want to. I want to, so badly. But I can't.

A terrible, ripping sound drowns everything out. He grabs me and forces me onto the floor, covering my body with his. Tears stream down my face. Fear and anxiety blur the edges of consciousness.

I love you too.

But I don't get a chance to say those words back to him before all hell breaks loose.

Chapter 41

Crutch

The quiet.

I've never been so glad to hear *nothing* in my whole life.

She's safe. And that's all that matters. The world around us may be gone. Imploded. But all that matters is she's safe.

I scoop her up from the hard floor, checking her for injuries even though I know she's just fine. Even though we just went through something traumatic, she doesn't want me to see her crying. She quickly wipes her eyes with her hands. The only light in the room is the glow from the flashlight on her phone. I glance around, spotting some candles on a shelf.

"Do you have matches in the Children's Wing?"

"We have a candle lighter. Carrie loves candles. There's a bunch more in the laundry closet."

Scooping the candles into my arm, I unlock the door and grab her hand. Nothing looks unusual in the hallway. I glance toward the Big House, not immediately seeing anything amiss, and pull her back into her section of the house. I need to assess the damage.

"Lulu, I need you to gather all the candles. Put them on the kitchen counter. I'll be back in a few minutes. I need to check on things outside."

She refuses to release my hand. Her lips purse into a thin line and she stares at me. "No. *We'll* gather the candles. And then *we'll* go outside. Together."

I growl. "Why do you keep giving me shit today?"

"Why do you keep trying to leave me today?"

I'll never leave you. Not in a million years.

Once we make it outside, I'm pleasantly pleased the damage isn't worse than it is. The house and cars are fine. The horrible, ripping noise that sounded like the world was splitting in two came from one of the pecan trees near the edge of the road. It's been completely upended from the roots and is now laying across Lulu's wide front yard. I look up and down the street. Some other people are walking around, surveying the damage. It looks like this neighborhood was spared from a direct hit. Or maybe the tornado was lifting back in the air at this point. I see a couple of downed trees and some downed power lines. Other than that, it's just a lot of limbs and shingles everywhere.

Lulu walks to the edge of the driveway to join me. She's cleaned the mascara from underneath her eyes, but they're still red-rimmed and puffy. She shivers. The storm brought with it a cold front, taking away the summer-like weather from this morning. The rain has stopped, and a few remaining sprinkles splatter in the puddles.

"I got ahold of Mom. Told her everything was okay with the house. She said she'll have Dad call someone about the tree. Harlan answered. They are fine. A tree fell on his son's car, but the house itself is okay. I still can't get ahold of Uncle Ray, Aunt Teresa, or Holt. It's making me nervous. I even tried Ridge. He didn't answer either."

"Maybe it's just the signal, everyone trying to use their cell phones at once."

She shakes her head, causing loose, wet strands of hair to fall from her scattered ponytail. She needs to change out of those wet clothes before she catches a cold.

"I don't think so. It would give me that weird beeping noise if that was the case. This just keeps ringing and rolling to voicemail." She taps her phone against her chin and reaches around to rub the scar on her neck. "Maybe some local news channels are already airing coverage." She starts to do a web search on her phone when it rings, making her jump.

"Raylee?"

...

"Yeah, we're okay. Mom and Dad are out of town. Me and Ry are at my house. Everything is fine here. Just some downed trees and power lines."

...

"No, I haven't been able to get ahold of them either, why? What's wrong?"

All of the color drains from Lulu's face. She looks like she's about to faint. I reach out, grabbing her elbows, holding her steady.

"We're on our way there now," she says, voice wavy and uncertain. "I'll call you as soon as we have news."

By the time she hangs up the phone, I'm already tugging her toward the car. We left everything in it. Keys, her purse. I open the passenger-side door, helping her inside. "Talk to me, Lulu."

She's in shock, and I have to call her name again before she shakes out of it. "Raylee saw her street. On the national weather broadcast. It's demolished. She said it looks like a war zone."

I glance around, trying to think. "Does your dad have any tools here? Like a chainsaw or an ax or anything like that?"

She nods, solemnly. "In the third garage." She points across the yard. "Other driveway."

I back out of her driveway on two wheels and drive up the road to the other driveway. She can't use her key code because the electricity is out, so she opens a side door with her key. Once we're inside of the garage, I pull the emergency cord and lift the heavy aluminum rolling door by hand. I grab everything I see that might be useful. A chainsaw, two axes, some flashlights, a ladder, some gasoline, and two large tarps, still in the vacuum packaging. We load everything into the back of the SUV. Lulu has to crawl in to lower the seats for the ladder.

We're driving down her street, trying to avoid the larger limbs when we pass a patrol cruiser with its lights flashing. A couple of seconds later, it beeps its siren, asking us over the loudspeaker to pull over. Are you damn kidding me right now?

"What? What's happening?" Lulu bounces in her seat, a nervous wreck. She checks her phone for the umpteenth time.

A policeman jumps out of the cruiser's passenger-side door and jogs over to my window. I quickly lower it. He looks at me and Lulu. "Officer?"

"Are you Ella Hill?"

"Oh no. What happened? Are they dead?"

The officer's face clouds with confusion. "Is who dead? Detective Marcum sent us to check on you. His cell phone was damaged. He's unable to make calls." He narrows his eyes. "Is someone you know injured?"

"We can't get in touch with our aunt and uncle. Our cousin called and said she saw their street on the news. Said it was demolished. We have to go check on them."

Since when are Teresa and Ray *our* aunt and uncle, instead of *her* aunt and uncle?

I guess since now.

"What street? What neighborhood?"

When I tell him, his own face blanches. "Listen, you need to turn around and head back home. You won't be able to get over there. That whole area is blocked off."

"No!" Lulu grabs my arm, digging her nails into my skin.

"No offense, Officer, but I will not take her home and make her sit there for hours, in the dark, wondering what happened to her family. No way in hell."

"Marcum said for her to stay put."

I chuckle, cynically. "Marcum knows her better than that."

He scrubs his face, looking back at his partner in the patrol car.

"Look," I say, lowering my voice, "if it's that bad, they need all the help they can get. I've got tarps, axes, gasoline, a chainsaw. And I'm able-bodied, strong. Let me help."

Sighing in resignation, he gives me directions to the back side of Ray and Teresa's neighborhood, where a small access road is usually blocked off from trespassers because it has a small electrical substation on it. "Go there. I'll radio ahead and tell the patrol unit to let you through. Be prepared to park and carry your stuff."

As we drive through town, the varying degrees of damage is astonishing. There are areas of nothing, areas that look like Lulu's neighborhood, and a few small areas where buildings are nearly flattened. We pass overturned cars. Parts of roof structures. There's even a patio chair in a tree. It looks to be in pretty good shape. Under different circumstances, I'd stop and get it for the homestead.

I don't have to ask Lulu to do anything for me while we drive. She takes it all upon herself. First, she calls the nursing home. It takes four tries to get through, but she finally does. Everything is fine with Grandma. The storm completely missed them. Biting her lip, she looks up the phone number for the gas station. Someone answers on the first ring.

She rubs the scar on the back of her neck. "Hello, yes, I was wondering if the station was okay from the storm. Did you receive any damage?"

...

"Good. So, it missed you?"

...

"And the body shop across the parking lot? It's okay too?"

...

She exhales in relief. "That's wonderful news, thank you. Um, was Trash at the gas station when the storm came through?

...

No, I don't wanna talk to—"

...

She can't hide the scowl on her face. "Trash, it's Ella Hill."

She squeezes her eyes closed, fighting her anger. Like me, she's probably grown to hate the sound of his voice in general. But... he's still my brother. Nice to know he's still alive.

"No. I'm just calling to make sure you weren't physically injured by the tornado. And Larry and Cindy?"

...

"No, he's with me. Town is a complete mess. We are trying to help where needed."

She doesn't mention Ray and Teresa. Smart move.

"Don't start with me." Her tone scares even me. "I'll let him know you're all safe." She hangs up the phone and just gives me a simple nod.

She's so damn remarkable.

I turn onto the small access road. I can barely function enough to lower the window, to talk to the officer. I give him our names, and he tells us where to pull in. "That's as far as you'll be able to drive. Clemson said you have a chainsaw and some axes?"

I clear my throat, trying to talk. I can't so I just nod. "Take them with you. Anything that can help."

I reach across the console, wrapping my hand around Lulu's. She's shaking like a leaf.

And as we approach what used to be the neighborhood that her aunt and uncle lived in, she gasps.

War zone doesn't even begin to describe it.

Chapter 42

Crutch

My shoulders ache.

I'm carrying the chainsaw on one shoulder and the two axes on the other shoulder. And Lulu actually took the belt from my jeans, slid it through the handle of the gasoline tank, and wrapped it caddy-corner around my body, like I'm some girl, carrying a purse.

She's hauling the tarp and flashlights. We've stopped here and there on our trek to the middle of the neighborhood to Ray and Teresa's house. Lulu gave away one of the tarps to someone whose roof was entirely missing from their living room. Apparently, the lady had antique furniture from her great-grandmother and she was terrified it would ruin in the elements. So many other people could use the other tarp, but Lulu refuses to let it go in case Ray and Teresa need it. I've already used the chainsaw and axes more in the past hour than I ever have in my entire life.

We've seen houses completely blown off their foundation, like someone picked it up and dropped it down, fifteen feet to the left. We've seen houses completely split in two from trees. One house even had a car in its bathroom, sitting right on top of the bathtub.

We turn onto Ray and Teresa's street, and Lulu immediately starts running. The sun is starting to set, casting everything in the glow of twilight, and she has a hard time seeing anything with all of the branches and limbs scattered everywhere. She stumbles a few times, the heavy weight of the tarp pulling her forward. I jog as fast as I can, but the sloshing gasoline makes me go slower. "Lulu, slow down!"

It's a moot point. Telling Lulu what to do on a day like today is like trying to tell the sun not to shine.

I can't believe my eyes when I get to the middle of the street. Standing there, like a flower among the weeds, are three houses, completely and totally unscathed from the damage and destruction. One of them is Ray and Teresa's house. I mean, it doesn't even look like one single shingle is missing. They have a few small twigs and leaves scattered across the groomed yard, but that's it.

Teresa has Lulu wrapped in a death grip when I finally make it up the driveway. I've barely put the chainsaw and axes down on the ground when Teresa flings her arms around me, enveloping me in a hug. Once again, I'm reminded of the family I should've had. And it makes me miss my grandpa and grandma.

"I'm so glad you kids are okay. I was terrified for you." She wipes the tears from her eyes. "For everyone."

"Raylee?"

Teresa turns to Lulu, holding her cell phone in the air. "I just talked to her about fifteen minutes ago. Service has been terrible for everyone in the neighborhood since the storm came though."

"I can't believe your house didn't get hit," I say.

She shrugs in disbelief. "It's unexplainable." She coughs, choking back emotion. She points to the house on the left. "The Conways are fine." She switches to the house on the right. "And Mrs. Tucker too. She's widowed. We actually had her with us when the tornado came through."

"Where's Uncle Ray and Holt? Ridge?" Lulu looks around, searching.

"They are out there helping. Some people are trapped in their houses by the trees. I was waiting here, trying to get ahold of Raylee and you."

I swing the chainsaw and axes back onto my sore shoulders. "Just point me in the right direction." Teresa points to the left. I stop in front of Lulu, lowering my voice. I don't think I've ever spoken so mean to her. "You *will* stay here. You will *not* come with me. You will *not* wander all over this death trap. It's too dangerous. So help me, Lulu, I will completely flip my shit. Night is falling, and I cannot help your uncle and cousin if I'm consumed with worry about you. Do you understand?"

She stares at me. Wide-eyed and innocent. Like she's never done a single thing to cause me one second of worry.

Hell, I've done nothing but worry about her since the moment I laid eyes on her.

Teresa places a hand on my shoulder. "She can help me. Several houses right around here have families with small children. We need to gather the little kids and bring them to our house so the parents can sort through what's left, put up tarps, cut trees, do whatever they need to do. We'll just hit a few houses. I promise we'll be back here before it's dark."

I turn back to Lulu. "Promise me."

She completely surprises me. "Ask me."

I don't have time for this, Ray needs my help. But how can I deny My Lulu. "Tell me something. Something no one else knows."

She kisses my lips. "From here on out, I'll never break my promises to you."

Hours.

We work for hours. Me, Ray, Holt, Ridge, Ridge's father, and Ridge's little brother, Cullen. And we are all covered from head to toe in complete filth.

Around midnight, when none of us can barely stand, we walk back over to Ray and Teresa's. We say goodnight to Ridge and his family and head inside. Candles are lit, casting a soft glow on the sleeping children scattered across the living room. If I had been thinking straight, I would've packed all the battery lanterns from the homestead, but they are all in the storage bins. Assuming, I still have storage bins left. I'm hoping the site and my truck made it out of the storm untouched since the body shop and gas station are fine.

I count seven slumbering little bodies. It looks like Teresa and Lulu made pallets for the children. The fixings for peanut butter and jelly sandwiches are spread out across the kitchen counter, and Teresa is stacking sandwich on top of sandwich on a large platter.

"I thought you all would be starving." She adds another sandwich to the pile. "The hot water heater already ran out of water, so you guys can either take a cold shower or just wash off. A sheriff's deputy dropped off several gallons of distilled water. We put a gallon jug in each of the bathtubs; at least it's room temperature."

Ray wraps Teresa in a hug. She holds him back like she hasn't seen him in ten years, not even caring that his sweat and filth are rubbing all over her. They intimately whisper to one another. I glance around, looking for my own woman to hug. A small sliver of worry pierces my heart when I don't see her.

"She's upstairs in Raylee's room, rocking the baby. Her room is the only one with a glider."

"Baby?"

She nods. "Neighbors five houses up have an eleven-month-old."

Holt bumps me on the shoulder, handing me a flashlight. "Come on, I'll show you. You can borrow some clothes too."

"Crutch, come back down and eat after you see her. You need your strength. Ray just said y'all are heading back out to meet the Conways at six in the morning for more work."

I nod, following Holt up the stairs. "Yes, ma'am."

We stop outside of his room. He grabs me a fresh T-shirt, pair of gym shorts, socks, and jeans. "Thought you'd wanna sleep in the shorts. The jeans for tomorrow may be an inch or two too short, but they should fit in the waist." He furrows his brow. "I didn't give you any of my underwear. You're a chill dude, but I don't think we're exactly there yet."

I chuckle, rubbing my hands across my face. "Smart move. Thanks." He points me in the right direction as he closes himself in the bathroom to wash up. I slowly push open the bedroom door. It was only closed halfway, but it still creaks.

She's standing in front of the large window, blinds raised, and she's looking out into the neighborhood. The cold front has pushed away the remaining clouds and the moon shines bright, illuminating the devastation in an eerie glow. Her thin hips and curved bottom sway from left to right as she rocks the baby back and forth in her arms.

Holy. Shit.

What a beautiful sight for sore eyes.

Wiping those thoughts from my mind and filing them away for the future—a long, long, long time in the future—I walk over to her, sweep her hair to the side and gently kiss the scar on her neck. She combed her hair. When I left her, it looked like rats had taken up residence in her ponytail. She's in the same clothes and smells like dried rainwater and ozone. She moans, leaning back against my chest. I can't smell good, but she doesn't seem to care. I peek over her shoulder at the sleeping baby. A little girl. Her small fist is balled up like she's about to punch someone and her little face is scrunched up like she's mad. All of a sudden, her face relaxes in her sleep and she smiles.

I laugh under my breath. That's pretty damn funny.

"It took forever for her to go to sleep. And she can't decide if she's mad or happy about it. I guess she's both." She nuzzles against my jaw. "Her name is Alexis. Her parents' house is bad, but not destroyed. The mom will come get her tomorrow morning. She said they'll go to her sister's house."

"Must be hard. I can't imagine having your life upended like this. Let alone while having to take care of a little baby." I reach around and run my finger across Alexis' smooth cheek, taking care not to get her dirty.

Holt leans in the bedroom, whispering. "I'm finished in the bathroom, man."

I squeeze Lulu's waist. "We haven't talked about it, but I assume we're staying here for the night, right? I'm supposed to go back out with the guys at six in the morning."

"Yeah, I can't leave Aunt Teresa with all of these kids."

"I'm gonna go get cleaned up and eat a few sandwiches. Are you hungry?"

She shakes her head, shifting Alexis into a more comfortable position. "No, I already ate. Can you tell Aunt Teresa that I'm gonna sleep up here with the baby? If she starts crying during the night, I don't want her to wake the other kids. There's one more sealed bottle of formula downstairs. Can you bring it up? Aunt Teresa has it."

"You got it."

I quickly rinse as much dirt from my hair and body as I can. I'm not sure what to do with my dirty clothes so I just toss them in the hamper with Holt's. I know he didn't share his underwear with me, but he has to give me a little bit of leeway with the deodorant. I rifle around in the bathroom drawers, find some men's deodorant, and lather it on before going downstairs.

Teresa sits with Ray, Holt, and me while we eat. I eat four sandwiches, and I know Holt eats more than me.

"Ella's gonna keep the baby upstairs in case she starts to cry during the night. She asked me to bring up a bottle of formula?"

Teresa nods, grabbing it from the counter.

Ray clears his throat. "There's a guest bedroom upstairs. I assume that's where you're gonna sleep tonight, right, son?"

I'm dying to wrap my arms around Lulu, hold her close and never let her go. I could've lost her today. That thought makes me want to collapse on the floor in a pile of tears and snot. Like a complete pussy. But... this is his house. And I have to respect his wishes. I just nod. "Sir."

Together, Holt and I climb the stairs again. By now, it's already one in the morning, so we've only got five hours to sleep before we head back out. The second I walk into Raylee's room, that big pussy heart of mine just melts even more.

Lulu's spread across the bed, cuddling Alexis in her arms. She changed into fresh clothes while I was gone—must belong to Raylee. The T-shirt fits fine, but the pajama pants are short, riding well above her ankles. There's a burning flashlight, sitting on the dresser. Lulu shined it at a small section of the wall, so there's just enough light to see in case she wakes up. But based on her heavy and even breathing, I don't see her waking up any time soon.

I gently place the formula next to the flashlight. I respect the hell out of Ray, but if he thinks I'm leaving my gorgeous girl alone after a day like this, he's a lunatic. I walk into the other room, grab a pillow, and rip the comforter and top sheet from the bed. I quickly make a pallet on the floor next to Lulu and Alexis. Giving them each a kiss on the forehead, I crawl into my makeshift bed and pass out.

It seems like only mere seconds tick away before someone is knocking me awake. I jump. Nothing like a toe to the shoulder to make a man really piss his pants in the morning. I open my eyes to see Ray standing over me.

He glances at the bed, and I assume Lulu and the baby are still sleeping. Whispering, he holds out a hand, helping me up. "Come on. It's six."

Grabbing my boots and the pair of jeans from the corner of the room, I follow him out the door, leaving Lulu softly snoring. I quietly close the door.

When we get out of earshot, Ray claps a hand across my shoulder. "I wouldn't have listened to me either."

Chapter 43

Ella

Night is starting to fall by the time we pull into my driveway from Uncle Ray and Aunt Teresa's house. Ry and I were glad to spend the day helping; the neighborhood really needs it. But we are beyond thrilled to finally have some down time. We've barely gotten a chance to talk or even really process what all happened.

Harlan went back to the garage today and confirmed everything was just fine. He has an extra key to Ry's truck and found it on the side of the road where we left it. Nothing was stolen. Nothing was storm damaged. The bed of the truck was waterlogged, and that's it. What a blessing. He drove it back to the shop and currently has the tent and foldable chairs set outside, drying.

I talked to my parents again. Not willing to cut their trip short since all immediate family members are still alive—not counting my sister—they said they'd be back in town on Sunday. Marcum and Leary and everyone else from the department made it through okay. Leary had a power pole fall across his driveway, but no one was hurt. I also talked to Kristie. She wanted to come over tonight, but I firmly told her no. And of course, Hudson called. He also wanted to come over tonight to check on me. You can imagine what I said to that.

I've never felt so dirty in my entire life, and I'm not even the one who was chopping trees and climbing over sheetrock all day today. I glance over at Ry, turning on the flashlight as he unlocks the door to my house. White plaster clings to his hair. His face is smudged with dark brown dirt, and chainsaw grease is caked against his neck.

"The hot water heaters keep a reservoir of hot water even when the power goes out, but I don't know how long it will last once the shower is turned on. You use my shower. I'll go over to the Big House and use one of the guest room showers. They're on different hot water tanks."

His brow furrows. "I don't want you walking through that house by yourself without the power on. You could hurt yourself."

I smile at his thoughtfulness. "It's okay. I'll use the guest bathroom closest to us."

He reaches in his back pocket and grabs his cell phone, turning on the flashlight. "No. You use your bathroom; I'll use the guest bathroom. I'll just follow the smell of entitled money until I come to the right door."

I snort. "That'll be the second door on the right, sir." I grab a candle from the counter, lighting it. I'm glad Ry had us gather them all yesterday after the storm. "Here, use this. You don't wanna kill your cell phone battery. It may still be a day or two before we get power."

He winks. "Good thing I'm with the only person I care to talk to."

He opens the back door and heads down the marble breezeway, searching for the guest bathroom. I holler after him, "I'll be sure to tell Harlan about that."

Twenty-two minutes. Twenty-two glorious minutes.

That's how long the water stayed hot. I shampooed my hair twice, I shaved every part of my body known to mankind, and I used a half a bottle of shower gel. I've never felt so clean in my life. What a difference twenty-two minutes can make.

I grab one of my sleep shirts from Ry. He only *gave* me one shirt. I commandeered three more. All Harlan Garage and Automotive T-shirts. I love them. The material is so soft it's like satin. Slipping it over my head and stepping into a fresh pair of panties, I open my bathroom door and smile when I see my bedroom. Ry must've finished before me. Seven different candles cascade dancing light across my bedroom.

I tiptoe down the hallway and stop when I see him in the kitchen. He's lit every single candle. The others are scattered across the kitchen and living room, lighting the space like a fairy garden in the summer. He's standing there, making sandwiches in his boxer briefs. Correction: in Holt's boxer briefs. Besides the T-shirts I sleep in, Ry didn't have any extra clothes here. Everything is in his truck. Before we left, he borrowed some more clothes from Holt, including boxer briefs this time. They're tighter across his crotch than his own boxer briefs.

Immediately, my mouth waters.

My eyes trail up the muscled V of his pelvis, to the firm lines of his muscled stomach. The tight lines of his pectorals flex when he reaches for the peanut butter. I engross myself in the strong build of his shoulders. His facial scruff is three shades darker than his hair. Sexy, dark, and mysterious. A stubborn water droplet falls from above his ear and travels down the thick cord of his neck. Even from across the room, the candlelight reflects against his eyes, turning the pale green shades of black and white.

I can't breathe. I can't function. I can't live one more second on this earth without knowing the feeling of him being inside of me. Being a part of me. I love him. And he loves me.

We haven't even talked about what he said before the tornado came roaring through our lives.

You're the love of my fucking life.

Well, right back at ya.

He doesn't even glance up when he notices my presence. "Your bananas were about to go bad. I'm making peanut butter and banana sandwiches. I know you're probably tired of peanut butter already. I promise when things are back to normal, I'll buy you a four-foot-long Philly cheesesteak."

When I don't laugh or respond, he glances over at me. "Lulu? Are you okay?" He sucks peanut butter from his thumb.

Wordlessly, I pull the shirt over my head and toss it over on the loveseat. The butter knife falls from his hand, clattering against the countertop. He loves my breasts. I know he does. He can't help it, but his cheeks turn pink every time he looks at my naked chest. It's so darn cute.

Grabbing the waistband of my panties, I slowly lower them to the ground. Stepping out of them, I kick them away. They crumple underneath the side table. From here, I watch as his erection grows, straining against the thin fabric of his underwear.

I'm really nervous. But I'm completely calm.

I'm really self-conscious. But I'm completely confident.

I'm really trapped. But I'm completely free.

He makes me everything. Everything all at once.

But what he really makes me is *wet*. Soaking wet. And ready to be loved.

His whisper is raspy and low. "Lulu."

"Yesterday was an emotional day."

He nods, staring at my naked body, like I'm the first girl he's ever seen. And we both know that's not true. "Yeah."

I suck in a breath, stiffening my spine. "Do you say things you don't really mean when you're emotional?"

His eyes dilate, and he slowly comes around the kitchen counter, lazily leaning against it, like he doesn't have a care in the world. Like his massive hard-on isn't bobbing up against his stomach like some sort of porno Heimlich maneuver. "No."

My heart stops beating. My nipples grow so hard, they become painful. "Oh."

He bites his bottom lip, driving me to the brink of hysterical lunacy. "Go ahead and ask me. I know you want to."

"I don't know what you're talking about."

He drags his hand over his jaw. "Don't beat around the bush, Lulu. I like you when you get to the point."

"Fine. That's the question then. Do you just *like* me?" Despite my best efforts, nerves get the best of me, and I catch myself rubbing my scar. I quickly put my hand down by my side.

"That's not the question you really wanna ask."

I lick my lips. "Do you love me, Ry? Are you in love with me?"

He pushes off the counter and slowly closes the distance between us. His chest grazes against mine. "You are the love of my fucking life, Luella Margaret Hill. Never before. Never after. You're my one and only."

Holy. Crap.

I press my body against his. We're still not touching each other with our hands. Only our bodies. "Ask me."

His jaw twitches, and his throat makes a loud gulping noise. "Tell me something. Something no one else knows."

"I love you, Ryland Joseph Crutchfield. Never before. Never after. You are my only reality."

His chest rattles. It sounds like he's purring.

I look down, mesmerized that our bodies are only separated by a thin piece of material.

"That's not the only question you wanna ask me," he whispers.

He's right. It's not.

Every part of my body is heavy with desire. Weighed down. Like trying to move in water. "Are you gonna have sex with me tonight, Ry?"

His sigh of relief would be comical if it weren't such a serious moment. "Hell, yeah, I am."

He gives me no chance to respond before hauling me into his arms and punishing my mouth with his. I wrap my feet around his waist, obsessed with how the motion spreads my innermost parts wide open. If that pesky underwear were gone, I bet his body would slip right into mine. He walks us back to my bedroom, only bumping into the wall twice, which is quite an accomplishment considering how ferociously we're attacking one another.

I lower my feet to the ground, anchoring myself as his kisses become more controlled, more time-consuming. Deeper. Better. His calloused fingers massage my breasts, making me moan. I can't stand it anymore. I quickly reach my hand down the front of his boxer briefs, grabbing him, and spreading his own moisture around the mushroomed head of his cock.

In one split second, Ry backs away from my touch. He drags his hands through his hair. Tossing his head back at the ceiling, he screams. "Are you kidding me right now!"

Who is he talking to? Me?

He looks like he's just been stabbed. Or shot. Or hanged. "Lulu, we can't have sex tonight."

The horror. "Why not? I swear I'm ready. I've been ready."

"I don't have a condom," he waves his hand at the bedroom door. "Condoms are in my truck. My truck is on the other side of the county." He swears underneath his breath. "Let me go find a store that's open."

I smile, biting my lip. "I have condoms."

His eyebrows rise into a new zip code. "Excuse me?"

"I bought condoms a few weeks ago. I didn't know when our moment would come so I wanted to be prepared. I don't wanna use condoms you bought for some other girl. In fact, those things get thrown out the second you get back to your truck, understand?"

He nods, watching me as I open my nightstand. I set all the boxes on the bed. He looks at the boxes and then at me and then back to the boxes again. He's taking forever to pick what he wants. I'm suddenly very aware of my nakedness, so I press my legs together and casually fold an arm across my chest.

He looks back at me. Back at the boxes.

"What's wrong, Ry? You're killing me."

"You bought nine boxes of condoms."

"Yeah."

He bursts out laughing, pulling my hand away from my chest and kissing my palm.

I pout, not understanding what's so damn funny. "Why? What's wrong?"

"It's so damn funny, Lulu. What did the cashier say? He probably thought you were filming a porno. Or running a condom distributing charity."

I look at all the boxes and start to laugh at myself. "Come to think of it, he did give me a weird look." By now, we're both laughing so hard, I'm afraid we may ruin the moment. "There's five-thousand different kinds. I wasn't sure what would be the best. I wanted you to have options."

Grabbing a black box that says '*XXL, New thinnest material ever*', he sweeps all the other boxes to the floor. If I thought our laughing fit would ruin the mood, I was wrong. The look on his face turns from good humor to carnal hunger in a nanosecond. The candlelight dances across his features, making his sheer beauty even more beautiful. Pushing me down on the bed, he crawls between my legs. He kisses from my neck, down my chest, and finally settles his face between my legs.

"I thought we were gonna have sex?"

"Is My Lulu impatient? Good things come to those who wait." He licks my wet folds, immediately sending an electric shock up my spine, freezing my movements. "But I'll probably only last two minutes once I'm buried inside of you, so I need to get you off at least one time before then."

Hearing him say that he's going to be 'buried inside of me' fills me with a yearning unlike any I've ever known. He could probably just blow cold air across my pelvis and I would immediately orgasm.

I'm luckier than that, though.

He takes his time.

Giving and pulling back. Giving and pulling back. Until I'm about to explode.

He's going back one last time to finish the job when I pull against his shoulders. "No. That's enough. I'm ready to come. But not on your face and fingers. On your cock."

His eyes widen and his chest heaves. He likes it when I talk dirty. And the more sexual we become, the dirtier I talk. He loves it.

He rips open the box, grabs a condom, and tears into the foil packaging. I stare in awed fascination as he rolls it on himself. I'm scared. But more than that, I'm excited. He's already broken me, but still, I know this will hurt. I pray it only hurts for a moment because I'm ready to feel pleasure. I wasn't kidding about wanting to come on his body.

Crawling over me, he leans his forehead against my own and lays his lips across mine, allowing us to breathe each other's air. It's one of the most intimate things we do. And the perfect beginning.

The beginning to the end of my virginity.

Chapter 44

Crutch

Fourteen days.

Twenty-three times.

I've had sex with Luella Margaret Hill twenty-three times over the past fourteen days, and I'm ready for a million more. I never wanna stop making love to her.

Never. Ever. Ever.

And that's what I'm thinking about as I try to drag my brain back into focus. I'm supposed to be studying for finals. My last two finals are tomorrow, on Friday. I thought about studying at the shop, but Lulu and I refuse to have sex on the little twin bed at the garage. We're too tall. Arms and legs would be everywhere. We have a hard enough time just actually sleeping in that bed, the few times we've stayed there. Plus, Harlan would *know*. He just would. And that's weird.

So, we came to the homestead because we both needed to have some immediate sex just to be able to function for the rest of the night.

Our first time was... I can't even put it into words. There's not a written or verbal word known to the human race that could describe it.

It did hurt her. And she bled a little. But stretching her all the weeks beforehand definitely helped. She didn't orgasm our first time together. But she did later that night. I was sound asleep, blissfully happy from our time together, and dog-ass tired from fighting the ravages of the tornado, when she reached across, rubbing my crotch until I woke up. When I rolled over, she looked just like an angel. Some of the candles had burnt out, shadowing her face in a haunted glow. Wordlessly, I put on a condom and slid into her. We didn't talk, we didn't whisper. We just stared at each other as I pumped into her. With every stroke, her core accommodated more and more of my body. I get hard even now thinking about the sound she made the first time she came all over my cock. Her orgasm moan from intercourse is fifteen notches higher than her orgasm moan from oral sex.

And I love it.

Just like I love her.

I look over at her now. She cuddles beside me on the loveseat, watching a crime show on her laptop. My own laptop is sitting on my legs, open to the website for one of my classes. The firepit crackles, sending a rush of embers in the air, and the cicadas of early summer chirp in the background.

I kiss the top of her head. "I love you."

She smiles and sighs in contentment. We decided that we wouldn't say 'I love you' back and forth to one another. If one person says it, the other person has to wait until a completely different moment to say it. That was Lulu's decision. She said saying it back and forth in response allows it to become automatic. Complacent. She doesn't want that.

Maybe she's afraid of becoming loveless. Like her parents.

"I can't believe your graduation is next Saturday. Are you sure you don't wanna walk?"

I shrug. "I could not care less about that. What am I walking *toward*? I've got some decisions to make, and walking across that stage would just remind me that I've procrastinated. Being clueless about your future and how to provide for your loved ones is nothing to celebrate."

She swings her legs down from the seat, clears her throat, and rubs her scar. "Ry, there's something I need to tell—"

The ringing of her phone startles us both. She grimaces when she looks at the home screen. Parents, Kristie, or Hudson. And the winner is...

"Hi, Mom."

I close my laptop, wondering what battle My Lulu will be fighting tonight.

"Mom, I already told you I wasn't going. Several weeks ago. So, I'm not sure where all this is coming from."

...

"Well, I'm really sorry that Hudson, for no reason whatsoever, thought we would be attending the prom together. He never asked me. I never asked him. And he knows that I'm in a relationship with Ryland."

Oh, shit. The prom. Is that even a thing anymore?

She sighs. "I know it's Saturday night, but that doesn't matter. He could ask any girl in school, and she would jump at the chance to go. I know for a fact that some of the younger girls bought dresses just in hopes that someone would ask them last minute."

...

"I'm not changing my mind. I made my decision, and it's final."

...

"Why don't we hang out instead? Me and you? We could get some takeout, watch a good movie, talk? We can go through the things that Caleb is giving us—Carrie's things."

I don't know why she does it. She always tries to establish that bond, and her piece of shit mother does nothing but turn her down. Even bringing Carrie into the mix, her mom will still turn her down. At least my mother would agree to hang out with me. Sure, she would only do it to try and squeeze some money out of me, but still.

Lulu is actually having dinner with Caleb tomorrow night. He's older than Carrie and is finishing his senior year of college. He graduates next week too. Of course, he has a four-year degree. Not two, like me. He wants to meet with Lulu to give her some of Carrie's things that he still has. I offered to go with her, but she wants to do it by herself, just her and Caleb. I'm fine with that. I'm proud of her for always being so damn strong.

Lulu points her chin in the air, swallowing. "No, I understand."

...

"I'm not even at home right now, Mom."

...

"Okay. Bye." Hanging up the phone, she looks battle wearied and drained.

"Prom?"

"Yeah. It's Saturday night. I'm not going. Hence, the drama."

I reach down beside me, grabbing my water. I drain half the bottle and hand the rest to her. "Why don't you wanna go to your prom? Isn't that some big rite of passage every high school student should experience?"

She smirks, lasering into my eyes. "Really. And how did your prom go? Did you have fun?"

Damn she-devil. She wins. "I didn't go to my prom."

"Exactly."

"Well, it's supposed to be different for girls. There has to be a reason you don't wanna go."

She makes a big show of standing up and stoking the fire.

"Lulu, do you plan on telling me the reason you don't wanna go to your prom?

"No."

"Well, I suggest you quickly modify your plans, then."

She stiffens her back and stares at me, planting her hands firmly on her hips. "Fine. The school has a stupid rule that no one over the age of twenty can attend the prom. Last time I looked at your license, that rules you out."

Oh.

She scowls, "And so help me, Ryland Joseph Crutchfield, if you say I should go with someone else, I will beat you to a pulp. The name Hudson Plott better never leave your lips."

I scoff. "Fuck no. I'd rather send you on a date with the weird-looking guy from the taco restaurant. The guy with the one eyebrow and the forked tongue." At least that gets a smile out of her. "Seriously, why didn't you just tell me about the prom and the age limit?"

She shrugs. "It wasn't important. It didn't have you there. So, it wasn't important."

Inwardly I groan. Shit. Looks like I'm throwing a prom Saturday night.

Chapter 45

Crutch

"I'm glad things went well with Caleb. I know it must hurt to see him leave. You were really close to him for a long time."

She swings her legs back and forth, sitting on the back of my tailgate in the warm, morning sun. We just visited my grandma, so we're sitting in the parking lot of the nursing home before going our separate ways for the day. I position myself between her legs, running my hands across the tanned, smooth skin of her thighs.

"He's such a great guy. I did love him. I mean, I just knew he would be in my life forever, you know? My brother. Part of my family. He's still devastated over Carrie. He's tired of being alone, but he's too scared to date someone else. He feels like he's cheating on Carrie. I don't know how to help him through that. Moving to Atlanta will be the best thing for him. New city. New job." She squints into the sun. "He had some of her clothes. Makeup. Extra cell phone charger. School notebooks. I haven't gone through it all yet, but it didn't seem like anything that would give me any further clues as to what happened."

"How'd your last meeting with Marcum go?"

She shrugs. "You know how it went—the same as always. I sit there and stare at the pictures, thinking something's gonna reach out and slap me upside the head, mocking me for missing it for so long. The only thing that's ever caught my eye was that her mint container was missing. But, like you and me talked about, she could've broken it and thrown it away and just not gotten a new one yet. Heck, maybe she was taking the drugs so fast before her disappearance, there wasn't even a need to hide them in her mint container. Maybe she sold or took everything the second she got her hands on it." She sighs so deeply she hurts her chest. I watch as she gives her sternum a quick rub. It's the same thing she did when she had a panic attack—or near panic attack—at the charity brunch when her parents basically announced Carrie's death to the world. "And there's nothing new on his end, especially since we decided to wait about submitting more evidence from her car for further testing. I mean, DNA testing is progressing so freakin' quick, year after year. I don't wanna mess up what evidence we do have if something better is just around the corner, you know?"

Lulu knows way more about forensics than me so I just nod in silent agreement. Besides, despite my desire that she find out the truth about her sister, I'm more concerned with keeping her safe... from Trey and everyone in his world. I know she hasn't mentioned the drugs to Marcum or any of the other detectives yet. How do I know? Because I'm fairly certain one of their first stops would have been to me. To ask me what I know about my brother, about the drugs, and about the gas station. And in spite of the guilt that's slowly eating away at my soul—the guilt I have for asking her to keep this information to herself—I wouldn't change a thing.

Why? Because four days ago, one of Trey's pushers went to the emergency room with two broken legs and a fractured skull. The "official" story is he fell off his roof when cleaning out the gutters. The "unofficial" word on the street is that he owed Trey some money. Apparently, Trey felt like beating the man within an inch of his life was the appropriate recompense. And the thing that worries me even more... this guy wasn't some lowlife from my side of the county. This guy has a wife and three kids and works in some accounting office. I mean, what the fuck. The guy wears a tie and goes to parent-teacher meetings.

I tuck a piece of bronzed hair behind her ear, quickly deciding to change the subject and bury the burning need to scoop her in my arms and run away from this whole shitty mess. "I'm sorry we can't spend the day together."

"Don't worry about it. Doesn't absence make the heart grow fonder?"

I grumble. "More like the balls grow bluer."

She bursts out laughing. "Forty hours doesn't constitute that much of a dry spell."

I grab her waist with my hands, squeezing tightly. Bending down, my hot breath rolls across the shell of her ear. "Your tight walls around me is heaven on earth. *Four* hours constitutes a dry spell."

She shivers. She blushes. But because she's My Lulu, she doesn't shy away. She stares deeply into my eyes. "Maybe I'm not that tight. Maybe you're just that big."

My dick jumps. I'm in agony. Kill me now.

She laughs, noticing my pain. Little minx.

She tries to get us back on topic. "Besides, you're right. Jackson, Mississippi, is too far for Harlan to drive on his own. I'm just glad y'all found the part you were looking for."

White lie. Hopefully, she'll forgive me.

I hold onto her as she jumps down from the tailgate. "So, what will you do today?"

She shrugs and then tilts her face back into the sun. "It's gorgeous. I'll probably just lay out by the pool and read."

I lift my eyebrows. "Read what?"

She ignores me.

"I guess that means your case file on Carrie."

"Maybe." She opens the back door of my truck and grabs a bottle of water from the cooler for the road.

"You should be studying for finals," I scold her.

"I'm Salutatorian. I could fail my finals and still pass. And they've already printed the graduation program. Stripping me of that title is the least of their concerns."

Like a lovesick school boy, I follow her to her car, watching her climb behind the wheel.

She furrows her brow. "Did you hear Grandma ask about the orange roses again?"

"Yeah, she misses her flowers. Can't remember to blink her own eyes, but she sure remembers those roses, knows they should be blooming now."

"We should get her a bouquet of orange roses next time we come."

This woman.

I lean into the car, kissing her goodbye. "I'll call you when I'm back in town."

"If you stop for food, don't let Harlan get anything too greasy. His acid reflux has been acting up."

I throw my hands in the air. "How the hell do you know how bad Harlan's acid reflux is? Do y'all really have nothing better to talk about at the garage while I'm working my ass off."

Once again, she ignores me. Slamming the door shut, she teases me with a wave as she drives away.

$145.

I was worried about what to do with my future. Worried how I could provide for Lulu. Build her that big house. Fill it with furniture. Fill it with kids.

Now, I know.

Own a damn tuxedo rental business.

This day is burning through my checkbook like a wildfire, giving me my own set of heartburn. Tux, corsage, food, and a whole new round of floating water lanterns. Harlan was still working at getting them all ready when I left. I'll text him when we start to head back that way so he can light them. With any luck, he won't burn the homestead down.

I straighten the lapel of my suit and knock on Lulu's door. "It's me, Lulu. Open up."

I hear the patter of her feet and the scramble of the lock. "Ry, I thought you were gonna call—"

She flings the door open and her jaw promptly hits the floor. After she digests her shock, it's pretty obvious she likes what she sees. Her eyes dilate, and her breath catches in her chest, expanding her large bosom like a balloon.

So, maybe the $145 wasn't such a bad investment after all.

"Ry," she reaches around, rubbing the scar on her neck. "What are you doing?"

I scan her pink shorts and white tank top, complete with blue sports bra straps peeking out of the top. Her cheeks are rosy and her lips are pinker than normal. She did lay out today. She looks good enough to eat. And I plan on doing just that in the not-too-distant future. "Well, you know I think you look great in anything, but you may wanna put on something a little more formal. You know, in case you wanna take pictures."

She shakes her head. "But we can't go to the prom. The school's rule? Everyone knows you're older."

I snort. "Who said anything about that bitch-ass school?" I smirk. "You deserve better. And I think I have just the place." Apparently, my smile is infectious because it quickly spreads to her face, and she jumps into my arms. I hug her tight, lifting her feet off the ground just the way she likes.

She wraps her hands around my neck and kisses my lips. She tastes like sunshine and chlorine and strawberries.

"You look so handsome."

"I'd better. I had to sell a kidney to rent this thing." We stumble through the door and I kick it closed with my shoe. I gently place her feet back on the ground. "You better go get ready. I'm like Cinderella. I turn back into a greaseball mechanic at midnight."

"Good thing I like greaseball mechanics." She folds her arms over her chest. "But I didn't get a prom dress because I knew I wasn't gonna go."

"You're telling me that out of all the stupid, fancy functions your parents drag you to, you don't have something that will work?"

She bites her cheek, fighting a smile. "I can find something."

I shoo her away. "Well, go. I'm setting a timer for forty-five minutes. Alarm goes off, and this chariot leaves."

She doesn't even make a smartass comment. She's already racing down the hall. Forty-two minutes later, she emerges. And forty-two minutes and fifteen seconds later, I officially turn in my 'man card'.

I'm over. I'm done.

I've stopped being a person of my own mind, body, and soul. Everything I have, everything I am, belongs to Lulu. She carries my heart around in her hand like a talisman, dragging me from place to place. I meant what I said to her. Never before. Never after.

Just like the first night I met her, everything about her screams money. She's curled her hair and piled it high into some sort of messy bun. Her eye makeup is a little heavier than normal, gray and smudgy, like she just woke up from a nap. Her black lace dress is short, but not obscenely short. Not like what most girls her age would wear. The straps on her dress are those string things that look like they may break if I tug too hard. Normally, Lulu would wear a sweater over something like this, favoring modesty in case she runs into one of those people she has to be 'Ella' with. But not today. Not tonight. And her heels are some of the highest heels I've ever seen her wear. She has to be nearly as tall as me.

I turn off the TV and flip the remote somewhere into the abyss of the room. She moves with such grace, such beauty. I can't take my eyes off her. Not even for one second.

"You're quiet. Do you like what you see?"

"Lulu, you're breathtaking."

She squares her shoulders and tosses her chin in the air. "And I still have two minutes to spare."

I press myself into her. She's so tall. With legs for miles and miles. "And just what can we do in two minutes?"

She presses her nose against mine. "Why don't you stick your tongue in my mouth and I'll show you."

Damn good plan with me.

Eventually we have to stop kissing. Literally. I'm dizzy. Low oxygen. "Alright, grab your things. It's time to get this party started. Mine or yours?"

"Yours! The truck is what we always have to drive for surprises," she says, confirming what I already knew she would say.

As soon as we're in the truck, I slide the white calla lily corsage on her wrist. She wraps her fingers around mine, refusing to let go of my hand. I have to drive the entire way one-handed. She's confused when I go past the turn for the homestead, though.

"Ry?"

I lift her hand, kissing her knuckle. "Just a little detour."

I pull onto the shoulder when we get to the small yellow house with white shutters. The long driveway is lined on either side with blooming orange rose bushes.

Her throat makes a strange noise before she whispers. "Orange roses."

"This was my grandparents' house. This is the place where I spent the best years of my childhood." A cynical chuckle rumbles low in my chest. "And, of course, Grandma was right..." my voice trails off as I wave a hand at the hundreds and hundreds of roses.

She remembers plants but not me.

Fuck Alzheimer's.

She touches the windshield. "It's a beautiful house. Which room was yours?"

I point. "Window on the left. And you don't have to say it's beautiful. It's small, nothing spectacular. But Grandpa took care of it. He took pride in everything, no matter how small. It was home. And it was filled with love."

"I'd rather live in a small house filled with love than a mansion filled with indifference." She turns, giving me a small peck on the cheek.

I need to find a way to give Lulu a mansion filled with love. She deserves both. I need to man up and provide that for her. Pulling back onto the road, I do a U-turn and drive to the homestead. Harlan is still there when we park. I should've known that he wouldn't sneak out early.

"Ry! Water lanterns." Lulu sits forward, literally on the edge of her seat in excitement. "Is that food?" She gasps. "Oh my god, Ry, the firepit has blue fire."

Normally, I'd back into my spot, but she's having too much fun looking at everything. I just turn the truck off, laughing. "I know. I soaked the wood in copper chloride. It does that."

Harlan opens the passenger-side door for her, holding her hand as she climbs out. "Harlan, the firepit is blue."

"I know; I see it. And you look beautiful, sweetheart."

Smiling, she wraps him in a hug, giving him a kiss on the cheek. "Did you help with my prom?"

"I'm the official water lantern boy. If I never see another lantern in my life, that will be fine by me."

"Well, thank you. So much."

I lean against the hood of the truck, watching her as she walks around the campsite. My eyes are glued to her every move. How did a poor bastard like me get so lucky?

She bursts out laughing when she gets to the food table. "A four-foot-long Philly cheesesteak? Really?"

I bite back my smile. No salad here. I've got all her favorites—the sandwich, pickle-flavored potato chips, gummy worms, and cantaloupe. Weird. I know.

She walks down to the dock, studying the glowing lanterns as they float around. Dusk is coming and the lights glisten off her skin like gold. Harlan slaps me on the shoulder. He winks, climbs into his truck, and drives away. I grab a beer from the cooler and walk down to one of the side tables. I open my laptop, turn the volume as loud as it will go, and hit 'Play' on the slow song playlist I made last night. It's really hard to find two hours' worth of slow songs that sound somewhat decent. The eighties proved very helpful.

She turns, watching me as I slug back half my beer. "So, what do you wanna do first? Eat? Dance?" I lick my lips. "Get naked? It *has* been a full forty-eight hours now."

"I did not spend all that time getting this good-looking to be undressed in less than an hour."

I pout, tossing back the rest of my beer. "Fine."

She holds out her hand, motioning for me to join her on the dock. "Let's dance."

We dance, we eat, we laugh, we talk. Trust me, there is no one on the face of this earth who is having a better prom than Lulu and me. And the songs aren't that bad; I get to hold Lulu close as I listen to them. That makes everything better.

Three hours in, it gets even better. She pushes me down onto one of the patio chairs and slowly removes her dress. Teasingly slow. She's playing our game just right tonight. Underneath, she's wearing a black lace strapless bra and black lace boy-cut panties. Those drive me crazy. And I guess, black lace is our theme for the night.

I chuckle to myself. If Lulu did believe in symbolism, something may be said for wearing the color of death to her prom.

She props her high heel up on the seat, allowing me to trace my fingers up the length of her leg, from ankle to crotch. When my fingertips skirt past the edge of her panties and into her moisture, she moans, but quickly lowers her leg before I can go any farther. Grabbing a seat cushion, she tosses it on the ground at my feet. Bowing before me on her knees, she slowly unbuttons my shirt, exposing my chest. She charts every line and muscle, before undoing my pants. I raise my hips, helping her free my throbbing cock. Folding me into her mouth like I'm the only flavor she's been craving for days, she forces me to the brink, but I stop her before I fall.

"No, Lulu. Tonight, I come in your pussy. Not your mouth. Let me go get a condom." I gently push her away, making room for me to stand up when she stops me. She reaches into the cup of her bra and pulls out a condom.

I can't help but smile. "Packing ahead of time. Presumptuous, don't you think?"

She stares into my eyes, tossing her chin in the air. "I figured you were a sure thing."

Oh, how you figured right, My Lulu.

Chapter 46

Crutch

Lulu's voice is raspy. She screamed so loud she actually made her throat raw. It's a good thing the homestead is isolated. A stranger would've thought I was murdering her. Three different times.

Damn women and their multiple orgasms. Don't get me wrong, I definitely plan on having another one tonight myself, I just need a few hours of recovery in between.

No two people fit together like me and Lulu. We were made for each other. Two halves, split right down the middle.

We're sitting on the loveseat, watching the blue flames dance in the firepit. My arm is flung around My Lulu, and she's snuggled against my bare chest, listening to my heartbeat. I slipped back into my underwear and pants—you can't go commando in a rental tux—and she put her dress back on, with nothing underneath. I take a pull of my cold beer, nudging her shoulder. "You need me to get you some water?"

"No, I'm good."

Something's bothering her. She's distracted, rubbing her scar.

"Are you happy, Lulu?"

"Of course, I'm happy. It's been one of the most amazing nights of my life. All of my amazing nights are with you."

"Then, what's wrong?"

Her voice squeaks out higher. "Nothing."

"Don't lie." I toss the possibilities around my brain. "Are you thinking about Carrie?"

"You know I always think about Carrie."

Trying a different tactic, I say, "Tell me something. Something no one else knows."

Her whisper is barely a sound, catching on the wind and flying on an angel's breath to my ears. "I'm keeping a secret from you."

Well, I wasn't expecting that. I grab her body, pulling her upright, planting her face to face with me. "Talk to me. What's going on?"

Her eyes fall down to her lap.

Shit. It must be worse than I thought.

She bites her lip. Taking a deep breath, she lifts her face, forcing herself into position. "I'm not going to the University of Virginia. I'm going to the university here."

At first, I'm taken aback by the news. I know she hated the idea of becoming an architect, but she never mentioned switching schools, never mentioned *not* leaving for Virginia. And as much as it pained me to think about her being ten hours away from me, I knew we could make it work. I love her that much, and she loves me that much. But I'd be lying if I said I didn't think this news was fucking fantastic. She'll still be moving forward with her plans for an education, but she'll be doing it from here. Next to me. Beside me. While I figure out my own shit.

I can't stop the smile from spreading across my face. I open my mouth to tell her how happy I am when she suddenly makes my jaw hang limp.

"And you'll be attending the university with me."

"Excuse me?"

She licks her lips. "I got us both in. Late admission. I know you were accepted before, so it was pretty much a given that you would be accepted again."

How?

What?

How in the hell?

I don't even know where to begin. I shake my head, unable to formulate an adequate response. "What are you talking about?"

"My father performed emergency surgery on the president of the university a few months back. Gallbladder removal."

And that's supposed to explain everything? "Well, I'm very happy to know the guy's stomach pain has resolved, but what the hell does that have to do with me? And you? And school?"

"I made an appointment with him several weeks ago. Late admission was already over, but the president can always make an exception. He agreed. We both meet with the academic advisor the week after I get back from the graduation trip."

"You just talked to him? That's it? You didn't fill out an application or provide transcripts or anything?"

She blushes. "Well, I did." She takes a deep breath. "I forged your application. And I ordered your community college transcripts online, pretending to be you. They already had your high school transcripts and ACT score from when you were accepted before."

I can't swallow. There's something stuck in my throat. I quickly stand up, unable to sit still. I pace around, dragging my hand across my face. "You forged my name? Pretended to be me?"

"Yes."

"Why would you do that!"

"Because," she says simply.

I'm about to scream that *'because'* is not an answer when she finally continues.

"I wanna stay here to be close to you. I know I need a college education. It's just like you said, people still wanna see that piece of paper, even though a real job, real life experience, is what matters in the end. And I know you want that too. You want a future for yourself. For us. You're just afraid to pull the trigger. So, I did it for you."

Anger flares behind my eyes, making me see red and black spots. My head swims in a fog. My blood pressure must be shooting through the roof. "Afraid? You think I'm afraid? I'm trying to be practical, Lulu! I want a future for myself. For us. But I was trying to think of the best way to do that. Not all of us have the luxury of doing anything we want, whenever we want. Real-world standards apply for the majority of us."

She doesn't like that insinuation. Her back stiffens and she sucks in a large gulp of air. It was an asshole comment. What can I say? I'm an asshole.

An angry asshole who feels like his balls have just been ripped off by his woman. "Just how do you expect me to pay for this fancy college? I didn't hear mention of the president doling out any scholarship funds. I already told you that I refuse to take on student loans that I'll never be able to pay back. And I swear on all that's holy, if you say you will pay for it, I will flip my shit."

"I know about the money. The money your grandpa left you for school. Follow through on his wishes. Use that."

How can she even suggest such a thing? I'm horrified. My whisper is low and mean. "That money is for Grandma. What do you want me to do? Toss her in some shithole so I can live high on my grandpa's dime?"

She shoots up from the loveseat, fists balled in fury. "I love that woman too. How dare you accuse me of not thinking of her. You're not tossing her out on the street. You can use the money to provide for both you and her. You don't have to sacrifice yourself in the process. You don't have to be a martyr. Your future and her care don't have to be mutually exclusive."

"There's not an endless supply of money, Lulu. We're talking about the sale of some rural property. Grandpa didn't sell a Rembrandt. She could live for another ten years with this disease. Fifteen. No one knows."

"There's options to help if the money starts running out. VA benefits, Medicare," she says, ticking items off her with fingers.

"Nothing that would keep her in that facility."

Lulu's face softens and she takes a step toward me, but I'm too mad. I take a step back. And that hurts her feelings.

"Ry, we'll figure something out, *if* and *when* that time comes."

"What about you? You turned down your full ride to the University of Virginia? All that free money, Lulu? I know you don't wanna be an architect. You could've switched your major, still taken the scholarship. You've already told them no?"

"I will. I'm gonna tell them no as soon as we set up classes with the academic advisor here."

I raise my voice. "There won't be a meeting with the academic advisor. At least not for me."

She squares her shoulders, preparing her defenses. She hisses at me, "What are you saying? You're just gonna squander this opportunity?"

I laugh, cynically. "So that's what this would be? Me not going to college? Me not following your well-laid—and might I add—deceptive plan? It would be squandering an opportunity?"

"Yes."

Sucker punch.

It's like I'm talking to a complete stranger. "Why can't you see how wrong this is? You did this without my permission. You forged my name and lied. But more importantly, you took away my choices, something you promised you would never do again. You took away my chance to plan a future for us. One where I could actually be the man of the relationship. Figure out how I'm going to support you, figure out how I'm going to provide a life for you. You cut off my balls and basically waved them in my face, telling me I'm doing a shitty job at being a man of integrity and honor. I wanna earn the respect of others. Really earn it. I don't want it to be handed to me on a silver platter just because I'm fucking the millionaire's daughter."

I can't believe I just said that. What the hell is wrong with me?

She points her finger in my face. The after-sex flush has left her body and beet red anger has replaced it. Like a car getting a fresh new coat of paint. "You're weak. A real man would realize that the guy and girl work together to make their dreams come true."

She's right. I am weak. I'm weak and poor and filthy. I'm white trash. A complete and total loser. Why did I ever think someone like her could love someone like me? I'm ruining her life. I'm dragging her from the mansion to the trailer park. Hell, I don't even own a trailer. I'm homeless. Living in a tent in the woods.

My heart is splitting in two, sending me into a whirlwind of wild thoughts and accusations.

I rub my jaw. "You're completely right. I am weak. You changed your entire future for me. Your scholarship, your school, your friends." I snort. "I even let you give up your comfortable bed, for what? A blow-up mattress on the ground. It doesn't matter what sheets we put on it, or what perfume we spray on it, it's still a blow-up mattress. And I'm still the poor mechanic. The guy who lives out of his car. The son of two addicts. The brother of a drug pusher. A drug pusher who may or may not have been involved in the disappearance of your sister. Don't you see how fucked up this is, Lulu? I've ruined your life."

Tears spring to her eyes. She quickly wipes them away, refusing to let me see them. "Don't you dare say that. You didn't ruin my life. You saved my life."

It's like I'm finally seeing clearly. Finally gaining clarity.

I'm the bad guy.

Here, I spent all this time worrying about her safety, worrying about her getting hurt. And I'm the one who has been hurting her all along. I've taken a beautiful songbird and captured her in a tarnished and used cage. I've plucked the sun from the sky and shoved it in a deep cave.

She's young. I took advantage of her. She's doesn't know what she wants.

Shit.

She's only eighteen. Seventeen when I met her! What the hell was I thinking. Eighteen may be an adult in the eyes of the law, but she's just a child. I was fooling myself every time I said she was the most mature person I ever met. It was just an excuse. An excuse to keep her with me.

I'm the bad guy.

It's time for me to be the good guy for once. It's time for me to save her life.

If I really love her, I will let her go. I will let her soar to her potential. Soar into the skies.

I can't keep her weighted down in the mud with me. Not if I love her.

And I do. I love her more than life itself.

I meant what I said. Never before. Never after. And I'm okay with that. I had *this*.

This gift. This gift of time with her.

I don't ever need to love again. This love is great enough to last me until I die.

But she's young. In ten years, she won't even remember my name. She'll love again.

I turn around, reaching for my shirt. "Grab your stuff, Lulu. I'm taking you home. I need some space."

"No, I'm not going anywhere."

I casually snuff out the fire in the firepit, casting us into darkness. Grabbing a battery lantern, I flip the switch. "Yes, you are. I said I need some space. I can't look at you right now."

It's true. I can't. Because when I look at her, I want to fall to my knees and beg her to never leave me.

But that's me being the bad guy again. Ruining her life.

She begrudgingly follows me to the truck. I'm in a daze. A walking zombie. I'm reaching for the door handle to the driver-side door when she pushes me back. Not anticipating it, I stumble. She jumps behind the steering wheel.

"You've had too many beers, I'll drive myself. You can come pick up the truck tomorrow. We can talk then. Get Harlan to drive you. Maybe sleeping in the woods by yourself will bring you to your senses."

She slams the door in my face and drives away.

My Lulu drives away. Taking my heart with her.

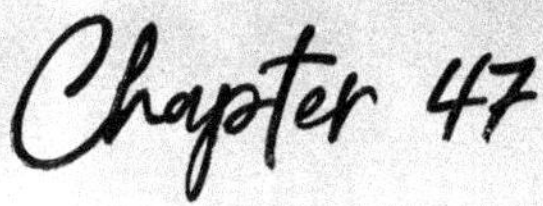

Chapter 47

Ella

Fourteen days.

Two weeks.

I haven't seen or talked to Ry in two whole weeks.

We shared a couple of short texts, but each time, he said he just needed some space, needed to get some clarity. He didn't even talk to me when he picked up his truck the day after our fight.

And now, here I am, about to stand up on this stage and give a speech to the graduating class, and he's not even here to see it. How can I forgive him for this? I look over at my family. Dad, Mom, Uncle Ray, Aunt Teresa, Holt, and Raylee. Even the Conways are here—Ridge, his parents, and little brother, Cullen. Dad's typing on his cell phone. Not surprising.

My throat starts to tickle and I pray I don't cough. Or worse, cry.

How can he not be here?

The audience applauds as my name is called and I walk to the podium. I open the folder that holds my printed speech and the words blur across the page. Taking one last scan of the crowd, my eyes catch someone by the back door.

His face is in the shadows, but I don't have to see his face to know it's him. I would know that body anywhere. I bite back a smile. Everyone here is dressed like we're at a fashion show in Paris, and he's wearing cargo shorts, a T-shirt, and flip flops. I'm surprised the school officials let him inside. He must have snuck in.

His presence steels my courage, fills my body with renewed hope. Everything is gonna be okay. With him. With us.

Licking my lips, I give my graduation speech.

Raylee nudges her way closer to Ry. "So, you won't set me up with your brother. Maybe you have a cousin who looks somewhat like you. Distant relative?"

Ry doesn't have to answer. Holt saves him. "Come on, Raylee. Stop being stupid. I'm starving."

My cousin pushes off the car, giving me a swift hug and kiss. "You were brilliant. I'm so proud of you." Jumping in the car with Holt, they drive off, leaving Ry and me alone in the mostly deserted parking lot.

He's so damn gorgeous. Even sexier than the first time I saw him. The green T-shirt he's wearing makes his pale green eyes even brighter. He pulls the ballcap down low on his head, blocking out the sun. "She's right, you were brilliant."

"I was afraid you wouldn't come."

"I'd never miss it. I'd never miss saying goodbye to you." He clears his throat and plants his fingertips on his firm waist. "When does your flight leave?"

"Not for six hours." I press my body against his, replacing his hands with my own. The band of muscles on his stomach feel even tighter than they did just two weeks ago. Has he been working out more than normal? "Why don't you come over? Give me a proper goodbye. I know a lot of things that can be done in the three-and-a-half hours before I leave for the airport."

He smiles softly but doesn't say anything. He's still a little mad. I can see it in his eyes. Read it on his face. Feel it in his touch.

I nuzzle against his neck, breathing his scent. "I know you're still mad. And you have every right to be. I've thought about it a lot. Every point you made was valid. But don't make up your mind about anything until after we meet with the academic advisor, okay? Just hear him out. There's no point in making a decision unless it's an informed decision. Okay, Ry?"

He nods. "Okay, Lulu."

I snake my arms around his neck, pulling him down to me. "We're gonna be fine. Everything is gonna work out. You'll see." I slide my lips across his. "Now, come on. I still have some packing to do and I hear packing while being naked can be fun."

He barely cracks a smile. "I can't. A shipment is coming to the garage and I have to be there. Harlan has a stomach virus."

"Oh no. Is he okay?"

"He'll be fine. Don't worry."

"But I leave for two weeks tonight. And we haven't even seen each other these past two weeks." I lower my voice to a whisper. "I can't make it a whole month without you being inside of me."

He moans. But it sounds different this time. Not like normal. Not happy and sexual and on fire. He sounds sad. Upset. Distant. I'll be so glad when this fight is finally behind us, once and for all.

He grabs his ballcap and spins it around backward on his head. "Then we better make this kiss count."

He grabs my body, wrapping me in a hug so tight I can barely breathe. Our kiss begins slowly. Licking, tasting, teasing. Eventually his tongue tangles with mine as we thrust against one another. He presses his erection into me so hard, it feels like it bruises me.

It's wonderful. Blissfully perfect and wonderful.

Kiss me. Kiss me forever.

My tiptoes graze against the pavement, searching for traction so I can delve my own tongue into his mouth even farther. I tug at the ends of his hair and drag my fingernails down his back.

Finally, we have no other choice but to pull away.

It's either that or suffocate to death.

"Bye, Lulu." He turns around and walks over to his truck.

My heart races in my chest and anxiety fires in the pit of my stomach, sending acid into my throat. I'm worrying for no reason. Everything is gonna be just fine.

His hand freezes on the door handle when he hears my voice. "Ask me."

He sighs. "Tell me something. Something no one else knows."

"I love you. I love you, Ryland Joseph Crutchfield."

His lip curves into a half-smile. "But I already know that."

I shrug. "I guess someone taught me how to break the rules."

Then My Ry drives away. Taking my heart with him.

Chapter 48

Ella

I'm gonna kill him.

Literally.

I've been home for twenty-four hours, and he hasn't called or come to see me. True, I was completely exhausted when I fell into bed the minute I walked through the door at two p.m. yesterday. I didn't even wake up until after eleven this morning. That stomach bug has really kicked my ass. I ended up getting the same stomach bug that Harlan had, apparently. I guess it was going around right before I left. I still had a great time, and it didn't prevent me from doing any of the charity work or the fun activities, but it left me drained and weak and exhausted. With not much of an appetite.

I fully expected to see dozens of missed calls and texts from him when I woke up, but there was nothing. And I called and texted him the second our wheels hit the tarmac. In fact, he should be here, banging down my door, demanding to be let in. Tired of waiting, I call the body shop. Harlan answers on the fourth ring.

"Ella! It's so good to know that you're back home, safe and sound. Was it fun, sweetheart?"

"It was absolutely amazing. I met some wonderful people and really feel like we made a difference. I'll tell you all about it, I promise. But first I need to kill him. He hasn't even called or texted. Put him on the phone so I can yell at him." I'm laughing at myself, so I miss what Harlan says. "Oh, sorry, what did you say?"

I'm having a really hard time hearing. Harlan sounds like he's whispering. "Why don't you just come on out here?"

"Sounds good. On my way. And I have souvenirs for you too." I grab my purse from the kitchen counter and race to my car. I smile during the whole drive. I can't wait to see Ry. Be with him. Touch him.

Maybe I won't kill him after all.

His truck is parked in its normal spot when I pull in. I run my fingers across the tailgate as I jog into the open bay. Harlan immediately wraps me in a hug. "You are one pretty sight for this old man's eyes. I haven't seen you in a month!"

"I know; I missed you too."

He holds me at arm's length, studying me. The trip bronzed my already tanned skin and left a scattering of sun freckles across the bridge of my nose. "You look great."

"Thanks. I feel pretty good. I did come down with that stomach bug you had before I left, though." His brow furrows in concern, but I ignore him, looking over his shoulder. "Where's he at? In the bathroom?"

"He's not here, Ella."

I shake my head, correcting Harlan. "Yeah, his truck is outside. The wrecker is here too, so he can't be out on a run. Did he just get back from one?" I raise my voice, hollering to him in case he's in the bedroom. "Ry!"

Harlan grabs my shoulders, forcing me to look at him. "Sweetheart, he's not here. He left. He left town."

Huh? What?

"What are you talking about?"

Harlan takes a deep breath. "He joined the Marines."

My jaw falls open. "Excuse me?" Am I dreaming right now? Am I still asleep in my bed?

"He joined the Marines."

Even though I don't believe Harlan, I can't stop the tremble that races through my body, shaking me to my core, like a hiker trapped in a snowstorm. My vision starts to fuzz around the edges. My blood pressure is rising. Or maybe falling. Who knows? All I know is I feel like I'm gonna faint and throw up, all at the same time.

"Ella, sit down, before you pass out." Harlan rolls my normal chair over, and I grab onto it with shaky hands.

"What? Are you lying? What are you talking about?"

He frowns in sympathy. His heart is hurting. I can see it on his face, plain as day, he's not lying. "I wouldn't lie about something like that."

I stutter over my words. "But... but... he never talked about joining the military. Never. He never said he wanted to do that."

"I don't guess he ever really thought much about it before. He always heard me and Michael talk about our time in the service, but he never openly expressed a desire to enlist."

"Harlan, don't get me wrong, serving in the military is an incredibly noble and selfless act, and I admire those who are called to do it, but you don't just walk in one day to join and then ship off. This stuff has to take time. I totally support him wanting to join the military, but we need to get everything in order. We need to figure out the process. Where he'll be... I have to coordinate a move and transfer to whatever school may be near there. Or maybe I can just take online classes. We need to call him and tell him to come back. We'll get everything ready, and he can join in a couple of months."

"It doesn't work that way, sweetie. He's already at Parris Island, South Carolina. Boot camp. Got there last Tuesday."

Today's Monday. He's already been gone nearly a whole week!

Holy shit. This can't be happening. I rub my breastbone with my hand.

I think I'm dying.

"Boot camp? For how long?"

"Yes, they call it MCRT, Marine Corps Recruit Training. He'll be there for thirteen weeks. Then, he'll go to SOI, the School of Infantry.

Depending on which school he is sent to, he will train for either fifty-nine days or twenty-nine days. I'm sure it will be fifty-nine days."

Tears are rolling down my face, I can't help it. I sniffle, "And then he'll be home?" I know it's a dumbass question. A girl can still hope, can't she?

"No, he'll receive his PDS. His permanent duty station." Harlan stands taller, making his voice firmer. "Ella, he signed up for six years active duty. Followed by two inactive."

Fuck me. Six years. Eight years.

I wipe the tears, spreading mascara all over my fingers. "I just don't understand. How can you sign up one day and be gone the next? Don't they give you time to prepare?"

"They give you time to prepare." Harlan drags his hand across his scruffy face. "If you *want* time to prepare."

My eyes grow wide and I cry even harder. "Ry didn't want time to prepare? He didn't wanna wait on me to get back?"

Harlan coughs, choking back his own tears. He hates delivering this news to me. I can't believe Ry would be so heartless as to make Harlan do his dirty work for him. What a bastard.

"No, sweetheart, he didn't want time to prepare. And I don't think he could stand to see you. If he saw you, he might have regretted his decision."

Slowly the pieces start to fall into place. The distance before I left for the graduation trip. The lack of communication. The lack of intimacy. "Harlan, when did Ry enlist?"

"The Monday after your fight. After the fake prom that Saturday night."

There was nothing fake about it.

Or so I thought.

Sucker punch. "So, he requested to leave as soon as possible?"

"He did."

I start to hyperventilate. Harlan races around, rubbing my back, pleading and begging for me to breathe and calm down. Seconds pass. Minutes pass. Hours pass.

Who the hell knows?

Eventually, my raw and chafed cheeks dry. My chest heaves for the last time. My throat finally swallows past the dry lump that's been choking me. I can handle this. I can do this.

"Okay. I'll call him and tell him that I'm okay with everything, that I fully support his decision. I guess that's why he didn't answer yesterday, he's busy at boot camp."

Harlan walks over to Ry's tall tool box, opens it, and pulls out the cell phone I gave him. "He's not allowed to have a phone."

"Seriously, so I have to wait for him to call me? When will that be?"

"They aren't really allowed to call out. Just the phone call to say he arrived safe."

I lean forward, pressing my palms against my eyelids so hard it feels like my eyeballs are going to pop out of my head. "So, I basically have to wait thirteen weeks before I hear from him? And *then*, I have to wait another fifty-nine days?" I stare at the ceiling and scream. It catches Harlan off guard and he jumps. "Now, I *am* gonna kill him! He is making it so hard to love him!"

I stand up and pace back and forth, rubbing my scar in thought. "Fine, when I finally get to talk to him, I'll tell him that as soon as he gets the information on his permanent place, I'll move wherever. I'll do a semester of school in-person, and then just start online classes so I can be ready for the move."

Harlan walks back over to the tool box and grabs a white envelope. His hand is shaking like a leaf. He lays it on my chair. He's afraid to actually give it to me. I flicker my eyes back and forth between the envelope and Harlan. I stiffen my spine, square my shoulders, and lift my chin. "Harlan, what is that?"

His voice cracks. "I'm not exactly sure. I haven't read it."

I purse my lips. Each syllable that rolls across my tongue causes a small part of my heart to die. Like a rot, it turns black and disintegrates. "Is that a 'Dear John' letter? Is Ry having you do his dirty work? Is he breaking up with me in a letter?"

Harlan won't lie to me. "I think so, yes."

I snatch the envelope off the chair and wad it in my fist, choking it like the vile piece of filth it is. Sprinting across the parking lot, I jump in my vehicle and speed to the homestead, driving so fast my tires actually squeal every time I turn. It's a blessing I'm not killed. Or kill someone else.

I sit in my SUV, frozen in place, frozen in shock, looking at the place I once called my home. Everything is gone. No furniture, no storage bins, no tent. The only things that remain are the poured concrete patio, the stone firepit, and the wooden dock. And those were only left behind because they are permanent. Hell, if Ry had enough time, he probably would've jackhammered the concrete.

But I guess he was too anxious to get away from me. Too excited.

I tear open the envelope, ignoring the tug of my heartstrings when I see his handwriting.

Hate me.

That's the only way I'll be able to survive.

I don't think I'd be able to live my life knowing that you're spending every day, every waking moment, loving me the way I will love you until the day I die. Don't love me. Stop. Find some-one worthy. Someone better. Someone who can give you what you need. Someone who can provide for you.

I'm a burden to you, Lulu. Don't you see that? I'm not the life-jacket; I'm the anchor. I'm drowning you, pulling you under. And I love you too much to do that. So, yes, I made this decision without you. But you have to know that I made this decision for the both of us. I need a higher purpose in life than just trying to survive the shit existence that surrounds me. I refuse to be like my parents or my brother. But I also refuse to have the woman I love give up the life she's been given. A life that's not a shit existence.

Let's face it, being born rich is a privilege. You are the most beautiful woman to ever walk the face of the earth. You are smart and funny and humble and fiery and passionate and... everything. My everything. You deserve every good thing that heads your way.

But the truth of the matter is, you will always have more opportunities than those who don't have money.

You're the one who told me not to squander an opportunity. And that's just what you're doing with me. You're tossing away a future of endless possibilities. You deserve happiness now. Not in ten years, when I hopefully have a good job. Not in fifteen years, when I hopefully have some money to call my own. Not in twenty years, when I hopefully have the land to build our dream home.

Now. You deserve happiness right now.

So, hate me. Move on with your life. Find love. Find happiness. Start a career, get married, have babies. Do all the things that Carrie won't be able to do. Make your sister proud. Take what should've been our life and make it your own. I give it to you. I'm giving you the life you deserve. It's the least I can do.

I won't lie and say I wish we had never met. Nothing could be further from the truth. The night I saw you on the back porch was the moment I actually started living. The night I started hoping, dreaming. Don't ever think for one second that I didn't love you, that I don't love you. Because I did. And I do. My heart will beat for you until the heavens cascade to the earth.

Your laugh, your kiss, your touch.

Mine.

You're mine. My Lulu. Never before. Never after.

And I'm content with that.

But I want you to have it all.

The fault lies with me. I made the gravest mistake of all. I told you I wasn't a fan of escaping from reality. And yet, I fell into my own trap. I escaped. With you held captive in my arms.

You're free now, Lulu.

Reality reminds you where you belong.

To be continued in...
Finding Our Reality: The Reality Duet Book Two
Available now.

Gratitude

Welp... I guess it happened. I wrote words (a lot of words) and put them out in the world for everyone to see. For everyone to love or hate. For everyone to laugh or cry. For everyone to share or hide.

I never saw myself as a writer. True, I did win two major awards in middle school. That's right, ladies and gentlemen—two, not just one. My first was in the sixth grade for an essay on the ramifications of drunk driving via the D.A.R.E program. (And if you don't know what that is, just search for "This is your brain on drugs.") The second award was in the seventh grade for a scary short story. Well, after those major accolades, who would need more, right?

Well, somewhere along the way, I guess *I* needed more.

So here we are.

No matter what happens, I crossed something off my Bucket List, and that's pretty amazing. I fell into my own world and found myself madly in love with Ella and Crutch. I can only hope you love them as much as I do.

I'd like to thank all of my sweet (and patient) family and friends who helped me throughout the process—voting on logos, voting on covers, giving me words of encouragement, beta reading, answering social media questions, testing the website and newsletter, spreading the word, and just being all-around cheerleaders and champions. Kuntry, Boo, Dandy, Big, Tonia P, Cassidy P, Aunt Karla, Kaleen G, Yolanda C, Ashley C.S., Adrienne C.E., Karisa B, Courtney W, Tanja E, Ashley R, Amy D, Misty M, Heather S.S., Casey Y, Amber M, Dani J, and Brooklyn W. And if I forgot anyone, please don't be mad!

A huge shout-out to all of my new followers on social media! Believe it or not, I was a social media virgin until I had to start marketing The Reality Duet. Why? As a self-proclaimed Nosy Nate, I was worried about the ramifications of social media on my psyche. Fortunately, I've been able to maintain a somewhat healthy balance—so far. If you see me slipping into a social media coma, please pick me up and throw me out!

Thank you to Tony B for looking at everything for me. And remember what I said about your art and romance novels. It could be a match made in heaven.

Thank you to Stacey Blake for accepting me as a client and designing beautiful covers for both novels. I appreciate you.

Thank you to the wonderful teams at Grey's Promotions (Jen and Olivia) and Give Me Books Promotions (Jo) for accepting me as a client and helping me with the ARC and promotional process. These two companies are on point!

Thank you to my new friend, mentor, and super-amazing author, Kelly Elliott. You have been sweeter than a candied apple, and I appreciate all your help—the phone conversations, the texts, the advice, and well... everything.

To Elaine York with Allusion Publishing... Holy freakin' cow, what can I say? I went looking for an editor, and I found an amazing friend. When I started the process of bringing The Reality Duet to publication, I was as lost as a Christmas goose. You have guided me the entire way. And by the entire way, I mean *the entire way*. When I was a hair's breadth away from posting to social media that I was backing out and publication would not happen, you talked me down from the ledge. You blessed me with the validation that I didn't even know I needed. You've filled a space in my writer's head and heart that I didn't even know was empty, and I will be forever in your gratitude for accepting me as a client. And a friend.

To Dandy and Big, the most amazing parents ever... Thank you for *almost* always buying me the Barbie doll. Like Dandy said, "I could entertain myself for hours with my imagination and a Barbie doll." Who knew that make-believe play would be a precursor to this? And thank you for always (not *almost* always, but *always* always) buying me the book to read. Considering I refused to check-out library books, you spent a small fortune on my book addiction. Books I voraciously—and quickly—devoured. Thank you for encouraging me to publish The Reality Duet. Thank you for loving me unconditionally, supporting me wholeheartedly, and singing my praises to anyone who will listen. I would be nothing without the two of you. I am beyond blessed that you are our best friends and that I have the privilege of seeing you every day. Thank you for loving my husband. Thank you for loving my son. Thank you for loving me.

To my Boo Boo Bear... I love you more than words can say. I've told you before and I'll tell you again—you are my heart. You are an amazing young man, and I'm beyond lucky to be your mom. You're filled to the brim with intelligence, empathy, and the best text-one liners known to mankind. I pray every single second of every single day for your happiness as you grow into the man you are meant to be. When I close my eyes, I see nothing but amazing things for your future, and I'm so excited for all the possibilities spread out before you. The love you give makes me a better person. Thank you for your hugs. Thank you for being my scary movie buddy. Thank you for being *you*—handsome, funny, smart, kind, and level-headed. And more importantly, thank you for making me a momma nearly eighteen years ago.

To Kuntry, my husband and my best friend... Thank you isn't enough. One party, and I was a goner. One look at that wonderful big butt of yours, and I knew you would be mine. We might've taken a little longer route to get back to each other, but the Lord knew what He was doing. If Boo is my heart, you are my soul. The way you love me brings me to my knees. You think I'm beautiful, funny, smart, crazy, and talented. You always treat me like I'm the only woman in the world. Literally. You only have eyes for me, and you have no idea how special that makes me feel. Not only that, you actually *like* me. Your favorite pastime is just being with us—me, Boo, Dandy, and Big. In a world where married people don't actually *like* each other half the time, you *like* me. That speaks volumes. You are the best husband, father, brother, son-in-law, friend, cousin, teacher… and the list goes on and on. Thank you for loving our son. Thank you for loving my parents. Thank you for loving me. You're stuck with me, baby.

To the Lord my God, my Almighty Savior Jesus Christ… Thank you. I am unworthy, but made worthy in Your eyes. You have blessed me beyond measure—with a family, with a home, with food in my (chubby) stomach, and with good health. I know it might seem crazy to some that I am thanking the Lord above when these novels are a little… 'unchurch-like'. But God gave me this imagination, and I am happy when I embrace it. Whether I sell one copy, one-hundred copies, or one-million copies, I am rich beyond my wildest dreams because I have an Eternal Home. My Granny went Home a few months ago. She's with You and Papa and her sons. I hear her. I feel her. And I miss her. Take care of her until I'm there.

About the Author

HALCIE DAWN is a happy and blessed wife and mother. She attended the University of Alabama where she graduated with a bachelor's degree in Business Management. A lifelong avid reader, her love affair with books started with the original *The Babysitter's Club* series when she was in the third grade and morphed into a love of all things romantic. After years of thought, she finally placed finger to keyboard and penned her first contemporary romance. When not writing or reading by the swimming pool, she can be found watching true crime documentaries or *Psych* (for the millionth time). Halcie lives in Alabama with her amazingly wonderful, funny, kind, and handsome husband and son. And she lives next door to her parents, whose antics often have her laughing so hard she pees her pants. But without a doubt, the star of the home is the family morkiepoo, Princess Doodle Fluffybutt.

Connect with me:
Website: www.halciedawn.com
Instagram: halciedawnromance
Facebook: www.facebook.com/halciedawn

www.ingramcontent.com/pod-product-compliance
Lightning Source LLC
Chambersburg PA
CBHW070511310726
48976CB00002BA/408